A STARTLING REVELATION

"No." The stranger's voice, while still a croak, was definite. Stubbornness glittered in his green eyes. "I'm not going. Just take me home."

"And where would that be?" Irritation overrode Valerie's fear, making her tone waspish.

He cleared his throat. "The Aurora Lodge."

"The Aurora Lo—" Valerie gasped.

Several moments passed before she regained speech. "That's impossible. No one lives at Aurora Lodge. It's been vacant since February."

The man's head dropped. In the silence, Valerie could hear him drawing deep, steadying breaths. Who was he, and why hadn't he heard of Arthur's death?

She cleared her throat. "Who are you?"

"Jack. Jack Wilder."

Valerie's eyes widened. Her heart thumped rapidly and her mouth grew dry. She stared at the injured male in the backseat of her car.

"Why—" she gulped, "why you're the person Uncle Arthur's lawyer has been trying to find."

She paused, then blurted out, "You and I have inherited Aurora Lodge."

NORAH-JEAN PERKIN

NIGHT SECRETS

LOVE SPELL BOOKS NEW YORK CITY

To Richard

A LOVE SPELL BOOK®

March 2002

Published by

Dorchester Publishing Co., Inc.
276 Fifth Avenue
New York, NY 10001

ISBN 0-505-52473-2

Visit us on the web at www.dorchesterpub.com.

NIGHT SECRETS

"The Yupik people of St. Lawrence Island say that the (Northern) lights used to have no colors. Children were warned to stay in at night so they wouldn't be stolen by the lights. Some children didn't listen and they were carried away. The colors we see now are the colorful parkas of the children as they dance in the skies."

"During powerful solar storms, animals sometimes become disturbed or act strangely. Homing pigeons, for example, have a hard time finding their way home."

—D. M. Souza, *Northern Lights*

Chapter One

A streak of yellow cut across the night sky, illuminating the stillness of the Northern Ontario lake far below. The light melted away and the deep waters, ringed by pine and maple forest and the age-old granite of the Canadian Shield, retreated into darkness.

Another streak flashed from the other side of the lake, before it too faded. Moments later, light breached the late June darkness yet again. Stronger rays, in glowing shades of sulphurous green and yellow, ranged across the sky, like the beams of giant spotlights in search of hidden secrets.

Slowly the light grew more intense, the ever-changing colors stronger and brighter, until they seemed to pulse across the sky, like a living, breathing creature on some unearthly quest. Their greenish glow reflected off the silent waters, bounced off the exposed granite worn smooth by the elements, and penetrated the deep woods. An owl, thrown off its pursuit of a rabbit, retreated to the dark recesses of a thick spruce tree. Everywhere the night creatures grew still.

1

The light, punctuated by a faint swishing and crackling, played across a small, sandy beach at one end of the dark lake, alternately bathing it in a golden glow and plunging it back into blackness. The moments of eerie illumination revealed motion, the motion of a dark form struggling to wrest itself from the lake's muddy bottom. Inch by painful inch, it clawed its way from the ooze into the shallows, fighting the weeds in the water that were reluctant to release what they had claimed for so long.

Finally the creature's appendages cleared the water, finding a home in the cool white sand of the beach. With the last of its strength, the creature heaved its upper body out of the water and collapsed onto the shore. Golden beams of light from overhead glanced off the beach, revealing in their glow the naked body of a man.

Several moments passed before the man raised his head. He braced his hands under his shoulders and, with painstaking effort, lifted his chest. He gazed up at the strange lights shimmering above him. He blinked and shook his head, then looked again. The Northern Lights danced across his dark, liquid pupils until he squeezed his eyes shut to lock out the sight.

"Oh, no," he groaned. "Oh, God, no. Not this. Not again."

His arms gave out, and he sank into unconsciousness.

The high beams caught the weather-beaten sign at the side of the dirt road. Valerie Scott slowed her Ford Escort from a crawl to stop. She squinted, looking through the scrub bushes that had grown up around the sign and obscured the letters burned into the graying wood. Was that an A she saw, followed by a U? And surely the last word read LODGE?

She sighed with relief and flexed her stiff shoulders. Aurora Lodge. It couldn't be anything else. Not this far along Lakeside Road, the dirt and gravel track that ended about halfway around Lake Aurora. It had been at least ten years since she'd set foot in the Muskoka lake country north of Toronto, but some things you didn't forget.

"We're here, Reddi. We're here." The young golden retriever must have sensed the excitement in her voice. He barked, then put his paws on her shoulder and licked her face.

"Whoa, boy." Valerie laughed as she pushed the gangly pup away. "Not now. In a moment you'll be able to get out. You're gonna love this place, I just know it."

She turned into the rutted driveway and carefully made her way along the winding road. Leafy branches of sugar maples and red oaks pressed in on either side and sometimes joined overhead, blocking out the startling display of Northern Lights.

Valerie glanced upward again. She'd never seen such a stunning display of lights, not even during the dozen summers she'd spent at this lodge with her mother and her Great-uncle Arthur. Only her anxiousness to get to Uncle Arthur's house, after two long days of travel from Chicago, had prevented her from pulling over at the side of the highway and stopping to gaze at the awesome and ever-changing play of shimmering colors across the night sky.

She continued along the dark, winding road, bouncing over the ruts and holes. As she rounded the last curve, the trees fell away, opening to the wide expanse of gravel and dirt parking lot and grassy playing field she remembered. In the dancing illumination overhead, she caught a glimpse of the chain-link fence surrounding the tennis court on the far side of the lot. And to the left, a welcoming beacon of light shone over the door to the lodge office and her uncle's adjoining house.

Valerie let out a breath she hadn't realized she'd been holding. It was a relief to see proof that her uncle's lawyer had kept his promise to have the power turned on and the house cleaned up. She didn't relish entering a dark, musty building that hadn't been lived in since her uncle's death in February.

3

She parked as close to the lit structure as she could. As soon as the car door opened, Reddi scrambled over her and leapt out. She followed him and watched as he raced around the parking lot. She smiled in understanding. It felt so good to be here. She'd had to grit her teeth to curb her impatience during the long meeting with Ed Grierson. She had stopped at the grocery store only long enough to buy the bare necessities. But no more.

They were here. It felt right, like coming home after a long absence.

Valerie blinked back the unexpected rush of tears. She breathed deeply, filling her lungs with the smell of clean, damp earth, cedar and blue spruce saplings, fresh water, and cool night air. She planned to soak up everything about Aurora Lodge as long as she could.

She slammed the car door and felt in the pocket of her cargo pants for the keys to the office. As she started toward the lit door, Reddi raced past her to the dirt path that snaked down the hill to the lake.

"Hey, Reddi. Here, boy."

The dog bounded back and leapt on her. Laughing, she pushed him down. It was clear the overgrown pup wasn't ready to be cooped up inside yet. Not after two days in the car. For that matter, neither was she. Especially when the Northern Lights beckoned.

She nodded to Reddi. "Come on. Want to explore? Let's go down to the lake."

The dog ran ahead of her as she picked her way out of the lot and onto the trail. The greenish-white beams of light crisscrossing the sky and pulsating with energy provided more than enough illumination.

Humming, she passed the dark main lodge building. She smiled when she saw the old shuffleboard court and the wooden swing where she'd spent countless hours with her summer friends. A dark hulk loomed ahead of her on the right. Pioneer, wasn't it? Each of the twenty cabins had a name; once she had known them all.

4

Valerie grinned as the name of each cabin she passed came tumbling back. Arrowhead, Centennial, Brown Bear— she ticked them off, one after another, pleased at her ability to remember. From the year she'd turned four until she was sixteen, this place had been one of the few constants in her life, waiting unchanged for her each summer.

She continued on down the path until the lake came into view, its glasslike surface shining with color from the sky above. She stopped. There was something about that first view of the water that had always moved her, filling her with such a strong sense of connection to the lake, the surrounding land, the unforgiving granite, and the vast tracts of trees, that she always felt invincible.

Invincible and safe. Always safe. Her hand moved to her throat, skimming the still-tender skin. She swallowed. Yes, safe. Here, alone in the middle of nowhere, bears and moose and God knows what else wandering around out there in the bush, and only a few cottages nearby. Safe.

Reddi circled back around to her for his customary scratch behind the ears. The comforting action, and the encouraging words she offered him, helped dismiss the unsettling thoughts. Not here. Not now. She had the whole summer ahead of her to sort things out. There was no need to spoil her delight in the fantastic show overhead.

With her head raised to take in the wonders above, she continued down to the beach. The beams of light wildly crossing the lake had settled into a mass of green and gold. The intensity changed from one end to the other, making the mass appear to pulse and move, like a living, breathing creature. It was strange. It was unreal. It was . . .

"Breathtaking!" Unaware she'd spoken aloud, Valerie stepped out of the trees and onto the sandy beach and an unobstructed view of the sky.

Splashing, followed by faint shouts and what sounded like a scream, broke her concentration. She peered at the opposite, tree-covered shore. Only three lights showed there, distant from each other and likely from some of the few cottages on the north shore of the lake. She couldn't make out any activity on the water, but the noises could have come from the far end of the lake. Probably just kids fooling around.

Valerie returned her gaze to the sky. The colors had changed once more, the yellows and greens overtaken by a stunning red that stained the darkness like flowing, pulsing blood.

She shivered, for the first time noticing the coolness of the night breeze. A mosquito buzzed her ear and she swatted at it. Somewhere to her left, Reddi growled.

Valerie edged toward the sound, her eyes still on the sky, her sandals filling with sand. "It's all right, boy," she murmured. "There's nothing to be afraid of. It's all—oomph!"

She tripped and went sprawling in the cold, wet sand. One hand slapped into the frigid water; with a start she pulled it back and pushed herself up to her hands and knees. Her right foot rested on something wet and grainy, probably the piece of driftwood she'd just tripped over.

She withdrew her foot and turned to look. "All right, Reddi, what did y—"

The words died on her lips. For a split second she stared. Then a bloodcurdling scream ripped from her throat.

Chapter Two

Moments sped by before Valerie could control the gut-wrenching terror that froze her to the spot. Oblivious now to the Northern Lights that played overhead, she swallowed and forced herself to look again at the mud-covered body resting beside her.

It was a man. A big, *naked* man, lying facedown in the sand. The flickering light alternately revealed the back of his head, then his torso, with its wide shoulders narrowing to lean hips and rounded buttocks. Water lapped quietly at the lower half of his partially submerged body, the light reflecting like sequins off his wet thighs and calves.

Swallowing again, Valerie reached out and gingerly touched his arm. Her fingers recoiled from the cold, wet flesh. *Is he dead?*

She grimaced. She didn't know. But she had to find out. Ignoring the trembling she couldn't stop, she forced down the wave of revulsion rising inside. She grabbed the man under the arms and, with a colossal effort, yanked him clear of the water.

Norah-Jean Perkin

She paused to catch her breath. He was tall, close to six feet, and from the effort it had taken to move him, likely 170 or 180 pounds. All of it muscle and sinew, if the firm flesh and sculptured body her brief perusal hadn't missed were any indication.

Even as the man's physical appearance registered, Valerie felt the hot flush rising up her neck; she cursed herself. Why, he wasn't even conscious—he was probably dead—and she was standing here grading his undeniably male, undeniably powerful physique!

Shaking her head, she grabbed one cold, sandy shoulder and hip and heaved the man over as carefully as she could. The only thing that mattered now was whether he was alive.

She inclined her ear over his head and listened. She felt the faint tickle of his warm breath before she actually heard it, faint and shallow but regular. He was alive! Thank God, he was alive.

Tentatively she patted his mud-encrusted cheek. Under the grime, his features appeared rugged, if a little grim. "Sir? Sir? SIR!" Her voice grew louder with each repetition. The earlier spurt of relief turned to desperation. What should she do now? Confused bits and pieces of information about hypothermia and drowning surfaced from long-ago swimming courses, none of it complete enough to be helpful.

"Reddi?" She looked around. She hadn't noticed the pup since tripping over the body. She saw Reddi about a dozen feet away. "Come here, Reddi. Here, boy."

An uncharacteristic growl met her command. Reddi stayed put.

Valerie frowned. This wasn't like her friendly dog. Normally he was all over her at the slightest encouragement. Maybe the body, er, unconscious man, had spooked him as much as it had her.

She sat back on her heels. "Reddi, I'm going to the car. I'm going to bring it down here so we can take this guy to the hospital. I want you to stay here. Stay, boy. Stay."

8

Valerie got to her feet. She swayed when an unexpected wave of dizziness hit her, then shook her head to clear it. This was no time to get squeamish. Using a firm voice, she pointed her finger at Reddi. "Stay." Reddi whimpered, but at least he didn't move. Valerie looked down at the motionless form at her feet once more. She hoped she wasn't too late.

She scrambled back up the hill. The Northern Lights had begun to fade and the darkness closed in on her. Twice she slipped into potholes; once she tripped over a rock. The bright eyes and dark shadow of what she sincerely hoped was a raccoon sent her jumping a foot when it emerged from the side of a cabin.

Out of breath, she reached the lot. Cursing herself for letting the battery on her cell phone die, she turned on the car and the high beams and drove down the winding path to the beach. She could have called an ambulance, but then again, how long would it take to get here? It didn't matter. The only option now was to get him to the hospital before it was too late.

At the bottom of the hill, just before the beach, the path turned right toward what had once been and might still be the boat docks and launch area. But here was good enough. She stopped parallel to the beach and jumped out, leaving the car running and the high beams on.

Neither the man nor Reddi had shifted position since she left. Valerie rested her hand lightly across the man's cold chest and turned her head to listen. She was relieved to feel the slight rise and fall of his chest, and to hear his shallow breathing, no less regular than it had been minutes before.

She sat back on her heels. There was nothing for it now but to drag him to the car. She didn't see any other way. The Escort would likely get stuck if she drove it onto the sand.

But he was a big man. And at five feet four and 115 pounds, she was no weight lifter. Could she do it?

She bit her lip: It didn't matter what she could or could not do. She had to get this man to the car, and to the hospital, now.

Taking a deep breath and steeling herself not to recoil from the coldness of the man's body, she grasped him under the arms again and rose slowly to her feet. She gasped with the effort. He was heavier than she'd thought. *A deadweight!* She shuddered. Not to mention clammy, wet, and muddy.

Gritting her teeth, she started moving backward in slow motion to the car. Each step took a supreme effort. Her breath came in painful gasps. Her back screamed. Still she carried on, wincing each time she hit an uneven bit of ground, or when half-buried sticks or stones scraped against the man's bottom and legs.

"I'm sorry," she whispered to the unconscious man between gasps. "I don't want to hurt you. But I don't know how else to do this. I'm afraid to leave you."

After what seemed hours, Valerie reached the side of the vehicle. Gently, she laid the man on the ground and stopped to rest. She leaned against the door and wiped the moisture from her forehead. She could feel sweat trickling down her back and between her breasts.

Catching her breath, she readied herself for the effort of putting the unconscious man into the backseat of her small car. Finally, after several gruesome minutes of lifting, tugging, pushing, shoving, and profuse apologies for knocking his head and twisting his shoulders and scraping his arms, she managed to get him into the back of the Escort, his head and torso on the seat, his legs and feet twisted into the legroom below.

Valerie hurried to the trunk and found a blanket. She tucked it around the man's shoulders and over his legs.

As she rose from the task, she blinked. Had he moved? She stared at him. Unlikely. The interior car light shone off his muck-encrusted features and hair. Mud and sand covered his face and hair and shoulders, and every body part that hadn't been scraped free by her dragging him over the ground to the car. She couldn't imagine how he could have gotten so dirty, like one of those old abandoned beach toys one finds buried in the sand, only infinitely more grisly. She shuddered.

After one last check to ensure he was still breathing, Valerie scrambled out of the car. "Reddi," she called.

From out of the darkness, a growl answered her, followed by a whine.

"Come here, Reddi. C'mon, boy, we've got to go."

Reddi crept into view of the high beams. Valerie frowned. "C'mon, boy. Here. Now. We've got to go."

Tail drooping and head down, Reddi slunk to the car. Valerie opened the front passenger door, but instead of bounding in as he usually did, Reddi hung back.

"Get in, Reddi." She grabbed his collar and pulled. He didn't resist, but he whimpered.

"There, there." Valerie scratched him behind the ears. "It'll be all right. I don't like this any better than you do. But we'll have him to the hospital in just a few minutes."

Valerie slapped at a mosquito that had landed on her cheek, and brushed off a couple more buzzing by her ear. Quickly she got in, reversed, and started up the driveway.

As she pulled into the parking lot, she glanced upward. Where earlier the sky had been alive with dancing color, now darkness reigned. Only a few faint pinpricks of light pierced the blackness. Even the light over the office door seemed dwarfed by the night.

Valerie shuddered again. Funny how everything could change in the space of a few minutes. She turned and looked into the backseat. He hadn't moved. She'd better hurry.

The car bounced over the rutted, winding driveway to the road. When it hit the graded gravel of Lakeside Road, Valerie sped up. Her pumping heart and jittery nerves urged her to go faster still, but she didn't dare top forty miles an hour on the unfamiliar, twisting road.

11

Reddi huddled in the passenger seat, refusing to respond or look at her. Had finding that unconscious man on the beach rattled him as much as it had rattled her? Valerie didn't know. She did know that she couldn't have just left that man lying unconscious on the beach, even to go for help.

But who was he? What was such an obviously fit and strong man doing on the beach, unconscious and naked? Why was he covered with mud from head to toe? If he'd been dead, maybe a drowning victim washed up during a storm, it might make sense. But where were his clothes? And why was sand ground into every square inch of him?

Valerie glanced in the rearview mirror. Lying on the backseat, the man was out of sight. Doubt, held in abeyance by the exhausting work of the last few minutes, assailed her. Had she hurt him by moving him? Maybe she should have tried to warm up his body first? Had she made everything worse, just as Reed always said she did? Visions of broken backs and severed spinal columns filled her head. She groaned.

The road grew more winding. Torn by guilt, Valerie slowed the car to less than thirty miles an hour. Some Good Samaritan she was! Maybe she'd crippled him for life. Maybe he was dying even now, lying on her backseat while . . .

A croak that sounded vaguely human crawled up her spine.

Valerie's heart flew into her throat. In the rearview mirror, she caught sight of a dark upright shape that hadn't been there before. Instinctively she screamed and shut her eyes.

A jarring thud and the sickening crunch of metal were followed by the cessation of motion, and then, silence.

Chapter Three

A deep throaty growl vibrated near Valerie's right ear. She opened her eyes. Her face was pressed against the steering wheel. The headlights illuminated a leafy wall of trees pressed up against the front bumper, as well as scores of dead bugs squashed on the windshield.

Dazed, she shook her head, and looked out the side window. At least the car hadn't plowed into a ditch. And she couldn't have hit anything too hard because the air bag hadn't deployed. Assuming the car would still run, there was a reasonable chance of getting it back on the road by herself.

Beside her, Reddi growled again, this time with a menacing note Valerie had never heard before.

She rubbed her neck and smiled at the pup. She still felt kind of woozy and . . .

Her gaze fell on the dark figure reflected in the rearview mirror. She froze. The source of the frog-like sound was now identified; the voice that had startled her so badly she'd driven off the road. The voice that belonged to the

13

body that had just come to life in her backseat!

Trying to tame the fear threatening to choke her, Valerie swallowed. There's nothing to be afraid of, she admonished herself. *He's a weak, injured man who's only now regained consciousness.*

She shushed Reddi. Schooling her features into a mask of calmness, she straightened her spine and forced herself to turn and face the stranger.

In the light reflected from the trees, the dark shape took form. Short, sand-coated hair stood out in every direction on the man's head. Light-colored eyes stared at her from out of the angular face, eyes reflecting the bewilderment— and fear—she suspected showed in her own.

Her hand shaking, Valerie reached up and clicked on the overhead light. The man jerked back and raised one hand to cover his eyes. The blanket had fallen to his waist, revealing his broad, mud-covered shoulders and lean chest.

After a long moment he dropped his hand. Eyes, startlingly green against the lightness of the dried sand that coated his face, blinked and then settled into a steady stare. Some of the mud around his eyes and mouth cracked and broke away from his well-defined cheekbones. His hands flexed in his lap, dislodging more grime.

Valerie swallowed again. Her fingers dug into the back of the seat. "How are you feeling?" she ventured.

"I'm fine."

Valerie cringed at his croak; the man grimaced, and more mud crumbled from his features. He looked around the car. He cleared his throat, with little effect. "What am I doing here? Where are you taking me?"

He eyed Reddi. The dog bared his teeth and growled.

"Stop it, Reddi!" Valerie glared at the pup, then returned her attention to the strange man in the backseat. "We're going to the hospital in Huntsville. I found you unconscious on the beach at Aurora Lodge, on Lake Aurora, just a few minutes ago."

The man frowned; more mud and sand fell away, revealing a clean-shaven, square jaw. "What time is it?"

"What?" The odd question jarred Valerie. "Oh." She glanced at her watch. "It's after eleven."

"No. I mean, what year is it?"

Valerie stared at him in distress. Didn't they say that head injuries or other severe accidents could disorient a person? That had to be the explanation for the man's disjointed questions. Still, she should answer. "It's the year 2000. June 2000."

"Two thousand," he repeated. He paused, then took a deep breath. "Two thousand." He said it in an odd fashion, almost as if he'd never heard the number before.

After a moment, he focused on Valerie again, his green eyes narrowed and wary. "Who are you?"

"Me? I'm Valerie Scott."

"Do you live here?"

"No, I'm just visiting."

The man lapsed into silence. He raised one hand to his shoulder to brush off some mud. The motion set off another round of growling from Reddi.

Valerie petted the dog until he subsided. She looked at the stranger again. "I'd better try to back onto the road so we can get you to the hospital. I don't know how long you were lying on that beach or how long you were in the water. You need to be checked over by a doctor."

"No."

Valerie frowned. "What?"

"No, I'm not going to the hospital."

"But who knows what's wrong with you?" Exasperated, she rose onto her knees. A body had come to life in her backseat. She had the jitters. Her head ached. Her back hurt from pulling this guy to the car. She'd driven off the road. And now her cadaver-come-to-life was refusing to co-operate for his own good. "You *have* to go to the hospital."

"No."

"Yes! I bet you don't even remember why you were in the water in the first place."

15

"I was swimming across the lake."

"So what happened to you?"

"I don't know."

"All the more reason for you to go to the hospital," she insisted.

"No." His voice, while still a croak, was definite. Stubbornness glittered in his green eyes. "I'm not going. Just take me home."

"And where would that be?" Irritation overrode Valerie's fear, making her tone waspish.

He cleared his throat. "The Aurora Lodge."

"The Aurora Lo—" Valerie gaped.

Several moments passed before she regained speech. "That's impossible. No one lives at Aurora Lodge. It's been vacant since February."

The man frowned. "Vacant? Where's Art?"

"Art? Oh, you mean Arthur Pembroke. My great-uncle. He died in February."

"Died . . ." The man's voice faded. He clutched the blanket at his waist. "But what . . . how did it happen?"

Despite the mud, shock and disbelief stood out on his face. Valerie, her own grief still near the surface, felt the sting of tears in her eyes once more. Her irritation fell away and she lowered her head. "He died in February. Of a heart attack. He was up here by himself. They didn't find him until . . . until several days later."

The man pressed his lips tightly together, and shut his eyes, but not before Valerie glimpsed the sharp stab of sorrow. Touched, she found herself offering him the comfort she herself needed. "The doctor said it was a massive coronary. He died instantly. He didn't suffer."

The man lowered his head. In the silence, Valerie could hear him drawing in deep, steadying breaths. Who was he and why hadn't he heard of Arthur's death?

She cleared her throat. "I need to ask." She paused. "Who are you?"

His lowered head muffled his response. Valerie couldn't hear. "Pardon?"

"I said my name is Jack. Jack Wilder."

Valerie frowned. She'd heard that name before, just recently. As recently, she realized with a start, as her meeting a few hours ago with her uncle's lawyer, Ed Grierson.

Her eyes widened. Her heart thumped rapidly in her chest and her mouth grew dry. She stared at the stranger in the backseat of her car.

"Why—" she said, "why you're the person Uncle Arthur's lawyer has been trying to find since February."

She paused, then blurted out, "You and I have inherited Aurora Lodge."

Jack stared uncomprehendingly into the darkness outside the car. *Arthur dead . . . the lodge empty . . . the lawyer . . . you and I have inherited Aurora Lodge. . . .*

He dropped his head into his hands. All the changes, the new information, the new faces, the dog—it was as bad as—no, it was worse than—the first time. Then he had been alone, bewildered, torn with guilt. But then Art had been there. Trusting, believing, always loyal Art. Now there was only this stranger, this woman who regarded him with fear and suspicion.

He swallowed, but couldn't rid his mouth of the gritty taste and feel of sand. Not for the first time, he wished he were dead.

"Are you all right?"

The gentle touch of a hand on his shoulder, together with the question, caused him to stiffen. He raised his head and his gaze collided with two soft brown eyes, eyes brimming with a sympathy and understanding that shocked him to the core. For a moment he could do nothing but stare at the woman—Valerie, she'd said—as she leaned over the driver's seat toward him. Her clear brow creased in a frown and she worried her full bottom lip with her teeth. Rich mahogany hair was pulled back by some means, but at least

17

half of the burnished strands had escaped to frame her pale, narrow face and smooth, pleasing features. A light floral scent wafted around him, a scent that spoke of life, and happiness, and hope.

He forced himself to go still, to push back the pain unbottled by her concern. Surrendering to self-pity was a weakness he could ill afford.

He shut his eyes for a moment and prayed silently. Prayed for an end to his torment. It was a prayer to which he no longer expected an answer. If there was a God, he had stopped listening long ago.

"Let me take you to the hospital."

The low, melodic voice washed over him again, reminding him of other times and other places. He gritted his teeth and forced himself back to the here and now. He opened his eyes and confronted once more that terrifying tenderness.

He blinked. The woman—Valerie—continued to watch him anxiously, her head tilted to one side and her full lips parted. Her eyes, like rich brown velvet, filled with the light of encouragement.

Something moved inside him, a spontaneous response to her beauty and caring that surprised and shocked him, both for its strength and the fact that it was there at all. He turned his head away. "No. Take me to Aurora Lodge."

From the corner of his eye, he saw Valerie worry her bottom lip again, making her look for all the world like an anxious little girl. Was she as young as she looked? he wondered suddenly. *Is she married?*

The ridiculous questions flashing through his head without rhyme or reason disoriented him further. He struggled for control, and cleared his throat in an effort to rid himself of his croak and the gritty taste of sand. "I'm sorry I disturbed your evening." He grimaced at the raspiness of his voice, and cleared his throat again. "But if we can get your automobile back onto the road, you can have me back at Aurora Lodge in a few minutes. And then you can be on your way."

Frowning, Valerie sat back on her knees. The retriever growled again, but she silenced him with a severe look.

She turned back to Jack. "I don't think you understand. I'm staying at Aurora Lodge too. In my uncle's house. The lawyer had the power and water hooked up. But he never said anything about anyone else staying there."

Jack's chest tightened. It was all he could do to keep a curse from leaving his lips. His fists clenched in his lap. "That's because he doesn't know." He paused. "Art—your uncle—we had a standing agreement. He kept a cabin ready and waiting for me at all times, in case I dropped by. Sometimes I didn't show up for a year or two, but he always kept it waiting."

He watched Valerie for signs of disbelief. She pressed her lips together and knelt up straighter, but not before a slight tremor gave her away. It was clear he was frightening her; he could hardly blame her.

She didn't quite look at him. "Which cottage did you say you were staying in?"

"Arrowhead. It's one of the one-room cabins right near the top of the hill."

"Oh. Yes." Her voice quavered. She swallowed, and said more forcefully, "I didn't see your car in the parking lot."

"I didn't come by car. I hitchhiked in this afternoon. Got a ride on a lumber truck."

"I see."

No, you don't. Even a dazed, half-drowned, mud-covered man could see she was growing more suspicious, and more jittery, by the minute.

He tried to allay her fears. "I'll get out and see what damage has been done to the car. Why don't you see if it will start?"

Jack grasped the blanket and awkwardly pulled it beneath him, the action dislodging yet more mud.

He opened the door and winced. Pain spurted through

his joints. Suppressing a groan, he eased himself out of the car and into the mass of raspberry bushes and tall grasses crowding the roadside. It was amazing he didn't creak from lack of use. He shoved the undergrowth out of his way in an attempt to examine the front of the car.

The roar of the engine caught him by surprise. He jerked back, crashing against the bark of a young oak tree. Pain arced through his back. Lots of pain. He groaned.

He glanced through the windshield. By the glow of the interior light, he saw Valerie busying herself with the controls of the car, straightening the rearview mirror, the side-view mirrors, anything but looking at him. The dog, his ears still flat against his head, watched him with suspicion. Jack suppressed an urge to growl back.

With clumsy motions, he pulled branches away from the grille. The crash had smashed the right headlight and dented the fender a little. Valerie must have been driving pretty slowly for the car to have sustained so little damage.

He pushed his way through the thick bushes on the driver's side of the car. Grimacing at the protests of his body, he knelt to examine the wheels and the ground beneath. They were lucky. Underfoot was a combination of gravel, crushed raspberry bushes, and dry, solid earth. There'd been little rain in the last week or two.

He got up and tapped on the window. Valerie opened it. "Well?"

"It looks pretty good. One headlight is out, and the fender is dented, but that's all."

"Good. Do you think you're strong enough to stand on the road and direct me?"

He nodded. Grasping the blanket around his chest, he clambered through the brush to the road. To his knowledge, no cars had passed since they'd crashed. And none were likely to appear this late, especially if it was a weeknight.

He gestured to Valerie to start backing up. Without warning, the engine roared, and the car jolted backward toward him. Jack jumped out of the way. He tripped over a rock and stumbled into a mass of raspberry bushes. Bits of gravel flew into the air and rained down upon him.

Groggily he rose to his knees. The rear lights glowed in his eyes, and his left temple throbbed with a familiar ache.

Before he had time to consider, the car door swung open. Valerie jumped out.

"I'm sorry. I didn't hit you, did I? I was afraid I wouldn't have enough power to pull out of those bushes if I didn't gun it."

"No." He shook his head and blinked. He felt one of her hands slide around his back and under his arm, its warmth penetrating the chill of his mud-covered skin, awakening glimmers of long-ago comfort and closeness and a life no longer open to him. She helped him to his feet.

"Are you sure you don't want to go to the hospital?" she asked.

Her dark eyes burned with worry, and her lips fluttered only inches from his. He could feel her sweet, warm breath, spiced with the faint aroma of what he thought must be coffee and cream, along with a floral scent from the cloud of hair framing her face.

Once more nerve endings tingled; there was a stirring in his groin. With a shock, he recognized the sensation for what it was: the beginnings of physical desire as his body responded to the tenderness and loveliness of the woman beside him.

"No." He stiffened and shrugged out of her grasp. "I'm fine."

He started for the car, aware she stood still, watching him. It made him feel . . . odd. As he reached the door, he heard her footsteps.

They drove in silence. The dog peered between the seats, fixing Jack with a menacing stare.

Several minutes later they pulled into the lodge parking lot. Valerie maneuvered the car into a spot next to the lit office door. In the faint illumination, Jack noticed little different since his last visit, except the absence of cars.

Valerie turned the key in the ignition. A popping sound made Jack jump.

"What's that?"

"The trunk. We'll need a flashlight to find your cabin."

Jack opened the door and eased out, pressing his lips tightly together against the screaming pain of his unused muscles and joints. Valerie got out, followed by Reddi, and proceeded to the trunk.

"Here it is." She turned on the flashlight and nodded to Jack. "I'll walk with you to your cabin. Are the power and water on there too?"

Jack grunted noncommittally. If she was still afraid, she hid it well. "You don't need to come with me," he croaked. "I know the way."

"I want to. I need to make sure you're safely settled."

Jack hid his dismay. With Art dead, who knows what had happened to the cabin? Maybe it was locked. Maybe it had been torn down. Maybe his clothes had been discarded. With so many unknowns, the last thing he needed was an audience.

He reached for the flashlight, but Valerie stepped back. Reddi growled.

Jack raised his hands placatingly, but then had to grab to save his falling blanket. "It's all right. Really. I know the way. I'm fine."

Valerie shook her head. Despite her earlier jumpiness, there was no missing the stubbornness in her stance now, or on her face. "I'm sorry. You won't go to the hospital. I almost ran you over with the car. The least I can do now is see you to your cabin and make sure you have everything you need."

Jack gripped the blanket. He'd hoped she'd be too nervous to escort him. But no. Unfortunately, her sense of duty overrode her nervousness.

He nodded curtly, turned on his heel, and walked unsteadily to the path. "This way," he threw over his shoulder. Valerie and the dog scurried to catch up.

Valerie managed to keep the shaky beam of the flashlight trained on the the ground before his feet. Barely daring to think, he passed the lodge, turned left at the shuffleboard court, and headed over the bumpy, rock-strewn terrain to Arrowhead. The grass was longer than usual, likely because regular upkeep had ended with Art's death. They passed the dark shape of the first of the three one-room log cabins, the trio built in the early nineteen-hundreds when Aurora Lodge initially opened as a hunting and fishing camp.

The closer they came to the cabin, the more his tension mounted. Would the door be open? Would his clothes be there? How would he explain if something was amiss?

The questions gnawed at him as they passed the second deserted cabin. His mouth, already gritty with sand, grew as dry as the Sahara. He clenched and unclenched the fingers of his free hand.

He hesitated on the first of six flat slabs of granite paving the way to the screened-in porch of the log cabin. Valerie flashed the light over the cabin, until she found the painted sign reading ARROWHEAD.

Jack turned. "Thank you. I appreciate your lighting the way. Good night."

Valerie shook her head. Her eyes darted back and forth, not quite meeting his. "I'm coming in," she said, a slight tremor undermining her firmness. "I want to see if you need anything. You know, towels, sheets, all that stuff."

"That's not nece—"

"I know." Her tone had regained its strength. "But I'd never forgive myself if anything happened to you now. Especially since I can't convince you to go to the hospital."

Jack turned back to the steps. The throbbing in his temple, before only a dull ache, had escalated into a painful drumbeat that bounced inside his head, matching the pounding of his heart. A stabbing pain gripped his chest.

Perhaps a massive heart attack was about to solve all his problems.

The chest pain passed, though the throbbing continued. No such luck. Jack squared his shoulders and lumbered forward. His hand closed over the cold, hard metal of the door handle. Taking a deep breath, he turned the knob and pushed.

The door stuck. Afraid to wait, he rammed his bare shoulder against its wooden frame with such force that the door slammed open and bounced noisily against the inside wall of the porch.

Reddi barked frantically. Jack swallowed. "Sticks sometimes." He didn't look at Valerie.

He eyed the remaining door, the one to the interior of the cottage. He'd forgotten. The screen door meant nothing. It had no lock, not even a hook to close it from the inside. It was the next door that locked, the door that would prove his flimsy story or reveal him a liar.

The flashlight glinted off the metal doorknob. Holding his breath, he stepped forward and reached for the handle.

His hand closed around the unforgiving metal. He paused. Then, gritting his teeth, he turned the handle and pushed.

Chapter Four

Swollen from years of extreme cold and heat and lack of use, the hinges creaked ominously. Then, with a squawk that was music to Jack's ears and a lurch that threw him off balance, the door gave way.

Jack let out his breath. *Safe . . . for the moment.* He stood unmoving in the doorway, blocking access to the cabin.

The flashlight flickered from behind and one side of him, bouncing erratically around the room, illuminating the bare log walls, the flagstone fireplace that consumed one wall, the painted plywood floor, the tiny kitchen area.

"Is the power on?"

With his left hand, Jack felt around on the wall. He found the smooth plastic of the light switch and flicked it on. Nothing happened. Another wave of relief surged through him. It was better this way. The less Valerie could see the better.

He cleared his throat. "It was so bright earlier I never bothered to check."

The explanation hung lamely in the air. After an awkward moment, Valerie asked, "Where are your things?"

Jack stepped inside and glanced at the spot where the wood table had been, and should still be. From the light of the flashlight, he made out the dark shape of what he hoped were the legs of a pair of jeans hanging over the edge of the table.

"There." He pointed to the table. Immediately the thin beam of light from Valerie's flashlight followed. The beam found the jeans, a pair of running shoes on the floor below, and then bounced back to the tabletop to reveal a neatly folded bundle of what appeared to be a T-shirt and sweatshirt. Beside the bundle lay a man's watch, the loops of its leather straps rising on either side like the undulations of a snake.

"You won't be able to stay here." Valerie's voice, small and stubborn, came from behind him, where she stood unmoving at the door. "Not without any power. Not in your condition."

Jack stuck out his hand. "Give me the flashlight."

He took it from her and flickered the beam over the wall to the left. The light revealed a narrow, shoulder-high wood shelf, and glinted off the glass of a sooty propane lamp.

"See?" he said, glancing back at her pale face. "I'll be fine." He directed the light at the fireplace. "There's kindling laid for a fire. And firewood, lots of firewood." A stack of split logs was piled against the massive hearth.

Reddi chose that moment to streak past Valerie into the room. He avoided Jack and ran straight to the fireplace and began sniffing.

Suddenly a scratchy, scurrying sound emanated from the fireplace. A tiny squeak, and the noise took off along the wall, followed by a fiercely-barking Reddi.

"What's that?" Valerie asked.

"Mice." Jack shrugged. "A lot of these cabins get infested with deer mice over the winter. Art sets traps every spring."

Or he used to set traps. Reality brought another stab of

grief, as well as the familiar bitterness. *Art,* Jack wanted to demand. *Why you? Why not me?*

Valerie interrupted his thoughts. "But without power, there's no water."

"That's all right. There's an old well around the side. It's got a hand pump."

"But you need a shower or a bath!"

"I can go in the lake."

Disbelief stood out on Valerie's face. From the doorway where she still stood she demanded, "You want to go in the lake *now?* After what happened?"

He shrugged again. "It's okay." Actually, it wasn't okay. The thought of that cold water lapping at the shore, lapping at his ankles, sucking at his limbs, filled him with dread. But at least it was a familiar dread, one he knew he could handle. Far better than dealing with the prying eyes and concern, however laudable, of this tenderhearted but far-too-persistent woman.

Slowly, one step at a time, Valerie advanced into the room. Jack glanced from her to the dog and back. She chewed her lower lip and twisted her hands. He felt a spurt of sympathy for her, and a return of the unsettling yearning he recognized but refused to accept. No doubt she was torn between doing what she saw as her duty and putting as much space as possible between herself and this stranger who'd washed up on her beach. But if playing on her jitters was what it took to get her to leave, then that's what it would be.

"I'm fine." He spoke firmly, the croak almost erased from his deep baritone. He straightened and looked at her as grimly as possible.

She paused, the weird shadows thrown by the flashlight obliterating all but fragments of the battle that raged across her expressive face, the battle between duty and fear. Reddi continued to snuffle along the wall in search of the elusive mouse.

27

"All right," she conceded, then straightened, as if to compensate for the concession. "But light the lamp before I leave."

Jack nodded. To refuse would only raise more suspicions. Grasping the blanket with one hand, the flashlight with the other, he made his way to the shelf. Beside the lamp, as usual, was a box of mantles and another, smaller box of wooden matches. He lifted the lamp down and set it on the table, away from the clothing.

He handed the flashlight back to Valerie. With fingers still stiff from disuse, he fumbled with the blanket in an attempt to fold it more firmly about his waist. Holding the lamp steady on the table, he pumped it until he had full pressure. Then he turned on the propane and lit a match.

The mantle burst into flames that flickered halfway to the ceiling. Jack jumped back.

"Is there a fire extinguisher?" Valerie shifted from one foot to the other.

Jack shook his head. "It'll die down in a moment. I should have lit it outside."

True to his word, the flames died a moment later, leaving only the mantle burning inside the glass globe and casting a steady light over the room. Too steady a light, as far as Jack was concerned. He glanced at the ceiling and the walls. Cobwebs hung in the corners, and a thick coat of dust covered everything. Art may have died only months ago, but it was clear no one had disturbed this cabin for years.

Jack turned down the lamp, hoping he'd done it before Valerie noticed the extent of the cabin's unlived-in state. But as he looked up, she had already approached the table and was reaching for his watch.

She picked it up. "Your watch is stopped. You'll have to—"

Her forehead creased in puzzlement as she examined its face more closely. "Why—"

"I'm not very good at keeping the dates and times in sync," he interrupted. He slipped the watch from her hand

and started winding it. He glanced at her. "What time is it, anyway?"

Valerie hesitated, then looked at her watch. "Ten after. Ten after twelve."

"Thanks." Jack set the time, finished winding, and buckled it onto his wrist. Unsmiling, he regarded Valerie. "It's late. I'll walk you back to Art's house."

Valerie shook her head, the strands of curly hair that had escaped their holder waving too. "No, it's all right. I've got the flashlight, and Reddi. I'll be fine. Come on, Reddi."

The dog bounded past her and out into the night. After a last quizzical look at Jack, she followed Reddi to the door. Teetering between relief at her departure and a strange sense of loss, Jack held his breath. The door shut behind her and he exhaled deeply, his head lowered.

Without warning the door swung open again. Jack jerked his head up, every nerve jarred.

"Sorry." Valerie smiled apologetically. "I guess you'll want to see the lawyer tomorrow. You know, about Uncle Arthur's will."

"Oh. Yeah." Jack swallowed. "I'll call on you about ten."

"Sure." She paused, her soft lips parted, as if she wanted to say something else. Her dark eyes, large in her pale and narrow face, shimmered with uncertainty. Finally, she bit her lip and nodded. "Good night."

"Good night."

The door shut again. Jack listened to her footsteps cross the porch. The screen door slammed. He heard her call Reddi. He waited until he could hear no more.

He pulled a chair out from the table, scraping its legs against the plywood floor. He fell heavily into it; then his upper body collapsed onto the table. His cheek pressed against the cool wood, oblivious of the dust. He lay there, unmoving, until sleep finally overtook him.

The twittering and chirping of birds just outside Valerie's second-floor window woke her from a restless sleep. Her eyes fluttered open, then blinked, adjusting to the gray first light filtering through the unlined cotton curtains. From the west of the house came the angry cawing of a crow, followed by a series of screeches from a bird Valerie couldn't identify.

She opened her eyes wide and scanned Uncle Art's guest room, where she had chosen to sleep last night. It was the same room, likely the same double bed, she and her mother had shared for the dozen years they'd summered here. She hadn't been here for a good ten years, but little had changed. She recognized the pink chenille bedspread and the soft cotton sheets, the maple dresser and desk with their scuffed and scratched finishes, the faded prints and inept oil paintings on the walls. The wallpaper, with its tiny, old-fashioned flower print, curled and buckled in spots, its greens and browns and whites now faded into soothing sepia tones. The painted plank floor gaped through holes in the braided rug where Reddi still curled up fast asleep.

Valerie wrinkled her nose in reaction to the faint musty smell clinging to the room despite the open window. She yawned and glanced at the bedside digital clock. It was new, the only new item in the room as far as she could tell. She yawned again and eased herself up from the crumpled sheets. It was only quarter to six but she might as well get up. She wasn't going to sleep, not now. She doubted she'd managed more than an hour or two of sleep since she'd fallen into bed shortly after one A.M.

She hugged her knees to her chest and shivered, but it wasn't because of the chill morning air. It was the thoughts she'd been unable to banish last night, and the uneasiness they had spawned. When she'd finally dozed off, her dreams had quickly turned into nightmares, worse than anything she'd ever experienced. The faceless man chasing her, his hands outstretched. No matter how fast she ran, he was always there, waiting around the next corner, in the room she had thought so safe, where her family waited.

She shuddered and tightened her grasp on her knees.

Being scared. She wasn't used to it. She didn't like it. But there it was, an uneasy feeling coiled in the pit of her stomach, grasping at her throat, making the hairs on the back of her neck stand up.

Is it because of him? Valerie wondered. Jack. Jack Wilder, he'd said. That man she'd found on the beach in such strange circumstances. She thought about his even stranger revival, and annoying refusal to go to the hospital. And the fact that Uncle Art had left half the lodge to him.

Valerie bit her lip. There was a time when she would have accepted Jack's story without doubt. But that was before the fear, the fear that had nothing to do with him, and yet everything to do with him. The fear she'd thought she had left behind in Chicago, with Reed and that one terrifying incident.

She flung back the covers and cringed when her feet hit the icy floor. Reddi opened his eyes and immediately bounced up, ready to play, his eyes alert, tongue hanging.

Despite herself, Valerie smiled. She liked having the playful pup around. He reminded her of her Grade Three students back at George Washington Junior School—and he took her mind off her troubles. She petted him as he danced at her feet. "I'll let you out in a minute. Just wait."

Reddi dashed out of the bedroom and down the hall to the stairs. Valerie knew he'd be back as soon as he realized he needed her to open the back door.

She glanced in the mirror above the scuffed dresser. The silver surface, pitted around the edges, showed a Valerie she knew she didn't like, one far too wan, with dark smudges under eyes filled with uncertainty.

Valerie edged closer to the mirror. She pulled down the neck of her sleep shirt and touched the tender skin at her throat. In the thin, gray light, only the faintest of shadows remained. But it didn't matter. In her mind's eye she could see them, the angry red marks that had circled her neck. Even worse, she could feel the terrifying panic as she couldn't catch her breath, couldn't break away.

31

Valerie shut her eyes and backed away from the mirror, fighting the panic rising inside. Her heart beat frantically; her palms started to sweat. She forced herself to take deep, calming breaths, to control the familiar anxiety attack before it devastated her.

Slowly, the anxiety released its hold, and her breathing returned to normal. Valerie opened her eyes and realized her hand still held her throat. Resentment flooded through her. Resentment at Reed and the violence that had destroyed her foolish sense of safety. Resentment at herself for allowing it to happen. Resentment at the unfairness of it all.

And now resentment at the man who had materialized out of the darkness to snatch away from her the one place where she'd always felt safe, the haven that she'd held in her mind for the last three weeks, a beacon guiding her through the long days and even longer nights.

Resentment flared into anger. He'll have to leave, she thought abruptly. I'll tell him to leave!

She swallowed hard and looked around. The room had brightened with the advance of the dawn. Somehow the brightness lifted her spirits.

Yes, that's what she'd do. She'd tell Jack to leave. She'd take control of her life again, re-invent herself as the strong, independent woman she'd always wanted to be. She'd left the nightmare behind in Chicago. She had no intention of inviting it into the one place that had always meant safety and happiness.

A knock on the kitchen door startled Valerie; she spilled the cup of coffee that had been halfway to her lips. Reddi leapt up from the spot in front of the Quebec heater where he'd been warming himself and raced barking for the door.

Grumbling at the coffee stains now marring her white sweatshirt, Valerie glanced at her wristwatch. It was twenty to ten. Jack was early.

She stood up, steeling herself for the confrontation to

come. She hoped Jack would accede to her request that he find somewhere else to stay. Especially since, as a half owner of Aurora Lodge—if he really was who he said he was—he had every bit as much a right to stay here as she did.

She swallowed. It didn't matter. For her peace of mind, she had to demand he stay somewhere else. And she had to demand it without letting on just how uneasy he made her. Likely he had family in the area, anyway. How else would he have come to know Uncle Arthur, and know him well enough to be left half of Aurora Lodge?

Plastering a strained smile on her face, Valerie grabbed Reddi's collar with one hand and opened the door with the other.

The greeting froze on her lips. Instead of Jack, a small woman in her mid-forties, dressed similarly to herself in a sweatshirt and jeans, smiled brightly. "Good morning. You must be Art's great-niece Valerie."

"Yes," was all Valerie managed before Reddi escaped her grasp and bounded up at the woman.

"No, Reddi, no." Valerie tried to collar him again.

The woman laughed and crouched down to Reddi's level. She petted him and looked up at Valerie. "It's all right. I've got a dog myself. They're so full of energy at this age."

She stood up and pushed aside a lock of gray-streaked hair that had escaped from an untidy ponytail. She smiled again, a smile that attractively crinkled the skin around her blue eyes. "I'm Velma Altenburg. Ed Grierson hired me to clean up the house before you arrived. I just wanted to make sure everything's fine. Do you need anything?"

In the face of the woman's friendliness and Reddi's obvious acceptance, Valerie's tension seeped away. "Oh, no. Everything's fine. I really appreciate how clean and tidy you've made it. I wasn't sure what to expect."

"I know." The woman nodded. "It's a little unsettling staying in a family member's house after his death. It helps if it's clean and cheery."

Drawn by the woman's warm practicality, Valerie invited her in for coffee.

"Why, thank you. I'd love some. I've been running errands all morning. This will be a nice break."

Velma sat down at the round oak kitchen table while Valerie fetched a mug and poured coffee. With the sun streaming through the east-facing windows and heat emanating from the small fire Valerie had set in the Quebec heater, the room breathed warmth and cheerfulness.

Feeling more relaxed, Valerie sat down across from Velma. She took a sip of her cooling coffee and regarded the woman. Although the gray streaking her almost-black hair and the lines around her eyes and mouth indicated she had to be at least forty-five, her slim figure and fluid motions were those of an energetic and enthusiastic young person. She radiated goodwill and friendliness.

"Is this the first time you've worked at Aurora Lodge?" Valerie asked, curious.

"Oh, no." Velma laughed. "I've been coming here on and off since I was eighteen. For years I worked as a maid on the weekends, cleaning the cottages after each family left and before the next one arrived. Sometimes, I worked the desk too, and ran the little convenience store. I remember Art pointing you out to me during one of your first summers at the lodge, but then I got married and wasn't around much. The last few years I've only been here every couple of months, just to clean this house for Art. You know he closed the lodge down three years ago?"

Valerie shook her head. She hoped the guilt she felt didn't show on her face. Perhaps her mother had told her that Uncle Arthur had closed the lodge, perhaps not. But even if she'd known, would it have made a difference? Three years ago she'd been immersed in her new job as a teacher, spending evenings and weekends marking papers and developing lesson plans, and summers taking courses. Any spare time had been spent with her friends or decorating her new apartment. There wouldn't have been a lot of time to think about a great-uncle she hadn't seen in years.

"Yes, Art turned eighty-one the year he closed the lodge. It was getting to be too much work for him. Everyone tried to convince him to sell, but he wouldn't do it. Said he planned to die here." Velma paused. "He got his wish."

She shook her head, shaking loose a couple more strands of hair. A faraway look clouded her blue eyes. "You know, it's odd," she mused. "Art always looked so worried whenever anyone suggested he wouldn't be around forever. As if no one else could take care of his precious lodge. Almost as if there was something here, some treasure or secret he couldn't bear to leave."

She smiled ruefully. "But I guess it was nothing more than the fact he'd spent his whole life here. He was born here, raised here, and worked here. He never married, though not for lack of interested women. I guess this place was his life and he couldn't imagine being without it."

"Yes, he certainly loved it." Valerie remembered many things about her uncle, but his love for Aurora Lodge stood out in her mind. She'd always accepted it as part of what made Uncle Arthur Uncle Arthur. But now her curiosity had been pricked. Was there something more to Uncle Arthur's attachment, something that as a child she might not have noticed? She made a mental note to phone her mother and ask.

Velma nodded. "It's not hard to see why. Aurora Lake is the most beautiful lake between Huntsville and Algonquin Park. The water's clean, the beach here is solid and wide, and the granite cliffs down the other end of the lake are magnificent. The fishing is good too, and so is the canoeing out on the East River. My husband and the kids like to come here as often as they can. Even after he closed it, Art let us stay here in one of the cottages down by the lake each summer."

"Where do you live?"

"Huntsville. It's only a twenty-minute drive. Even staying

out here, my husband could go into work each day."

Valerie wondered if Velma was angling for a cottage again this summer. Not ready to relinquish her privacy, she resisted the impulse to offer one. "Where do you work now?"

"I've got a job as a waitress at a restaurant on the highway. You've probably seen it. Three Guys and a Stove?"

At Valerie's nod, she continued. "I work the lunch shift." She glanced at her watch. "Which means I should probably head home now and get changed for work."

She tipped her head and drank the remains of her coffee, then stood up and rummaged in her pocket. She handed Valerie a card. "Here's my phone number and address. If you need any help out here, or if you want to know about anything in the area, let me know."

"Why, thank you." Valerie stood up too. Velma's warmth made it impossible to suspect any ulterior motives. But recent experience had made Valerie cautious. She'd check with her uncle's lawyer first before even considering asking Velma if she'd like to take a cottage here for a few weeks. Aurora Lodge encompassed more than a dozen acres. There was plenty of room.

Velma scratched Reddi behind the ears and headed for the door. She touched her head in a jaunty wave and shut the door.

Valerie sat down again. She picked up her mug and gazed at the last few swallows of coffee. What was Velma's relationship with Uncle Arthur? More importantly, what was Jack Wilder's relationship with Arthur? And why had Arthur left him half the lodge?

She shook her head. What a fool she'd been to think she'd find peace and solitude here. People kept turning up—some in the most unlikely ways—each with a story and a relationship to Uncle Arthur. It was only natural, of course. Uncle Arthur had spent his whole life here. She just hadn't anticipated all the complications returning to the lodge would entail.

A firm knock on the door disturbed her revery. Reddi flattened his ears and growled.

Jack, thought Valerie. She took a deep breath and rose.

Velma whistled as her running shoes crunched across the gravel parking lot to her tiny Datsun. She was glad she'd made the trip to Aurora Lodge. Art's great-niece, while understandably reticent, had grown into a lovely young woman. She even looked a bit like Art. Something around the eyes, though Velma wasn't certain whether it was the shape or just the way Valerie had of looking at you, as if she were looking deep within for something not visible on the surface. It certainly wasn't the color: Art's eyes had remained a startlingly clear blue until his last days.

Shaking her head at her fancy, Velma opened the car door. She had slid onto the seat, one hand on the handle of the open door, when her eyes caught movement coming up the hill.

A tall, well-built man, wearing jeans and a blue plaid shirt, walked up the path from the lake toward her. His blond head was down and Velma couldn't see his features, but it didn't matter. The impression his presence evoked was immediate and unmistakable.

Her heart skipped a beat, and she gaped. *Could it be . . .*

Unable to draw her gaze away, she watched as the man turned at the shuffleboard courts and disappeared behind the lodge common room. He appeared to be headed for the kitchen door from which Velma had just come.

Velma slowly shut the car door. Valerie hadn't said anything about a boyfriend or a husband staying with her. Ed Grierson hadn't mentioned it either. But that didn't mean that Valerie hadn't brought someone with her. There was certainly no reason why she should have told Velma about it.

But it wasn't the fact that someone else was staying at Aurora Lodge that had given her such a start. No. It wasn't that.

It was the unbelievable familiarity of the man. Everything

about him, from his hair color, his broad shoulders, lean waist, and long legs, to the way he walked with his hands held easily at his sides, said he was a man Velma remembered all too vividly from the past.

But that was impossible. And no one knew it better than she did.

Chapter Five

Valerie grabbed Reddi's collar with one hand and reached for the doorknob with the other. The way Reddi was growling, she feared he might take a piece out of Jack's leg.

Holding on to the headstrong puppy, she pulled open the door. "Would you mind waiting outside?" she asked without glancing up. "I'm going to put the dog in another room."

She pulled Reddi past the stove and around the table to the hallway to the lodge office. She shooed him inside, then shut the door. Immediately Reddi's growls turned to whimpers.

Valerie winced. She hated shutting him up. She'd had trouble ignoring his whimpers from the first time she'd looked into his big, soulful eyes when he was four weeks old. But as much as she'd appreciate his presence, she wasn't taking him to town. Not with Jack in the car. "It won't be for long, boy," she called through the door.

She returned to the kitchen and stepped out onto the deck and into the warm sunlight streaming over the

Norah-Jean Perkin

beeches and oaks on the east side of the lodge grounds. The freshness of the air enticed her senses, and she couldn't resist taking several deep breaths.

She saw Jack standing beside the deck rail with his back to her. The clean line of his hair across the back of his neck indicated a fresh haircut, likely yesterday or the day before. His blue plaid flannel shirt fit snugly across broad shoulders, then tapered to faded jeans that molded to a firm butt and long, long legs, ending at scuffed brown work boots.

She swallowed. "Jack?"

Slowly he turned. Valerie blinked. This couldn't be the same man she had hauled from the beach last night. "Jack?" she repeated incredulously.

It had been clear last night that Jack was a lean, hard, well-built man. Now, in the daylight and without the mud, he seemed taller, more robust, and infinitely more alive.

But it was more than that. He was also surprisingly handsome, in a rugged, outdoors sort of way. His tanned face was clean-shaven, and with those broad cheekbones, full lips, and square jaw, would have looked good on the cover of any hiking or climbing magazine. An ugly purple and yellow bruise on his left temple, hidden last night by the mud and now partially covered by a shock of sun-streaked light brown hair, only added to his overall impression of tough competence.

Shock gave way to a familiar ripple of feeling. Despite Valerie's surprise, she recognized it instantly for what it was: attraction. Even with all her fears, she wasn't immune to the man's physical presence.

She raised her eyes from his boots to his face. "But . . . but you're so . . . so . . ."

"So clean?" Jack raised one dark eyebrow. Though he didn't crack a smile, a hint of laughter danced in those strange eyes that now appeared more blue than the mint green of the night before.

Valerie laughed nervously and shook her head. "No, it's

40

not that. It's just, well, I wouldn't have recognized you."

Through the long, sleepless night, she had built him up from merely a man she had found unconscious on the beach to the focus of all her fears, past and present. It was a relief to see that, under all the grunge, he wasn't a monster. Just a man. A man with an ugly bruise, with a toughness and strength that could be dangerous, but still, just a man. A man, Valerie reminded herself as fear nibbled at the edges of the mental pep talk she was giving herself, that Uncle Arthur had liked and trusted well enough to leave a half share in Aurora Lodge.

"It took a while to get the mud off," he said.

Valerie had a sudden and all-too-vivid picture of a naked Jack washing the dirt off his impressive body in the cold lake. She felt an embarrassed heat rise up her throat, and she forced herself to concentrate on the fully clothed man before her.

The silence between them grew longer and more awkward. Valerie knew she had to broach the subject of his leaving Aurora Lodge, but she wasn't sure how or where to start.

A howl echoed through the air, Reddi's escalating complaint against being locked up in the office at the other end of the house. Valerie frowned. Jack chuckled. "Sounds like your dog wants to get out."

Valerie nodded. "I'm going to leave him here while we go into town. He'll be all right."

Recollection of Reddi's odd behavior toward Jack last night bolstered her decision to ask Jack to leave. Reddi usually liked men, or at least he had until . . . Valerie skipped over the memory she didn't want to dwell on. Yes, Reddi had never been as hostile as he'd been when they discovered Jack on the beach. The dog's reaction alone should be enough to persuade her.

Valerie glanced at Jack. He leaned against the deck rail, regarding her intently with those strange eyes.

She cleared her throat. It was now or never. "Are you ready to go into Huntsville?"

"Sure."

Valerie rushed on. "Look, Jack. I'm happy to drive you to Huntsville to see Ed Grierson. He'll be glad to know you've arrived. Maybe you should go see a doctor too." She gestured to his forehead. "That bruise looks pretty bad."

She lifted her chin. "After that I'd like you to leave."

"Leave?" Jack's face darkened. He straightened and moved away from the rail.

Valerie focused on the empty space beside his head. "I know you've got a right to be here." She considered whether to give him a reason, and decided against it. "But I'd appreciate if you'd stay somewhere else until your claim is established and we've decided what we're going to do with the lodge."

Jack stiffened. A muscle visibly throbbed in the center of the bruise on his left temple. The light eyes narrowed, changing from a bluish green to the color of stormy seas.

"Why?"

Valerie winced at the flat harshness of the one-word question, and the terrifying flash of memory it evoked. Her legs started to tremble. She clenched her fists in an effort to stop the shaking. She wasn't about to tell him he scared her half to death, especially when it had nothing to do with him.

She raised her head and forced herself to look into his face, to confront those cold eyes. She swallowed again. "That's none of your business." An unfortunate quaver undermined her firmness.

Jack continued to regard her with a cold, assessing stare. He looked as if he were about to argue, to insist that he had as much right to stay there as she did. Valerie could hear a rushing sound in her ears as her nerves threatened to overwhelm her, but she managed to continue to hold his gaze.

Without warning, he turned away. "I see. I'll get my

things together now. After we go to the lawyer's office, you can drop me at the bank."

"Thank you." Valerie's words came out on a whoosh of breath. She didn't know why he'd given up without a fight, but she was grateful.

"I'll be back in five minutes." Jack tromped down the stairs and disappeared around the side of the house.

Valerie followed to the edge of the deck and watched as he jogged out of sight. Jack's immediate compliance with her wishes left her feeling a little guilty, but also proud of herself. She could do it. She could.

Resolutely, she pushed away the niggling guilt about Jack and his well-being. He was an adult. He'd lived in this area before. He could take care of himself.

Just as she could.

Valerie shuddered at the radio announcer's words, something about bodies being found in a home outside Huntsville. Though she lived in a city known for its violent crime, she'd never really paid much attention. Until now. Until the moment three weeks ago when violence crashed into her life in a way she couldn't ignore. Now violence seemed everywhere, more dangerous, more personal than it had ever been before. No matter where she went, no matter what she did, she couldn't escape it. Even here.

She shuddered again and turned down the volume. She could do without the details. She'd turned the radio on only to relieve the strained silence that had settled over the interior of the car after she'd turned out of the lodge driveway onto the lake road. She'd hoped for soothing music, not news of even more violence.

The low drone of the announcer continued as Valerie cast about for something, anything to talk about to tune out the ever-present violence. With Jack filling the seat beside her, his head almost touching the roof, her usually adequate Escort felt cramped and uncomfortable, the stranger beside her unbearably close.

But even with her nerves on edge, she couldn't resist surreptitiously studying him whenever the road and the traffic allowed the chance to glance away from the wheel and the front windshield. Unwilling to chance a collision of their gazes, she'd examined his worn jeans, only to catch a glimpse through a hole in the left knee of another fresh bruise and nasty scrape. The hand resting easily on his left thigh also appeared battle-scarred, the knuckles bruised, scraped, and swollen.

"Were you in a fight?" She could have bitten her tongue. This wasn't the kind of question you asked a stranger, especially one you'd just thrown out of his lodging. Nor was it a question you asked when you wanted to avoid violence.

"Why?" His tone was blunt.

Oh, she was in for it now. Her stomach clenched. "Well, that bruise on your head—and your hand and your knee look pretty bad too." She paused, waiting for his reaction. When none came, she plowed on. "So were you in a fight last night?"

"Not last night." Jack turned his head and looked out the window.

What's that supposed to mean? Valerie turned her attention to the road. Jack's unwelcoming tone didn't encourage more probing. And given her sensitivity to violence these days, it was just as well. After a moment, she glanced at him again, and then at the worn backpack on the floor between his legs. It was khaki green, far smaller than she'd expect for someone on the road, and the shoulder straps and corners were worn right through in spots. In fact, it looked as if a mouse, or perhaps a dog, had been chewing at it recently, making Valerie wonder exactly where Jack had been before the lodge.

When she looked again, Jack was staring straight ahead, his gaze on the road. He sat erect, his profile with the straight nose, broad cheekbones, and angular jaw perfectly still. Another twinge of nervousness prompted her to start a new line of conversation. "You said you'd just arrived," she tried. "Where were you?"

"In the States."

"Whereabouts?"

"Florida."

Valerie's hands tightened on the wheel. Jack's stilted answers to her stilted questions were almost as bad as the previous silence, and were doing nothing to calm her nerves.

She tried again. "Which part of Florida?"

"The Keys. The Gulf."

"Were you working there?"

He nodded. "I'm a fishing guide, among other things."

In her peripheral vision, Valerie noticed with a start that Jack's hands were balled into tight fists.

She looked at his face. His expression remained impassive, with no indication of the tension reflected by his fisted hands.

"So you come back here to work for Uncle Arthur every summer?"

For only the second time since they'd entered the car, Jack looked at her. His forehead creased and his eyes darkened with reluctance. "No. Not every year. Only once in a while. I do odd jobs for him. Sometimes I take out fishermen or lead canoe or hunting trips. Whatever's required."

With a pang, Valerie realized they'd both spoken of Arthur in the present. For a moment she saw a clear picture of her uncle the way she remembered him, elderly but robust and well-tanned, his brilliant blue eyes twinkling with that teasing light that always meant he had a surprise in mind.

Jack's lunge forward, followed by the blasting voice of the radio announcer, startled her, jarring her back into the present.

"*. . . and the dazzling display of Northern Lights last night was the best we've seen in this area for at least eleven years. Astronomers say the unprecedented sunspot activity they've noticed on the sur-*

face of the sun in recent days is likely to continue for several weeks, resulting in many nights of excellent aurora viewing. So far—"

Jack turned the radio back down, and Valerie wondered if he was interested in astronomy. "Did you have a chance to see the Northern Lights last night? I mean, before you had your swimming accident?"

"No."

"They were wonderful from the beach." Valerie silently cursed her faux pas. Jack wouldn't be there to see them tonight. "They'll probably be good from town too," she added.

Jack shrugged. Valerie noticed the muscle still jumping in his forehead, though his fists had relaxed and were now stretched out on his thighs.

The news faded seamlessly into Paula Cole's "Where Have All the Cowboys Gone?" and Valerie was thankful for an excuse to end the conversation. The farther they drove from the lake, the guiltier she felt about asking Jack to leave, especially when she considered his brush with death last night.

After five minutes of nonstop music, she turned off the highway and drove past the two grocery stores and the mall into town. "Ed Grierson's office is in an old building just off the main drag," she explained.

She parked the car in front of an unassuming two-story brick building that also housed the offices of a doctor, a dentist, and another lawyer.

Conscious of Jack following her, she led the way into a small lobby and then up the single set of stairs. Ed Grierson's office was the first one to the right, and consisted of a small reception area with yellowing wallpaper, decrepit vinyl-covered chairs, and an end table that looked as ancient as Mr. Grierson himself. Next to the shiny, new computer, the youngest thing in the office had to be Lynn, Mr. Grierson's secretary.

"Good morning, Valerie." Lynn gave them her best small-town friendly smile.

Valerie couldn't help noticing how the copper-haired secretary's gaze flew to Jack, where it remained far longer than necessary, taking his measure and obviously finding it more than satisfactory. Lynn tilted her head and ran one hand through her glossy pageboy, before returning her attention to Valerie. "What can I do for you?"

"I was hoping I could see Mr. Grierson. I don't have an appointment, but it's important."

"Ooh, I'm sorry." Lynn sighed and looked at Jack. "Mr. Grierson's in Orillia today on business. He's got a daughter there, so he won't be back here until after the weekend."

Valerie frowned. Orillia was more than an hour away. And she'd wanted so badly to have the lawyer confirm Jack's identity so they could start discussions on what to do with the estate.

"Well, I guess it can't be helped. But can you call Mr. Grierson? I think he'd like to know that Jack Wilder has turned up."

"Jack Wilder?" Lynn's blue eyes widened. She looked at Jack with renewed interest. "You're Jack Wilder? The co-inheritor of Aurora Lodge?"

Jack nodded. "I'm Wilder. As for being a co-inheritor of the lodge, I'll have to talk to Mr. Grierson about that."

"Wouldn't it be great if you opened it up again?" The secretary leaned toward Jack. "They used to have some great dances there when I was a teenager."

More than a little annoyed, Valerie stepped forward. "Why don't you make us an appointment for Monday morning? Is Mr. Grierson free at eleven?"

Lynn scanned her day book. "Looks like it. I'll put you down and phone if there's any change."

"The phone isn't connected yet, but you can call me on my cell. Here's the number." Valerie handed her a card. "If I don't hear from you, we'll just come, all right?"

Sure." Lynn flashed her most alluring smile at Jack. "Have a nice weekend, Mr. Wilder."

"You too, Miss Scott," Valerie muttered under her breath

as she turned to leave. Jack was good-looking—even she wasn't immune to his charms—but she didn't appreciate being treated like the invisible woman once he appeared on the scene.

Valerie left and headed down the stairs to the parking lot. Oblivious to the brilliant June sunshine and balmy air, she waited by the car for Jack, who had apparently stopped to flirt with the awestruck Lynn.

When Jack strolled out the door a moment later, Valerie bit her tongue to keep from loosing a sarcastic comment.

"Where's your bank?" she demanded.

"It's the National Trust branch. It's only three blocks from here. I'll take my pack and walk."

Not a hint of rancor showed on Jack's face. Suddenly, Valerie felt ashamed. He hadn't done anything to her, had only had the misfortune to show up, unconscious and naked, on the beach they now jointly owned. He'd acceded without argument to her demand that he leave. She was letting other people, other places, control her reaction to him and to the present situation.

She let out a long breath and twisted the keys in her hands. "No, it's all right. I'll drive you."

Jack paused. Under the ugly gash, his green/blue eyes regarded her levelly, making her throat constrict once more. Finally he shrugged. "Sure."

They got in and Valerie started the car. "Turn right and go back the way we came two blocks," he directed. In the light traffic, Valerie followed his instructions easily. The true summer rush wouldn't hit until after Canada Day on July first and the American Fourth of July.

"Turn left here, and then left again at the first corner. It's the second building on your right."

Valerie stopped the car before a glass-fronted, one-story building whose front door was propped open. People streamed in and out, brown paper bags and boxes in their hands.

The homey aroma of fresh-baked bread wafted around

them. Valerie took a better look at the building. It was a bakery, not a bank. Billie's Bakery, to be exact. She glanced from side to side. As far as she could see, no bank stood on this street.

"Are you sure you've got the right place? Jack?" When he didn't answer, she glanced at him. Jack stared at the bakery, his mouth set in a grim line.

"Jack," she repeated. "Maybe we're on the wrong street. Maybe it's the next one over."

"No. This is the right place. At least it was the last time I was here."

"When *was* the last time you were here?"

Jack flipped through the passbook. "I made a deposit eight months ago. The bank hadn't moved then."

"Maybe it's moved to another building somewhere else in town. Maybe—"

"I'll go inside and ask." Jack hurried out of the car and into the bakery.

Valerie watched the door. A moment later, Jack appeared. He filled the doorway, creating the same impression of lean, hard, capable masculinity that had stolen her breath this morning. She swallowed. Maybe she shouldn't have been so hard on Lynn after all.

But something was wrong. Jack walked woodenly to the car, the bankbook crushed in one hand.

She got out and regarded him over the Ford's roof. "What's wrong?"

"The bank closed this branch. The closest location now is in Orillia."

Valerie frowned. "So we'll just go to another bank and you can use your ATM card to withdraw money from your account."

"I don't have an ATM card."

"You don't have an ATM card?" Valerie repeated, dumbfounded. But then again, she was from a large American city. Maybe it was different here. She didn't know. She couldn't imagine functioning without her bank card. "Well, what about a credit card? You could get a cash advance."

He shook his head.

No credit card? How did he survive without a credit card?

"I move around a lot," he said in answer to her look of disbelief. "It's too hard to keep up with the bills when you don't stay in one place. Easier to pay cash, sometimes even to barter."

Barter? Valerie raised her eyes to the sky. He bartered?

With motions that spoke of a deep weariness, Jack opened the car door and lifted out his pack. He hoisted it over one shoulder and raised his eyes to Valerie's. It was like looking into a cold, murky sea, tinged with bitterness.

"Thanks for the ride. I'll see you at Grierson's office Monday morning."

He turned and strode out of the parking lot.

Chapter Six

Numbness slowly gave way to bitterness as Jack walked away from Valerie and one of the few remaining links to his past. The street dimmed around him. He stumbled over a break in the sidewalk, and jogged awkwardly to the left to miss two pedestrians.

Art is gone. The reality hit Jack now in a way that it hadn't last night. *Arthur Pembroke is dead.* His friend, his supporter, a man whose understanding and practical help had made life bearable.

But now Art was gone. There was no one left who knew Jack, who knew his unbelievable story, and yet believed him without fail. No one.

Most important of all, gone was Art's unflagging optimism, his belief that somehow, somewhere, they would find a solution. Never before had Jack realized how much Art's optimism had buoyed him up, had prevented him from giving up and sinking into despair.

But Art was gone.

At the corner, Jack stopped. He jingled the four dollars

and thirty-three cents in his pocket. He looked around, unseeing. Which way should he go? Where? Did it even matter?

His throat filled with the sour taste of loss. Loss and confusion. He'd forgotten what it was like. This terrible aloneness that had assaulted him the first time. The knowledge that he was alone with a secret no one would believe, much less understand. A secret he didn't understand himself.

He looked up at the sky. Overhead a hawk, away from its usual haunts, glided in deceptively lazy spirals. Was this hell? He'd often thought so. His own private hell on Earth, a punishment crafted to fit his particular crime. He—

"Jack!"

His attention jerked from the sky. Hair flying in a cloud around her face, Valerie charged to a stop beside him. "Where are you going? The bus station?"

He fingered the change in his pocket. "No. I don't have enough money."

Still breathing heavily from her run to catch up with him, Valerie gasped out, "Can I lend you some?"

He shrugged. "Don't bother. I'll hitchhike to Orillia."

He turned to cross the street, and Valerie gripped his left arm above the wrist. "Where will you stay?" she asked. "Do you have family here?"

He shook his head and regarded Valerie. Wild mahogany curls framed her furrowed forehead. Her dark eyes blinked uncertainly, then settled into a steady gaze, full of a conviction and concern that suddenly reminded him of Art. Art had worn that expression, had gotten that determined Good Samaritan look, whenever he'd decided to offer help, wanted or unwanted.

But Art's voice hadn't squeaked as Valerie's did; his chin hadn't trembled like hers, betraying her reluctance. Jack didn't know why she was so frightened, but she was. No matter what his problems, no matter what his reason for being here, he had no intention of scaring an already frightened woman even more.

"I'll be fine." He forced a smile.

"You're not going to go to a motel?" Her liquid brown eyes widened.

"No."

She frowned. "Then where will you go?"

"To Orillia. To the bank." It wasn't an answer, but it was all he had at the moment.

He looked down at his arm. Her fingers were still digging into his skin. Gently, he pried them loose. For a moment he held her small, soft hand between his two larger ones, savoring the human contact, a passing moment of sweetness so long denied to him. But when he realized she was shaking, he released her.

"Go home, Valerie. I'll see you Monday at Grierson's."

Despite her trembling, that stubbornness that reminded him of Art flared in the soft brown eyes and the set of her mouth again. "No. Look, Jack. I'm sorry I told you to leave. I didn't know. . . ."

She straightened and met his gaze again in an obvious attempt to show she meant what she said. She cleared her throat and spoke firmly. "You have as much right to stay at Aurora Lodge as I do."

Jack hesitated. It would be so much easier to return to Aurora Lodge. To hole up in that cabin and wait. He'd heard the radio report. Perhaps he'd be gone by Monday, anyway.

But was she still scared of him? Was the new firmness in her voice all show, or had she actually conquered her uncertainty? He shook his head. "It's better this way."

"Jack. I want you to come back. Please."

He made the mistake of looking at her again. The earnest determination and concern he saw on her face touched the raw and lonely spot deep inside him. He swallowed as that strange feeling stirred inside once more, that yearning for someone to care about him, to want him, for whatever reason. Maybe what he saw in her eyes wasn't what was really there, but it was so hard to resist.

He made one last attempt. "You don't have to do this."

Valerie's lips curved in a gentle smile that lit her whole face. "I know. But I want to."

The tenderness went straight to Jack's heart, momentarily dislodging the bitterness. His throat tightened. He shifted the pack on his shoulder. "All right. But first, I'll go to Orillia."

"You're going to hitchhike?"

He nodded.

"I can drive you."

He shook his head. "No, I'll hitchhike. With any luck, I should be able to get there and back by six."

"Okay. But when you get back, let me know. I can make dinner."

"That's not necessary."

"You're right. But I want to. We can talk more about Uncle Arthur."

Jack nodded. "All right. See you later."

He turned and took a deep breath. One step at a time, he reminded himself. One step at a time.

The welcome sunshine still played warm on Jack's bare arms and head as he exited the mixed stand of maples, pines, and yellow birches separating his cabin from Art's house. He looked up at the blue sky and took a deep breath, savoring the tangy smell and aliveness of everything around him.

He had started to take another deep breath when what he saw made him forget to breathe.

Was that some kind of wood nymph washing Art's windows, spirited into his view in the same inexplicable fashion in which everything else seemed to function in his life these days?

He swallowed. She wore a two-piece bathing suit of some shimmery chocolate material, in the skimpy style to which he'd never become accustomed. Her skin glowed, whether from the rays of the sun in the western sky or from good health, he didn't know. She was small but perfectly made, her breasts rising and falling with each scrub of the window, her limbs slim and shapely and delectable, her belly flat and firm.

Desire hit him like a punch to the gut, hard and disabling, with a sweet, sharp edge that was as unexpected as it was pleasurable. He gritted his teeth, but didn't stop looking. Was this just more torment, enticing him with what he could never have, a reminder of what he had done and how he would pay for the rest of whatever it was he now lived?

He swallowed again and forced himself to call out. "Hey, Valerie."

With a shriek she jumped away from the window. She collided with the bucket of sudsy water, overturning it and herself onto the deck.

In a flash Jack crossed the clearing, leapt onto the porch, and reached for Valerie. Kneeling in the dripping water, he grasped her wrists and helped her to her knees. "Are you okay?"

She grimaced. "I don't know why I did that."

Because you're terrified, Jack thought, feeling her trembling. But why?

"Are you hurt?" Jack knew he shouldn't, but he brushed at the cloud of hair around her face. His hand lingered for a moment, drawn by her summery scent and the heat he could feel radiating from her body, so close to his. He looked at her full, wet lips, then let his gaze travel downward, along her throat to the golden swell of her breasts above the shimmery brown material. A drop of soapy water followed a slow trajectory along the curve of one breast.

Abruptly, Jack looked up. As he raised his eyes, he saw the faint shadow across the base of her throat and the scratches under her ear. Alarm undid his reticence. He touched the scar, then looked into Valerie's eyes. "What's this?"

For a split second, panic flickered in her eyes. Then she

shoved his hand away and turned her head. "Nothing." She stood up. "Nothing at all. What time is it?"

"I think it must be close to seven. My watch stopped working." Jack watched her with a mix of curiosity and concern.

"Then I'd better get changed. Sorry. I lost track of the time. I'll get changed and then we can start dinner."

"Sure." Jack got to his feet. It was clear she wasn't going to reveal anything. And why should she? Especially to a stranger who'd arrived under suspicious circumstances. "Anything I can do?"

"The barbecue's around the corner. D'you mind checking that it has propane and is still working?"

Jack nodded. He watched as she rounded the corner, water dripping down the backs of her slender legs. He frowned.

Apparently, he wasn't the only one with a secret.

Valerie tugged at the neck of her turtleneck and glanced in the mirror of the golden oak sideboard before heading out to the deck to meet Jack. Why had she reacted like that? It was so stupid. Here she was, trying to take control of her life, to act in the friendly, forthright way she'd always acted. And what did she do? Respond in sheer, unthinking terror to Jack calling her name. How could one insignificant event affect her so deeply and for so long?

Because it wasn't insignificant. The truth wouldn't be shoved aside. No matter how she pretended, even the thought of what had happened—of what might have happened—terrified her all over again. In the space of thirty seconds, one event had changed everything. How she thought, how she acted, how she felt, deep inside. No matter how hard she tried, the fear refused to go away.

She swallowed and patted her hair, now loose around her face and neck, covering any telltale shadows. Compassion had moved her to ask Jack to stay here and to have dinner. Compassion, and a sense that she was punishing him for something that had nothing to do with him. But so far, her high-minded plans weren't working. She was rattling herself, and probably him too. Either that, or he thought she was some kind of wuss.

Valerie squared her shoulders. Maybe if she pretended, long enough and hard enough, that everything was all right, it would be.

She opened the door and stepped onto the deck. Jack leaned against the railing, his arms outstretched on either side. The neck of his shirt stood open, revealing a strong brown throat. Muscles stood out on his forearms, exposed by the rolled-up sleeves of his plaid shirt. He gazed skyward, his angular jaw raised, his bruised forehead hidden by a shock of sun-streaked brown hair, his expression far away.

Once again Valerie felt a tug of attraction, indicating that she wasn't immune to his rough appeal. She started to smile, but then caution—a caution born of fear—struck, cutting dead the warmth growing inside her, stopping the unfurling of her natural feelings toward him. He's a man, she thought. And she'd already lost far too much to one man to get involved with another. Her stomach roiled; her fists clenched; she had to fight to keep from turning and running.

The screen door slammed behind her. Jack's gaze dropped. The smile forming on his face turned to a frown. "Is something wrong?"

"No. No. I'm fine. I just . . . no, I'm fine."

Jack straightened. "You don't look fine." His eyes narrowed. "Maybe we should forget dinner. My being here upsets you."

"No." Valerie winced at her yelp. "I'm fine," she repeated. She took a deep breath, then a stab at telling him a portion of the truth. "I am a bit jittery, that's true. But it has nothing to do with you."

Jack continued to study her, his chiseled features and hard eyes alive with a skepticism that said he didn't believe her for a minute.

Valerie plowed on, ignoring his doubtful look. "So does the barbecue still work?"

Jack glanced at the barbecue and back. "Oh, it works. But you're out of propane. Do you have more in the house?"

"No." Valerie sighed. "Too bad. I've really been looking forward to my first barbecued steak of the season. I guess we can broil the meat in the oven."

Without warning, Jack swung over the deck railing onto the grass. "Maybe not. Art stored an old hibachi under the deck. At least he used to store it there. Let me look."

He disappeared, and Valerie heard scraping and rustling underfoot, then a crash and a muffled curse. A moment later Jack reappeared, his arms streaked with dirt, and soggy leaves and twigs clinging to his shirt and jeans. But in his hands he held a small, black metal hibachi. He pushed it across the deck toward her. Then he loped to the stairs and jogged up, brushing himself off.

"I hate to tell you this, but I don't have any charcoal," she said.

"Spoken like a true city girl. There's plenty of dry wood around the back of the house. If you'll get me Art's ax—it should be in the closet just inside the door—I'll chop up some kindling and start a fire in the barbecue. It will take a little longer, but you'll still have that barbecued steak."

Valerie opened the door and found the ax, just where Jack had said it would be. She brushed aside the disquiet sparked by his apparently intimate knowledge of this house and of her uncle. If anything, this evidence of their close relationship should reassure her, not make her more suspicious.

She turned; in the open doorway stood Jack—big, male, and scary. She bit her lip to keep back the squeak of fright.

"Good. You found it." He reached out to take the ax. His warm hand touched hers, and she dropped the ax. Jack grabbed it before it hit the floor.

When he straightened, he studied her for a moment,

frowning. Finally he said, "Where's your dog?"

"He's in the office."

"Why don't you let him out?"

"He doesn't like you."

"He'll get used to me. Besides, he's not going to attack me as long as you're here." He paused, and his eyes flicked over her with a shrewdness that made her uncomfortable. "I think you'd be a lot more . . . relaxed if he was out."

Valerie wavered. She would feel better if Reddi was around, and she appreciated Jack's acknowledgment. Still, she hesitated. "I wouldn't want him to hurt you."

"It's all right. I'll move slowly and stay away from him. That should work. He's not the first animal to dislike me."

Valerie frowned. "Don't you like animals?"

"Sure. They just don't like me."

Don't animals usually sense cruelty or other negative features? But Reddi had always liked Reed, at least until . . . Valerie shook off her doubts. She had no reason to see anything in Jack beyond what he presented—a rough and capable drifter whom Uncle Arthur had known and liked. Liked well enough to leave him a half share in the possession most dear to him in the world. That had to count for something.

Valerie nodded and went to release Reddi. The pup leaped joyously about her, licking her hands and jumping up on her until she pushed him away.

The moment he reached the kitchen, he stopped. The hair along his back stood up and he growled, his eyes narrowed menacingly on Jack.

Jack shook his head. "See what I mean? But he'll get used to me. You'll see."

Not taking his gaze off the dog, Jack walked to the door. "I'll be a few minutes chopping the wood. We should be able to get the steak on in a half hour."

Valerie nodded, her attention on Reddi. The dog continued to growl, but at least he hadn't sprung on Jack. She wasn't anxious to take Jack to the hospital with dog bites. On the other hand, it would get him there to be checked out. The bruise on his forehead still showed ugly and purple whenever he brushed his hair aside. And who knows what latent effects he could be suffering as a result of his near-drowning?

A few minutes later, Valerie joined Jack on the deck, where he had set the hibachi on a picnic table and was arranging kindling to start the fire. Valerie clung to Reddi's collar.

Jack didn't look up from breaking and arranging the kindling. "Let him go. He's just a pup. He wants to run around and explore."

Valerie looked at Reddi doubtfully. This aggressive behavior was new for Reddi. She petted the pup. "It's okay, Reddi. Relax. Stay."

Reluctantly, she released her grip. To her amazement, Reddi didn't move. He seemed mesmerized by Jack, unable to take his eyes off him. He continued to growl, but he didn't lunge.

Jack retrieved matches from his pocket and lit a few crumpled-up sheets of old newspaper he'd found to start the fire. He talked as he waited for the wood to catch. "See? Reddi and I will just stay our distance. Right, Reddi?"

His directed a steady and uncompromising look at Reddi. To Valerie, it seemed as if a form of silent communication, from which she was excluded, took place. Whatever it was, a moment later Reddi stopped growling and began to sniff around the edges of the deck. He didn't present the welcoming, puppy-dog behavior he exhibited with most of her friends, but at least he wasn't theatening. As he explored around the deck, he stayed a respectful distance from Jack.

"How'd you do that?"

"Let's just say that we reached an understanding. I agree to stay away from him and he agrees to stay away from me. Whatever. It works."

Valerie puzzled over that one, but let it go. She contented herself with watching Jack build the fire. The tiny flames had already spread through the kindling, while Jack gradually added larger pieces of wood. The flames grew higher and hotter, changing from red to orange to white. The dancing light reflected off Jack's tanned forearms and hands, the fingers long and supple and confident as they moved about their task. The fire seemed to hold him in thrall, and Valerie took the opportunity to study him.

How old is he? she thought. He had a few tiny lines at the corners of each eye, likely from being outdoors so much, but his build and the fluidity of his movement suggested he was in his late twenties or early thirties. At the same time, there was something about him that suggested a bone-deep weariness. As if he'd experienced all that life could offer, and had had his fill. It wasn't anything Valerie could put her finger on, but it was there all the same. Deep and intriguing, raising her curiosity and sending a shiver down her spine.

Had she seen Jack before? Was he old enough to have worked at Aurora Lodge when she'd summered here? Surely, if he'd been here when she was fifteen or sixteen, she would remember.

Before she could voice her questions, Jack broke into her thoughts. "When's the last time you were at Aurora Lodge?"

She looked up to find Jack studying her with an acuteness that suggested he'd been wondering about her too.

"Ten years ago, the summer I turned sixteen. It's the last time I saw Uncle Arthur too."

"So that would make you twenty-six?"

She nodded.

"And not married?"

"No." She reined in the retort that rose to her lips. Next he'd be asking if she had a boyfriend.

But he didn't. In the silence that followed, she felt compelled to tell him more about herself. "I'm a teacher. I teach Grade Three in North Chicago."

He didn't pursue that topic, but another. "So how often did you come here?"

"Every summer since I was four. As soon as school was out for the year, my mother and I always drove up here from wherever we were living. We stayed right until the end of August."

Jack's inscrutable gaze focused on her once more. "What about your father? He didn't come?"

Involuntarily, Valerie stiffened. "No. He was in the Army. He didn't like it up here anyway."

What she didn't say was that, as the years went by, she'd come to realize that the summers at Aurora Lodge were an escape. For her mother and, eventually, for her too.

"So why'd you stop coming?"

"I started working summers. Then I went to college. Now my parents are retired and live in Florida, on the Gulf side, in Panama City."

Jack's attention returned to the fire. He added a larger log of birch, then looked up at her once more, his gaze flicking over her face and her neck before settling at the base of her throat.

"How'd you get that bruise and those scratches on your neck?"

The edge of anger in his voice startled her. She looked straight into his eyes and saw the same hard anger reflected there.

She turned her head away. "It's nothing. I don't want to talk about it."

She knew he watched her, still and assessing, but she said no more.

"So which is it?" he persisted. "Nothing? Or you don't want to talk about it?"

The new and surprisingly gentle tone unnerved her even more. "It's nothing." She stood up. "I'll go get the meat now."

She escaped to the kitchen.

*   *   *

Jack pushed his empty plate to the side and leaned forward. He rested his elbows on the picnic table and his chin on his hands and looked out to the lake and the darkening sky. Though it had to be close to ten o'clock, only the first glimmers of stars were visible and the mosquitoes had yet to come out en masse.

Even as he gazed up at the sky, he was aware of Valerie. Despite his tense state, she was hard to ignore. The porch light shone off her pale but lovely face, with her dark eyes focused so intently on her plate and her soft pink lips glistening with moisture. The light also illuminated her far-too-transparent attempt to pretend that his presence didn't bother her.

He sighed. On the one hand, he could understand her fear and reluctance to be around him—a stranger found in odd and unsettling circumstances. Especially given those suspicious marks on her neck, and the nasty business they suggested, a business that cut too close to his own memories for comfort.

On the other hand, he had to think about himself. Especially now that Art was gone. He needed time to adjust, time to figure out how he would manage. What better place to do it than familiar Aurora Lodge? And what better time to start than right now?

He picked up his plate and rose.

"Wait!"

He looked at Valerie.

She smiled. "Sit down," she coaxed. "You can do that later. We need to talk."

Jack sat down. He'd all but interrogated her; it would look odd if he denied her the chance to question him. But he'd have to be careful. He quashed the impulse to drum his fingers on the tabletop. Or worse, to jump up and run.

Valerie lined up her knife and fork in the middle of her empty plate and pushed it to one side. She lifted the bottle of French Burgundy and gestured to Jack. He shook his head. The one thing he didn't need was fuzzy thinking.

Valerie poured herself a half glass more. She set down the wine and looked at Jack, with a directness he suspected was more show than real. He couldn't help being impressed at her attempts to present a brave face.

"So you grew up in this area?" she asked, resting her chin on one hand, her brown eyes wide. For the first time Jack noticed the gold flecks softening the dark eyes.

"Yes."

"Right in Huntsville?"

"No. Outside it, on a farm. Or what passed for a farm in those days. The land around here isn't much good for farming, as Pa soon found out. Too many rocks. Too thin. Not good for anything."

"Your parents still live in this area?"

"No."

"They've moved to Toronto or Ottawa?"

"No." He paused. "They're dead."

"Oh, I'm sorry." Genuine dismay filled Valerie's eyes.

Jack shrugged.

"What about other family? Brothers, sisters. Aunts, uncles, grandparents. Any of them around?"

Jack should have been prepared for the predictable questions. Experience and time should have supplied him with plenty of armor against the pain and sense of loss the familiar questions provoked. But he wasn't, and they didn't. Maybe he never would be prepared.

"No," he said hoarsely after a moment's pause. "They're all gone. Either dead or moved out of the province. I haven't kept in touch."

Valerie frowned again. Jack could almost see the wheels in her head turning, as she tried to place him and figure out what kind of a man he was. Why he had no family. What was wrong with him.

"Did you know that Uncle Arthur—I mean Art—did you know he was going to leave you Aurora Lodge?"

"No. Truth is, I never thought of Art dying. Stupid, I know. Everyone has to die sometime. But Art seemed, well, indestructible. Or maybe that's just what I wanted to think."

"You were close?" Valerie tilted her head, in a gesture that reminded Jack of Art. The resemblance was faint, but it was definitely there, something in the way she held her head, the way she looked at you as if she really wanted to know.

"Yes," Jack said slowly. "And no. I didn't know Art that well. It's been a long time since I've seen him last. But I've never met a more loyal or trusting man. Once he decided to be your friend, that was it."

"I know what you mean." Valerie leaned closer, so close that her clean, fresh scent filled his senses, the sheen of her skin dazzled his eyes. "For a long time, the only place I really thought of as home was this place, because of Uncle Arthur. We moved a lot. My dad was in the Army. My parents didn't get along that well. They still don't, though somehow they're still together, even in retirement."

Valerie paused and looked past Jack, out to the lake. "Uncle Arthur was always so glad to see Mom and me. It was as if he kept a space just for us. Just for me." She looked at Jack and curved her lips into a wistful smile, one that indicated how much the memory meant to her. "Like the cabin he's always kept waiting for you, he always seemed to have a special place in his heart for us. He remembered everything I'd told him the summer before, everything I liked. The oatmeal, for example. He remembered to make oatmeal in the morning, just for me, oatmeal with brown sugar and exactly the right amount of milk. I don't know how he remembered. It wasn't as if he wasn't busy enough with the lodge guests."

For a moment Valerie seemed to forget Jack was there. She spoke as if to herself. "I feel badly, though. It's been a long time since I saw him last. Sure, I wrote the occasional letter. But I was your typical self-absorbed teenager, more interested in myself and my own pursuits rather than some ancient uncle far away in another country."

"You were a kid," Jack said flatly. "He was an old man. The Art I knew would have understood."

"I still think I should have behaved better." She tilted her head, and her eyes met his for a long moment. "But thank you, anyway." A tiny smile lurked about her lips.

The smile did strange things to Jack's insides. Warmth started to curl upward from his belly. He knew that he'd like to see more of those smiles, that he'd like to trace those lips with his fingertips, and feel their texture and their movement as they curved upward in that inviting smile. He'd like—

"When was the last time you saw my uncle?"

Jack forced his thoughts back on track. "Five years ago. 1955, I believe."

"Were you ever here as a young man? I mean in your late teens or early twenties? I'm sure I'd remember if you were here when I was fifteen or sixteen. But if I was only seven or so, probably not."

A muscle pulsed in Jack's jaw, and he gritted his teeth. "I don't remember you," he lied. "I must have started after you stopped coming."

"So that makes you?"

"That makes me?" Jack repeated, clenching his fists in his lap. Then he clued in. "Oh, my age. I'm thirty-two."

Valerie took another sip of her wine; Jack prepared for another question. It didn't come.

Instead, Valerie looked up at the dark blue night sky. Her eyes widened. "Oh, wow! This is even better than last night."

Jack followed her gaze, knowing already what he would see. He'd heard the radio reports. He knew what was coming, and what it meant.

Green and yellow spotlights, pulsing with movement and life, ranged across the sky over their heads. The spotlights seemed to dance to a rhythm of their own making, a rhythm that had already begun to pulse in Jack's blood. He could see it with his eyes, but he could also feel it throbbing in the bruise on his temple, and through his chest, his arms, and his legs, each pulse increasing his sense of foreboding.

"Oh, but I guess you didn't see it last night," she said. "You'd already had your accident by the time the aurora borealis had started, right?"

Jack nodded, his body tensed, ready for flight.

Valerie, focused on the wonders overhead, didn't notice Jack's stiffness. "I've never seen them like this," she added, "not even when I was a child and came up here with my mother. This is fantastic."

She leaned forward. "Did you know that the Northern Lights can cause power failures? Just before supper, on the radio, the announcer said they'd caused a huge power failure in Quebec about eleven years ago. They knocked out power across the province for five hours. Can you imagine?"

Jack nodded stiffly, glad that the deepening night hid his expression.

Valerie raced on. "They said that the Northern Lights can confuse animals, make them lose their sense of direction too. Apparently, homing pigeons can't find their way home during a severe aurora borealis."

Jack rose from the picnic bench. He couldn't listen to any more. "Thank you for dinner. I'd better be going."

"Don't you want to watch?"

"No."

In the silence that followed his blunt reply, Jack climbed over the bench. He forced himself to walk along the deck, down the stairs, and off to the right and the path to his cabin.

"Good night," he said.

He knew without looking that Valerie had risen and stood by the railing, watching. Watching and wondering. He could feel her gaze on his back, hear the unspoken questions on her lips.

But it didn't matter. Nothing mattered now.

Nothing except holing up in his cabin and waiting. Waiting for what had happened before, and what would happen again.

Chapter Seven

Monday morning in Chicago

"Here are those plans you wanted, Mr. Vogler."

"I'd appreciate if you'd knock—" Reed halted when he looked up and saw *who* had interrupted his reading of *The Tribune*. It was Tracey, the new girl the architectural firm of Vogler, Earheart, and Jamieson had hired last week. A slim, young woman of no more than twenty whose silky blond hair and smooth, tanned skin glistened with an irresistible combination of all-American good looks and sex appeal. An appeal she showed to good advantage with a low-cut, tight top that revealed enough to be interesting, and a short skirt that made her legs seem to go on forever.

And sweet too. "Oh, uh, I'm sorry Mr. Vogler. I didn't realize you—"

"It's okay. I'm a bit testy in the mornings." Reed shaved the edge from his voice, replacing it with firm good nature. He rose in one smooth motion that he knew showed his six-foot-plus build and dark good looks to advantage. He allowed his gaze to roam leisurely over the young woman before him, from her large baby-blue eyes and pouty lips to her long, shapely legs, and back to linger on the delicious swell of breast. Would those breasts be as pouty as the lips, the pink nipples swollen and hard to the touch? Would she scream or cry when he pinched or bit them? When he dug his fingers into her ass, pinned her writhing body under his?

He raised his gaze in time to catch the deep flush rushing up her throat, burning in her cheeks. He shot her his most devastating smile. "How do you like it?"

The girl's eyes grew round. Two red blotches appeared on each cheek. "Like . . . like what?"

"The job." He pretended innocence. He knew his thoughts had been written all over his face.

"Oh, the job." The girl—Tracey was her name, wasn't it?—fluttered her long lashes as she tried to regain composure. "Oh, it's great. Everyone here has been really nice."

"I'm glad to hear that. If you have any problems, or any questions, I'd like you to come to me. I can give you the lowdown on everyone in this firm, tell you all the ins and outs."

Tracey smiled uncertainly and started to back toward the door. "Thank you, Mr. Vogler. I—"

"Call me Reed. Everyone does." He smiled, pumping up the voltage for her benefit.

"Reed," she repeated. Her smile strengthened. "All—"

The sharp ring of the phone interrupted. Reed dismissed her with a nod. He picked up the phone. "Vogler here."

"Reed. Good. I was afraid you'd be out of town."

Reed frowned. It was Gord Vickers, his lawyer. Not the firm's lawyer, but his own personal lawyer. He couldn't think of any reason he'd be calling now. "Well, I'm not," Reed said cautiously. "What's up?"

"Probably nothing, but I thought you should know."

For something Gord described as nothing, he sounded more than a little worried. "Yes?"

"It's been what, five years now since your wife's death?"

"Yes."

"Well, some new questions have cropped up about her death. The police have interviewed a couple of your friends. They're talking about getting an order to exhume the body."

Reed swore. "Why? It was an accident. Everyone knows that. She fell down the stairs. The medical examiners, the police, everyone agreed. Why are they looking at it again?"

The silence at the end of the line deepened. Finally, Gord responded. "Apparently a childhood friend of your wife's returned to Chicago a few weeks ago. She'd been out of the country for the last six years and hadn't heard the circumstances of Melinda's death. When she did, she contacted the police and told them you were a wife beater. It seems she has some influential friends at the district attorney's office." He paused. "Did you abuse Melinda?"

"Of course not!" Reed exploded. "I loved my wife. Ask anyone. I was devastated by her death. Sure, I blamed myself. But I wasn't even home when it happened. It was an accident. A terrible accident."

"Calm down, Reed. I had to ask, that's all. Because it's a pretty safe bet the police are going to be at your door soon asking the same question. Going over the death and your whereabouts at the time. You need to remember as much as you can about it."

Reed expelled air with a whooshing sound. "All right. But I don't understand why they're willing to reopen this case because of one person's vindictive accusations. It was five years ago, for Chrissake!"

"Are you seeing anyone now?"

"No."

"What about in the years since your wife's death? How many women have you gone out with?"

"Do you mean dated, or had longer relationships with?"

"Both. But I'm more interested in any long-term relationship. Weren't you going out with some schoolteacher from the North Side for quite a while?"

"Yeah." Reed frowned. "But we broke up about two weeks ago."

"Did you part on good terms?"

Reed's grip tightened on the receiver. "What's this all about, Gord?"

"Did you part on good terms?"

"More or less. Why?"

"Because the police are likely to interview your old girlfriends and any current girlfriends to see if you abused them. If there's any evidence you did abuse any one of them, it will make them look all the harder at your wife's death."

Reed raised one hand to his forehead, then yanked it away and looked at it. Despite the air-conditioning, he was sweating. He swallowed. "Well, that shouldn't be a problem. Valerie and I got along great. In fact, we were engaged for a few months."

"Maybe you should talk to her. Let her know the police may come knocking on her door."

"Can't right now. She's out of town for the summer. Someplace up in Canada, I think.

"Well, I suggest you try to find her. Let her know what's going on. Right now you need friends in your camp, not enemies. Particularly not disgruntled girlfriends."

After a few more comments, Gord said good-bye and hung up. Reed put down the phone. He advanced to the window of his corner office, the one with the wide-angle view of the Chicago River as it wound its way into Lake Michigan. He didn't see any of it, just stood there thinking, his hand on his jaw.

Would Valerie mistake their little tiff as something more serious? He'd tried to tell her, again and again, that it had been an accident. That he hadn't meant it. That she was imagining things. Sometimes he lost his temper, his self-control. But only for a moment. That was all.

72

He winced. But Valerie had refused to take his calls. She wouldn't let him into her apartment. She'd told him to go away, that their engagement was finished. Over the intercom, for Chrissake!

He clenched his fists as he gazed unseeing out the window. If only she'd listened. If only she'd done what he wanted.

He turned back to his desk. Now he would have to find her. Find her, and make sure she understood exactly what had happened between them.

Monday morning at Lake Aurora

With the wind blowing in his face through the open window, Jack watched the scenery go by. The twisted pines clinging to massive rocks, the bulrushes and grasses in the ditches and low, swampy areas, the oaks and maples fighting for mastery of the roadside, so perfect against the clear blue sky that they seemed unreal.

He glanced at Valerie maneuvering the curves of the road. The only unreal part of the scene was him. In fact, he was surprised he was still here. No one had been more shocked than he had been to awaken Saturday morning in his bed in the small cabin. Based on experience, all the conditions had been there for him to disappear.

But he hadn't. Perhaps the Northern Lights hadn't been strong enough, however dramatic they had looked against the night sky. He had watched them, drawn by some perverse need to observe and understand the distant beauty that was tied to him, and to his life, such as it was. He had once loved the Northern Lights, but now they were forever and inextricably linked with the events of that terrible night so long ago.

The soft strains of a song about change filled the car, one that Jack recognized immediately as stolen from Ecclesiastes, Chapter Three, verses one through six, courtesy of his mother's insistence that he and his brothers and sisters study the Bible: "To every thing there is a season, and a time to every purpose under heaven. A time to be born, a time to die . . ."

Hmph, Jack thought, unable to stem the flood of bitterness. When will it be my time? The song continued inexorably ". . . a time to kill, a time to heal . . . a time to weep, a time to laugh . . ."

As the music faded away, Jack glanced at Valerie. Despite his own bitterness, he hoped she would enjoy the good things of life—love, kindness, happiness—everything that had passed him by. Whatever was bothering her—and it was clear something was—he hoped she wouldn't let it poison her life.

Without warning, Valerie glanced his way and smiled. The expression lit her narrow face and sent light shooting through her dark eyes, like a meteor shower across a dark sky. And just as unexpectedly, it lifted his spirits and sent the bitterness wafting away.

For the first time in a long time, he smiled. "You seem more relaxed today," he commented.

"Yes. It always takes a few days after the school term ends before I unwind." Valerie tossed her head, setting the waves of burnished hair swinging about her face and loosing a hint of floral scent that teased his senses. "This year it's probably taken longer because of driving up here alone and having to deal with the details of Uncle Arthur's estate."

She paused. "I hope Mr. Grierson will be able to clear up a lot of things today. For both of us."

Jack nodded. For reasons he refused to examine, he wanted to see things go well for Valerie. But he suspected his inheritance—if indeed Valerie was right—would only complicate the situation. Art had always meant well, but occasionally he overstepped and presumed too much.

A sigh escaped him, and Valerie glanced his way once more. Before she could say anything, the dying strains of music from the radio were interrupted by a booming voice:

"The top story in the news today is the release of the names of the mother and two young children found shot to death in their home off Highway 8 last Friday. They've been identified as Catherine Vanderstone and her children, six-year-old Stephanie and four-year-old Justin. Police are looking for Jack Vanderstone, the husband and father. Mr. Vanderstone has not been seen since late Thursday evening.

"Mr. Vanderstone has been described as a . . ."

Valerie lowered the volume. With a shudder, she turned to him. "Isn't that terrible? I know things like that happen in big cities all the time, but you never think of them happening in a quiet little place like this."

"Just because it's small doesn't mean that people don't have the same passions and frustrations. People are pretty much the same all over." Jack knew he sounded harsh and bitter, but it was the truth, and no one knew it better than he did. "Maybe they just keep their dark secrets to themselves for—"

Jack halted as the word "aurora borealis" caught his attention. Without apology, he leaned forward and turned the sound back up.

". . . currently at the solar maximum, the peak period for sunspot activity that occurs every eleven years. The sun sends out a stronger solar wind, which spews energy-charged particles into our atmosphere. The earth's magnetic field channels those particles to the poles, where they slam into molecules of gas and make them glow, producing the aurora borealis.

"What this means for us, folks, is that you're likely to see some stunning Northern Lights this summer, especially when you're away from Toronto or Ottawa. Unfortunately, there's no way to predict them more than a day or two in advance, but we promise to keep you posted.

"Now, in other news . . ."

Jack snapped off the radio. "I guess that explains why we've been having such great light shows."

Valerie raised one eyebrow. "I thought you didn't like the Northern Lights."

"I didn't say that."

Valerie turned off Highway 60 onto King William Street, the road leading into Huntsville. As they passed the first grocery store, Jack glanced at the car clock. Five to eleven. His gut tightened. Five minutes to a meeting that could only make his life worse.

The blue eyes assessing Jack and Valerie from out of the bronzed and lined face were shrewd and lively. Despite his age, which Valerie guessed at somewhere between seventy-five and eighty, Ed Grierson didn't miss a thing. His navy suit might be worn and out of style, his silver-gray hair a little too long for fashion, but it was clear he hadn't lost his grasp of the law. Whether it was his small-town friendliness, his friendship and regard for Uncle Arthur, or simply his kind and efficient manner, Valerie had immediately liked and trusted him.

Now Mr. Grierson leaned back into his simple black office chair. He folded his hands, as bronzed as the rest of him, across the small belly that protruded from his pants. He looked from Valerie to Jack. "I'm so glad you showed up," he said, nodding at Jack. "I was running out of options for finding you. I'd advertised in the big papers across Ontario and Canada, even a few in the States. Art didn't leave any information about you except your name."

Frowning, Jack looked up from the copy of the will Mr. Grierson had given him. "I didn't know Art intended to leave me anything. He never mentioned it. If he had, I would have talked him out of it."

Mr. Grierson chuckled. "Now that's a first. Though I doubt you would have been successful. To my knowledge, once Art made up his mind, no one talked him out of anything. No, he would have made you an heir whether you wanted it or not."

Mr. Grierson leaned across his desk. "Do either of you have any idea what Aurora Lodge is worth?"

Valerie shook her head.

"One-point-eight million dollars. I had it appraised right after Art's death." He nodded at Valerie. "Of course, that's in Canadian dollars. But it's still nothing to sneeze at."

Valerie struggled to keep from gaping. She grasped the arms of her chair. She'd always loved Aurora Lodge, but she'd never considered its monetary worth.

She glanced at Jack. He sat still as a statue, his face as impassive as if he had heard nothing. Wasn't he shocked?

"Of course, that's only the appraised value. You might get more, or less." Mr. Grierson paused and looked directly at Valerie, his piercing blue eyes taking her measure. "You know, it was Art's fondest wish that the lodge be kept open, and in family hands. It always was a family resort."

Valerie felt her heart sinking. She'd never . . .

"He never actually said, but I think that's why he left the place to you and Jack, rather than to your mother, Valerie. He knew there wasn't a chance your mother would keep it open, especially now that she and your father are retired in Florida."

"What happens if only one of us wants to keep the lodge?" Valerie asked. She didn't dare look at Jack.

"The heir that wanted to keep it would have to buy the other heir out. That means that one of you would have to pay the other nine hundred thousand dollars, or whatever you agreed upon as a selling price."

Nine hundred thousand dollars! Valerie doubted Jack had that kind of money. She knew she didn't. She changed tack. "If we were to sell it—I mean if we both decided we couldn't keep it, do you think it would sell quickly?"

Mr. Grierson tented his fingers and studied them for a moment. "It's hard to say. Good resorts are hard to come by. Aurora Lodge has a great location, wonderful waterfront, and a good reputation based on close to a hundred years of taking in paying guests. But there's no doubt it's old-fashioned. Rustic, I guess is the word. There are no TVs, no satellite dishes, no hot tubs or pool, no fancy game rooms. And most of the cabins, except the newest ones, are pretty basic, right down to the spare kitchens and steel bunk beds. I don't know if it would be as attractive to guests as it once was, especially with the Deerhurst Inn and Grandview Resort so close by."

Valerie bit her lip. She'd seen both those resorts on the drive from Huntsville to Aurora Lake. She vaguely remembered at least one of them from her last trip to Canada, as well as all the hoopla about the pricey resort. She frowned. Didn't at least some people still like to get away from all the amenities of modern life and rough it out in the bush?

"So you think it could take a long time to sell the resort, maybe even a couple of years?" she asked slowly.

Mr. Grierson nodded. He looked at Jack, who had said nothing so far and sat unmoving in his chair. "I was hoping—assuming we could find Mr. Wilder here, which we have—that perhaps you might both be interested in hanging on to it. I know you're a teacher, Valerie, and you live in the States, but Jack—well, managing this place would seem to be a perfect fit, what with you being a carpenter and hunting and fishing guide. You could keep it open the whole year if you winterized the cottages. And Valerie could come up from Chicago in the summers to help."

Mr. Grierson looked expectantly at Jack. Jack remained silent. To Valerie, he looked grimmer than ever, his tanned face now pale, a muscle twitching from the center of the ugly bruise on his forehead. "I'm not sure that's possible," he said abruptly.

Mr. Grierson turned to Valerie. "What about you?"

"I don't know. It's all so sudden."

"Fair enough. Why don't you both think about it for a few days? Neither of you is rushing off anywhere?" He looked pointedly at Jack. "You're not heading back to Florida, are you?"

Jack shook his head."

"Good. Take the time to consider what you're going to do. The estate has already paid capital-gains tax on the increased value of the lodge and grounds. If you sell it, though, you may have to pay additional tax if you get more than the appraised price."

Mr. Grierson paused, and looked from Valerie to Jack. "I should tell you, I'm planning on retiring by the end of this year. I'd like to have this pretty well wrapped up by then."

Valerie nodded and stood up, her head whirling with all the details and Grierson's proposition. *Run Aurora Lodge?* The thought had never entered her head. But now that it was there . . .

"Oh, wait! I almost forgot again." Mr. Grierson pulled open a desk drawer, withdrew a file folder, and looked up at Valerie. "I am sorry I didn't give this to you the first time we met. I didn't remember it until after you had left. I kept it in a separate file from the will. It appears that at the time of his death, Art had been writing you a note. Must have had a premonition that the end was near. From what's written here, it seems he wanted to tell you something he considered very important. Unfortunately, he never finished the letter. We found it on the floor by the table where he'd slumped after the heart attack."

He opened the folder, took out a sheet of plain white writing paper, and handed it to Valerie.

Valerie focused on the few lines of script written there. She noted the shakiness of the spidery handwriting, far more feeble-looking than the penmanship in any letter she'd ever received from her great-uncle. Her chest tightened. Poor Uncle Arthur. Had he known the end was coming and pushed himself to get down on paper his last words? Had he been in pain the whole time he was writing? She'd never know.

She blinked to push back the tears that had sprung into her eyes, and she began to read.

Dear Valerie,
    I wish you were here so I could talk to you in person.

*I guess it won't surprise you to know that I never much
thought about dying. I was too busy living.*

Valerie brushed a tear away, and blinked again to clear
her eyes.

*But now I know I don't have much longer to live. I must tell
you something I should have told you long ago. It's important
and inextricably linked to the reason I have left you my dear
Aurora Lodge. I know you love this place, as I always have,
and I trust you will help guard its one unbelievable secret, a
secret that revolves aro*

The message ended there, with the ink skidding in a long
line diagonally across the page. Valerie closed her eyes to
shut out the awful picture of her uncle clutching his chest
in pain and falling to the table.

When she was able to control herself, she opened her
eyes. Mr. Grierson smiled sadly at her from across the
room. He shook his head. "We'll never know what he was
going to say. But it certainly leaves you with a horrible picture of Art's last pain-filled moments. I shudder every time
I read that note. And I wonder too. Wonder what secret
he was talking about. Do you have any idea?"

Valerie shook her head, not trusting herself to speak.
After a moment she swallowed. "Thanks for giving me this
letter. Even if he didn't finish it, it means a lot."

The lawyer nodded. Valerie jerked as a warm hand
closed around her upper arm. She looked up in surprise
at Jack. She'd forgotten he was there.

"Come on," he said quietly. "I'll buy you a coffee."

Ed Grierson watched as the tall, blond man and the pretty
young woman with the amazing cloud of burnished hair
filed from the room. Though they were a study in contrasts,
the pair made a striking couple, no doubt about it. For a
moment he'd thought there might be something between

the taciturn outdoorsman and Art's friendly, sweet niece, a relationship that might help make Art's last wish to keep the resort in family hands a reality.

But no. He sighed and walked to the window and peered out between two slats of the blind. Valerie and Jack stood beside her dark red Ford. Jack, his face as expressionless as it had been throughout most of their meeting, was reading Art's note. Finally, he looked up and shook his head.

Then he did something that surprised Ed, and made him reconsider his assessment. Jack touched Valerie's cheek. From here it was hard to tell, but he seemed to be brushing tears away.

"Hmm." Ed turned from the window. Perhaps he wasn't quite the old geezer he'd felt himself to be the last few years. He was seventy-eight, but still not too old to recognize the most basic attraction between a man and a woman.

He smiled to himself. He remembered, all right. He and his Katie. How could he ever forget? If only he hadn't insisted on working, working, working. He'd wasted so many years. And now, well, it was too late. She was dead, and he'd never half appreciated her or what they'd had together.

He walked more slowly to his desk than he had to the window. Something was nagging at him. Something about Jack. The man's taciturn, almost angry silence reminded him of someone. Someone he'd seen somewhere before. And just recently too. Someplace mundane, like the grocery store or the mall.

But Jack said this morning he hadn't been in Huntsville for five years. And he certainly had all the proper identification.

Ed frowned. He traipsed across the office once more to the window. When he parted the blinds, Valerie and Jack and the car were gone.

He dropped his hand and the blinds snapped shut. He winced at the noise. His housekeeper was right. He was an old fool. Time he stopped confusing who he'd seen and when. Time he retired.

But first, he'd wrap up this Art Pembroke business and see, as far as he was able, that his friend's beloved Aurora Lodge ended up in good hands.

"I must tell you something I should have told you long ago. It's important and . . ."

The words on Art's last message to Valerie blurred before Jack's eyes as one indisputable fact took hold: Art had meant to tell Valerie about him—about him and the bizarre secret he'd lived with so long.

The truth jolted Jack. *Did this mean . . .*

He looked up from the letter. The transformation in Valerie shocked him. Where before she'd been calm and controlled, now she appeared pale and unwell, her lips bitten, tears pooled in her dark eyes. Her hands were clenched at her sides, and she looked on the verge of losing the battle to keep from bursting into tears.

"What's wrong?" he asked in alarm.

Valerie sniffed and half turned away as a lone tear escaped and started a slow trip down her cheek. "I just—it makes me feel so bad that he died like that. All alone. No family around. No friends. Maybe someone could have helped him, if only they'd been there."

Gently, Jack turned Valerie back to face him. He touched her cheek and wiped away the tear, glad to see she no longer jumped away from him. He resisted the sudden, compelling desire to pull her into his arms, to press his warmth against hers, to tell her everything would be fine.

"Valerie, it's okay," he said quietly, loath to remove his hand from her smooth, wet cheek and break the physical contact, however tenuous. Instead, he cupped her narrow chin, tilting it upward when she would have looked away. "Truly." His gaze locked with hers. "You heard Ed Grierson. He said your great-uncle died instantly. He suffered a massive heart attack. No one could have helped him. There was nothing that could have been done."

Valerie's chin wobbled. "I guess I know that. I just don't like to think—" Her voice cracked and the tears started to fall in earnest.

"Hey. Don't cry." Jack forgot his qualms. Awkwardly he bundled her into the circle of his arms, pulling her close, offering comfort the only way he knew how. He held her close, trying to reassure her and still her silent sobs with the strength and solidity of his body. But he couldn't help savoring the dangerous awareness of her warm and pleasing curves, the sweet scent of her glossy hair, the curve of her neck just a whisper away from his lips. He couldn't help wishing he could hold her in his arms forever.

When the sobs subsided, he dropped his arms and stepped away. "Give me your keys. There's a park down by the river. We'll stop there for a while."

A few minutes later they stopped near the banks of the North Muskoka, the river cutting through the center of Huntsville and linking Lake Vernon with Fairy Lake. The waterside park was cool, shady, and quiet, away from the hustle and bustle of the main street and the tourists stocking up on supplies or looking for souvenirs. Jack led Valerie along the cinder path around the curve of the river, to a tiny sanctuary out of view of the Main Street Bridge and the people eating at the pizza shop patio. He gestured to a cedar and wrought-iron bench and they sat down, a polite distance apart.

Valerie leaned back and sighed. She shut her eyes and breathed deeply. Jack took the opportunity to study her. He liked looking at her. With the shiny, wavy hair swinging about her face, the low-necked and short-sleeved cropped T-shirt, and the jeans that hugged her hips and shapely legs, exposing her navel and an enticing strip of flat, smooth belly, she looked young yet shockingly provocative. He'd seen enough in his two visits to town to realize there was nothing out of the ordinary about her dress. It appeared to be the current, if revealing, fashion for young women, and not all that different from what he remembered from the last time.

His gaze traversed her throat, searching for and finding the faint shadows he had noticed the other day. He tamped down the familiar spurt of anger; then his gaze traveled lower still, caressing the swell of her creamy breasts until they disappeared beneath the dip of her shirt. He felt a familiar tightening in his groin; he smiled grimly. Would he never learn? He'd been a sucker once for a sorry story and a pretty face. Hadn't that experience been enough of a lesson, a lesson for all time?

Valerie opened her eyes. Her gaze collided with his, then, with a spark that could have been alarm, bounced away. She looked around at the maples and blue spruce to each side, the rocks near the river's edge, the water as it ran downstream. "It's beautiful here."

Jack nodded. He'd hoped the magical quiet of this special place would help heal the pain in her heart. He cleared his throat. "Yes."

After a moment of awkward silence, he broached the subject they needed to discuss. "How well did you know Art?"

"Not that well, I guess. I mean, I was a kid most of the time I was here. I loved him, yes. He was good to me, giving me special treats, taking me out in the boat, going for walks. And he always listened, no matter what I had to say. But how well did I actually know him? Not that well, really. Kids are pretty self-absorbed."

"Well, I *did* know him. For most of my life, and as an adult too. Art had lots of friends—he even had a couple of long-term girlfriends up until a few years ago. But he was also comfortable with his own company."

Jack fixed Valerie with a stern look. He wanted her to understand the way it was. He didn't want her feeling guilty about something for which no guilt was required. He reached for her hand, clasping it in his. "Think about it,

Valerie. Would you have preferred that your great-uncle died in the sterile environment of a hospital hooked up to resuscitators and machines, surrounded by strangers in masks and white coats? Or alone, yes, but in the place he loved, surrounded by the mementos of a lifetime, and writing to someone he loved?"

Valerie's eyes shimmered with new tears. "When you put it that way, I guess you're right."

Jack squeezed her hand. "Of course I'm right."

The grin he sought broke across her face, shining through the tears in her eyes. She tugged her hand free of his. "A typical male, always right."

Jack laughed. He was relieved that she was bouncing back; he admired her spirit and courage. The strength of her love for Art evoked a tenderness he hadn't experienced in a long time. He could understand why her uncle had wanted to trust her with their secret.

The thought sobered Jack once more. But Art was dead.

"Do you have any idea what Uncle Arthur wanted to tell me in that letter?" Valerie asked.

"No," Jack lied.

"I feel badly about his wish to keep Aurora Lodge in the family."

Uneasiness started to percolate inside Jack. "Why would you feel badly about that?"

"Because I can't keep it. Unless you want to buy my share, we'll have to sell it."

"You can't do that!" The words ripped from Jack before he could stop them.

Chapter Eight

The vehemence of Jack's reply startled Valerie.

"Yes," she repeated, "I have to sell Aurora Lodge. My share in it, at least."

"Why?" Jack's light green eyes turned the cold gray green of stormy seas.

"I live in Chicago, Jack." Her voice grew sharp. "I'm a teacher. I can't run this place, not from there. Besides, it's just not something I'm prepared to do now, however much Uncle Arthur wanted it. No, I have to sell."

"You can't."

"I don't have a choice. I have to sell it."

"Art wanted you to keep it. I thought he meant something to you."

Valerie flushed. She could see how Jack might think she was a hypocrite. But it didn't matter. For sentimental reasons she'd love to keep the lodge, but it wasn't practical. Besides, she'd had enough of a man telling her what to do, a man undermining her self-confidence, making her feel incompetent. She couldn't let the wishes of another man, even Uncle Arthur, whom she'd loved dearly, sway her now.

She raised her chin. "There's nothing stopping you from buying me out and running the lodge yourself."

Jack's mouth tightened into a thin, stubborn line.

"Well, is there?" Valerie demanded. How could he blame her for not caring when he wasn't prepared to take the lodge on either?

He met her question with stony silence.

"You don't want to be tied down, do you?" she persisted.

Silence again. His rigid stance and harsh expression radiated accusation.

"Don't you have enough money?" The words escaped before she could stop them.

He flushed, but still said nothing.

Shame stabbed Valerie. *Of course he doesn't have enough money. He's a self-admitted drifter, working at seasonal jobs. For that matter, I don't have enough money to buy him out.* She softened her tone. "Look, if that's the case—if you don't have enough money—maybe we could work something out, something along the lines of what Ed was suggesting. You could stay here and run the lodge, and I could keep my share, at least for now. Be a silent partner . . ."

Her words trailed off as his expression grew harsher, his eyes colder and darker.

"That's impossible," he said flatly.

"Why?"

"It just is."

Valerie frowned. Why, oh, why did Jack have to be so difficult? Why couldn't he take on the lodge? She liked him, but she wouldn't, she couldn't let him make her feel guilty. Not the way Reed always had.

Before she could jump into the fray again, he stood up. He fixed her with a look full of a terrifying bleakness she'd never seen before. Despite his height and his youth, he looked old, old and weary.

He held her gaze for one long moment. "Don't sell the lodge," he said finally. "That's all. Just don't sell it."

He turned away. "We should go back," he said. "May as well check out that inventory that Ed gave us."

Valerie watched as Jack strode away, his back ramrod straight, as uncompromising as his position seemed to be. Confused and a little surprised by his reaction, Valerie stood up too. Finally she sighed and followed him.

Why was nothing ever easy, nothing ever as simple as it first seemed, even here in her childhood retreat?

In the early afternoon sun, under a hazy sky, Jack gestured to the small log cabin beside his, then turned to Valerie. "This is one of the first cabins built by Art's father in the early nineteen hundreds. That's when this place was mostly a hunting and fishing camp, not a cottage resort."

He walked up to the log walls and examined them. "Old, but sturdy. With the right care, this place will likely last another hundred years."

Valerie winced. Was that reproach she heard in Jack's voice? She couldn't be sure. Ever since their impasse in the park, he'd remained cool. No matter how she had approached it, he'd refused to discuss Aurora Lodge or why he wouldn't take it on.

She watched him now as he examined the wall for chinks or rotted wood. His bare legs, baggy shorts, loose shirt, and the beach-boy blond-streaked hair, suggested a man relaxing at his summer home, an image completely at odds with the hard-edged, brook-no-nonsense, let's-get-to-it air he'd adopted since they'd returned and started to review the inventory and cottages. An attitude that was a perfect barrier to intimacy or discussion of any kind.

With a sigh, Valerie looked down toward the lake. From here atop the hill, she had a panoramic view of the beach and the brilliant blue waters lapping at the cream-colored sand. Halfway across the bay, she could see the tiny rocky outcrop of Blueberry Island, and beyond that the tree-lined edge of the distant shore. How she'd love to be down there, swimming in the cool waters, rather than up here going through the hot, stuffy, closed-up cottages.

She sighed again, then fiddled through the numerous keys attached to a big ring her uncle had hung in the office. Each key bore a number corresponding to a different cottage. She found number one, for Flintlock, then pushed through the unlocked outer door onto the wide, screened-in porch. Two heavy wooden Muskoka chairs sat on either side of the entrance, facing the lake and that enticing view. How lovely to sit here on a warm summer's night, keeping watch for boats and listening for the haunting call of a loon.

The lock to the cottage door turned easily, but the door stuck and required a hefty shove before it opened on a large, bright room. A granite fireplace took up one end wall. Another corner was sectioned off for the bathroom, and the other featured a small kitchenette. A set of bunk beds, a sofa, an upholstered chair, and a square wooden table with four chairs made up the rest of the furnishings.

"You take a look at the furniture and appliances. I'll check out the fireplace and the stove."

Valerie started. She hadn't heard Jack enter, but now that he was here, awareness of his closeness set her nerves tingling. She turned, then blinked, her gaze drawn to the ugly, bruised gash standing out on his forehead. "That bruise doesn't look as if it's getting any better," she blurted out.

Jack shrugged, as distant as ever. Obviously another topic he had no intention of discussing.

Valerie stiffened, her irritation growing at his stubborn refusal to talk. She held out her hand for the inventory list and Jack handed it to her. Reddi was still outside exploring the distant reaches of the lodge grounds.

She headed for the kitchen cupboards. Inside were neat stacks of mismatched dishes, glasses, and cups, enough, Valerie estimated, to handle four people, with a little juggling.

She opened a drawer under the counter beside the sink and jumped back with a shriek.

"What is it?" Jack crossed the room in two strides.

Embarrassed, Valerie shrugged. "A mouse." She looked into the drawer again. Dish towels had been chewed and made into a tiny nest, empty now except for a welter of mouse droppings.

Jack yanked the drawer out of the cabinet and riffled through the towels. "Well, it's gone now."

"He ran over there." Valerie pointed to a crack between the counter and the wall. The mouse, probably as startled as she'd been, had leapt out of the drawer, shot across the counter, and disppeared into that crack.

Jack shrugged. "Most of the older cottages and cabins have mice. Art sets traps in the spring and gets rid of most of them."

Jack's voice cracked and Valerie glanced at him. Acute sorrow was etched across his face. He cleared his throat. "If you want, we can set traps. I'm sure there's a slew of them in the equipment shed."

Valerie nodded, her irritation with Jack and his frustrating remoteness ebbing away. No matter what, it was evident he cared deeply for her uncle and mourned his death, just as she did. She couldn't hold his refusal to discuss the reasons for his incomprehensible decisions against him.

Jack closed the drawer and returned to the fireplace. Gingerly, Valerie continued to investigate the kitchen. She saw no more mice, but plenty of evidence of their activities. She shuddered. She didn't envy whoever got the job of cleaning up these cottages for sale or rental.

A muffled curse from the fireplace drew her attention. Jack pulled his upper body out of the fireplace and brushed at his soot-covered hair and face.

Valerie couldn't help it. She laughed. "What were you doing, climbing up the chimney?"

Jack shook his head and brushed his cheeks, succeeding only in rubbing the soot into his skin, softening his harsh features and making him look as if he'd been rolling in a coal bin. He coughed. "I was checking the flue. Sometimes there's a creosote buildup; other times chipmunks or birds build nests inside. There's nothing worse than starting a fire and filling the room with smoke."

"No, I guess not." Valerie choked back another laugh. "Are you okay?"

"I'm okay. Just dirty." For the first time since the park, Jack grinned, with an ingenuousness that cut through his remoteness and went straight to Valerie's heart.

"You want to go back and wash it off?"

Jack shook his head. "Nah. It'll probably happen again. I'll wait till we're finished."

Her heart lighter, Valerie returned to her task. A few minutes later they were finished. Except for the mouse droppings, and the toaster electrical cord chewed right through, everything was in good shape and nothing was missing.

"Once it's dusted and cleaned up, it would be a lovely place to stay," Valerie commented as she locked the door.

"Art kept this place in good shape. That's one of the reasons his guests kept coming back. They must have been pretty disappointed when he closed it down."

Valerie glanced at Jack, looking for criticism in his words. She'd suffered years of subtle comments aimed at winning her compliance through guilt. Was this one of those comments? She wasn't sure. Nothing in his soot-covered face or in his voice indicated he'd meant anything other than what he'd said.

"Can these cottages be used in the winter too?" she asked as they headed to the next one on the list.

"They've never been kept open much past the end of October. None of them are winterized. But it's a good idea. This place could easily be used as a winter resort. Guests could toboggan on the hill, skate and ski on the lake. And there's good downhill skiing just fifteen minutes away at Hidden Valley."

Norah-Jean Perkin

"So why don't you stay here and keep it open?" The question popped out before Valerie could stop it. She wasn't sorry.

"I can't." The closed mask descended on Jack's face once more. Without another word, he strode to the door of the next graying log cabin. He held out his hand for the keys.

Valerie passed them over, but refused to drop the subject. She'd let too many things go in the past, first with her father, and then with Reed. "I don't understand why not," she persisted. "You'd be perfect in the job. We could work out something. You wouldn't have to buy me out. We could—"

"No." Jack unlocked the door and went inside.

Valerie gritted her teeth. What was it? For a moment there, Jack had seemed like an open, approachable man, one she could understand and appreciate. One she found herself liking more by the moment. Until she'd trespassed once more on the forbidden subject, or should she say one of *many* forbidden subjects. Certainly he was entitled to his privacy, but this was ridiculous. For the moment, she bit back her questions, but she hadn't given up. One way or another, she intended to find out why Jack resisted taking over the lodge.

Reddi nosed his way in behind her and began his own exploration of the room. Jack and Valerie repeated the tasks they'd handled in Flintlock. This building was in better shape than the first one, with little sign of mice. Only the queen-size bed, with its broken leg and lumpy mattress, needed replacing.

Slowly Valerie and Jack worked their way from cottage to cottage, examining, assessing, and noting on the inventory anything that was missing or in need of repair. They had finished ten of the twenty-one cabins when they finally arrived at the beach. It was just after four o'clock.

Valerie glanced up from the inventory sheets. She mentally ticked off the tiny shed and the two docks. "Where are the boats? It says here there should be two paddle boats,

92

four canoes, three kayaks, and three aluminum dinghies with nine-horsepower motors."

Jack nodded to the top of the hill. "Up in that big metal storage shed near the tennis court. We can take a look now, if you'd like."

"No. I'm too hot. I'm going for a swim."

Jack took the inventory sheets from her and flipped through them. His green eyes looked lighter than ever in his still-soot-stained face. "I wonder if the rope's still here."

"The Tarzan rope . . ." Valerie smiled as a childhood memory came flashing back. "I hope so. Let's go see."

"It's not part of the inventory."

Valerie glanced at Jack in surprise. It was the first hint of humor to break through since she'd pressed him about the lodge.

She tossed her head and adopted a falsely official tone of voice. "An obvious oversight. It would be irresponsible not to check it out." Without another glance at Jack, she whistled for Reddi, then set off at a trot across the beach, past the sunning platform, the fishing docks, and the poles for the volleyball net. She hit the packed dirt area once used as a helicopter landing pad, and started to run toward the wall of trees on the other side.

"Hey, wait."

Valerie stopped and Jack caught up with her. They entered the cool shade of the trees together, walking along a well-worn dirt path under the pines and maples and birches while Reddi took side trips after startled chipmunks and deer mice. She and Jack leapt the tiny creek where, Valerie remembered, she and her summer friends had played at make-believe, concocting elaborate stories of castles and dragons and knights in shining armor. Such an innocent time.

Suddenly the canopy of branches overhead grew denser, blotting out the sun. In an instant the dark woods seemed to swallow them up into a world of shadows, one redolent with the damp smell of earth and pine, the ground spongy underfoot with decomposing leaves and needles, and an air of mystery hanging in the air.

Valerie shivered. A sudden image of swirling blackness seized her, accompanied by a choking sensation and that terrifying panic. Sweat broke out on her forehead and her hands rose of their own accord to her throat. She halted and Jack plowed into her from behind.

"What?" He grabbed for her as she teetered and would have fallen to the ground. Warm, rough hands grasped her arms and pulled her back to her feet, back from the terror. As quickly as they'd reached for her, the hands released her and she felt an unexpected sense of loss.

Dismayed at the unexpected flash of terror, and her re-action to it, she swayed a little. She felt the sweat slick on her throat and self-consciously dropped her hands.

"What's wrong?"

Jack's alarmed voice cut through the swirling emotions she couldn't control. She raised her eyes, only to drop them again at the worry she saw on his face.

"Uhh, nothing. It's nothing."

She turned away. She swallowed, struggling to push away the fear, a fear that had nothing to do with the moment. *Stupid, stupid, stupid.* Especially when she knew she was safe, knew no one was going to hurt her. Not here.

She shuddered again and straightened. Ahead, through the trees, she could see the sun shining into a small clear-ing, and farther along, glimpses of sparkling water. She hurried toward the light, looking back only once.

When she did, she paused. Jack hadn't moved. He stared after her, a deep frown creasing his tanned face. Quickly, she turned away. His concern was comforting, but also em-barrassing. She didn't want him to think she was a mouse, afraid of every noise and dark corner.

At last Valerie came out of the trees and into the full sun of the tiny beach behind the curve of the shoreline and out of sight of the lodge buildings. She let out a breath she hadn't realized she'd been holding and shook her head.

God, she was a fool. Since when had a little darkness and a couple of shadows bothered her?

Shading her eyes, she looked upward, glad to be distracted. There it was, the Tarzan rope, a thick length of line knotted around the branch of an enormous birch tree. The branch extended out over the water and the rope was tied back to a ramshackle platform closer to the base of the tree. A series of boards, hammered at odd angles together and into the tree, provided the ladder to the platform, as well as different levels from which to swing out over the water.

"So who's first?" Jack's voice came from behind her.

Even if he hadn't spoken, even if she hadn't heard the crackle of twigs as he stepped from the trees onto the beach, she would have known he was there. Ever since he'd held her outside Mr. Grierson's office, she had been aware of him in a different way, a much more physical and sensual way than before. She had not been immune to his solid strength, or the gentleness of his touch, so different from much of what she had experienced in the last two years. Even their disagreement and his lack of communication hadn't shaken her growing interest.

She swallowed. "You, of course." She turned and forced a grin. "Someone has to climb up and unloop that rope."

Jack glanced toward the top of the tree, then started up the man-made ladder. He moved slowly, testing each board before putting his weight on it. Finally he reached the top, untied the rope, and yanked on it to test its strength. "Everything's fine here," he called down.

Reddi chose that moment to leap onto the beach. The pup looked upward, then ran back and forth barking at the base of the tree.

"Shhh, Reddi. Stop it." Valerie grabbed him by the collar and petted him until he calmed down. "Watch this."

Jack shucked his shirt and tossed it over a branch. He sent an ingenuous grin Valerie's way, as startling for its unexpectedness as for its effect on Valerie. She felt her spirits soar.

"So do you want the whole show, the Tarzan yodel and everything?" he called down.

Valerie allowed herself the luxury of enjoying the moment and the view. As Jack stood there, waiting, his shorts low on his narrow hips, his muscled chest and broad shoulders bare, his blond hair falling in his eyes, he could easily have been a real-life Tarzan. Another shiver ran through Valerie, this one a shiver of sheer delight, one she imagined wasn't much different than Jane's when she first met Tarzan. Her mouth turned up in an impish grin. "I don't think so. Just swing."

Jack raised his hands on the rope, backed up to the far edge of the platform, then ran forward and leapt into space, his knees raised and clasped around the rope. He swung out in a wide arc a good forty feet from the shore. Not until the line started to swing back did he let go and hit the water with a mighty splash. He surfaced seconds later, treading water and shaking the wet hair out of his face. "Now it's your turn, Valerie."

Emboldened by his success and her own memories, Valerie kicked off her shoes and grabbed the rope, now hanging over the sandy beach. Holding it, she climbed about halfway up to the platform, then turned to face the water.

"What? You're not going to the top?"

"Not this time."

Valerie raised her hands as high as she could on the rope. She pressed her lips together and watched Jack as he swam toward shore. It seemed higher, and scarier, than she remembered.

She took a deep breath—and jumped. She swung out, high above the ground and then over the water, the sun shining on her face, the wind ruffling her hair, her heart singing with exhilaration. When the rope reached the end of its trajectory, she let go, soaring free for a moment before she splashed down into the cold water.

She surfaced immediately, shaking back her hair and smiling. "Ahh, that's wonderful." She dived, then swam underwater to the shore. Reddi ran to greet her, licking her face as she turned and sat in the knee-deep water. She laughed and pushed him away. "Stop it, Reddi."

Jack offered his hand. For a moment she just looked at it; then she grasped his fingers and let him pull her to her feet. Water streamed from her cutoffs and her halter top was plastered to her like a second skin. It felt great to be alive. She couldn't remember the last time she had experienced this life-affirming joy. Certainly not in the last two years.

Jack squeezed her hand. His green eyes, unguarded for once, sparkled with amusement. "Ready for the big one?"

"The big one? Oh." Valerie looked from Jack to the top of the tree. She paused. Right now she felt as if she could scale any mountain. "Sure."

"Atta girl. You first."

Valerie took the rope in one hand and climbed the haphazard ladder. On the platform she gazed out at the landscape. This time it *really* was a long way down. She pulled on the rope, testing its strength. She wouldn't want to fall from here onto the beach.

Jack's head appeared at the platform, and he rested his arms on the edge. Valerie couldn't help but notice the sprinkling of blond hair on his arms, or how sculpted and strong they looked.

"Having second thoughts?"

Valerie made a face. "No, I'm invincible. Didn't I tell you?"

She gripped the rope with both hands and backed to the far side of the platform. She took a deep breath, then ran and jumped into space.

This time it truly was like flying, high, high into the air. And with the sensation came that same wonderful feeling of sheer exhilaration. Valerie grinned, released the rope, and smacked into the water. She popped up and swam to one side to watch Jack.

Jack already stood at the back of the platform, in the deep shade of the trees. With his arms raised high over his head, he looked the quintessential hero, ready to leap tall buildings, or in Tarzan's case, to whiz through the air. Then he too was flying, his extra weight carrying him higher and farther out than Valerie. He let go and sailed straight into the water.

When he surfaced, he grinned at Valerie.

She smiled her agreement. They swam side by side to the shore, then sat half in and half out of the water. Pushing wet strands of hair out of her face, Valerie turned to Jack. "I'd forgotten how much fun this is."

Her heart did a little flip when he smiled back at her, freely and widely, sparks of light shooting through his green eyes. The grin spread across his still-sooty face.

Impulsively Valerie reached out and rubbed at the soot. His cheeks and chin were rough with five-o'clock shadow under the sensitive pads of her fingers. "Too bad we didn't bring some soap."

Jack laughed, grabbed her wrist, and stopped her ministrations. "Just like my mother. Can't stand a dirty face."

His laughing gaze traveled across her face, focusing for one long moment on her lips, then dropping lower to her throat, and then to her breasts, covered with the thin, wet cotton, before rising back to her face again.

Valerie felt his gaze like a hot breeze, blowing over her body, awakening every cell, building a liquid warmth within her. She focused on his lips, full and alive, and on the fire she could see darkening his eyes. For the first time she noticed blue rimming the soft green of his irises. Enticed, she leaned toward him to take a better look as his hand flicked to his chest and her attention followed.

She blinked, his eyes forgotten. A thick red scar crossed the left side of his chest, just above the nipple. It had to be three inches long and at least half an inch wide.

She reached out and touched it. The skin felt rough and uneven under her fingertips. Still touching it, she looked up at Jack. "That looks terrible. How'd you get it?"

"Hunting accident."

Before her eyes, all the warmth and closeness in Jack's expression evaporated. He was slamming the door again. Just as he'd done when she'd asked about the lodge, or about the bruise on his forehead.

She splayed her fingers across his chest, the roughened skin of the scar under her palm. "But—"

"I thought I heard laughing and splashing from over here."

Valerie dropped her hand. A woman stood on the beach, smiling. For a moment, Valerie's mind refused to work. Then it clicked in. It was Velma, her uncle's cleaning lady. Velma Altenburg.

Valerie scrambled to her feet.

"Oh, hi."

"Hope I'm not interrupting." With one hand, Velma shaded her eyes against the late afternoon sun.

"Oh, no. We were just swinging on the rope."

Velma chuckled. "Oh, yes. The famous rope. Wouldn't mind trying it again myself."

"Can I help you?" Valerie hid her disappointment at the interruption. She would take care of Velma as quickly as possible and send her on her way.

Velma walked out onto the beach. Reddi ran around her, leaping into the air. Laughing, she pushed him down.

"I feel a little awkward asking this, but I was wondering if you planned to rent cottages this summer."

Valerie heard Jack rising from the water. "I hadn't planned on it. Why?" she asked.

"I told you my family and I have stayed here many summers. The kids love it here, and it's real handy for my husband and me to commute back and forth to work. We were wondering if we could rent one of the bigger cottages for August. We'd pay the going rate, of course."

Valerie looked behind her. "Jack? What do you think?"

Jack made a noise that sounded like a grunt, and which Valerie interpreted as assent.

She turned back to Velma to find her staring at Jack as if he had two heads.

"Velma?" she said.

The older woman stepped closer, but she wasn't looking at Valerie. She stared at Jack. "Is that Jack Wilder?"

"Yes."

Valerie looked from Velma to Jack. Not a glimmer of recognition showed on Jack's face. "Do you know each other?"

"Yes," said Velma.

"No," said Jack.

Valerie frowned. What was going on?

Velma started to sputter. "I'm sorry. Of course you're right. It's just—you look just like a Jack Wilder I met here, at Aurora Lodge, the summer I was eighteen. He was working here. But that was thirty years ago. You can't be him."

"No, I can't."

Valerie looked at Jack. His face could have been cut from the bedrock of the Canadian Shield, for all the expression it showed.

Velma apologized. "I'm sorry. It's just, well, I've never met anyone who bore such a striking resemblance to another person. You wouldn't have had an uncle or cousin in this area living here thirty years ago?"

"The Wilders did come from around here, but to my knowledge no one ever worked at Aurora Lodge. Not then."

Valerie looked from Jack to Velma. The conversation, and Jack's resemblance to another Jack Wilder, made her uneasy. Just one more strange thing about the excessively private Jack Wilder. She cleared her throat. "What cottage did you want to rent?" Valerie asked.

"Hackamatack. It's big, and the most like a house."

"It's fine with me. Jack?" Valerie turned to him. "What

about you? Can you see any problem renting the cottage to Velma?"

Jack shook his head.

"Why are you asking him?" Velma piped up.

"It's up to Jack too. My uncle left the lodge to both of us."

Velma's expression registered surprise. After a moment's silence, she fumbled out a response. "Uh, oh, that's great. I'll come back next week to work out the terms. See you later."

Velma backed off the beach and disappeared down the path. Valerie watched with curiosity. Why did Jack's resemblance to another Jack Wilder disturb the woman so much?

Chapter Nine

Reed smiled as he put the phone down. He leaned back in his plush leather chair, a growing sense of satisfaction warming him all the way through. He stretched his arms over his head, clasped his hands, and made a gesture of triumph. He'd done it! He'd ferreted out Valerie's location, and without raising any suspicions in the mind of her gullible friend Suzanne. All he'd had to do was tell her he'd misplaced Valerie's address, and the woman had fallen all over herself to find it for him.

He lowered his arms, picked up the yellow notepad, and examined the information he'd written there. Aurora Lodge, Lake Aurora, RR 4 Hunstville, in Ontario, Canada. Valerie's summer hideout.

Hideout. He frowned at his inauspicious word choice. Definitely not the right term to describe where Valerie had gone. Retreat would be better. Summer home, maybe. But not hideout. Why would Valerie want to hide, from him or anyone else?

Still, he'd have to be more careful. It was important to

give the right impression. Just as he had with Detective McCallum.

He stood up and ambled to the window. His corner office provided a stunning view of the Chicago River as it wound its way into Lake Michigan. Far below the traffic flowed through the business section and he could see tiny people scurrying across open plazas and spaces, going about their business like ants around an anthill. The combination of his bird's-eye view and the everyday, orderly nature of the streets and activity below increased his sense of well-being, helping to restore the sense of control that had gone slightly askew in the past few weeks.

From up here he felt calm, powerful, in command. The universe was unfolding as it should, and he was playing his part, taking the reins, making things happen.

The interview with Detective McCallum, for example. Reed hadn't wanted any part of it, but as his lawyer had pointed out, to refuse to talk would suggest guilt, however unfounded.

The visit had proceeded smoothly; in fact, Reed had emerged feeling stronger and more invincible than ever. He'd repeated his reluctance to dredge up the horrors of five years ago, a tragedy from which he still hadn't recovered. Maybe he never would. He had expressed his shock and dismay that anyone, anywhere, might think he could have harmed his wife. Certainly, they'd had the odd disagreement, some of which had escalated into arguments. But to suggest that he had hit his wife—that he might have pushed her down the stairs in the heat of an argument—was unthinkable.

He clenched his fingers at his sides as rage flared up. At least now he knew who to blame for the reopening of the investigation into his wife's death. When this issue was put to bed, as he expected it would be soon, he'd have to look into that. Consider an appropriate *reward* for unsettling his life and blackening his name.

He snorted, then took a deep breath. Everything was

fine, and would be fine. He didn't lose control, he'd told the detective. He was calm, gentle, together. He would never hit a woman. It was out of character. Ask anyone.

Reed took another deep breath, then returned to his desk. He glanced at the notepad again. No phone number, but he'd get it, right now. He picked up the receiver, tapped out the numbers to long-distance information, then barked out the area and name.

"We're sorry, sir. That number has been disconnected. If you—"

Reed hung up with a curse. Then, fueled by anger, he punched out the number to Valerie's cell phone. She'd stopped answering his calls after they broke up, but maybe she had her phone on now and would pick it up.

"The person you are calling is out of the calling area or away from the—"

Reed slammed down the phone. "Shit!" He didn't want to drive up to some godforsaken place in Canada just to talk to Valerie. He remembered her mentioning this lodge and seemed to recall it was somewhere north of Toronto. But how far north?

He gritted his teeth and flipped open his daybook. He had an important meeting with the Addison Group Wednesday, but after that he could probably clear his schedule and get away for a few days. He could fly to Toronto, then rent a car and drive to wherever Valerie was hiding.

That word again. He grimaced, but went on with his calculations. One day to get there, one day to get back. But how many days to convince Valerie to reinstate their engagement?

He rose and pondered. Ah, he could probably do it in half a day.

Because he always—always!—got his way.

"So what do you think?" Valerie asked.

Jack scanned the bookshelf that covered the wall above

Art's old desk in the living room. In addition to the scores of paperback mysteries that Art had read by the armful, the reference books about Muskoka and Huntsville and fish and wildlife, and the assortment of business and management texts, there was a whole row of titles that startled Jack out of his after-supper contentment.

Books with titles such as *Reincarnation through the Ages,* an *Encyclopedia of the Occult, The Truth about Ghosts,* and *Time Travel: Truth or Fantasy.* Books on fairies and leprechauns, New Age healing, aliens and UFOs, dragons and alternate universes. Books on mysticism and the Book of Revelations. The breadth of Art's apparent interest in the odd and supernatural was amazing—but to Jack, not altogether unexpected. Hadn't Art always insisted there had to be an answer to Jack's predicament, and that one day they would find it?

Jack clenched his fists at his sides. Art was dead now. If he'd found the answer, he had taken it with him to the grave. Unless, of course—

"Well?"

Valerie's amused voice brought Jack back to the present. He dragged his gaze away from the titles. Her eyes sparkled with good humor and a smile lit up her narrow face. Was it his imagination, or had she been less edgy around him since they left Grierson's office this morning, the underlying fear that had marked all their previous encounters gone or at least lessened? He'd felt something else too, a—

He refused to let his thoughts go there. Instead, he glanced at the shelf of books, and then back to Valerie. "Art had a great hunger for knowledge. He was interested in everything, and not afraid to look outside the limits of what we all accept as real."

Valerie shook her head. "Well, it's a surprise to me. His interest in these areas seems so out of character. He always struck me as so practical, so down-to-earth. But look."

Valerie stepped over to the bookcase and reached up to the middle shelf. "There's everything here from aliens and

UFOs to ghosts and reincarnation. I can't help wondering what he actually did believe."

Jack's pulse quickened. "You don't believe in any of that?"

"Of course not. I know Americans have a reputation around the world for weird cults and beliefs in strange or New Age ideas, but not me. I believe in God, but the rest of this stuff? Ghosts, werewolves, fairies? I don't think so."

The glimmer of hope within Jack died. He glanced back at the titles, his eyes scanning the material. He wasn't sure he remembered what Art's journal looked like. As he searched for it, he asked, "Does this change your opinion of your uncle?"

"No!" Valerie was adamant. "No matter what his interest, he was a wonderful man. There was nothing flaky about him."

Jack's scan stopped at a faded brown, cloth-covered book, its spine bare. Casually he raised his hand and withdrew it. The cover was as plain as the spine. His stomach clenched. Quickly he slipped the slim, worn volume back between two books. Later . . .

He turned and sat on the edge of the desk. For a brief moment, he drank in Valerie's beauty, reveling in the forbidden pleasure the way a starving man relishes his food. Tonight she wore jeans with a pale green T-shirt that gently molded to her womanly curves. In the light from the lamp, her hair glistened with red and gold, framing her face in an angel-like halo, her sweet full mouth and eyes alive with laughter and a touch of the day's sun.

Almost immediately, his appreciation was marred by the bitter realization that love—with Valerie or anyone else— could never be his. He balled his hands into fists and forced himself back to the issue that had been hovering between them since this morning.

"About the lodge," he said slowly.

Immediately the laughter fled from Valerie's eyes, replaced by alertness. "Yes?"

"I know you have questions. You want to sell the lodge. You want to know why I won't—can't—take it over. Why I don't want you to sell it."

His gaze locked with hers. In the depth of the dark pools of her eyes, curiosity glistened, coupled with wariness. Wariness of him, the strange man who had washed up on the shores of Aurora Lodge.

He took a deep breath. "You deserve answers to all those questions. You'll get them. But first I'm asking you to give me a little time, a few days at least. I need to . . . consider a few things, investigate the options . . . think."

Maybe what I find in that book will help me to tell you the truth. To convince you to hang on to Aurora Lodge until I discover the key to my future. Or until I disappear.

His gaze met Valerie's once more. "What do you say?"

He watched as her eyes widened, curiosity and newfound acceptance of him warring with her remaining wariness. Her forehead furrowed and she chewed on her lower lip. Finally, she reached a decision. Her mouth edged up into a soft smile and the furrows disappeared. "Well, I had planned to stay here to the end of August. I think I can wait a few days for you to figure out what you want to do."

Relief sailed through Jack. Relief and an unexpected glimmer of anticipation—anticipation of a few more golden moments with Valerie, filled with the same kind of laughter and warmth they'd experienced at the Tarzan rope this afternoon. He shoved aside the niggling voice of his conscience: *But what if you disappear?*

Impulsively, he grasped Valerie about the waist, lifted her into the air, and spun about the room until they were both breathless and laughing. Unceremoniously, he dumped her onto the couch and flopped down beside her.

Valerie's dancing eyes met his. "Well, you certainly know how to show your appreciation. I wonder what you'd do if I did something really wonderful."

"You don't know?"

She shook her head, but her eyes sparkled and the corner of her mouth twitched suspiciously.

Drawn by some inner devil, Jack leaned forward and brushed his mouth over hers, a quick kiss that was long enough to let him know that he wanted more. Far more.

If he'd had any doubts about his reception, the widening of Valerie's eyes, and the curve upward of her lips, dispelled them. Gently, he framed her face with his hands and reclaimed her mouth, this time savoring the honey hinted at in his first pass. Her lips softened under his, pliant and welcoming, and something like a sigh escaped between them.

Encouraged by her response, he deepened the kiss, exploring her honeyed mouth, the long-forgotten sensations quickening his pulse and sending his blood pounding through his veins, awakening what had long been dead.

He ignored the dim bleating of his conscience and slipped one hand behind her head, tangling in her silky hair. His mouth clung to hers, stoking the fire in both of them, filling him with the sweetness of life and living that he craved. His other hand closed over her breast, feeling its fullness swell under his touch, the nipple harden and come to life through the thin material of her T-shirt and underclothes.

He raised his fingers to her smooth throat to caress it. Without warning, Valerie froze. She jerked away, breaking off the kiss, then scrambled to her feet and turned her back. But not before Jack saw the fright in her glazed and disoriented eyes.

He stood up too, but she didn't turn around. He saw that she was shaking, and he cursed himself for being every kind of fool. And worse.

"I'm sorry," he said quickly. "I shouldn't have done that. It's not—not my place."

For a long moment Valerie said nothing. Finally, when she turned around and faced him, she seemed to have regained control of her fears. Her full lips still glistened from their kiss. Her eyes, big and dark in her small face, regarded him steadily.

"It's all right. It's not you, Jack." She paused, then looked down at the ground. "I just ended a long relationship with another man in Chicago. It wasn't . . . it didn't end happily. I'm not ready to start something else new. It's not you. It would be the same with any man. I just don't want any encumbrances right now."

With each word she spoke, the fear Jack thought had fled grew more evident, endowing her actions and expression with a nervousness that hadn't been there only moments before.

His gaze dropped to her throat. The dim living room light hid the shadows he knew still marred the whiteness of her skin. Were those shadows the reason for her fear? He felt certain they must be. But it didn't matter. There were far more compelling reasons why he shouldn't touch her.

When he raised his eyes, he knew she knew where he'd been looking, what he'd been thinking.

"You're right," he said quietly. "We have a lot of pressing questions to settle right now. Business matters. Better we don't cloud matters any more than they already are."

Wrapped in her housecoat, warm wooly socks on her feet, her hands clasped around a mug of hot chocolate, Valerie curled up on a chair at the kitchen table. Except for the light overhead, the house was dark, as were the deserted lodge grounds. Reddi lay asleep on the floor in front of the Quebec heater, the remaining embers of a fire still casting a little heat into the cool night air. Outside, Valerie could see only blackness, not even a hint of light from the direction of Jack's cabin.

Why would it be otherwise? Unlike her, Jack was probably asleep. It was well after two in the morning and normal people were sleeping. Unlike her. Her mind was running like a train on a one-stop track, round and round in circles, never getting anywhere.

Once more, as she'd done several times tonight, Valerie touched her lips. The pressure of her fingers sent a tingle of memory through her, along with the delightful sensation of a kiss that shouldn't have happened, a kiss about which she couldn't stop wondering.

She ran her tongue along the sensitive inside edge of her lips, then exhaled sharply. She didn't understand why Jack had kissed her—or why she had kissed him back.

But she did understand why she'd frozen the moment Jack had touched her neck, why she'd jerked away in something close to panic. She understood exactly.

She shivered, not from cold, but from the debilitating fear she couldn't seem to shake. No doubt she was still too raw, too frightened by what had happened only a few weeks ago. Frightened not only by the incident, but by the fact that she had failed to recognize all the little signs of potential danger. Now she needed time to get over her fear, and time to build up her confidence again. She needed to decide who she was, and what she wanted from life. Over the past two years she'd pushed aside too many of her own desires, allowed her independence to be threatened. But it wouldn't happen again. She'd struggled too hard to free herself in the first place, to stand on her own two feet without the constant criticism and put-downs of her father.

Funny, though. She took a sip of the hot, soothing chocolate. Despite all her questions about Jack, his arrival at Aurora Lodge, his past, his secretiveness and refusal to provide explanations, he didn't frighten her.

Quite the contrary. She frowned. No doubt the fact that they shared a love for her late uncle, and a heartfelt sorrow at his death, made her feel a certain bond with him. But Jack, despite his stubbornness, had also been kind and supportive. More importantly, he hadn't pressured her, hadn't belittled her feelings or ideas. Hadn't insisted she do everything his way.

Unlike her father. Unlike Reed. She couldn't imagine Jack exploding in rage as Reed had during that final, terrifying moment, the moment when he'd realized she was refusing to do what he wanted.

Restless, Valerie stood up. She'd gone over this ground a dozen times, to what end she didn't know. She needed something to distract her.

Cup in hand, she fled to the darkened living room. She snapped on a table lamp, and made her way to her uncle's desk and the bookshelves over it. Resolutely, she focused on the row of strange volumes that had so surprised her earlier today.

She tilted her head to better read the titles. She couldn't quite picture what she sought. Jack had withdrawn a small brown book while they were talking this evening, then slipped it back into place. She'd meant to ask what it was, but had forgotten after he kissed . . .

Determined to think about something else, she stood on the desk chair to get a closer look. Her fingers moved from book to book, pulling this one out, then that, marveling at how clean and dust-free they were. Velma really had done a good job cleaning.

But no matter how many books with brown covers Valerie examined, none seemed to be the one that Jack had examined. Maybe she'd imagined it. Or perhaps, she thought, scanning the shelf below, he'd actually placed it somewhere else.

Tired of the search, Valerie stepped down. As she replaced the chair, she noticed a a cupboard door built into the wall beside the desk. She tugged on the handle and it opened, revealing two shelves filled with scrapbooks and photo albums.

Excitement spurted through her. Had Uncle Arthur kept pictures and mementos from the early days of the lodge? She hoped so. She vaguely remembered looking at photos from "the old days" with her mother. Valerie had been seven or eight, and not much interested in pictures of people she didn't know or recognize.

That was then. Now, driven by curiosity about the lodge and her uncle's life here, Valerie removed several scrapbooks from the bottom of the heap. A puff of dust escaped the yellowing pages and she sneezed. Velma must have missed this storage space.

Back in the kitchen, Valerie spread the volumes across the table. On the cover of the three scrapbooks, in a neat hand not her uncle's, was written "Aurora Lodge." The scrapbooks were labeled "1906 to 1913," "1920 to 1927," and "1928 to 1937."

Valerie sat down with her mug of chocolate. She chose the earliest scrapbook and, like a scholar about to read a long-lost text, contemplated the cloth cover with anticipation.

Gingerly, she opened it. The first page held a hand flyer, advertising the opening of the lodge in May 1906. "Wilderness Lodge for Hunters and Fishermen," the ad proclaimed. "Proprietors Newton and Emma Pembroke. Home cooking, good beds, expert hunting and fishing guides. Fair prices. Americans welcome."

Valerie smiled at the last line. Americans from New York and Michigan and Illinois had constituted a sizable group of guests during the years she'd stayed here, though they'd come chiefly for the cottage life and beautiful, clean lake rather than hunting or fishing. It was interesting to see Americans had been guests here from the start, even in the days when a hunting or fishing trip into the "wilderness" had involved a long train trip, from Chicago or Buffalo north to Toronto, and then up to Huntsville and Algonquin Park.

Each page revealed another fascinating segment of the lodge's history. Invitations to fishing derbies, newspaper clippings about hunters bagging record numbers of deer or bears, a summer dance and barbecue, the catch of a forty-two-pound bass, the accidental wounding of a hunter by his companions, the addition of new, one-room log cabins for the guests, the launching of two new fishing boats and three canoes. Each year seemed to bring a new idea or improvement.

When Valerie closed the first book and reached for the next, several yellowed newspaper clippings fell out onto the floor.

Valerie retrieved them, unfolded the first one, and smoothed it flat on the table. The headline blared a stark message: THREE DROWN IN BOATING MISHAP AT AURORA LAKE. In pen, at the top of the article, someone had written, "Thursday, July 14, 1927."

Valerie started to read.

Police recovered the bodies of two people and are still searching for a third after a boating accident at Aurora Lake two nights ago.

The bodies of James Redden, 35, and his wife Louise, 29, both of Buffalo, were found late yesterday afternoon near the west end of the lake. The coroner has determined they died of drowning.

Mr. and Mrs. Redden were regular guests at Aurora Lodge, and had been coming each summer for the past five years. Lodge owners first realized they were missing Wednesday morning when they didn't come to breakfast. A check of the boathouse revealed that two canoes had not been returned the evening before. Shortly afterwards, staff spotted the overturned canoes floating near the swamp at the west end of the lake.

"This is a terrible tragedy," said lodge owner Newton Pembroke. "I can't believe this has happened. Mr. Redden was an experienced canoeist and I'm certain he could swim too. And Jack. I just don't understand how Jack could be missing too."

The second man Mr. Newton referred to was Jack Wilder, 32.

113

Valerie's mouth dropped open. Jack Wilder?
More intrigued than ever, she read on.

Mr. Wilder was a hunting and fishing guide and experienced outdoorsman employed by the lodge for the last eight years. He had taken Mr. Redden, and occasionally his wife, out on several fishing trips. The night of the accident, it appears the three of them had gone on a pleasure trip around the lake.

Valerie frowned. What an incredible coincidence. Not only the same name, but the same age and occupation as the Jack Wilder she had just met. She turned her attention to the rest of the article.

Mr. Wilder's body has not been recovered yet but police are still looking. They fear his body may have been trapped in one of the deep holes in the lake, some of which are more than two hundred feet deep.

"Jack is an excellent swimmer. He's won regatta races. And he could handle a canoe better than any man I know. I can't imagine what could have happened," said Mr. Pembroke. "I won't believe he's dead until someone actually shows me the body."

Police have contacted Mr. and Mrs. Redden's relatives in Buffalo and arranged for them to take the bodies home for burial. Mr. Redden was the owner of a hardware store. He and his wife had no children. They are survived by . . .

Valerie's eyes misted over and her throat filled up. It didn't matter that she knew nothing of these people, or their lives. She could imagine the sorrow and suffering of their families.

Anxious for more, she unfolded the next clipping. She cringed at the heading. POLICE CALL OFF SEARCH FOR MISSING MAN'S BODY.

She scanned the rest of the article.

Yesterday police called off their search for the body of local fishing and hunting guide Jack Wilder.

Mr. Wilder, 32, is presumed drowned in a boating accident last week that also took the lives of two American tourists, James Redden and his wife Louise. Despite a search involving a team of six officers and three boats, no sign of Mr. Wilder's body has been found or any other evidence that would explain how the boating accident occurred.

"We haven't even discovered a scrap of clothing . . . the only reasonable explanation is that Mr. Wilder drowned along with the Reddens, but for some reason his body got carried into a deeper part of the lake and sank . . . we don't have the equipment or resources. . . ."

Mr. Wilder's family is planning a memorial service next week to be held at . . . His brother Vincent Wilder, a carpenter and farmer, continues to insist Mr. Wilder could not have drowned, but he admits he doesn't know what could have happened. "I just know Jack didn't drown. That's all."

Valerie shuddered. Bad enough to drown, but to fail to find the body? She could sympathize with his brother's insistence that he hadn't drowned—how do you have closure when you don't have a body?—but it seemed the only logical explanation.

Police still have no idea how the accident occurred or what events led up to it. All anyone knows is that sometime around seven P.M. on Tuesday, July 12th, the Reddens took out one canoe. A few minutes later, Mr. Wilder took out another canoe, and was last seen paddling in the same direction.

"It's a mystery, all right," Police Chief Reginald Cotter said. "I don't think we're ever going to find out what happened that night, or how the three of them drowned. Mrs. Redden is the only one who couldn't swim. The others?"

Chief Cotter shrugged. "We'll never know."

Valerie wondered if Jack had ever heard of this tragic accident. It had to be one of his relations, maybe a great-

great-great uncle. Perhaps even his namesake. But what a coincidence—same age, same name, and same occupation!

She folded up the articles and placed them back in the scrapbook. She could hardly wait until the morning to tell Jack.

Chapter Ten

When Jack didn't answer her knock, Valerie tried the door. It was unlocked, so she pushed it open and stuck her head inside. "Jack? Jack, are you here?"

Her voice echoed in the empty room. She glanced from side to side. The room looked larger and cleaner in the early morning light. The dust had been swept away and the cobwebs knocked down since the night she'd first seen it. Clean dishes were stacked neatly in the drainer, a box of cornflakes and a loaf of brown bread sat on the counter, and the bed in the corner was made up. Valerie slipped inside, a scrapbook in one hand, and shut the door behind her. "Jack," she called again.

The bathroom door swung open and Jack emerged. His damp hair was combed back, and shaving lather covered the bottom half of his face. He wore no shirt, and a stray droplet of water wandered leisurely down his brown, scarred chest and across his washboard-lean stomach to jeans worn low on the hip and only half buttoned.

Maybe it was because Valerie hadn't thought about meeting a half-naked Jack. Maybe it was the lingering effects of last night's kiss. Whatever the reason, Jack's nakedness struck her like a physical blow, provoking an unexpected flush of desire, one that shook her from head to toe and stole her breath away, leaving her deliciously dizzy.

She reached for the door frame to steady herself, trying to catch her breath and regain her equilibrium. What she wanted to do was touch Jack, splay her hands across his warm, wide chest, follow that droplet with her lips, tenderly exploring his skin, the sweet saltiness of his firm, lean flesh. And more.

"It's only seven. What's your rush?"

Jack's comment cleared her fuzzy head, put bone back into her liquid limbs, quelled the earthquake that had rocked her. She swallowed again, and remembered the scrapbook clutched in her hand.

She raised it. "I found this last night. D'you know what's in it?"

Jack shook his head. Amusement glinted in his green eyes. "No, but it must be good to get you here so early." He glanced back at the bathroom. "Can you tell me while I'm shaving? I'd like to finish up."

"Sure." Valerie followed Jack to the tiny bathroom. With a narrow shower stall, toilet, and free-standing sink, it was cramped with just one person. A small window at shoulder-height catercorner to the sink hung half open on rusted hinges, but did little to relieve the closed-in feeling of the still-steamy room.

Valerie stood in the doorway while Jack peered into the mirror and raised his razor. She tried not to stare at his chest. Given her current state of mind, she needed to fix her attention elsewhere.

She cleared her throat. "It's this clipping I found. It's about some drownings on the lake a long time ago."

Distracted from her purpose, she watched as Jack drew the razor slowly across his chin, and then under it. She'd never thought of shaving as an erotic activity before, but now she followed every stroke with breathless anticipation.

She shook her head, hoping to knock some sense into it, and tried again. "I couldn't sleep last night so I started looking through some old scrapbooks I found in a cupboard by Uncle Arthur's desk."

"Uh-huh." In the mirror, Jack's eyes met hers, only for a moment, but a moment electric enough to derail her train of thought once more.

She dropped her gaze to his jaw, and the slow sweep of the razor across his face. *No, that wouldn't do either.* She focused on the window instead, noting the absence of a screen.

"I found this old newspaper clipping about a drowning on the lake in 1927. Three drownings, actually." She paused. "One of the people who drowned was a Jack Wilder."

The razor jerked sharply. Bright red blood spurted from a nick in Jack's chin. "Ouch!"

"Are you okay?" Valerie inched forward.

"I'm fine." Jack stanched the blood with a tissue; then his gaze flickered to Valerie's reflection in the mirror, avoiding her eyes. The ugly bruise on his forehead seemed to stand out more vividly than before.

"I guess it's startling to hear about the death of someone with the same name." Valerie paused. "Who was it, anyway? A great-grandfather or uncle?"

"Don't know." The last of the lather disappeared from Jack's jaw. He picked up a towel to wipe his face and looked away.

"You know the weirdest thing," Valerie continued. "This Jack Wilder was a hunting and fishing guide at Aurora Lodge. Just like you. And he was thirty-two years old. Aren't you thirty-two too?"

"Mm-hmm." Jack flexed his shoulders, setting off a chain reaction of rippling muscles that Valerie couldn't ignore. He didn't turn around.

Disappointed by his response, Valerie pressed on. "Are

you sure you've never heard about this? Uncle Arthur never mentioned it?" She calculated in her head. "Let's see, he would have been about ten years old when this happened."

"No."

The bluntness of Jack's reply startled Valerie. She watched as he pulled a white T-shirt over his head, but his expression revealed nothing.

"That's too bad." She sighed. "No one could figure out the details of the boating accident that killed him and two other people. They were a man and wife, and apparently both men were good swimmers." She sighed again. "I guess it's going to stay a mystery."

Jack's green eyes, shuttered once more, said more loudly than words that he wasn't about to be drawn into this conversation. His gaze flickered past her. "Guess so," he said.

Straight ahead, the sun rode low in the sky, casting long dark shadows on the water from the tree-studded shoreline. To the left was a tiny island, not much more than a large hunk of rock, with a couple of hardy white pines clinging to it. Beyond it, waves lapped against the top of dark, submerged shards of granite, clearly visible during the day but dangerous at night. To the right, the open water gave way to a profusion of swamp grasses and bulrushes. Inland, the lighter green of the tamarack punctuated the darkness of the woods behind. Somewhere in there flowed a river connecting Lake Aurora to another lake.

With a sigh, Valerie laid the paddle across the bow of the fiberglass canoe, resting her weary arms for a moment. Actually, more than her arms were weary. Her back had started to ache and her knees felt permanently frozen into a crouch in the bottom of the canoe. And one pesky horsefly kept buzzing around her head, waiting for a chance to take a hunk of her flesh.

She turned slightly and glanced at Jack, still paddling steadily. "I thought you said it was an easy paddle to the end of the lake."

"It is." He paused. "For me."

Despite his straight face, Valerie could hear the restrained laughter in his voice.

"Once you get some more practice, build up those city-girl muscles, you'll be able to do this by yourself, easy."

"Yeah. Sure." Valerie wasn't convinced. She rolled her shoulders, then stretched her arms out on either side and looked eagerly around. "So where do you think those drownings took place?"

When he didn't answer, she turned again and regarded him. He continued paddling as if she hadn't spoken.

"Jack, those drownings I told you about this morning. Where do you think they happened?"

"Don't know."

Frustrated by his continuing lack of interest, Valerie turned to face the bow once more. She puzzled over the deaths, speaking out loud. "I wonder how it could have happened. I mean, even in the middle of the lake, it's not that far to shore. The stories didn't say anything about high winds or the boats crashing into rocks. Surely if one of the canoes had flipped, they could have hung on or swum to shore. It was summer. The water wouldn't have been that cold.

"And why did they take two canoes? Three people could easily fit into one canoe, even a small one."

Realizing that Jack had no intention of trying to figure out what had happened here so many years ago, Valerie stopped talking. Reluctantly she picked up her paddle and started to raise it, then noticed that the canoe was no longer traveling toward the western shore, but was making a wide arc, turning back the way they had come.

She turned again. "Where are we going?"

"Back."

Valerie stared at Jack. He was paddling harder and faster than before, literally stabbing the paddle into the water, with a savagery that would have done harm to any other substance. His face was set in harsh, almost angry lines.

Norah-Jean Perkin

"But what about the river? I thought we'd go through the swamp and try to find the river to the other lake."

"Not now."

"But—"

"Valerie, you can go there later this summer. Right now in any swampy areas the mosquitoes are fierce. At the end of the summer, preferably during the day, when the water's down a bit more, you'd probably enjoy it. But not now."

Jack didn't break or slow his stroke the whole time he spoke.

As the canoe changed direction, the rays of the sinking sun shone into Valerie's face. She shaded her eyes against the glare, but Jack's face was now hidden to her, plunged into shadow.

She turned to face the front of the boat again and raised her paddle once more, her muscles screaming in complaint. Grimly, she dipped her paddle into the water, determined to contribute to their forward motion, but not attempting to match his breakneck pace.

By the time they reached Aurora Lodge, the sun had disappeared behind the tree line and the sky behind them was streaked with hues of gold and pink and purple. Checking her watch, Valerie realized they'd made it back in less than half the time it had taken to paddle to the west end of the lake. Of course, on the way there, they had stopped to look at cottages, at the granite cliffs, at the public beach. Their pace had been leisurely, not driven.

The canoe ran aground with a thud, jerking Valerie forward. A second later the small boat floated again, as Jack leapt out into the knee-high water. He pushed the craft forward, close enough to the shore that Valerie could jump out without removing her running shoes.

"Thanks." She nodded and reached back to grasp the canoe and help haul it farther up onto the beach.

Jack's large brown hand covered her much smaller one. "I'll do it."

"No, it's—"

122

Jack gently eased her grip on the canoe. "I know you can do it, Valerie. So do you. But let me."

Her lips parted and her forehead creased in puzzlement. She didn't begin to understand this man, why he acted the way he did, or anything about him.

She stepped back and he pulled up the canoe until it cleared the water by several feet. He removed both paddles, flipped the boat over, then nodded at Valerie. "I'll put the paddles in the shed."

They headed up the long hill to their respective lodgings. They had passed the fourth cottage along the gravel road when Valerie stopped to catch her breath. "I'd forgotten how steep this hill was." She raised her arms over her head and stretched. "Especially when you're tired and stiff from three hours of canoeing."

Without a word, Jack took her hand. As the warm, rough flesh closed securely around her, a glow of happiness shimmered through her. How could the mere touch of a hand, from a man so silent and so strange, fill her with such a good feeling, such a sense of rightness? Valerie squeezed his hand as they continued up the path, which no longer seemed quite as steep.

They trudged companionably past several more cottages and two giant hunks of granite, then cut across the shuffleboard court in front of the main lodge building. As they approached the deck of Art's house, strains of music greeted them.

Valerie frowned. "I must have left the radio on. It's sitting on the picnic table."

A few feet from the deck, Jack stopped. He turned to Valerie. She was shocked by the earnestness of his expression. He took her hand between both of his, stroking each finger, studying the appendage as if it were a marvel of life. Finally he paused and looked straight at her.

"Valerie, I nee—"

The music abruptly cut out, replaced by the boom of a male announcer's voice. *"In news today, police have issued a warrant for the arrest of Jack Vanderstone for the murder of his wife and two young children. Catherine Vanderstone and the children, Stephanie, six, and Justin, four, were shot to death last Thursday night in their home just outside Huntsville.*

"No one has seen Mr. Vanderstone since about ten P.M. Thursday night, when he was out drinking with his buddies at The Rusty Spoon. The murder weapon has not been found."

Valerie shuddered, the dire words reminding her all too vividly of her own brush with violence. "I still can't believe something like that happened around here," she said. Then, thoughtfully: "I wonder if he's still somewhere in the area."

"Not likely. He's probably hundreds or thousands of miles away by now." Jack squeezed her hand. "Besides, it sounds like one of those family-violence cases. I doubt he'd harm anyone else. You're not worried, are you?"

She shook her head, sending her private dark memories on their way. Perhaps she should be concerned, but she didn't think so.

"That's good. But if you are nervous, you can always stay in a motel in town for a few days until they find the guy."

Valerie shook her head once more. "It's not as if I'm alone here. I've got Reddi. And besides, you're here, just a few yards away." She smiled. "Who's going to bother me with all that protection?"

Her comments didn't bring the light response she expected. Instead, that earnest look took over Jack's expression once more. "Valerie, you can't count—"

"The best show in North America tonight is going to be right outside your windows and over your heads," boomed the voice of the announcer. *"Astronomers predict clear skies and a stunning display of Northern Lights, one of the best yet as we approach the eleven-year maximus in which the electromagnetic activity of the sun reaches its peak. So, folks, head outside and . . ."*

Jack listened intently, his forehead furrowed. And that bruise! To Valerie, it looked far angrier and uglier than before, almost throbbing with the sounds coming from the radio.

As the newscast ended, Jack dropped her hand and started to turn away.

"Jack? Where are you going?"

She grasped his arm, forcing him to stop. "Where are you go—"

The bleakest expression she'd ever witnessed on a living person took her words away. Finally, she whispered, "Jack?"

He cleared his throat. "You can't count on me, Valerie. I—I'm not—"

Without warning he pulled her to him, his hands hot on her arms. His mouth descended on hers, with a desperation and a raw hunger that was as unexpected as it was shocking.

Despite her surprise, she responded eagerly, with a hunger as heated as his. She welcomed his embrace, holding him tightly, kissing him back, her mouth opening under his, offering herself to him with all her heart.

His arms wrapped around her, pulling her hard against him. She could feel the muscles of his chest pressed against the softness of her breasts, his groin resting against hers, the heat and strength of his erection. She could smell his maleness, musky and hot and appealing. Electricity sizzled through her nerve endings and raced through her veins, signaling her desire for him.

Then, as suddenly as he'd embraced her, he let her go. She stood there, dizzy and wanting, her lips parted and her eyes dark with confusion.

The bruise on his forehead visibly throbbed. He swallowed and stepped back.

He started to raise his hand as if to touch her, then quickly dropped it.

"I'm sorry," he said. "Good-bye."

He turned and walked away.

Too stunned to stop him, Valerie watched him disappear into the trees.

Chapter Eleven

Leaning against the kitchen counter, Valerie peered through the morning light in the direction of Jack's cabin. No smoke rose above the trees, no familiar form exited into the clearing.

After a moment, she slapped the dish towel onto the counter and pushed herself away. Enough craning out of windows. Enough waiting to see if Jack would come by and explain his behavior. Enough worrying about why he'd left so abruptly, and behaved so strangely last night. The best way to dispel these foolish wonderings was to march right over to Jack's cabin and say hello.

Sure he'd kissed her, after they'd agreed it wouldn't happen again. But she'd kissed him back. And she'd wanted to kiss him back. So why had he literally turned and run?

"Hey, Reddi."

Reddi, always eager to go outside, leapt up from the rug in front of the stove.

Once outside, Valerie headed for the stairs and the path to Jack's. Two rose-breasted grosbeak flared out from a

126

sumac bush as she walked by. The fresh scent of water carried on the breeze, ruffling the grasses and leaves.

As she came out of the trees, Valerie could see no sign of activity around Jack's cabin. She glanced at her watch. It was after ten. No way he'd still be in bed. From what she'd seen, he rose at the crack of dawn.

She traipsed up the granite stone path, calling to Reddi. The puppy came to the edge of the clearing around Jack's cabin, but refused to move any closer, growling and crouching down on the ground defensively. Valerie shook her head. She'd never figure out what it was between Reddi and Jack. After letting herself onto the screened-in porch, she knocked briskly at the door and waited.

Suddenly, she remembered Jack's odd choice of word last night, and the uneasiness it had spawned. *Good-bye.* Why had he said good-bye instead of good night? Impatiently, she pushed the question aside. Jack had used the wrong word, that was all.

Thirty seconds passed. She knocked a second time, and waited at least as long again. Finally, she opened the door and stuck her head inside. "Jack?"

Her voice echoed through the cabin. She stepped inside and scanned the room. The door to the bathroom stood open, and it was empty. The drainer by the sink was cleared of dishes, and the bed was made, though it bore the imprint of a body. A pair of worn, brown leather loafers could be seen under the bed, and the jeans and T-shirt he'd worn yesterday hung over the back of a kitchen chair.

Valerie glanced at the corner where she'd seen Jack stash his backpack. It was bare.

"Good-bye!" The word rang through her head. Her uneasiness flared to fear. He couldn't have left. Not without telling her.

"Good-bye!"

But maybe he had. She just hadn't understood. That was why he'd acted so strangely last night. He'd planned to leave but he hadn't wanted to tell her.

But why would he do that? What about the lodge? What about the decision he had to make? Valerie stood still in the middle of the room while she grappled with what had happened and her conflicting emotions.

Finally, she straightened and shook her head. She was being foolish. Likely Jack was out fishing, or had gone to town, that was all.

She glanced at the table. Her heart leapt. *His watch!* If he was leaving, he'd have taken his watch. But hadn't he said something about it not working? She shook her head.

Likely his backpack was stashed in a drawer or cupboard. Her eyes automatically scanned the walls, finding a likely closet near the bathroom. She started toward it, then stopped.

She couldn't go rifling through Jack's things, invading his space.

"Good-bye." The word crept into her head again. She gritted her teeth.

Now she *was* being ridiculous. Just because Jack hadn't told her his plans, it didn't mean he was gone. He was bound to show up later this morning or afternoon.

She ignored her uneasiness and stomped to the door. She wouldn't invade Jack's privacy, that's all there was to it.

Especially not to assuage a silly fear that had no basis in reality.

Shivering from the early morning chill, Valerie knocked on Jack's door again the next morning. *Where is he?* As she waited, she mentally ticked off the number of times she'd come looking for him yesterday: once in the morning, twice in the afternoon, four times over the course of the evening.

Valerie pushed open the door and looked around. Nothing had changed. The bed was made, the watch lay on the table, the bathroom door hung open at the same angle. And Jack was still gone.

But where? And why? Why hadn't he told her he was leaving?

The worries she'd managed to keep at bay yesterday and through the night came flooding in. What if something had happened to him? Had he tried another cross-lake swim, only to drown? What if he'd blacked out as a result of some unseen injury, or a concussion they hadn't known he had? Oh, God—what if he'd run into that Vanderstone man? The one the police wanted for murdering his wife and kids?

A cold shudder ran through Valerie. She shut her eyes and took a deep breath, then opened them, struck by the incongruity of *her* worrying about Jack. She really was being ridiculous. The most logical explanation was that Jack had gone into town, maybe met up with a friend, and decided to stay overnight. Maybe he'd hitchhiked to Lindsay and couldn't get a ride back. Maybe . . .

"Good-bye." The nasty word that had tormented her for the last twenty-four hours surfaced again. Roughly, she shoved it away. She wouldn't believe he'd just left. Especially after his kindness to her, the fun they'd shared. And that kiss . . .

But he's a drifter. A drifter who said he doesn't want to run the lodge. Why wouldn't he just up and leave?

Valerie exhaled and slowly unclenched her fists. This worrying was getting her nowhere. She looked at the cupboards and drawers, and resisted the urge to investigate, to see if she could find a clue to where Jack had gone. Not yet. Jack was a private man, and she wanted to respect his privacy. She'd hate for him to return to find her snooping through his things.

Quickly, before she could do anything she'd later regret, she left the cabin, shutting the door behind her. But there was one thing she could do. Call Ed Grierson. Perhaps Jack had gone into town to see the lawyer and discuss the sale of the lodge. After all, he'd said he needed to think. He probably needed legal advice too, before he made a final decision.

If Mr. Grierson hadn't seen Jack, perhaps he might know where he'd gone or what she should do to find him.

At the house, Valerie dug out her cell phone and turned it on. She'd been careful to keep it charged, just in case. The signal was weak, but it improved when she went outside and moved away from the house and rocks and into the parking lot.

On the second try she got through to Grierson's line. The phone rang and rang and rang. Valerie glanced at her watch. Oops. It was only quarter to eight. Likely neither Lynn nor Mr. Grierson were in yet—

"Hello."

The familiar voice broke into her thoughts.

"Mr. Grierson?"

"Yes."

"This is Valerie Scott, Mr. Grierson. I was wondering if you'd seen Jack Wilder yesterday."

"Wilder? No. Not yesterday." Mr. Grierson's voice sounded rusty, as if these were the first words he'd uttered this morning.

"Does he have an appointment with you today?"

"I'd have to check with Lynn, but I don't think so." There was a pause. "Why? Is there a problem?"

"Actually, I'm not sure, Mr. Grierson. I'd like your advice."

She gulped. "You see, he's staying at Aurora Lodge, in one of the cabins, while I'm in the house. But yesterday morning when I went to his cabin, he was gone. And he hasn't come back."

"Mmm. Did he tell you where he planned to go?" Mr. Grierson's gravelly voice cracked.

"That's just it. We've spent a fair amount of time together, reviewing the inventory, examining the cabins. He didn't say anything about leaving."

"Hmmph. That is odd. But he is a drifter. Always was,

according to your uncle. Maybe he got a little restless, and took off for a couple of days."

"Maybe you're right," said Valerie, not convinced. "But he's left things behind, like his watch."

"Tell you what, Valerie. Wait until tomorrow. If he hasn't returned by then, call me and I'll phone the police. I know most of the men on the force. All right?" The kindness in his voice, one of the first things Valerie had noticed about him in their initial meeting, flowed across the line, soothing her jangled nerves.

"I guess so." Valerie's tension eased slightly.

"He's likely to show up anytime, so don't you worry. By the way, have you two decided what to do with Aurora Lodge yet?"

"Not yet. Jack wanted a few days to think about it."

"There. You see? That's probably it." Mr. Grierson sounded triumphant. "He's left to think things over. When he shows up again, you'll likely have his answer."

The sound of gravel crunching under tires intruded. Valerie jumped, then turned around to see a small-model car slowly driving into the parking lot.

"I've got to go now, Mr. Grierson. I'll call you tomorrow."

She punched an end to the conversation. The car halted only a few feet away. The door swung open and the driver jumped out. It was Velma.

Valerie managed to hide her disappointment behind a welcoming smile. "Hi, Velma."

"Mornin'." Velma's gaze dropped to the cell phone in Valerie's hand. "I thought I'd drop by to firm up the cottage rental we talked about the other day. Am I interrupting?"

"No." Valerie shook her head. "Just a short call. I came out here because the signal's clearer."

Velma nodded, her ponytail bouncing on her neck. "Good, now about August. The whole month at Hackamatack? Is there any problem with that?"

"No."

131

"Now about the rate—"

"Oh, you don't have to pay. Jack and I aren't sure what we're going to do with the lodge yet. Probably we'll sell it, but not until the fall. If you pay all the expenses—you know, like the hydro hookup—and you clean it before and after, that's fine with me. You'd have to provide your own towels and sheets too, and do your own laundry."

Velma beamed. "Wonderful! But are you sure? Maybe Mr. Wilder would prefer if we paid."

Valerie shook her head again. "Don't worry about Mr. Wilder. He's not here now, but I'm certain he wouldn't mind."

"Good."

Velma shifted from foot to foot, with the look of someone who had something to say but didn't know how or where to start. Finally, when Valerie was about to say goodbye and return to the house, Velma blurted out, "D'you mind if I ask you a question? It's about Mr. Wilder?"

"Mr. Wilder?" Valerie tensed. "You can ask, but I'm not sure I'll be able to answer it. I met him only last week."

Velma twisted the keys in her hands. "That's kind of what I was wondering about."

Valerie felt her face flush. Of course. Small-town curiosity was at work already, wanting to know the connection between Jack and herself. She straightened. Well, there was nothing to tell. "Why?" she asked, her tone cool.

Velma twisted the keys. "I know this sounds odd, but I almost fell over the first time I saw him. I told you he's the spitting image of a Jack Wilder who worked here, at Aurora Lodge, the summer I turned eighteen."

"Yes, I remember," Valerie said cautiously.

Velma screwed up her face. "I know it sounds ridiculous. But it's true. I didn't know *that* Jack Wilder well, but I, well, I guess you'd say I had a crush on him. I've never seen him again since that summer, but I've carried a picture of him around in my head all these years. Which is why it shocked me so, seeing him here after all this time."

"But Jack can't be the Jack Wilder you're talking about!"

Velma swung the keys. "Of course. I realize that. It's just freaky, he looks so much like the Jack Wilder I knew." She paused, then looked at Valerie point-blank. "Do you know whether his father or uncle worked here, oh, thirty years ago?"

Valerie blinked. "Didn't Jack already tell you no?"

Velma nodded. "I thought it might have slipped his mind."

Valerie considered whether to mention the Jack Wilder who worked at Aurora Lodge in 1927 until he drowned, then decided against it. "I could ask him again," she offered. "Maybe your question has jogged his memory. Or maybe there's someone else around here he could ask."

Velma nodded. "Yes. Do that. I'd like to know. It's such a strange coincidence, especially when they look so much alike."

As Velma turned to leave, a question occurred to Valerie. "What kind of work did the Jack Wilder you knew do for Uncle Arthur?"

Velma paused, one hand on the car door. "Oh, you know. Odd jobs. Repairs to the cottages. He took the kids fishing, taught anyone who wanted how to canoe. If I recall, that summer he helped Art rebuild two of the docks. Parts of them had rotted away and needed to be replaced."

Velma nodded, got into her car, and drove away.

Valerie stood in the parking lot, ostensibly watching the older woman leave. But her mind was reeling with the puzzle of Jack Wilder.

Odd jobs. Fishing. Canoeing. Just like today's Jack Wilder.

With a start, Valerie halted her pacing and looked around. Darkness had taken over the living room; she could have sworn that it was still light when she'd started walking back and forth across the room, trying to work out the puzzle of Jack Wilder and where he might have gone.

She shook her head and advanced to the window that

133

looked out over the deck and down the hill to the lake. Ever since her phone conversation with Mr. Grierson, she'd tried, she'd really tried, to put Jack's disappearance out of her mind and assume he would turn up again soon.

But it hadn't worked. Lying on the beach sunning, cooling off in the lake, eating lunch and dinner alone, taking Reddi for a long walk back on one of the trails beyond the road, she'd kept wondering. Wondering where he was, what he was doing, when he'd be back.

And damnit, why he hadn't told her!

Cupping her eyes to block out the light from the fireplace, she pressed her face to the window and gazed upward. After a cloudy night yesterday, this evening's dark sky pulsed with an amazing display of Northern Lights. After the show two nights ago, when the sky had shimmered with gold and green, it was hard to believe anything could top it. But tonight's aurora borealis did. Beams of blood-red light swept across the sky in arcs, staining the sky with a design that was as eerie as it was impressive.

Involuntarily, Valerie shuddered and pulled back from the window. As beautiful as it was, tonight's show made her uneasy. She shuddered again.

What if Jack doesn't come back? The unexpected question set her worries in a new direction. She started pacing again. He was a drifter after all, never staying in one place for long, never committing to anything. Had the question of assuming responsibility for the lodge sent him running?

Valerie shook her head. Drifter or not, running away didn't jibe with the Jack she knew, however briefly. He'd fixed any problem that had come up at the lodge. He knew so much about the area, and he could do so many things, from canoeing and fishing to building and organizing, it was impossible to believe he'd run from a little responsibility.

Nor did running away fit with her gut feeling about Jack, about his honesty and dependability. She was trying so hard to pay attention to her feelings, to trust and believe in them. After two years with Reed, it was a struggle to believe that her opinions counted, that she could be right. She couldn't—no, she wouldn't—be wrong this time, not on her first test.

But then there was the coincidence of the three Jack Wilders. The Jack Wilder who drowned in 1927. The Jack Wilder of Velma's crush thirty years ago. And today's Jack Wilder, who apparently was the spitting image of Velma's Jack Wilder.

A new, unbidden possibility struck Valerie. *What if today's Jack Wilder isn't the right one? What if Uncle Arthur had actually left the lodge to the Jack Wilder that Velma knew?*

The idea derailed her thoughts. For a long moment she stood there, unable to think, unable to move.

Finally, she swallowed and forced herself to examine the unthinkable. Velma's Jack Wilder would be close to sixty now, far closer in age to Uncle Arthur, and more likely to be his friend and co-inheritor of the lodge. But if that was the case, where was he? And why had Velma never seen him except for that one summer?

And what about Jack? *My Jack,* thought Valerie. If he isn't the right Jack, if he hasn't worked for my uncle, how does he know so much about him? How does he know so much about this place?

Valerie shook her head. The only answer could be a coincidence, an incredi—

Fierce barking interrupted her musing. *Jack!* It must be Jack to set Reddi off like that.

Valerie flew to the kitchen door. Reddi was barking frantically and leaping at the door.

Valerie collared the pup with one hand. With the other she grabbed the doorknob. She didn't want Reddi taking Jack's leg off.

She turned the knob, and opened the door. As she looked up, she started to smile in welcome.

The smile froze on her face. "What—what are you doing here?"

Chapter Twelve

Reed smiled. The light from the kitchen's overhead fixture reflected off his blue/black hair and his strong, patrician features. In his arms he held a huge bouquet of at least two dozen blood-red roses. He ignored Valerie's question, instead crouching down to offer the straining pup his favorite doggy treat.

After Reddi gobbled up the bribe and started licking his hand, Reed looked up at Valerie, his expression amused. "Aren't you going to ask me in?" He glanced upward as a trio of moths fluttered to the light, followed by something that looked suspiciously like a mosquito. "So far your only houseguests are bugs."

Valerie swallowed. She tried to calm her frantically beating heart and overcome the paralysis seizing her vocal cords. "I don't think that's a good idea," she managed.

With a last pat for Reddi, Reed stood up. As he loomed to his perfectly proportioned height of six feet two inches, Valerie could almost feel herself shrinking. Angrily, she forced herself to stand straighter. She *wouldn't* be afraid.

He couldn't make her do anything she didn't want to do.

"I brought you flowers." Reed held the peace offering out to her. The overpowering smell of roses, his favorite flower, nauseated her. When she made no move to take them, he lowered them and sighed.

"Valerie, please. After all the time we've spent together, surely you trust me enough to at least let me through the door."

"No."

"Please, Valerie."

Valerie blinked. Had she heard right? Was Reed *asking* her? Was he actually begging?

"We need to talk," he said. "About what happened. You have to at least give me that. Please."

The uncharacteristic pleading shocked Valerie. She wavered. She was right to be afraid, but was she also being unfair? Should she at least give him a chance to apologize in person? And to prove to herself that she could stand up to him?

She took a deep breath. "All right. You can come in. But only for a few minutes."

Valerie stepped back into the room. The relief on Reed's face as he crossed the threshold was almost palpable, and an emotion she'd never seen there before. Despite relenting, she remained tensed, like a spring, ready to recoil at the slightest provocation.

Reddi, yipping happily, danced around Reed's knees as he entered the room. Valerie watched her pup with dismay. *How could he?* After all that had happened? The dog's joyful welcome to Reed cut like a knife blade, an unbelievable betrayal of his mistress and a repudiation of what she had suffered.

Reed pulled out a chair and sat down at the table. He laid the flowers down. Then, in the proprietary manner that Valerie had only recognized of late, gestured for her to sit down.

It's my house, she thought bitterly, not his. "No, I think I'll stand."

Reed shook his head as if she were a recalcitrant little girl who didn't know what was good for her. Then he smiled, with an openness and lack of guile that would have convinced the perpetrators of the Inquisition that he was without fault. The same look with which he had met Valerie's accusations, the look that sometimes made her wonder if she and Reed were living in alternate universes. Once again, it struck her how much he was like her father, though to her knowledge her father had never lost control and exploded in violence. No, her father had relied on guilt and manipulation.

"I'd like a beer," Reed said.

Valerie slipped to the fridge. Go away! she thought. Then: What's wrong with me? Why did I let him in? Why am I doing this? As she passed him, she realized she was shaking, and her hands had turned cold as ice. She found the beer, twisted off the cap, and set the bottle in front of Reed, keeping as far away as possible. But she couldn't avoid the spicy smell of his aftershave, the almost physical sense of confidence and power that emanated from him, dominating the room and everything in it.

Reed glanced pointedly from the bottle to Valerie, one eyebrow raised in displeasure. For a moment, Valerie didn't understand.

Then it hit her. A glass! Reed wanted a glass, of course, and was letting her know as only he could that she had failed him. Again. She considered ignoring him, then rejected it. Better to get him the glass, have him drink his beer, make his apologies, and get out.

Without a word, she moved to the cupboard and brought down a glass. She swallowed, bolstering her strength to approach him again. She set down the glass beside the beer and stepped back.

Suddenly Reed grasped her wrist. She started, her throat constricting and her stomach clenching.

Reed regarded her with a warmth and sincerity in his deep blue eyes that should have kindled fire in the coldest rock, but only frightened her. "I missed you," he said simply.

Valerie avoided his gaze. She forced herself to peel his fingers away from her wrist, silently berating herself for the trembling that slowed her motions, the trembling that Reed couldn't miss. Once freed, she backed away to the counter. She swallowed and raised her head, making herself look him full in the face. "You said you wanted to talk?"

Once again Reed flashed that sad little smile. He shook his head, as if sorrowful at the need to play this little charade. "I had a devil of a time finding you."

"How did you?"

"Suzanne. She told me."

Valerie winced at her failure to tell Suzanne the truth. But she'd been in such a hurry to get away, she'd left her address—without any explanations—on her friend's voice mail.

She swallowed again and forced herself to repeat her question. "You still haven't told me what you're doing here."

He waved his hands in a gesture of openness. "You were so upset when you left. So confused. I wanted to clear everything up." He paused, and his blue eyes, serious and pleading, zeroed in on her. "I wanted—needed—to make sure you know how much I love you."

"Our engagement is over, Reed." As if she were in a dream, Valerie heard her voice, small and far away. But she'd said the words. Again. That was a start.

Reed shook his head, his expression one of forbearance. "I don't know why you keep saying that. You know I love you. You know we're perfect for each other."

His quiet insistence, his apparently unassailable sincerity, hit Valerie, striking a chord of fear deep inside her. He hadn't changed. He didn't want to apologize. He wanted to manipulate her, as she'd let him do so successfully for most of the last two years. But not now. Now she recognized his tricks. She should. She'd had plenty of practice. Her father had been a master at inspiring doubt, doubt and guilt, whatever it took to make her feel small, stupid, and insignificant. When she'd left for college, she'd finally escaped his influence. How had she ever let herself get involved with a man not only just like him, but far worse?

"I don't want to get into this again," she said quickly. "It's over."

Reed's dramatic sigh filled the room. "Valerie," he said, with patented patience, "I've come all this way. I've taken time off work during our busiest season. All to ask you for a second chance. Can't you at least think about it? Can't we spend some time together for the next few days, talk about our problems and what we each want?"

As he spoke, he scratched Reddi behind the ears. The pup panted contentedly at his feet.

Valerie watched with bitter resentment. What was it about Reed that always made her feel so unreasonable? Made her feel as if she were the one at fault, when it was the exact opposite?

"I don't think so," she managed, then stopped, horrified at how tentative, how weak, she sounded.

A flash of impatience crossed Reed's face, but it was gone so quickly Valerie wondered if she'd imagined it. His voice rang with reason and patience as he repeated his plea. "Valerie, it was a little thing, a tiny, meaningless incident that should never have happened and never will again. For two years we've had a great relationship. I've never—never—hurt you. After all this time, how can you blow something so small so out of proportion? Be reasonable. You know I love you. And you love me. That's all that should matter."

Valerie gaped. For one horrifying second all she could see was the rage contorting Reed's face. His refusal to let her go. Panic rose in her throat as his hands tightened around it, cutting off her air, leaving her gasping, on the edge of blackness.

She shook her head and called on all her strength to cast off the terrifying flashback. She knew what had happened, even if Reed pretended it hadn't. She still felt those hands around her neck, even if Reddi, wooed by a doggy treat, now welcomed Reed.

But even if she was wrong about what had happened, it didn't matter. She'd already realized that Reed was bad for her, in every way. Nothing would change that.

She swallowed once more. "I don't—"

"Then it's settled." Reed, his voice firm, stood up. "I'll go and get my bags."

"Your bags?" Valerie's mouth went dry.

"They're out in the car."

"You can't stay here!" Her heart thumped frantically, beating out her alarm.

Reed frowned. "Why not?"

"There are good motels in Huntsville."

Reed moved closer, his hand capturing her chin. Valerie jerked away as if he'd slapped her.

He frowned again; his eyes narrowed. Placatingly, he said, "Valerie, sweet, you know I'm not going to hurt you. I'll sleep on the couch down here, or in another bedroom if that will make you happy."

With each word he uttered, Valerie could feel the noose tightening around her neck, could feel herself getting mired ever deeper in the quicksand of their past relationship. She opened her mouth to deny—

A menacing growl diverted her attention to Reddi. Was the pup finally recognizing Reed for what he was?

But no. Reddi's attention was focused on the door. His growl grew louder and his ears flattened on his head.

"What the—"

Reddi poised to leap. The door flung open and the dog rushed forward with a snarl.

"Whoa!" Jack fended Reddi off with his bare arm. "Hey, boy, I thought we had an agreement." He grabbed the dog by the ruff of the neck and stared at him.

141

In a reversal as stunning as it was swift, Reddi started to whimper. Jack released him and the dog crept from the room.

Jack straightened and looked from Valerie to Reed. "Good evening."

"Who are you?"

Reed's rude demand barely penetrated the wave of relief that swept over Valerie at Jack's arrival. She took a deep breath to still her quavering and put bone back into her legs.

She beamed at Jack, the most beautiful sight she'd seen in a long time. "Jack Wilder, meet Reed Volger. Reed, this is Jack Wilder."

Reed glared, his dark brows bristling as he surveyed the intruder. Finally, with what seemed to Valerie an unusual ill grace, he recomposed himself. With a casual gesture to Jack, he turned to Valerie. "So is Wilder the lodge's maintenance man?"

Valerie glanced at Jack. If he had noticed Reed's intentional slur, he didn't show it. His expression remained open and friendly.

Valerie straightened, amazed at both the relief she felt and the accompanying spurt of joy at Jack's arrival. Yes, she was relieved that he had interrupted her confrontation with Reed. But it was more than that, and she knew it. She'd been so worried that something bad had happened to him, and now he was here. Only Reed's presence stopped her from throwing herself into Jack's arms and kissing him senseless.

She contented herself with smiling warmly at Jack while she answered Reed's question. "Jack and I have inherited the lodge."

Reed's gaze returned to Jack, this time with undisguised surprise. "So is he going to manage the lodge?"

Jack spoke up, ignoring the fact the question had not been directed to him. "Valerie and I haven't decided yet whether to keep the lodge or to sell it. Until then, the lodge is closed."

"You're here together?" Reed stared at Jack, another, more proprietary question implicit in his words.

"Not here. I've got one of the cabins a couple of hundred yards over." Jack gestured over his shoulder.

Reed digested that in silence. Then he turned to Valerie. "I'll get my bags."

"No!"

Embarrassed by her yelp, Valerie tried to soften it. "Look, Reed, I already told you I'd prefer if you stayed in town, at a motel. You'll pass two on the way back, the Grandview and the Deerhurst."

"I'd feel better if I was closer. I don't like you being out here alone in the middle of nowhere."

"I'm not alone." With each word, Valerie felt herself growing stronger, her self-confidence and assurance returning. "I've got Reddi. Jack is nearby. And I've been here for a week without any problem. I can't see why there'd be one now."

"But we've got so much we need to talk about."

"Not anymore."

Reed plowed on as if she hadn't spoken. "We can't leave it like this, Valerie. Not now."

When she didn't say anything, he frowned, then raised his hands in apparent concession. "All right. You're tired now. I can see that. I'll come out tomorrow morning."

"No." Valerie paused. "I'll come into town. We can talk there."

"Okay. Dinner then."

"Lunch."

Reed shot daggers at Jack, clearly blaming him for the impasse. But he merely said, "All right. We'll do lunch. Where?"

"Phone me in the morning. I'll have my cell phone on."

When Reed nodded, Valerie blinked in surprise. It was unlike Reed to give up, ever. Whether it had anything to do with Jack's presence, she didn't know. She was just glad that Reed had stopped fighting her.

She watched as he nodded to Jack, then made his way out, slamming the door behind him.

The second Jack had stepped into the house, he'd known something was wrong. Valerie's pale face, Reed's angry glares and rude comments—they pointed to a confrontation, something simmering below the surface, something at which the stilted conversation only hinted and which his arrival had interrupted. Jack had watched the interplay with growing concern, disturbed by the undertones of fear, and by the reminders they generated of other confrontations, in other times.

Now, in the echoing silence, he stuck his hands in the pockets of his jeans and jerked his head at the closed door. "A friend?"

"Yes."

"From Chicago?"

Valerie nodded. She sat down heavily at the kitchen table, looking for all the world as if she wanted to burst into tears.

"Just a friend?" Jack asked softly, cursing himself even as he did. *It's none of my business.*

Valerie twisted her hands on the tabletop and looked at her lap. After a moment of silence she looked up at Jack, her eyes dark and weary.

"No. More than a friend. We were engaged. Until about four weeks ago. Remember I told you I just ended a relationship with another man? It was Reed."

Jack leaned against the wall. He knew he should walk—no, run away, put as much space between himself and Valerie and whatever troubles she was suffering. It was all too reminiscent of a past he'd just as soon forget, a past that was responsible for his current predicament. But one look at her pinched, pale face, at the dark eyes full of that painful vulnerability, and he knew he wasn't going anywhere anytime soon. At least not of his own free will.

He cleared his throat. "Seems like a pretty high-powered guy."

Valerie nodded miserably. "He is. He's a partner in one of Chicago's top architectural firms. Does projects all over the world."

"He doesn't look too happy right now."

Valerie looked away. "He wants our engagement back on. I told him no. It's over."

The words hung in the air between them. But it was what remained unsaid that interested Jack, the unspoken fear that still lingered in the room. The electric current of fear that he had felt the second he stepped through the door.

The shadow of a bruise filled his mind's eye, and he glanced sharply at Valerie. In the bright kitchen light, no trace of bruising remained on her delicate throat.

"You told me *you* broke up with him. Why?"

She shrugged, but didn't quite meet his eye. "Lots of reasons."

"You're afraid of him. He hurt you, didn't he?"

His angry statement clearly startled Valerie. It surprised even him, welling up from somewhere deep inside, reverberating with echoes from the past. But he had no doubt it was true. He'd seen how Valerie had shifted from fear to bravado and back in Reed's presence. He'd seen her relief at his departure.

"That's ridiculous," she sputtered.

It was on the tip of his tongue to ask why she denied what was so clearly true, but he stopped himself. Instead he asked, "Are you planning to get together with him again?"

"No!" Valerie yelped, then turned bright red.

"Good." Jack smiled thinly. For her sake, for her safety, he was relieved to see that she had the sense not to return to a man who had hurt her like that. "That's pretty definite," he allowed.

"It *is* definite." Valerie jumped up from the table and

glared at him. "No one's pushing me around."

Jack raised one eyebrow at her choice of words, but let it go. He was relieved to see she was standing up for herself, protecting herself. He couldn't stand to see a replay of the past that had haunted him for so long, a past that would continue to haunt him for the rest of whatever it was he lived.

But more than anything else, he was relieved that Valerie was still here. That so little time had elapsed since he had disappeared. And that she appeared so happy to see him, something he had never expected.

"So where the hell were you?"

Jack blinked. He'd known he wouldn't escape questioning for long. But Valerie's flip from welcome to anger startled him, and raised his spirits another couple of notches. Had his absence meant that much to her?

He stared at her, enjoying the transformation. Anger flashed in her brown eyes and splashed color back into her pale cheeks. Her bottom lip jutted out, full and lush and inviting, so inviting. Wisps of hair escaped from the ever-present ponytail, calling to him to push them back from her face.

A wave of desire washed over him, sharp and burning, testimony to the life and desire for life pounding in his veins, a desire reawakened inside him the moment he'd met Valerie, and growing stronger each day as he discovered new and wonderful things about her. He didn't want to answer her question. He wanted to sweep her into his arms, to kiss her as she'd never been kissed.

With an effort he forced himself to focus on her question—and the answer he had yet to formulate. He couldn't tell her the one thing he wanted to tell her, the one thing he needed to tell her. Because the moment he did everything would end. He was selfish enough to want his relationship with Valerie—whatever form it took—to continue.

"I'm sorry," he finally said. "It was a last-minute decision. I went . . . I went to visit an old friend in Lindsay."

"You could have told me!"

"You're right. It was . . . inconsiderate."

"Yes. It was."

For a moment Jack thought she might not forgive him. But then the anger blazing from her eyes slowly subsided. She lowered her clenched fists, took a deep breath, and regarded him with an expression that was part wistful, part puzzlement. "I wish you'd told me. I was worried," she said.

Jack's chest tightened. He swallowed the lump that had risen in his throat. "You were worried?"

"Yes." Valerie held his gaze, the emotion in her eyes simple and honest, there for him to see. "Yes, I worried about you."

"Why?"

Valerie raised a hand and ticked off the possible reasons. "I thought maybe you'd drowned. That you'd run into that man who killed his family. That you'd been hit by a car. That you'd got lost in the woods." She paused and narrowed her eyes. "That you'd been carried off by killer bees."

"Killer bees?" Jack raised his eyebrows in mock alarm.

"Why not killer bees? Haven't you heard? They're swarming up from the Southern states to the Eastern Seaboard. At this very moment they're probably crossing the border to Canada, just looking for likely victims."

"Bees, huh?" Jack suppressed a laugh.

Valerie bit her lip. At first Jack thought she was trying not to laugh. Then he saw the tears glittering in her eyes.

"Are you crying?"

"No." She sniffed and brushed at her eyes. "Of course not. I'm just glad you're okay." Then she smiled at him, a little shakily, but a smile all the same. "You don't know how glad I am that you're back."

For one long, yearning-filled moment, Jack held himself in check. From across the room he devoured her, taking in everything about her, from the soft pinkness of her lips to the velvet shimmer of her eyes, from the swell of her breasts above her low-cut T-shirt to the way her jeans clung to her shapely hips. The pulse in his forehead throbbed, a throb that was repeated through his chest and his groin and his legs. He couldn't quite put his finger on it, but something about her had changed since he'd left, something indefinable. As if, perhaps, she'd come to some new understanding of herself. And of him.

He swallowed, then crossed the room, not taking his gaze from her. "I'm glad I'm back too," he said, his voice husky. "You don't know how much."

God help me. His hunger was so strong, his need to touch her so powerful, he couldn't resist raising a hand to her cheek, catching a tendril of hair, and carefully securing it behind her ear. He told himself he'd step away then. But he didn't.

And then it didn't matter. Valerie, taking matters into her own hands, rose on tiptoe. Her arms encircled him, her hands warm and tender on his neck. Then her lips brushed across his, welcoming him, telling him she was as glad to see him as he was to see her. Her lips whispered their welcome to the corner of his mouth, then nuzzled his chin, while the fingers of one hand brushed aside the locks of hair covering his forehead.

Suddenly she halted. "Jack!"

His eyes flashed open at the horror in her voice. Valerie stared at his forehead.

"That bruise! It's worse than ever. What did you do to it?"

Jack raised one hand to his forehead. Indeed, his temple did feel swollen and tender, and he could feel the rough edge of the scab where the rock had broken his skin. He frowned; it didn't hurt any more than usual, just the dull throb that he almost didn't notice anymore. But it probably did look worse, just as it always did whenever he returned.

"Nothing."

She reached out to touch his forehead, but he grabbed her hand, then lowered it to his lips. He raised his eyes and smiled at her worry. It was a wonderful sensation, this being worried about. "It's all right," he said softly. "It doesn't hurt." *Much.*

He rubbed the smooth warm softness of her hand against his lips, savoring the taste and feel of her skin. He took a knuckle into his mouth and suckled it, shutting his eyes to better enjoy the sensation. He opened his eyes and pressed her palm against his cheek. He smiled faintly. "It's all right. Really."

Uncertainty flickered in Valerie's eyes, then faded. She smiled. She framed his face with both hands, her skin gentle against the roughness of his face. "Good. Because I wouldn't want to take advantage of an invalid."

Her mouth dipped to his once more, this time for a lengthy taste of all he had to offer. He met her stroke for stroke, his tongue dancing with hers, exploring the sweetness of her mouth and building his hunger for more.

Once more she broke away, this time to follow the line of his chin to his ear. He shivered with delight as her tongue darted inside and her warm breath tickled.

"Hmmm," she whispered. "Sand. You taste sandy." She pulled away, her eyes narrowed. "You been playin' in the dirt again, boy?"

He would have laughed, except for the reminder of where he'd been and what was still ahead. He shut it from his mind and smiled. Her teasing was infectious. "Never."

This time he claimed her lips, with an urgency and firmness that made it clear just how much he enjoyed her, how much he wanted her. His hands slipped to her breasts, cupping them through the thin material of her T-shirt.

Gently, she grasped his wrists. He stilled, hoping against hope that she didn't plan to end it all now.

"Stay with me."

His heart leapt. "Now?"

"Now."

"Are you sure?"

"Yes."

Norah-Jean Perkin

Her gentle smile filled her face, and his heart, with happiness. Until he remembered. He frowned. "What about Reed?"

"That's over. He and I have no relationship now nor will we ever again."

Could it be true? Jack studied her face, searching for reluctance, a hidden message. He'd made a terrible mistake once, a mistake with deadly consequences. For Valerie's sake, for her continued safety, he had to be sure. He couldn't make that mistake again.

"You're sure?" he repeated.

Silence filled the room. Jack waited, not daring to hope.

Valerie tilted her head. Her gaze held his for a long time. "I've never been more certain of anything."

Chapter Thirteen

The pounding of her heart echoed so loudly in Valerie's ears that she was certain Jack must hear it. But she didn't care.

A smile split her face, sending ripples of happiness through her, lighting her eyes, warming her chest, putting a tingle in her limbs and on her lips, building a fire in her belly. Fear had given way to relief, then to gratitude, only to explode in joy. Joy that Jack was here, that he was all right. Joy that he wanted her, and that she wanted him.

She slipped her hand into his, shivering in anticipation as the warm flesh closed over her own. She raised her eyes to Jack's once more, and what she saw in those blue-rimmed emerald pools sent sparks along her nerve endings. He wanted her, needed her, as much as she wanted him.

She started to tug him into the living room, but he stopped her with a growl. One hand was tangled in her hair, grasping the remains of the ponytail and twisting it gently around his fist. His lips came down firmly on hers once more, as if he couldn't wait, as if he'd already waited far too long. With his other hand, he pressed her body against his, lifting her upward until her breasts flattened against his lean chest, and she could feel the strength and the heat of his erection against her belly. He massaged her bottom, pushing her thighs apart until his hand claimed the space between, sending a flash of sheer pleasure spiraling upward through her.

Through her already fogged senses, Valerie heard Reddi growl. Reluctantly, she drew back. "Just a moment. I'd better take Reddi upstairs." She bit her lip. "I don't want an audience, not even a dog."

Jack threw back his head and laughed. "Good idea." He leaned against the kitchen table, his tanned arms crossed over his chest, his eyes bright and smoldering. "But hurry."

Valerie didn't need to be told twice. She grabbed Reddi's collar and rushed him up the stairs, following behind. With a pat and a scratch, she shut him in her room, then remembered. She reentered, retrieved what she sought from the dresser drawer, and raced downstairs.

The kitchen was empty.

"Jack?"

Arms closed around her shoulders from behind. "Mm-hmm?" Jack nuzzled her neck, his lips rasping along the side of her throat. She leaned back into him, a sigh escaping like a whisper from her lips. She shut her eyes to the sensations enveloping her, lulled by the safety and security she felt in his embrace.

He rubbed her bare arms, alternately squeezing and stroking, the roughness of his hands creating a friction that set her blood boiling. He slid his hands from her arms to cup her breasts, slowing lifting them, the heat of his hands burning a pathway around them. She arched into his hands, wanting him to touch her, needing him to touch her. He complied, palming her breasts in wide concentric circles until she thought she would swoon.

But it was only the beginning. Slowly his hands, hot now,

dropped to her waist, then slipped under the bottom of her short-cropped T-shirt. She gasped from the heat, holding her breath as he pushed the tight material higher, pausing beneath her breasts, then continuing his upward path. Behind her, his erection nudged against her round bottom, and she couldn't help squirming against him.

His hands closed over the round globes of her breasts, naked but for the thin lacy cups of her bra. But it wasn't enough. She wanted bare skin against bare skin, his hands holding her. "It undoes at the front," she gasped.

She felt his smile against her neck, his warm breath as he continued to taste her. Unerringly, he found the clasp and released it. Her breasts bounced free, the nipples tightening in the cool air, straining forward for the touch of his fingers.

"Mmmm," she murmured as his hands closed around her once more. Slowly, gently, he massaged them, stroked and pulled at the nipples, before holding her breasts in his palms almost as though weighing them. Somewhere in the back of her brain it registered that nothing hurt, that she felt no pain, but she pushed the thought away, a thought from another time that didn't belong here. Not with Jack. Not with her.

One hand dropped to her waist, the fingers splayed wide, burning a path along her abdomen. Then Jack lowered his hand, resting it between her thighs, cupping the juncture between her legs, then stroking, long slow hard strokes, until everything inside her seemed to melt into steaming liquid.

Valerie shut her eyes and moved against his hand, her breath coming fast and ragged. She'd never felt so good, so safe, so relaxed yet full of tension and anticipation. Her knees weakened and delightful dizziness flooded through her.

"Jack," she murmured, undulating her behind against his belly, "Jack, honey, we need to lie down before I melt and slide to the floor."

Laughter, low and delighted, reverberated beside her ear. He nipped it, before turning her to face him. "I'd never let you fall," he said, his gaze hot and sultry. "Unless it was with me."

His hungry eyes devoured her, starting with her swollen lips, and falling to her breasts, bared and full below her T-shirt, then sliding and lingering on the jean-covered apex of her legs, before returning to her mouth.

Under his gaze Valerie felt wanton, and sultry, and wanted. Oh, so wanted. She lifted her face to his, slanting her lips over his, wanting to take as much as she wanted to give. He tasted so good and the texture of his mouth and lips on hers made her head swim. She raked her hands through his hair, pulling his head down to meet her, for once not afraid of what was to come.

She felt him lifting her, big hands cupping her bottom and bringing them together in the most intimate of embraces. Automatically, her legs clasped his waist. He started to walk, and she leaned back, her arms around his neck. "Where we going?"

"The living room." His eyes, simmering with promise, settled on her face. He flicked his tongue along his full lower lip. "I want to see you naked," he said, his husky voice vibrating with need. "In the firelight."

They stopped in front of the stone fireplace. Jack's mouth descended on hers once more, this time with an intensity that seared everything it touched, starting brush-fires that raced off in every direction. She kissed him back, with everything she had, and still, it didn't seem to be enough. They clung together, learning each plane, each valley and peak of their bodies, and rejoicing in them.

Jack withdrew his mouth and Valerie followed him, like a moth to a flame. Laughing, he reached for her T-shirt, tugged it up over her head, and tossed it aside. The bra followed. Then, his eyes locked with hers, he knelt before her. He undid the snap of her jeans, pulled down the zipper, and slowly tugged the jeans down over her hips, then to her knees. When they reached her ankles, she stepped out of them, and kicked them aside.

All that remained was her pale pink lace bikini underwear. Still kneeling, Jack grasped her hips in the gentlest of embraces. He lowered his head to her waist, his lips settling on the bare skin, making her gasp. He kissed his way to her navel, and then his tongue dipped inside, lightly flicking over her until his mouth moved lower still, his warm breath alternately tickling and burning her. He dragged his lips along the top edge of her panties, and Valerie thought she would die of wanting. Her hands had drifted to his hair, and she didn't realize she was gripping him fiercely.

Just when she thought she would collapse in a puddle on the floor, Jack dragged his mouth back to her waist. This time his hands settled on the elastic tops of the panties, and he slid them down over her hips and cheeks, along her legs to the floor. He followed their descent with his mouth, kissing his way along her inner thighs, behind her knees and her calves.

Then he stopped, picked up the panties, and tossed them over one shoulder. He raised his head, the firelight gleaming off the blond highlights in his hair, making him look for all the world like a god of the summer. He took his time, his gaze following the line of her ankle, along her knees and the smoothness of her eyes. He lingered at the shining chestnut curls at the center of her womanhood, then meandered upward still, detouring at her navel, then carrying on to settle on her full, rounded breasts, the nipples straining forward for his touch. His full, generous lips parted slightly; then his examination continued, burning its way across her throat, to her swollen, wanting lips, before coming to a full halt at her eyes.

For one brief second, Valerie faltered, seized by a lingering insecurity that Jack didn't like what he saw, just as Reed had never—

"God, you're beautiful. So, so beautiful."

The words, spoken in a voice husky with admiration, killed the fear before it had a chance to take hold. If Valerie had had any further doubts, she needed only to look in Jack's eyes. There, in the deep green pools, glittering now like cut emeralds, raged a feverish desire and hunger for her, a hunger she knew was reflected in her own eyes.

Her heart swelled, and she grew warmer still. For this alone, she would love Jack forever. And right now, with all her heart and soul.

She licked her dry lips. "I—I need to take off your clothes now too."

"You do, do you?" Jack grinned, the fires in his eyes growing brighter still. He ripped off his running shoes and socks, rose to his feet, and raised his arms to the side. "Well, here I am. Come and get me."

Valerie couldn't help grinning back. She tugged his plaid cotton shirt free of his jeans, then slipped her hands inside. His skin was heated, but smooth and muscular under her fingertips. She explored further, her hands crossing his chest. Her fingers touched his nipples, and then found the roughened skin of the scar on his chest.

"Hey! Slowpoke. Can't we hurry this along?"

Valerie bit her lip to keep from laughing. "Anxious, are we?" But she started unbuttoning his shirt. When the last was undone, she shoved the shirt back from his broad shoulders. She spread her hands across his chest and kissed her way down to his belly, where a pale arrow of hair disappeared beneath his waistband. Quickly, she slipped the belt open and unzipped his jeans. She slid one hand inside, over the smooth, hard length of his erection.

A murmur of pleasure escaped Jack and she repeated the motion, harder and faster, until he grasped her wrist once. "Enough," he growled, softening the command with a smile. "I thought you were taking my clothes off."

"I was. I am." She smiled sweetly. "I got distracted, is all." She raised her hands to Jack's chest once more, spreading her fingers and reveling in the feel and smell of him. "There's so much to be distracted by."

"You said it." Jack framed her face with his hands once more, then dipped his head toward her. His mouth slanted over hers, and he tasted and drank of her until her head swam with dizzy delight, obliterating everything but the taste and scent and feel of Jack's mouth on hers.

She didn't realize they were moving until the backs of her thighs hit the couch. Jack slowly lowered her onto the cushions, then stepped back. With a smooth economy of motion, he stripped off his jeans and jockey shorts. For a long moment he stood and regarded her, while the golden light from the fire licked his bronzed body, flickering over his biceps, the lean musculature of his chest, his trim hips and strong legs. Valerie's mouth grew dry with want. She held out her arms.

Jack lay beside her, pulling her into his arms. Her mouth joined with his, her breasts crushed against his firm chest, her abdomen pressed against his erection. They fit together perfectly, hard to soft, tough to sweet, floral to musk.

Valerie's conscious thoughts slowly receded as sensation after sensation swept over her. Greedily, her mouth and tongue danced with Jack's, stroking, sucking, nipping, tasting, her hands buried in his hair, pulling him closer still. He stroked her body, caressing and palming her breast, slipping his hand over her belly, through the dark curls to her slick inner folds. Slowly and repeatedly he stroked her, building the fireworks within her. She moved against him, trying simultaneously to escape and get closer, wanting more and less, wanting higher and lower at the same time, until finally, the ultimate explosion occurred, setting off lights behind her eyes, and shock waves through her chest and belly and everywhere else. Almost in tears, she clung to Jack, waiting to regain her equilibrium, to catch her breath, to slow her heartbeat.

Gradually the fires dimmed, her head cleared, and a

wonderful feeling of satisfaction settled over her. She nuzzled Jack's cheek and slipped her hand over his erection, still hard and throbbing. "Jack," she whispered, "what about you? Don't—"

He stilled her hand, swiftly rolled her under him, and gazed down at her. "It's all right. I haven't done this in a long time. I don't have any . . . protection."

"But I do." Valerie's heart swelled with Jack's generosity and his admission. Somehow she'd known he didn't make love lightly, and the knowledge filled her with gladness. She raised her head and shoulders, resting her weight on her forearms, then collapsed back onto the couch. "But I don't have the strength to go and get it."

She smiled sweetly. "I'm sure *you* do. There's a condom in the pocket of my jeans somewhere"—she tossed her head in the general direction of the kitchen—"over there."

Jack grinned down at her with mock accusation. "So why didn't you say so sooner?"

"I was busy," she responded primly. "Very busy."

He chuckled and eased himself away from her and the couch. Valerie shivered as the cool night air hit her heated body. A moment later she welcomed him back, her body reacting hungrily as his hard, warm length settled over her once more.

Jack nuzzled her nose; then his mouth claimed hers again, slowly and surely restoking the fires that had ebbed only moments before. Valerie wriggled beneath him, arching her back, wanting to get closer, to ease the emptiness that only he could fill.

Finally, he positioned himself over her, the planes of his face and his upper body sculpted in the firelight. He watched her face as he eased inside. His eyes burned and his lips glistened. But it was only when he was buried to the hilt within her that he smiled, ever so faintly, and began to move, slowly at first, and then more quickly, building the pace, the rhythm, steadily upping the ante in the fiery game of love.

Valerie's gasp was lost as his mouth covered hers for the last soaring rush. Her fingers dug into his firm buttocks and she met and rode each thrust. Her heart soared, her senses went crazy, and then exploded in wave after wave of torturously wonderful sensation.

When Jack's sated body settled over hers, his large hands clasping her wrists and his lips nuzzling her neck, Valerie sighed with satisfaction. She wriggled underneath him, savoring the feel of body against body. *Her* body against *his* body.

Could there ever be anything more wonderful?

Valerie stretched and wriggled under the warm, sweet-scented sheets and blanket. She'd never felt so good, in all the right places, filled with the languid contentment that came only from loving, and being loved. For the first time, ever, she wasn't worried about her performance in bed, wasn't tensed for the morning-after critique that was sure to come.

She wriggled farther under the sheets. Beside her, she could feel Jack's comforting heat; gradually, she became aware of the sound of his breathing, quiet and steady.

As she fully awoke, she opened her eyes and turned to him. In the morning light streaming through the window of her room, he lay on his side, facing her, his eyes shut. The sunshine created a halo around his blond hair, bathing his skin in a golden hue that made him appear heaven-sent.

A rush of tenderness followed that thought. Valerie smiled, her heart full of the gift Jack had given her, even if he didn't realize it. He had accepted her, loved her just the way she was, with all her imperfections. He'd made her feel special, wonderful, and silently bolstered her faith in herself to know a good man when she found him. Because this time she had.

Her gaze wandered to the stark bruise on Jack's forehead, partially hidden by the golden hair. It looked worse

159

Norah-Jean Perkin

than ever. Her inspection traveled lower, to the scar slashed across his left breast, and she wondered once more how it came to be there. It struck her suddenly as strange that a man so marked by violence could be so gentle, so tender, yet so confident in his lovemaking. While others, unmarred by knife or stone or bullet, could take delight in inflicting emotional and physical pain.

Tentatively, Valerie reached forward to trace the ugly slash, as if mere touch could somehow heal it. But before her fingers could reach their target, Jack's hand snapped to life and waylaid her.

"Oh!" Valerie squealed in surprise.

Jack regarded her through eyes narrowed against the sun. His broad lips turned upward in an engaging grin. "Good morning." He lifted her hand to his lips, his eyes sparkling with good nature.

"Good morning to you too. How's your head?"

"My head?" Jack raised one eyebrow. "Oh, that." He shrugged. His eyes gleamed suspiciously. "You haven't given me much time to think about it."

Valerie flushed at the reminder of last night. What had begun in the living room had continued until only a few dying embers remained in the fireplace. She remembered Jack carrying her upstairs, along with at least some of their clothing, and then falling into bed in a laughing heap. And then, *ohh!*—they had started all over again.

She breathed in deeply, raised her chin, and issued a challenge. "Is that complaining I hear?"

"Never." Jack shook his head and tenderly squeezed her hip.

Her heart swelled. Impulsively she bent forward and kissed him. She felt his immediate reaction, as well as her own, a thrumming that began deep inside and began to spread outward. Before she could do nothing but surrender to it, she withdrew. There was something she wanted to say.

For a moment she examined his sturdy face. The dark

160

brows, those incredible green eyes, the firm full lips, but most of all, the appreciation of her that seemed to radiate from all his features, infusing her with self-confidence and contentment.

"You're so different," she whispered.

"Different?" He stiffened in a manner she hadn't expected.

"Oh, not in a bad way," Valerie rushed on. "In a good way. You're in great physical shape. You're big enough and strong enough to do anything you want. But—"

"But what?" Jack frowned, a question in his eyes.

"You're—you're so gentle. You don't—push me. You're not critical of everything I do. You treat me as if . . . as if I'm a priceless treasure."

Jack exhaled slowly. He regarded her steadily. Finally he said, "You *are* a treasure. One I never expected to find, much less deserve."

His voice dropped so low, Valerie had to strain to hear. "When you find treasure, you take care of it. You love it."

Valerie's heart skipped a beat. She let his words settle deep inside her, trying them out for fit and color. He thought she was *treasure?*

Gladness swelled inside her, and she smiled with delight when Jack rolled over and trapped her between his arms. She felt his hardness against her belly, and as he dipped his head to capture her lips, she couldn't resist saying, "Keep this up, and I'll think I've died and gone to heaven."

Jack's head jerked up. "Don't say that!"

"What? What did I say?"

Jack sat up and looked down at her, his expression fierce. "Never be sorry you're here, now, alive and well. Never."

He turned away, grabbed his jeans from the end of the bed, and yanked them on. "I'm going downstairs to start the coffee and let Reddi out."

Then he was gone.

*   *   *

Stunned, Valerie stared at the door closing behind Jack. What had she done to make him leave abruptly?

Determined to find out, she scrambled into jeans and a sweatshirt, and quickly combed her hair. The cold floor chilled her bare feet, but she didn't take the time to don socks. She wanted to know what had changed Jack's mood from amorous to—to what? She wasn't sure.

She found him in the kitchen, filling the coffeemaker with water. "Reddi's outside," he said, without turning around.

"Thank you." Valerie stared uncertainly at his bare back. Despite his unyielding stance, she approached. She slipped her hands around his middle, then rested her head against his warm, muscled back, breathing deeply. He smelled good, of the warm bed they had shared for so many hours and the love they had made.

At her touch, he tensed. Valerie bit her lip. What was wrong? She swallowed, then forced out the words. "What's wrong? Did I say something? Do something?"

He didn't move. With her ear pressed against his back, she heard and felt him sigh. "No. You didn't do anything."

"Then what was it? We were about to make love—I thought—and then wham, you're gone."

"There's something I need to tell you."

A suspicion popped into Valerie's head. She dropped her arms and stepped away from Jack. "It's the lodge, isn't it? You don't want to sell it, and you don't want to tell me."

The muscles in Jack's back tightened visibly. He gripped the counter but did not turn around.

"Whatever you decide about the lodge, it doesn't matter," she blurted out. "It won't change anything between us. Not now. We can find some way to work it out."

Jack raised his head. Slowly he turned to face her, rearranging her arms around his waist, and placing his own around hers. The soberness of his expression shocked her. "That's very generous of you," he said quietly. "But it's not about the lodge."

162

"No?"

"No. It might explain why I'd prefer you not to sell it, but that's only a small part of what I need to tell you."

Trepidation gripped Valerie, like a hand clutching her stomach and squeezing hard. She stared at Jack, uneasy at the seriousness of his tone, a seriousness repeated in his stance and in his expression. She couldn't imagine what he might tell her that could provoke that level of tension, that level of somberness. She swallowed. "So tell me. I can be trusted."

Jack frowned. "It's not a matter of trust."

"What is it then?"

He paused. "It's more a matter of . . . of belief."

"Belief?" It was Valerie's turn to frown. She was getting more confused by the second.

Jack scowled. He raised his hands to his forehead and shoved the hair away from the ugly bruise, then raked his fingers through his hair. "I don't know how—"

"Jack." Valerie reached out and grasped his arm. "Jack, you can tell me anything. I know we—"

"Oh, isn't this cozy!"

The growled comment startled Valerie into dropping Jack's arm. She knew who it was. Her face flaming, she turned to greet Reed.

"You didn't tell me you had breakfast together," he said acidly before she could open her mouth. His scorching gaze raked over Valerie and then Jack, lingering on his bare chest, before returning to Valerie.

With an effort, Valerie shook off the unreasonable guilt Reed's comment inspired. She didn't have to worry about what Reed thought. Not anymore. She straightened and regarded him with as cool a look as she could manage. "Sometimes. When it's convenient."

Reed's upper lip curled. He glanced pointedly at the Rolex on his wrist. "A little late, isn't it? It's after ten-thirty. I told you I'd be by to take you into town."

Valerie shrugged, her guilt replaced by growing irritation. "No, you didn't. We agreed I'd come into town to meet you. Besides, I'm on holiday. I sleep in."

Reed glared at Jack, who now lounged against the counter, looking as comfortable as if he'd spent years in this kitchen. At Jack's nod of greeting, Reed's eyes narrowed. His expression clearly asked, "With him?"

Jack smiled at Reed. "How'd you like some breakfast?" He glanced at Valerie. "You've got eggs and bacon in the icebox, haven't you?"

At her nod, Jack continued. "I'm starved." With impeccable politeness, he directed his attention to Reed. "You're welcome to join us, of course." But underneath the polite words, the careful nonchalance, Valerie sensed the challenge, heard it ringing through the strained air.

"I've already eaten." Reed tapped his foot on the floor. "Besides, Valerie and I are having lunch in town."

"Coffee, then?" Jack turned back to the coffeemaker. He pressed the on button. "Be ready in three or four minutes."

"Good." Valerie looked from Jack to Reed. She wanted a shower, but was it safe to leave the two men alone together? The atmosphere was so fraught with tension, it wouldn't take much to set off a detonation. Damn Reed! Why did he have to show up now?

"I'm going upstairs to shower," she said finally. "I'll be down in about fifteen minutes. Jack, don't bother making breakfast for me."

Reed harrumphed, then yanked out a chair at the table and dropped into it. Jack crossed his arms and leaned back against the counter. "I was thinking," Jack drawled. "I've got some business in town." He glanced from Reed to Valerie. "How about you two giving me a lift?"

"Sorry," Reed snapped. "This is a private trip. Valerie and I have a lot of things to talk about."

"Reed!" Valerie remonstrated. "We're having lunch together. We've got lots of time to talk. And Jack doesn't have a car."

Reed glanced at Jack with a look of unbelievable scorn.

Grudgingly he gave in. "All right. But we're not taking the dog."

With exaggerated casualness, Jack set about making his breakfast under the silent observation of Reed. Despite the other man's silence, Jack could feel his antipathy, lacing the already tension-laden air with hostility.

Reed made no attempt at conversation, sitting like a frozen image of dark, picture-perfect, male good looks. Jack was glad. It was difficult enough to hide his agitation over Reed's intrusion, over his interruption of what was likely the most important conversation he would ever have with Valerie.

Jack broke two eggs into the frying pan and put bread in the toaster, then paused. He had been about to tell Valerie the truth, a truth that in all good conscience he should no longer avoid sharing with her, no matter what the consequences.

But Valerie's ex-fiancé had intervened. A wave of anger surged through Jack; he gripped the handle of the pan until his knuckles turned white. Reed, the man whom Jack would bet his life was responsible for that shadow on Valerie's throat. The man who likely had put the flicker of fear in Valerie's eyes, made her jump at every noise and unexpected motion.

Jack gritted his teeth. Control. He had to maintain control. Once before he had let emotion rule his actions. And that emotion had destroyed his life, along with the lives of other people. This time, he had to remember who he was, *what* he was. And the limited options open to such as him.

Slowly he expelled his breath. He flipped over the sizzling eggs, oblivious to their aroma as he tried to logically think his way through the current impasse. Could Reed's arrival this morning actually be for the best? Had the man saved him from telling Valerie something she would never have believed, something that would have ended, immediately and abruptly, the brief but wonderful love they had shared?

He eased the eggs onto a plate and retrieved the toast, which had popped up. Still standing, he balanced the plate in one hand and attacked the food with the fork in his other, though his hunger had long fled. As he chewed, he studied Reed, who continued to ignore him.

Despite the man's immobility, there were definite signs of tension. The muscle pulsing in his temple, the way he pressed his lips together, the hands locked together in his lap, all testified to a battle to maintain an outward picture of calm and to pretend the source of his irritation didn't exist.

And he did it amazingly well, conceded Jack. Reed acted as if Jack were as invisible as your stereotypical ghost.

The irony of that thought caused Jack to sputter, earning him a glare from Reed.

In that instant, in that poisonous glare, Jack saw the truth. He saw the reality of the rage simmering in Reed just below his polished surface. In a rage, Reed had tried to choke the life out of Valerie. In a rage, he had terrified her, leaving deep-seated internal scars long after the outward marks were gone.

Jack's stomach clenched. He clutched the forgotten fork so tightly it cut into his fingers. His vision blurred with renewed anger, the same anger convulsing his gut and racing through his veins like a heat-seeking missile in search of its target. Silently he dumped his half-eaten eggs and toast into the garbage, then dropped the plate and cutlery into the sink with a clatter.

He straightened, and regarded Reed through narrowed eyes, all pretense of friendliness gone. Jack's hands clenched and unclenched at his sides, itching with the desire to pick up this scum who had dared to hurt Valerie and bodily throw him out of the house.

Reed was clearly here to win Valerie back. Even if Jack hadn't cared deeply about Valerie—and he did, more than

166

he could ever tell her—he would have opposed Reed's campaign. Any man who'd hit a woman, much less try to crush the life out of her, didn't deserve that woman. Should be kept away from her by any means.

And I'll do it! But even as he thought the defiant words, Jack recognized the fatal flaw in his spontaneous impulse. He would protect Valerie, he would keep her out of harm's way, he would love and cherish her, as long as he was here. *But how long would that be?*

Bitter reality twisted Jack's insides. He turned away, grasping the counter for support. The truth—the unpalatable truth—was that he was close to powerless, as powerless as he'd been so many years before when he'd been unable to save the woman he loved.

Only now it was worse. Because then, at least, he'd had a life.

Chapter Fourteen

The blue of the sky, the fresh breeze off the lake, the straightness of the towering pines convinced Reed that everything would work out in his favor. As he walked in silence to the car with Valerie and Jack, his confidence reasserted itself. He was one of the beautiful people, living in a beautiful world where success was preordained. He was a *winner*, for God's sake! Not a loser like—he shot a sidelong glance at the man walking on the other side of Valerie—like Wilder.

Jack Wilder. Reed suppressed a snort of anger. It was clear to him that Valerie and Jack had just tumbled out of bed before he'd arrived. He didn't know why Valerie had been drawn to a man like Wilder—an inarticulate man who apparently had nothing to recommend him besides passable looks and a little knowledge of the outdoors—but it didn't really matter.

Because she *would* come back to him. One way or another, he would get her back. She would recognize his superiority; she would realize what she'd lost by running away; she would come crawling back. He had no doubt whatsoever.

And then . . . He smiled faintly, savoring his anger and the adrenaline it was releasing into his system. Once the little problem with his ex-wife's death was put to bed, then he'd make Valerie pay. After she had returned to Chicago, and after she was safely married to him. There would be nothing overt, of course. But numerous subtle ways existed to exert control, to show who was in charge, to brand her as his property and to ensure she never forgot it.

Or perhaps, he thought with a savagery that put new sparkle in his eyes and lightness in his step, perhaps he'd just dump her once and for all.

They reached the lot, and Reed, buoyed by the image of his success and Valerie's downfall, unlocked the black Jeep Cherokee he had rented in Toronto. He opened the passenger door for Valerie. With a silent glance at Jack, she climbed into the front. Jack got into the backseat.

The look rubbed Reed the wrong way. With a spray of gravel, the car shot out of the parking spot, turning sharply onto the dirt road around the lake. Within a minute they were traveling sixty miles an hour along the winding cottage road, the Jeep wildly taking the corners on two wheels.

Valerie grabbed the door handle. "Shouldn't you slow down?"

Reed glanced at her, satisfaction warming his smile. He liked seeing the shadow of uncertainty on Valerie's pretty face, and liked knowing that he had put it there. "Don't worry. I know what I'm doing."

Valerie bit her lip. In the rearview mirror, Reed saw Jack's frown. Even better.

Buoyed by a sense that all was right with the world, Reed started to talk. "I can hardly wait until you're back in Chicago, Valerie. I'm working on a new project in the downtown core—a combination retail, office, and residential complex. If we get through all the approvals, work should start this fall. Wait until you see the plans. The publicity

169

alone will be worth millions to Vogler, Earheart, and Jamieson.

"The site is right near the river at—"

The blare of the radio drowned out his comments.

"Oh, sorry." Valerie adjusted the volume downwards. "I haven't been watching TV or reading any newspapers. About the only way I get any news is when I'm in the car listening to the radio."

Before Reed could signal his annoyance, Valerie turned to the backseat and Jack. "Where do you want to be dropped off?"

"The mall is fine. I'm transferring my accounts from the Lindsay bank to another bank here."

"That shouldn't take long. Do you want us to pick you up afterwards?"

"Valerie!" Reed objected.

"What? Why shouldn't we pick Jack up? We have to go back to the lodge anyway."

Jack leaned forward between the two seats. "Why don't you wait for me at the bank? I'll only be a few minutes. Then I can join you for lunch."

It was all Reed could do to keep from snarling. Instead, he gritted his teeth and enunciated each word as if he were addressing an idiot. "Valerie and I have a lot to discuss. In private."

"Reed's right." At Valerie's unexpected agreement, Reed sneered at Jack. But the sneer died as he watched her gently place her hand on Jack's bare arm. "It's all right. I'll be fine. But we do have to talk. We can meet you later." She squeezed his hand.

Jack glanced at Reed, then back to Valerie. He didn't smile, but nodded solemnly. "If you say so. Where are you going for lunch?"

"Three Guys and a Stove. That place out on the highway."

"Good. I'll meet you there at one-thirty."

"I don't want to be rushed," said Reed. He was losing

the threads of control, and he didn't like it. "That's not much time."

"It's enough," said Valerie flatly. "I think we can discuss everything we need to in two hours."

Reed's hands tightened on the steering wheel. Inside he was fuming. "We have a lot to talk about. An awful lot." He paused, taking time to perfect an expression of patience. "But if that's all the time you can allot for something as important as our relationship, well, I guess I have to accept that."

Having shown he could be gracious in defeat, he cleared his throat and went on as if the discussion hadn't taken place. "As I was saying, Valerie, the firm has some exciting projects on the go. We're in demand now, for work but also on the social circuit. There are at least three black-tie events I want us to attend in September."

"Hmmm." Valerie didn't look at him or offer any sign of interest. A lock of hair had escaped from her ponytail, and lay across her rounded cheek.

The sight of it there, compounded by his defeat and her obvious disinterest, sent his blood pressure soaring. His foot pressed down on the gas pedal harder than ever and the car spurted ahead. Valerie should never wear her hair like that. She looked best with it either loose, or pulled into a smooth chignon—the way she used to wear it whenever they were together. And ignoring him. She'd never dared to ignore him or his wishes like this before. Never.

The loose strand of hair swinging across her face, Valerie leaned forward. The radio blared once more, a brash announcer's voice booming through the car. She glanced at Reed. "It's just for the news. I don't want to miss anything."

"The top story in today's news is the cross-Canada warrant issued for the arrest of Jack Vanderstone. Vanderstone, an unemployed carpenter, is wanted in connection with the murder last week of his wife and two young children.

"The OPP have found no trace of Vanderstone since the night of the murders. He is missing, as well as his car and hunting rifle.

Police believe he may be driving his dark green older-model Subaru to the Maritimes, where he is said to have friends and relations.

"His mother, Emily Vanderstone, disputes the police contention her son is on the run. She has publicly appealed for him to surrender to the police and face questioning. She fears her son may be dead, murdered by an intruder who killed his wife and children, and then transported her son's body in the family car and dumped it somewhere deep in the woods before fleeing. She does admit her son was troubled in the months preceding the murders."

Reed tried to wrest control of the situation once more. "All the more reason why you shouldn't be staying at that lodge. Who knows who's out there, waiting to pounce."

"I'm fine, Reed. Besides, Jack is staying only a few cabins away. Nothing can happen."

The chilling howl of a wolf burst from the radio and echoed through the car, followed by the jovial voice of the DJ. *"Well, I guess I've got your attention now. What better way to announce the wolf howl scheduled for tonight at ten o'clock at Algonquin Park, with a talk beforehand at nine o'clock. Actually, it's a double feature. At eight-thirty, a park ranger will give a talk on wolves. It's at the park's outdoor ampitheater. Afterwards, everyone can stay for the wolf howl. The wolves aren't guaranteed to howl, but given the record lately, the chances are pretty good."*

Valerie turned down the radio. "Oh, that sounds good." She twisted in her seat. "Want to go to that, Jack?"

"*I'd* love to go," Reed intervened sharply.

Valerie shot another one of those expressive glances at Jack, a glance that clearly excluded Reed. Reed gritted his teeth once more in an effort to hold back the venom threatening to drown him. You'll pay for this, he thought, his fingers digging into the steering wheel.

Reed took the road into Huntsville. "Where's the mall?" he ground out.

"Just up the street."

A moment later, Reed turned into the crowded parking lot. It looked as if everyone in cottage country was doing their shopping this morning. He pulled up in front of the main entrance.

"Thanks." Jack got out.

The door had barely shut when Reed sped off, wheels squealing.

The sharp crack of the putter as Reed slammed it down onto the counter of the mini-putt booth made Valerie wince. She glanced at him warily. It was unusual for Reed to make his irritation quite so obvious.

"So are you ready for lunch now?"

"Yes." Valerie nodded. They'd arrived at the restaurant a half hour before it opened. Playing mini-golf on the course behind it had been merely a delaying action, a way to put off and shorten the time available for this talk with Reed. Actually, she'd been surprised when he'd agreed. In the past, Reed had rarely agreed with anything she suggested.

Reed stood beside Valerie, inspiring an immediate, and uneasy, awareness of his closeness. Like it or not, she was still afraid of him. He was taller than Jack, by a good two inches, and all dark, sophisticated good looks beside Jack's less-polished roughness.

Reed's hand snaked to Valerie's lower back. A subtle pressure drew her closer. She flinched and stepped away.

Fist clenched, Reed dropped his hand to his side. "I wish you wouldn't do that," he ground out.

"Do what?"

"Jump every time I touch you. Act as if you're afraid of me. As if . . . as if I'm some kind of monster."

Valerie glanced at his face, then blinked. She couldn't believe it. Reed looked genuinely hurt. She opened her eyes wide and stared.

Surprise prompted her to apologize. She stopped just in time and reminded herself of what he'd done. What he was trying to convince her had never happened. Maybe the bruises were gone, but she hadn't forgotten. She wasn't about to play into his little game. Even if he hadn't hurt her, she'd had enough of his constant need to control, his desire to bend her to his will in every little thing.

And then there was Jack. Jack who was quickly pushing all thought of Reed out of her head. Even a confrontation with Reed couldn't prevent her from smiling at the thought of Jack.

She turned away and continued walking around the building to the front door. Reed followed, remaining silent as the maitre d' showed them to a table for two in a shaded part of the restaurant's patio, overlooking the mini-golf course and Fairy Lake.

They sat down. Valerie picked up her menu and opened it, but the words blurred before her eyes. She'd like to think that Reed wanted to apologize, to beg her forgiveness. But unless Reed had changed drastically, that was unlikely. She feared she was in for a repeat performance of the argument that had escalated into that terrifying moment of violence.

She swallowed and moved restlessly in her seat, trying to still her trembling. Despite her show of bravery, anxiety gnawed at her insides. It was easier to be strong, to confront Reed, when Jack was around.

But still, she had to be fair to Reed, to acknowledge the time they'd spent together. He'd come all this way. Maybe he really did want to do the right thing.

"I'll have two glasses of the California zinfandel."

The order jarred Valerie from her thoughts. She set down her menu and gathered her courage. She looked pointedly at Reed. "Are you planning to order my lunch too?"

Reed's dark brows came together over the top of his menu. He lowered it to the table, and then sighed. "Valerie, why are you so combative? You know you like zinfandel. You always have. Why bother with the unimportant details when someone else is willing to take care of it?"

He reached across the table and covered her hand with

his own. The touch she'd once thought so loving, repulsed her now, and she tried to pull away. But he moved more quickly, seizing her fingers with an iron grip.

Reluctant to cause a scene, she stilled. "You're hurting me."

"Oh, forgive me." He dropped her hand like a hotcake, then patted it before moving back. "Sweetheart, don't put up a fuss," he continued. "I'm only thinking of you. This way you—we—have more time to talk about the important stuff." His deep brown eyes connected with hers. His tone, his expression, his demeanor, all communicated his sincerity. "Important stuff. Like us."

Valerie held his gaze for a moment. Despite her resistance, it was impossible not to admire Reed's charm and the hypnotic quality of his sincerity, real or feigned. Only now she knew the truth.

She looked away.

Reed's voice rose. "Which is why I don't like this . . . this thing you've got going with Jack."

Valerie's gaze flashed back to Reed, searching for signs of that uncontrollable rage. She saw none, but it didn't matter; her imagination filled in the spaces. The hair on the back of her neck prickled, and she started to quiver again. She hated herself for her fear, and hated Reed for being able to provoke it.

With great effort, she managed to control her shaking. "I like Jack," she said. "He's my friend."

A slight flaring of nostrils was the only indication of any change in Reed's sincere, concerned expression.

"I noticed," he said simply. His eyes darkened with meaning. "I know why too."

"What do you mean? You know why? Why what?"

Reed shook his head. "It's obvious, isn't it?" Smugness tinged his voice. "You were distraught when you left Chicago. You were really upset with me. And now that I'm here, you're trying to hurt me. You're using Jack to get back at me, for what you mistakenly perceive as the wrong I've done you."

Before Valerie could correct him, he continued in the same patronizing tone. "But it's all right, Valerie. I understand. I forgive you."

"You forgive me?" Valerie repeated, her voice rising.

"Of course. Because I love you."

Valerie was so taken aback, she was speechless. How could he possibly have such a skewed view of reality? And worse, how could he sound so reasonable, so sincere?

"I don't want your forgiveness." She cleared her throat and straightened, forcing herself to meet his gaze. "What I want is for you to accept that our engagement is over."

Reed smiled faintly. "Of course it's not over. We spent two years of our lives together. Two years of good times, shared experiences. I'm perfect for you. You're perfect for me. Everyone says so."

Valerie blinked. In just a few short weeks, she'd forgotten Reed's tunnel vision, his ability to ignore everything else but what he wanted to see. His ability to paint a picture that bore no relationship to the truth, and yet everyone— even she—had believed it. His ability to convince her again and again that he was right, and she was wrong. That he knew best and she was . . . young and foolish. Or perhaps merely stupid.

But not this time. She closed her eyes in an attempt to gather her resolve. But all she saw was the rage burning in his eyes, the contorted mask that had replaced his face, the swirling room and blackness while she gasped and struggled for breath. Her eyes flashed open. Her heart banged against her ribs, and her throat felt thick and constricted. "Reed," she gasped, "no—"

"Your drinks, ma'am, sir."

Valerie's words sputtered to a halt as a woman set a glass of white wine before her, and one before Reed. She swallowed and glanced at the server. A rush of relief struck her. "Velma! What a pleasant surprise!"

"Oh, hi, Valerie. We're so busy in here today, I didn't even notice it was you." The older woman, in a crisp uniform of black pants and white shirt, glanced across the table. Her eyebrows rose appreciatively. "And your friend?"

Reed stood up. "Reed Vogler. I'm Valerie's fiancé."

Valerie bit back her irritated correction. Time enough for that later. Through gritted teeth, she said, "Reed's here from Chicago."

Velma gave Valerie an odd look. "Where's Jack?"

"He's in town. Had some banking to do."

"You didn't have a chance to ask him again about his namesake, did you? The other Jack Wilder?"

"Sorry. No, I didn't."

Velma's shrug set her ponytail swinging. "That's all right. I've got to run now. Just tell me, should I speak to you or Jack about the details of the rental?"

"Either of us is fine."

"Right. I'll be in touch. Your waiter will be by in a moment to take your order."

Uneasily Valerie watched Velma's disappearing back. What she wouldn't give to have the older woman join them for lunch. Because it was becoming increasingly clear that Reed didn't plan to apologize. He didn't want to talk about how he would change, what he was doing to control his temper. All he wanted was what he'd always wanted: to be right, to be on top, to be the one in control.

The waiter arrived to take their orders. Her appetite gone, Valerie asked for only a small salad and a roll.

"What was that woman talking about?" Reed nodded to the kitchen door. "Velma?"

"Oh, that. Velma used to work at Aurora Lodge. She's renting a cottage at the lodge for the month of August."

"You can't possibly stay until August."

"Why not? I'd planned to stay until school starts."

"I miss you, Valerie." The beseeching tone in Reed's voice shocked her. For a moment, she thought he looked almost desperate, but she dismissed the idea. Reed? Desperate?

Valerie toyed with her unused fork. "Actually," she said slowly, "I might be staying here longer than that."

"What? What are you talking about?"

"I told you Jack and I are co-inheritors of the lodge. I don't think Jack wants to sell it, and I can't afford to buy him out."

"That's ridiculous." Reed threw his napkin onto the table. "You're not going to let him dictate your actions, are you?"

No more than I'm going to let you. The thought surprised Valerie and gave her strength. "It's not just that. It was Uncle Arthur's wish to keep the lodge in the family. I'm the only family he has left. I'm not sure I want to go against his wishes."

Saying the words out loud made Valerie realize just how true they were. Something inside her didn't want to let this last little bit of family history escape into the hands of strangers. Memories of so much of her life, of her uncle and her mother, of . . . of Jack were tied up in Aurora Lodge.

"You're kidding, aren't you?" Reed stared at her as if she'd lost her mind. "Sure, it's lovely around here, for a summer home or a cottage. But it's not your home. You can't possibly be thinking of staying here."

"Well, I am." A surprising sense of satisfaction settled over Valerie as the words sank in. Did she really mean them? Or was it just the opportunity to thwart Reed? She hadn't realized until near the end how much she had let him dominate her life, control her actions. It had started innocently, with a simple desire to please him, to play to his desire for her. But by the time she'd realized she had to get out, it had degenerated into a real fear of offending him, of garnering his displeasure and resulting sulks.

An unexpected sound broke into her thoughts. Reed was

laughing. "Oh, Valerie. What makes you think you could ever run a lodge?"

"What?"

Reed fell back in his chair, shaking with mirth. "It's one thing to run a class of eight-year-olds. But running a business requires business sense, marketing, and money skills."

Valerie straightened, seeing no humor in his comments. "And I suppose you think I don't have any of those skills?"

Reed sputtered. When he finally managed to control himself, he leaned across the table, his blue eyes intense. "With the right help, I'm sure you could develop them. But you don't really want to do that, do you?" He strained closer. "Valerie, if it's money that's the problem, I can help. I can buy Jack out, and then we can put the place up for sale. If it's important for you to retain a stake in it, I'm sure we can arrange that too."

"That's very kind." Valerie took a deep breath before she plunged on. "But we aren't engaged anymore. We aren't getting married. And I don't think you'd make this offer to an ex-girlfriend."

"I'm only suggesting this because I love you. You're upset now, a little deluded. But believe me, I know what's best for you."

"I assume you knew what's best when you put your hands around my throat and—"

"Stop it." Reed's voice guillotined her comment before she could finish. Rage momentarily blazed in his eyes, only to be replaced with that patronizing look of ultimate reason she was coming to hate. "We both know you're blowing everything out of proportion. I would never hurt you. That was an . . . an aberration."

"An aberration? You call almost choking me to death an aberration?" Valerie was so livid she could barely talk.

"All right, all right." Reed held his hands up in supplication. "You're right. Of course, you're right. It was more than that. I . . . I lost it. I'm truly sorry. It will never happen again."

179

"You're right." Valerie's voice had dropped to a harsh whisper. "Because we're never going to be alone again, d'you understand? We're finished. Even if that hadn't happened, we'd still be finished."

She repeated the words she'd already said more than once, the words Reed refused to hear. That she didn't like the person she'd become around Reed. From an independent woman, she'd reverted to the girl of her childhood, terrified of her father's disapproval and loss of affection. Just like her mother, the woman that, no matter how much Valerie loved her, she'd always sworn she wouldn't be like.

Reed bowed his head, his shoulders slumped. Was he finally getting it?

Finally, he raised his head and leaned across the table once more, his expression more earnest than she'd ever seen it. "Valerie, please. All I'm saying now is give what we had a chance. Forget that incident. Spend some time with me alone. See how good it can be again. Even your dog likes me. Which is more than you can say for Jack. That alone should tell you something."

Valerie stared at him in dismay. She tried to see him as the rest of the world saw him. A handsome, smart, young businessman with the world by the tail. Oozing confidence, especially in himself and his own power. Dark and sexy.

But however hard she tried, all she could see were those hands coming at her, threatening her, the light growing dim, Reddi barking in the background.

She bit her lips and shook her head. "No, Reed. No."

After a silent car ride, Reed dropped Jack and Valerie back at the lodge. Valerie returned to the house to take Reddi out for a run. Though he knew she wanted to talk, Jack declined her invitation to accompany her, saying he wanted to work on one of the canoes. He needed time—time to figure out what he should tell her and how he could keep her safe.

An hour and a half later, Valerie found him kneeling in

the sun on the dock, sanding the gunnels of one of the lodge's oldest canoes.

"Needs new stain and varnish," he pointed out in answer to her question. "Besides, I like to keep busy."

Valerie nodded. While Reddi sniffed his way across the sandy beach, she settled herself on the sun-warmed dock, sitting cross-legged, a bare foot pressed against one thigh. The scratch of the sandpaper and the lap of the gentle waves against the shore were the only sounds in the late afternoon quiet.

Valerie watched in silence as Jack methodically sanded his way along one side of the canoe. Despite his concentration on his work, he was painfully aware of her presence only a foot or two away. Out of the corner of his eye he could see the breeze blowing strands of hair about her face. Her chest, firm and rounded under the bright pink T-shirt, gently rose and fell with each breath. Her long smooth legs, folded gracefully beneath her, gleamed with the first gold of a suntan, while her slim, delicate hands sat quietly in her lap.

He took a deep breath. It was now or never. He—

"Did you get your banking done?" she asked, preempting him.

"Yep." The flutter of her soft lips held his attention.

"Which bank?"

"What? Oh. Bank of Montreal." He watched as she wet her lips with her tongue, the motion setting off the first tremors of want within him. Damn, he didn't want to talk about banking. Fascinated, he continued to watch her soft, pliable mouth. He could think of a hundred things he'd rather be doing than discussing his finances.

Valerie shifted one leg out from under the other. "Reed offered to buy your share of the lodge."

"What?" He stared at her, his hot daydream exploded. "And?"

"I told him no." She took a deep breath. "I told him I hadn't decided myself about whether I wanted to sell the lodge. That I might like to stay here and run it."

Jack frowned and sat back on his haunches. "You told him that? Why?"

"Because it's true. I haven't made up my mind yet. I keep thinking about what Uncle Arthur wanted."

Jack tossed the sandpaper into the canoe, then fixed Valerie with a sober look. He paused. "Valerie, you're not letting what happened between us last night change what you want to do, are you?"

"I might be." Valerie's eyes narrowed. She stiffened. "There's nothing wrong with that."

Jack groaned, then immediately wished he hadn't. Valerie drew back, hurt and surprise written all over her face.

"That's not what I meant." Jack reached across and took her hand, unwilling to let her believe he didn't care, even for an instant. He clasped her less-than-willing hand in both of his own, then raised it to his lips and kissed the palm. He lowered her hand to his lap and regarded her. "Don't get me wrong. Last night was wonderful. It meant a lot to me, far more than I can tell you. But . . ."

He paused. He needed to tell her the truth. But before he did that, he needed to make sure she'd be okay.

"Reed," he said abruptly. "He's not coming back, is he?"

"What?" Valerie pulled back her hand. "No. At least—"

"I don't like him." The savagery of his words startled Jack.

Valerie bit her lip, but she couldn't keep back the smile trying to break through. "I wouldn't expect you would," she said softly. She tilted her head. "You and I made love last night, Jack. Then my ex-fiancé shows up."

Jack shook his head. "No, it's more than that." He stared hard at Valerie. "He's the one who put those marks on your neck, isn't he?" He continued relentlessly. "He's the reason you're so jumpy, so scared by every little thing."

A deep flush engulfed her face and neck. Her dark eyes glowed suspiciously; for a moment Jack thought she might burst into tears.

But she didn't. She lowered her head. "I . . . it's not something I want to talk about."

Jack frowned. Was she embarrassed? In the past, most people had looked the other way when it came to violence against women, treating it like a dirty, shameful secret. Even he'd been guilty of that attitude, at least until the end. But today? He'd thought the world had changed.

Whatever. Her embarrassment, her shame—if that's what it was—Reed would pay for those too. Jack clenched his fists, but all he said was, "Valerie, it's all right. You can tell me. You—"

"No!"

Jack paused. He didn't understand why she wouldn't admit what Reed had done, unless . . .

"You still love him, is that it?"

"No." She looked up, a lone tear running down her face. "No, I haven't loved him for a long time. Even before . . ." Her voice trailed off.

Relief zinged through Jack, but he continued. Too much was at stake, and there were too many variables, for him to let anything as important as Valerie's safety ride.

"Do you expect Reed back?" he asked again.

"No." She shook her head. "I told him not to come back. But . . ."

"But what?"

"I know Reed. He'll be back anyway."

"Why?"

"He doesn't take no for an answer. He—"

"I can make sure he won't come back," Jack said flatly. Adrenaline surged through him and he flexed his fingers.

But Valerie shook her head. "Thank you. But no. I've got to do it myself. I've got to get it into Reed's head once and for all that we're finished. That I don't want to see him anymore. It's no good if I don't do it myself."

"Why not?"

"It's just something I have to do. For me. Besides, until Reed really believes I don't want him anymore, nothing will

183

keep him away." One corner of Valerie's mouth turned up and she looked pointedly at the fists still clenched by Jack's sides. "Even your rather formidable form of persuasion."

Jack admired her strength, and he wanted to believe her, but he'd seen something similar once before, and the disastrous results. To make everything worse, now he didn't have the luxury of time, of waiting to see what happened. He grimaced, then slowly released his fingers. "All right," he conceded. His chin jerked up and his eyes narrowed. "But if he bothers you at all . . . if he so much as lays a finger on you, I'll make him sorry he ever left Chicago."

Tears shimmered like diamonds in Valerie's thick lashes, but her smile shone with gratitude and the light of the sun breaking through the clouds.

She reached out and grasped one of his hands, her gaze steady and warm. "Thank you. You don't know how much that means to me."

The sight that met Jack's eyes as he and Valerie walked to the lodge parking lot early that evening raised every hackle he possessed. He jerked to a halt. What was *he* doing here?

"Hi, Valerie. Hi, Jack." Reed leaned against his black Jeep, his arms crossed and one foot pressed back against a tire. "Thought you two would never get here."

Beside him, Jack felt Valerie hesitate. Then she moved forward, brushing his arm. "What are you doing here?"

"I told you I wanted to go to that wolf howl. You're going, aren't you?"

"Yes, we are."

"Well, I'm sure it's no problem if I tag along."

"Yes, it is." Jack loomed behind Valerie. "You're not coming."

Reed pushed away from the car and raised his hands to Valerie. "Come on, Valerie. I'm going home soon anyway. What's it to either of you if I go along to see the local sights?"

"Reed, I—"

He cut her off. "We spent two years together. Surely, it wouldn't kill you to spend another couple of hours with me before I leave? I think you owe me at least that."

"She doesn't owe you anything," Jack snarled, his fists clenched at his sides.

"Jack."

Jack felt Valerie's hand, cool and restraining, on his arm. He glanced at her. Why was she wavering? Did Reed have some kind of hold over her he didn't know about?

"Please." She turned to Reed. "All right. You can follow us in your car."

Jack reeled to face her. "Valerie, what are—"

A shake of her head and press of her lips silenced him. He didn't understand. He just hoped it didn't mean she still harbored feelings for Reed.

Reed smiled expansively. "Why don't we all take the Jeep? There's no point taking two cars."

Valerie shook her head and turned towards her small Escort. "I think—oh, no!"

Jack followed her stricken look. The rear passenger side tire sagged flat on its rim. He tamped down the suspicions that immediately arose. "D'you have a spare in the trunk?"

"Yes, but by the time we change it, we'll be too late for the wolf howl."

Jack shrugged. If that was the way—

"That's okay. I can take you."

Jack glared at Reed. Triumph glowed in his dark eyes, and a smile that bordered on a sneer creased his handsome face. But the expression he turned to Valerie was all gentle humility. "Come on, let's get going."

Valerie bit her lip. Finally, she looked at Jack, her eyes filled with a silent apology. "Come on, Jack. Let's go. It's better this way than not at all."

Jack narrowed his eyes. He couldn't believe Valerie was doing this. A sinking feeling seized his heart. Was history about to repeat itself?

* * *

185

"Reed, I think you'd better slow down." Valerie's voice rose and she gripped the Jeep's door handle.

In the rearview mirror, Jack saw Reed's dark eyes narrow obstinately. The Jeep surged forward faster than ever, flying on two wheels around a curve through towering walls of cut granite.

"Reed!" Valerie protested again.

"You worry too much," Reed said smoothly. He turned to Valerie and smiled with absolute confidence. "This is a four-wheel-drive, and the road surface is new."

"That's not the point," Jack said, glancing out the window. At twenty to nine, daylight held strong, but the sun was beginning to sink below the tree line in the west. "It's almost twilight and the moose start coming out to the road. If you come around a curve going a hundred kilometers, you'll never be able to avoid hitting one."

"Well, that'd be one dead moose," Reed quipped, not dropping his speed one iota.

"A moose is big," Jack continued. "A full-grown moose can weigh about thirteen hundred pounds. If you hit a moose, you'll likely kill him. But you'll also kill yourself, either on impact or when you spin off the road into one of these granite cuts."

"Reed, please slow down. We've got plenty of time to reach the outdoor theater before the wolf presentation starts." Valerie's voice sounded strained, and her expression was pleading as she glanced at Reed.

Jack saw the speedometer fall from one hundred to ninety to eighty to the seventy kilometers recommended through this part of the park. But Reed's compliance didn't reassure him. No matter what Valerie said, his gut told him Reed was dangerous, and that Valerie needed to stay as far away from him as possible. Any contact, no matter how minor, was playing with fire.

Jack glanced down at his balled fists. What he wanted to do was punch Reed out, then resume where he'd left off with Valerie. More importantly, he wanted to keep her safe.

Instead, he was sitting here in the backseat, alternating between frustration and anger, helplessness and fury, while the clock ticked away his precious time.

Because like it or not, Jack knew he would disappear again soon. The only question was when. At least no Northern Lights were predicted for this evening. He would be able to watch over Valerie one more night.

Traffic grew heavier, and Reed was forced to slow to a crawl as they turned onto the road to the park's outdoor theater. "How many people are coming to this thing, anyway?" he muttered.

Valerie consulted the flyer she'd picked up at the park gates. "It says there have been as many as three hundred and fifty cars at these wolf howls, and more than fifteen hundred people."

"Fifteen hundred! What in God's name for?"

"Most people have never heard a wolf howl, much less a chorus of wolf howls," said Jack. "It's an awesome sound. Primal. Romantic. And very wild. Reminds people that not that long ago this whole area was nothing but wilderness. Much of it still is."

From the parking lot, already two-thirds full, they proceeded on foot along a dirt path winding through groves of sugar maples, which gradually gave way to spruces, balsam firs, cedar, and hemlock. They reached a natural hollow near the eastern end of Lake of Two Rivers. Trees had been removed from its sloping edges and replaced by long wooden benches, rising on three sides of the ampitheater. At the bottom, on a cement dais, a projection screen faced the audience, which already numbered in the hundreds. Families, couples, gatherings of adults, and what looked like organized groups of children from nearby summer camps lined the seats.

On a bench about halfway up the hollow, they found seats, Valerie sitting between the two men. Jack scanned the cloudless sky, slowly darkening with the setting of the sun. Suddenly he had a bad feeling about tonight. Wolves wouldn't howl during a strong display of Northern Lights, and none was predicted, but still. The hairs on the back of his neck tingled with awareness and a faint nausea took hold.

For the first time in a long, long time, he prayed. Prayed that he would be given the time and the strength to assure Valerie's safety. Prayed that Reed would leave her alone, once and for all.

The benches were full and twilight had faded into almost complete darkness when a light flashed on stage. "Good evening, ladies and gentlemen."

The form of a young, bearded man, wearing the khaki uniform of the park staff, was illuminated. "Thank you all for coming. If we're lucky, tonight will be a night you'll never forget—a chance to hear and communicate with wolves, animals whose ancestors have roamed these forests and bogs for centuries. . . ."

What if I'm condemned to roam these forests and bogs for centuries too? The question that Jack had never been able to answer surfaced again, shutting his ears to the forest ranger's words. He couldn't prevent the shudder that shook him, the clenching of his fists, the sick feeling pooling in his stomach, as the full impact of his fate struck him anew. But why, *why?* he wondered, screwing shut his eyes against the question, growing angry that it remained unanswered.

"Hey, you're missing the slide show!"

Slowly Jack became aware of the pressure of Valerie's fingers on his forearm. He opened his eyes and tried to clear the fear and the angst from his mind. He turned to her, barely able to make out her features in the faint illumination from the projection screen far below.

The pressure of her fingers on his arm increased. "Are you okay?" she whispered. "You've been sitting there with your eyes shut for the last five minutes."

Jack blinked. Had it been that long? Was he losing his mind too, in addition to everything else he'd lost? "I guess

I didn't get enough sleep last night," he whispered back.

"I guess not." In the darkness, Jack could hear the smile in Valerie's voice. His hand covered hers and he took what comfort he could.

"Watch the slide show," she whispered. "It's interesting."

Jack forced himself to pay attention. The slides, narrated by park staff, didn't tell him anything he didn't already know about timber wolves—their mating and family habits, how they hunted, where they roamed—but the photography was stupendous, catching the beauty, the grace, the playfulness, and the ferocity of the timber wolf. In his day, Jack had killed more than one wolf, but he'd also had the good fortune to observe the wild creatures at play and at hunt. He had nothing but respect for the wolf.

Finally the slide show ended. The park ranger instructed the audience on the meeting place several kilometers away, and the need for silence once the cars were parked and everyone was standing and waiting. "Once we're all settled, I and another naturalist will howl to the wolves. Wolves responded to our howls last night in that spot, so we expect they will respond again tonight."

Then, without warning, the naturalist placed his hands around his mouth and emitted an amazingly accurate rendition of a wolf howl, chilling enough to make the hairs on the back of Jack's neck stand up.

From the other side of Valerie, Jack heard Reed snort. "Oh, wonderful. Not only do we need to listen to a pack of wild dogs yowling, we get to hear people too."

The park naturalist issued one last warning. "We believe we have an excellent chance of communicating with the pack of wolves. However, there is one factor over which we have no control. And that's the Northern Lights. If they start up, it's unlikely we will hear from the wolves."

His words sent more chills through Jack. *Not tonight. It couldn't be tonight.* He swallowed and stood up. How could he leave Valerie alone out here with Reed?

In the silence recommended by the nauralist, the audi-

ence began to file from the ampitheater to their cars. Once
they reached the parking lot, attendants with flashlights
directed them to follow a lead car. Tonight there were
about two hundred cars. Near the turnoff to the Spruce
Bog Boardwalk, they would be divided into two parking
groups, one for either side of Highway 60.

No one spoke as they waited in the Jeep to join the car-
avan to the wolf howl site. From the backseat, Jack scanned
the clear night sky, just now starting to dot with stars. So
far no hint of boreal light tinged the sky, no faint spotlights
danced anywhere. But despite what his eyes told him, his
stomach churned, his tension heightened by his fear for
Valerie. His mouth ran dry and a cold sweat broke out on
his forehead, where the ugly bruise that never went away
began to throb to the beat of his heart.

Reed followed the line of cars for several kilometers until
an attendant wielding a flashlight signaled them to park on
the right-hand side of the road, behind a line of cars
stretching off into the darkness and around a curve of
road. They remained in the car for five minutes, until the
traffic had stopped and all the engines had been shut off.
Quietly they exited the Jeep and stood beside it, facing the
dark, towering pines on the far side of the road. It was from
there, somewhere in the bug-ridden expanse of the dank
spruce bog, that the naturalist had said they could expect
to hear the return call of a pack of wolves.

Jack, his hands clenched at his sides, stood in silence
beside Valerie. He scanned the sky, unable to shake his
uneasiness despite no hint of shifting lights on the horizon.
The hair on the back of his neck tingled and he gritted his
teeth. *Not now!*

Finally, the first howls of the naturalists split the night
air, only to be quickly swallowed by the deep forest. For a
moment, silence reigned.

Suddenly, a tremendous clamor of wolf howls broke out,
so loud, so clear, they seemed breathtakingly close, perhaps
just behind the curtain of trees on the far side of the road.

Silence fell again, unbroken by the waiting humans, awe-stricken by a sound as wild and ancient as all time.

As he always had, Jack felt a kinship with that sound, a closeness that told him he was as much a part of this time and this land as the oldest denizen of the forest. But this time the kinship encompassed far more. This time, deep at its heart, it held the woman standing beside him, the woman he wanted to love and protect more than he'd ever wanted anything in his life.

Awed by the realization, he turned toward her, ready to take her into his arms.

Then he felt something else. A faint tingling in his hands, a turning in his stomach. He scanned the sky, watching for the telltale glimmer that could seal his fate.

Another chorus of howls broke out, splitting the sky and sending chills up and down his spine. At the same moment, he saw it. A spoke of light far off to the right, caught only by his peripheral vision, but there all the same. And as clear and full of meaning to him as the brightest beacon.

The symphony of wolf howls continued, voices together and separate creating a cacophony of music at its wildest and most primal. Jack glanced at Valerie in the faint light of the stars. She stood spellbound, her eyes wide and full of awe.

He raised his hand, then dropped it. He daren't touch her. Instead, he tried to freeze-frame that impression, that memory, to carry with him always.

Please let her forgive him for deserting her. He kicked himself for not trying to tell her the truth this afternoon. It was just another failure to add to his already long list of regrets.

He swallowed, clenched his fists, and slipped quietly around the edge of the Jeep and into the spruce forest. *God protect her!*

Chapter Fifteen

The black silhouette of the trees against the star-studded night sky held Valerie's attention as the last of the wolf howls faded and were swallowed into the depths of the spruce bog. As silence fell over the throng of campers and other people standing in tiny groups by their cars, Valerie exhaled long and low.

Something about those wolf howls—the loneliness, the raw power, the sheer primacy of the sound against the quiet night—had touched Valerie in a way that both startled her and filled her with wonder. It wasn't so much that she'd been afraid, though the first howl had sent terror coursing through her veins, but something deeper still. A wordless recognition, perhaps, of all the wolf and humans had once shared, long, long ago when the world was young, an ancient memory that truly could not be erased.

"That was incredible," she whispered. She turned to Jack, certain that he would understand what she was feeling. "Jack, don't you—"

"You're right, it's incredible." Reed gripped her arm.

"Come on, let's get in the Jeep. We can talk about it on the way back."

A car door slammed in the distance, and then lights flickered on, cutting through the darkness and breaking nature's spell. Valerie resisted Reed's tug, turning to Jack. "Jack, have you ever heard anything like that before?"

When he didn't answer, she narrowed her eyes and searched the darkness, now lit by numerous headlights and brake lights. "Jack? *Jack!*"

She pivoted back to Reed. "Where's Jack?"

"I don't know." Reed waved his hand to the pines on the other side of the ditch. "Probably he's just gone into the trees for a leak."

"Oh."

"Come on. Let's wait in the Jeep. The bugs are starting to get bad."

Valerie shook her head. "You get in. I'll be there in a minute."

"Suit yourself." Reed got in and slammed the door.

Valerie walked around the rear of the Jeep and studied the trees. She couldn't make out much besides the motley forms of spruce and twisted pines, thick stands of sugar maple, scrub, and grass, and a couple of huge boulders. She shivered. She doubted even the undeniable urge to relieve herself could entice her into the forest at this time of night. Especially after listening to those wolves.

She shivered again and hugged herself to keep warm. The night air had grown chill through the course of the presentation and wolf howl, but she hadn't noticed until now. The cool air, along with an errant mosquito, crawled under the edges of her sweatshirt.

Cars passed as campers began leaving to return to their sites. With each passing headlight, Valerie scanned the trees, looking for a sign of Jack in the shadows and open spaces.

Minute after minute ticked by, until almost all the parked cars were gone. Valerie had vaulted from panic to nonchalance, and then back to panic again. *Where is he?*

A car with the Ministry of Natural Resources logo on the side stopped beside their parked Jeep. Valerie recognized one of the naturalists when he rolled down the window and leaned out. "Is there a problem, ma'am?"

"No," Reed's voice issued from the Jeep.

"Yes!" Valerie said, contradicting him. Her words came out in a rush. "We had another man with us, a Mr. Jack Wilder. He was here just a few minutes ago, but now he's gone. I don't see him anywhere."

The naturalist frowned. "You don't think he might have gotten into another car, maybe met up with a friend, and decided to go back with him?"

"That's probably it," Reed responded smoothly. "Thank you for your inter—"

"I don't think so," Valerie answered. "I'm sure he wouldn't leave without telling me."

"Well, ma'am, you can wait a while. The park staff will be patrolling the area for the next half hour or so. If we see him, we'll pick him up and bring him to the office. What's he look like, anyway?"

"About six feet tall, blond hair, plaid shirt, a big bruise on his forehead," Valerie offered.

"He didn't have a medical condition, or any problems, something that would cause him to wander away?"

"No."

"His name again?"

"Jack Wilder."

"Wilder, huh? Okay, we'll keep an eye open for him." The naturalist rolled up his window and drove away. Her anxiety rising, Valerie watched the car disappear around a curve.

"Valerie, get in the Jeep. Standing out there isn't doing any good."

"I know. But I don't want to leave. What if something happened to him? What if—"

"Valerie, use your head. What could have happened to

him? He's an adult. You said yourself he knows this area, he's an expert outdoorsman. Be realistic."

"Okay." Valerie bit her lip and looked up at the clear sky. Now that the cars had all but disappeared, darkness had returned. Out of the corner of her eye, she caught a gleam of light. She turned to the east and saw it again, a greenish-yellow beam that stretched upwards like a spotlight before disappearing, only to reappear in a different place a few seconds later.

"Why, the Northern Lights. I guess we're getting them after all," she said, for no reason in particular.

"Yeah, I guess so. C'mon, Valerie. Get in the car. You can wait inside. It's getting chilly out."

The cold, and a fear that hadn't been there before, settled in Valerie's heart. This time she didn't resist; instead she scurried around the edge of the Jeep and climbed into the passenger side. "All right," she said as she settled into the seat. "But we need to wait. I'm sure he'll be back soon."

Reed turned the ignition key and the engine purred to life. He flicked on the lights, and they sat in uncomfortable silence as the minutes ticked by. Reed said nothing, but it wasn't long before he started drumming on the steering wheel. Finally Valerie opened the door.

"What are you doing?" Reed demanded.

"I'm going to look around some more. I'm going to call his name."

"What good will that do? Face it, Valerie, he's gone home with someone else."

Valerie shut the door without answering. She walked to the rear of the Jeep and peered into the bush. Unable to see anything, she cupped her hands to her mouth and called Jack's name, then waited. Her voice sounded puny and ineffectual in the dark maw surrounding her. She walked to the front of the Jeep and tried again. Still nothing.

Back and forth, back and forth. She kept it up for at least fifteen minutes before giving up. She felt sick inside, but she had to face facts. Jack wasn't coming.

She didn't look at Reed as she got back into the Jeep. "We may as well go. We can check at the gate on the way out."

Reed's smug look screamed, "I told you so!" He put the Jeep into drive and spurted away from the roadside, spraying gravel in every direction. As they drove along, Valerie scanned the roadside as Reed hummed a series of upbeat popular songs, one after another, until she wanted to scream.

Forty-five minutes later they reached Algonquin Park's western gate. Much to Valerie's surprise, lights still shone from the gatehouse. A white police cruiser, with the OPP logo on the door, was parked and running at each side of the road.

Reed stopped and rolled down his window. A man in police blue, a flashlight in his hand, approached the Jeep and bent over to peer into the open window. He flashed the light into the backseat.

"How are you this evening?"

"Fine. What's this all about, officer?" Reed asked.

"We're checking all the cars coming in and out of the park at the west and east gates," the officer said. His gaze focused on Reed, flicked to Valerie, and then back to Reed. "We had a reported sighting of Jack Vanderstone, the man wanted for the murder of his wife and two children near Huntsville. Have either of you seen him? He's blond-haired, about six feet tall, a hundred and eighty pounds, and likely driving a green 1994 Subaru."

Reed shook his head. "No," said Valerie. She scanned the area, then looked over at the officer. "Has anyone been waiting here for a ride while you've been here?"

"Nope. You expecting someone?"

Valerie frowned. "Hoping, more like." She didn't pursue it. It was clear Jack wasn't there.

The officer stepped back, and signaled to the gatehouse

staff to open the gate. He waved the Jeep on. "Have a good night."

It was after one A.M. when Reed finally drove into the parking lot at Aurora Lodge, empty save for Valerie's small car. With a jerk, he halted the Jeep beside the other vehicle, then snapped off the ignition.

"You don't have to see me to the house," Valerie said, her hand on the door handle. "I know the way."

"But I'm going to anyway." Reed flung off his seat belt, opened the door, and got out. Across the hood of the Jeep, he regarded Valerie. "I don't feel good about you being here alone."

"I'm not alone. Jack—"

"—isn't here," Reed snapped. "And even if he was, how reliable is he, Valerie? Look at what he's done tonight. Disappeared without any warning. How reliable is that? Besides, what exactly do you know about him?"

"I know—"

"—nothing!" Reed hit the car for emphasis. With satisfaction he noted the way Valerie bit her bottom lip, a definite sign of her uncertainty. Thanks to Jack, Reed's arguments were finally cracking her defenses, making her doubt her decisions: about him and about Jack. About everything she'd thought had or hadn't happened. If he hit all the right notes tonight, things couldn't help but work out in his favor.

Reed strode around the Jeep and took Valerie's arm. Buoyed by the turn of events, he nudged her toward the path. "C'mon. Let's go."

Reed's hand gripped Valerie's upper arm. Though she still said nothing, for the first time he didn't sense any resistance. *Good.* Perhaps she was finally starting to face reality, to realize what she'd almost thrown away.

No lights shone from the house or lodge building, but after a moment of adjustment to the darkness, they were able to pick their way along the path around the lodge to the back deck and the kitchen door.

Reddi could be heard barking on the other side of the door as Valerie pulled out her keys. Immediately Reed took them, unlocked and opened the door, and flicked on the kitchen light. Reddi leapt around their feet.

Valerie knelt down to her dog and hugged him. "Good boy, good boy." She stood up and held out her hand for the keys. "Thank you. Have a good trip back to Chicago tomorrow."

Reed suppressed a flash of irritation. When was she going to stop playing this stupid game? He shook his head. "Valerie, I'm not leaving."

"But I don't—"

"We both know you're upset tonight. Upset and confused. You need someone here. You need *me* here. You're just too stubborn to admit it."

"I—"

Reed took advantage of her floundering to advance and claim her. Unerringly his mouth captured hers, his tongue thrusting inside with the righteousness of an owner whose possession had just been restored. His arms closed around her, and he pressed her against him, his growing arousal hard against her groin, her soft breasts crushed against his chest.

She stiffened, jerking her face away from his and pushing against his chest. Surprised, he let her go.

She swallowed, her eyes big in her small face, her lips wet from his kiss. "I . . . I think you'd better go."

He closed his eyes briefly. He took a deep breath. It was important to remain in control, to refrain from doing anything that would frighten her off, especially when he'd come so close.

He opened his eyes and regarded her sadly. He reached out and touched her cheek with the tips of his fingers. "We're so good together, Valerie. I want to stay here tonight, with you. I could make it wonderful for you . . . for us."

He trailed one hand down the silky skin of her cheek, along her neck, suppressing his anger when she flinched. He gritted his teeth, then continued in a smooth, assured voice. "We could get up in the morning and drive to Toronto, then fly to Chicago. By tomorrow night we could be married. Then, if you'd like, we could come back here for our honeymoon. Whatever you want."

Valerie blinked. "Reed, how many times do I have to tell you? It's over. I'm not coming back to you."

Despite her refusal, the weakness of her voice encouraged him. He reached for her again.

She backed away, her eyes dilated.

Turned on by her fear, he raised his hand, then thought better of it and relented. As annoying as she could be, he couldn't lose control now. He needed her compliance now. Her willing submission now. Later, when they were married, it wouldn't matter. But for now he needed to woo her, on her terms.

He willed his arms to his sides, and stepped back. He swallowed and struggled to control his ragged breathing and runaway desires. "Forgive me, Valerie. I don't want to rush you into anything. But I want you so much. You know that. And I know that, deep inside, you want me too. You love me, as I love you.

"But I'm willing to wait. I know you're confused. I know you're upset about Jack. But it's okay. I'm here for you."

He took a deep breath and stared at her. She looked small, alone, and confused. It wouldn't be long now. It was clear she couldn't hold out much longer. If he pressed too hard now, he might lose everything.

And I never lose. A smart man knows when to retreat. And I'm a smart man.

"Good night, Valerie," he said softly. He didn't touch her, just stared hard at her lips and her throat until he saw her answering tremble.

He opened the door, nodded, and left. As he walked away, he started to whistle.

A moment later, Valerie opened the door and slipped out onto the deck, Reddi snuffling along beside her. She followed the wall of the house to the other side of the deck, and listened.

Finally she heard the sound she'd been waiting for: the roar of the Jeep's engine, and the crunch of gravel as it crossed the parking lot. She waited, hands at her sides, fingers dug into her palms, until she could no longer hear the sounds of the vehicle.

With a sharp expelling of breath, she leaned back into the house. He was gone. Thank God, Reed was gone.

For one awful moment she'd feared a replay of the violence that haunted her still, the violence that she couldn't shake, no matter how often she told herself it had been a momentary insanity, one Reed would never dare repeat.

Since his unexpected arrival at the lodge, she'd tried so hard to be fair, to give him the benefit of the doubt, even if she didn't want him back, ever. She'd done it for herself, to prove that she could face her fears, but she'd also done it for him. Despite that terrible night that ended it all, they'd spent two years together, not all of it bad. The least she could do was hear him out.

But she was wrong. If she hadn't realized it before, she knew it now. Perhaps she should have let Jack "convince" Reed to go away once and for all.

The thought of Jack brought a new pang all its own. She looked up at the dark sky, still clear and studded with stars. Not a trace of the Northern Lights remained. Was she wrong about Jack too? Had she foolishly and blindly misjudged Jack, seeing a kind, decent, and reliable man where nothing of the kind existed?

"No!" The cry ripped from her of its own accord. She couldn't believe it. She wouldn't believe it.

She staggered away from the wall, then gained her equilibrium. She returned to the kitchen, grabbed a flashlight, and gestured to Reddi. "C'mon, boy. Let's go. Let's go see for ourselves exactly what kind of man Jack is."

She ran down the steps of the deck to the path, Reddi dancing around her. She strode toward Jack's cabin, aiming the flashlight at the ground. Whatever she found, doing something about it—herself—definitely made her feel better.

They arrived at Arrowhead, only to find it dark and silent. If Jack had returned, he'd already gone to bed.

Not to be deterred, Valerie marched up the steps and onto the screened-in porch. She tried the door; it wasn't locked. Cautiously, she turned the knob, then pushed hard at the door that still had a tendency to stick.

"Jack?" she called as she stuck her head through the doorway. A quick circuit of the room with her flashlight revealed it to be empty, the bed still made, clean dishes stacked on the drainer by the sink. Valerie felt the wall for the switch; she'd had the power to this cabin turned on after Jack's arrival.

Her spirits plummeted as two lamps came on and Reddi exploded past her into the deserted living space. Wherever he'd gone, Jack certainly hadn't returned to his cabin.

Dejectedly Valerie scanned the room. If only he were here. If only she could talk to him.

She sank down onto Jack's single bed. She touched the worn plaid bedspread, soft and comforting from untold numbers of washings and dryings out in the fresh air and warm sunshine. It reminded her of Jack—straightforward yet intriguing, strong yet gentle, confident and capable yet not pushy or controlling, without an ounce of cynicism or a jaundiced eye.

She gripped the spread in both hands. But what if she were wrong? Wrong about Reed, wrong about Jack? What if she'd misjudged Jack completely? Reed didn't like him, but that was to be expected. But Reddi didn't like Jack either, even after all this time.

Whether she wanted to admit it or not, she knew things about Jack that should make her suspicious. Things like his strange, and still really unexplained, appearance on the beach, naked and sand-covered. His refusal to go to the hospital. His numerous wounds and that bruise that never seemed to get any better. Even his life as a drifter and his relationship to Uncle Arthur were difficult to understand.

If that wasn't enough, what about the coincidence of his name being the same as that guide who drowned with those two other people so many years ago? And stranger still, the same name as that other Jack Wilder, the one who apparently had been the spitting image of Jack, Velma's teenage crush almost thirty years ago? What about Jack's vehement refusal to sell the lodge?

Still, despite all these oddities and unanswered questions niggling away in the back of her mind, she believed Jack was a good man. No, it was stronger than that. On an instinctual level, a gut level, she *knew* he was an honest, decent man, in much the same way that she *knew* the fingers gripping the bedspread were her own. She'd never felt as close to anyone, as connected to anyone, as she had to Jack during the wolf howl.

But then she'd turned to him, and he was gone.

With a groan she fell back onto the bed and shut her eyes. She pulled the soft folds of the blanket into her arms. She didn't want to believe she was a fool, any more than she wanted to believe Jack was a no-good drifter with felony on his mind.

But why had Jack disappeared? Where was he when she needed him so badly?

Valerie rolled over, stiff and cold.

She blinked, absorbing just enough of her surroundings to shock her into complete awareness. She jerked upright and looked around. She was in Jack's cabin, on his bed, and the sun was streaming through the windows.

But still no Jack.

She rubbed her eyes and shivered in the morning coolness. Reddi, seeing her awake, padded over to the bed and snuffled at her jean-clad knees. She caught his collar and scratched behind his ears. "Oh, Reddi," she said, eyeing him with reproach, "why didn't you wake me up? I can't believe I fell asleep."

She looked around the large room once more, willing Jack to appear. But it was not to be. Grimacing, she swung her feet to the floor. Despite the brightness of the day, and the fact that she'd actually slept, she felt depressed and out of sorts.

Jack wasn't here.

She dragged herself to the sink, poured a glass of water, and rinsed her mouth. As she looked around the room, her mood began to change, anger seeping in, slowly at first, then more quickly, until the growing weight of it shoved aside the depression and reenergized her. Anger at Jack. Anger at his disappearance. At his unreliability. Anger for all the things he hadn't told her about himself. Anger that he'd said he loved her, but obviously didn't mean it. *If he did, he'd be here now, wouldn't he?*

She banged the glass down on the counter. Well, if he wouldn't tell her anything, she'd find out for herself. He wasn't here. What was to stop her from doing a little snooping? It would serve him right if she found out all about him on her own.

As she opened a drawer under the counter, she suppressed a spark of guilt. Why should she feel guilty? The drawer revealed only the usual cottage cutlery.

Slamming it shut, she surveyed the room. Nothing jumped out at her as being unusual, or remotely personal, only the furnishings and odds and ends similar to those in every other cottage on the lodge grounds. She walked over to the shelf holding the propane lamp and several ancient-looking, cloth-covered books. Standing on tiptoe, she dragged her hand along the shelf, only to unearth a cloud of dust and wooden box of matches. She examined the

203

matches. The box looked as old as the cottage itself, and the label read "E. B. Eddy."

Next, she explored the small dresser beside the bed. It was painted the shade of dried mud, and its three drawers contained only two T-shirts, a sweater, a couple of pairs of boxers, some jeans, a pair of socks, and a bathing suit. Not a letter, or a bill, or a form, or photo, or anything personal of any kind was hidden away there.

Miffed, she headed for the narrow closet. Two plaid shirts, both of which she recognized, hung inside. A pair of work boots, as ancient-looking as the matches, sat on the floor. The chewed backpack Jack had carried the day she'd asked him to leave hung on a hook just inside the door, but it too was empty.

She frowned. There had to be something, somewhere, that said, "I am Jack Wilder and this is what I'm all about." Certainly, anyone searching her uncle's house would find items not only revealing his personality and interests, but hers. The clothes she'd brought, the makeup, the books and CDs. Even the food in the fridge and the cleaning products left in the bathroom said something about the present and former occupants.

Her interest spiked when she opened the tiny drawer under the old-fashioned wood table. Jack's bankbook. Finally. She hesitated only a moment before picking it up, self-righteously telling herself he'd forfeited any right to privacy by his behavior.

Valerie flipped to the first page. Her eyes widened when she saw the amount: one hundred and twelve thousand dollars and twenty-three cents. Whatever Jack might be, he certainly wasn't standing on poverty's doorstep.

Only the one entry showed on the page, from the other day when Jack said he'd transferred his account in Lindsay to a bank in Huntsville. This must be the new account, which explained the fact there was only one entry.

Replacing the book in the drawer, Valerie pondered. With this much money, why hadn't Jack invested it? Everyone knew savings accounts were the worst place to keep money. Unless, of course, he was planning to do something with his money now. Like make a start on buying her portion of the lodge?

She frowned. But why hadn't he told her?

Still frowning, she surveyed the walls. For the first time she noticed the hunting rifle hanging on the wall over the mantel. Why hadn't she seen that before? Was it new? She approached the fireplace from the side, staring at the rifle. She was only a foot away when a board wobbled under her foot, sending her pitching forward. Waving her arms frantically in the air to try to catch her balance, she just managed to prevent herself from crashing headfirst into the stone mantel.

Annoyed, she examined the offending floor. One painted board, marginally shorter than the rest, sat incongruously between its longer brothers, sagging at one end. The supports beneath it must have rotted away.

Valerie knelt and slipped her fingers into the narrow space where the board ended. She tried to pry it loose. To her surprise, it came up easily. She set it aside and peered into the dark hole she'd uncovered. The end of a plastic bag showed, and she wondered if several had been stuffed inside as a temporary fix. Despite her reluctance to stick her hand under the floor, she reached inside to pull out what she thought might be several bags. She felt something hard inside the plastic, maybe a brick or a box.

There was only one bag in the hole, and she yanked it out and dumped it onto the floor. Instead of a brick, an old tin cigar box fell out.

"Go away, boy." Valerie pushed away the inquisitive Reddi, his wet, black nose already sniffing the unexpected find. She shook the box. There was definitely something inside.

Rising, she carried the rusted tin over to the table. She stared at it for a moment, debating whether to open it or not. Oh, why not?

Despite the rust, the lid opened easily and Valeried eased it back onto the table. Inside were what appeared to be a number of personal papers and cards. On the top sat a white and red Canadian Social Insurance Card, with the name Jack Simon Wilder written in black letters across the bottom and a small Canadian flag in the upper left-hand corner. It was the equivalent of an American social security card.

"Well, now we're getting somewhere!" Valerie reached for the pile of cards and papers. She placed the social insurance card on the table—remembering with a grin that Canadians called them SIN cards.

The next two were Ontario Health Cards, the identification necessary for Canadians living in Ontario to gain access to their much-vaunted free health care. One of them appeared much older than the other, and carried two numbers. The other was green and white, with large and small photos of a white and gold trillium, as well as a hologram—probably, Valerie supposed, to prevent fraud. She wondered why Jack hadn't destroyed the first card when he'd obtained the second.

Shrugging, she set those two beside the SIN card. Next in the stack was an Ontario driver's license, showing a sober-eyed Jack staring straight ahead. Why wasn't he carrying his driver's license? Or his health card, for that matter? Valerie wondered. She noted the birth date, then started to set it aside.

Suddenly she pulled it back. The birth date of 1965 would make him thirty-five years old, not thirty-two, wouldn't it? Quickly she repeated the math in her head. Yes. She frowned. But why would he have told her the wrong age? He had definitely told her thirty-two.

Puzzled, she moved on to the next card. It was another driver's license, with what looked like exactly the same photo of Jack. She picked up the first card again, examining it more closely. It *was* the same picture. But why? Surely the government here took new pictures each time they re-issued a license?

Valerie looked at the second card again. The number was the same, the address the same. Her gaze raked over the birth date, then returned. Her eyes widened. This one showed a birth date of 1974, which would make Jack only twenty-six.

Her heart started to hammer in her chest. Slowly, she turned the card over. Then she swallowed, stunned, unable to believe what her eyes read.

On the back, the card showed that it had been issued in the year 2006—six years from now—and would expire in the year 2010.

The license fell from Valerie's numb fingers. It was a fake, an obvious fake.

But why? And why so far in the future?

Chapter Sixteen

Shock turned to dismay as Valerie regarded the fraudulent pieces of identification spread on the table before her. Who was Jack Wilder? What was he doing here? Was Reed right? *Oh, Lord, don't let Reed be right!*

With shaking fingers she picked up the last driver's license, the one issued in the year 2006. Could it mean anything but deceit, anything but that Jack was an imposter of some sort, an imposter who had not only taken her in but Uncle Arthur as well?

She shut her eyes. God, she didn't want it to mean that. But what else could it be?

As the implications of the fake I.D. assembled one by one before her, a sliver of fear pierced her heart. If Jack was an imposter, what would he do if he found her here, rifling through evidence of his guilt?

The sliver split and grew until it formed a gaping chasm; her stomach started to churn. She had to get out of here, fast.

With shaking, uncooperative fingers, she scooped the

pieces of I.D. together and threw them back into the box. It took several attempts to close the lid. She dumped the tin back into the bag, ran over to the hiding space, dropped the package in with a clatter, then shoved the floorboard back in place. She had to get out of here before Jack returned and found her snooping, before . . .

The bang echoing through the cabin sent her jumping a foot in the air. Clammy and cold, she turned to the door—and saw that Reddi had knocked over an unoccupied plant stand.

"Oh, Reddi." The words came out a sigh of relief rather than a reproach. With one hand she straightened the stand. With the other she grabbed Reddi's collar. "Come on, boy. We're leaving."

She pulled the pup through the doorway and shut the door behind them. So far so good. She released Reddi's collar and headed for the screen door. Just one more minute, she prayed. *That's all I need to get away.*

She opened the screen door and let Reddi and herself out, then turned back to shut it properly. When she faced outward again, she raised her eyes—and froze.

There, on the path less than thirty feet away, stood Jack.

The terror disappeared in an instant, buried under one of Valerie's controlled smiles.

But not before Jack saw it. He would have had to be blind to miss the flash of fear that had contorted her features the second her gaze fell on him.

His gut constricted and he had to fight to prevent himself from grabbing her and demanding to know what she'd found—what she'd found out about him—that had frightened her so.

His fists clenched, his expression under tight rein, Jack approached Valerie. As usual, Reddi growled and his ears flattened against the back of his head. For the first time, the dog's behavior irritated him; it reflected Valerie's expression too clearly.

Jack stopped about three feet away from Valerie. "Good morning. Were you looking for me?" He noticed that Valerie's ponytail was untidier than ever, and her clothes crumpled, as if she'd slept in them.

"No . . . yes." Valerie's smile was strained and didn't reach her eyes. She straightened and studiously avoided meeting his gaze. "I was just wondering if you'd come back yet."

"Well, here I am."

She nodded, then moved to one side and started past him on the path. He reached out to stop her. As his fingers closed around her arm, she started; alarm raced across her face. Reddi barked frantically at her side.

Appalled by the response his touch had provoked, he loosened his grip but didn't let go. He was afraid she'd run the moment he dropped his hand. He searched her face, only inches from his. "Aren't you going to ask where I was?"

She tossed her head and laughed nervously. Briefly, her eyes connected with his; then she looked away. "Okay. Where were you?"

"It's a long story. It has to do with what I started to tell you the other morning, when Reed interrupted."

"Oh, you mean about the lodge? Your decision?" Valerie voiced the question with a brightness that was as chirpy as it was false.

Jack grimaced. "That's part of it. But only a small part."

He watched as Valerie's dark velvet gaze darted nervously across his face. She bit her lip. "So tell me."

"It's a long, difficult story. How about if I make us some coffee?" He was delaying the inevitable, but he still didn't know how he was going to tell her.

"All right."

He released her arm. "Come in."

"No!" Valerie must have regretted her yelp the moment it came out. She gave him another strained smile. "I mean, I'd rather stay outside."

Jack studied her. What had she found that had made her

so afraid? A half-dozen possibilities came to mind, each more incriminating than the next.

He shook his head, trying to shake off the deep hurt welling inside. It was clear that her fragile trust in him had crumbled, and her initial fear and suspicion had returned, stronger than ever. And he could blame no one but himself. He should never have made love to her. He should have stayed with her last night, no matter what he feared. He should have told her the truth from the start.

He swallowed. "All right. You wait here. We can take the coffee down to the beach, and sit in the sun and talk."

"Okay."

Jack regarded her assessingly. "You're not going to take off as soon as I go in the door?"

She shook her head. For a second their gazes connected. He saw how troubled, how frightened she was, and his heart ached. "Is that a promise?" he asked.

"Yes." She looked away.

As she waited outside on the doorstep, Valerie wondered why she hadn't made a dash for her car and driven into town to the police station the moment Jack had gone inside. Why was she sitting here on the doorstep, waiting for a man who obviously had lied to her before and was likely to tell her even more lies now?

Because, she thought as she dropped her head into her hands. Because she still couldn't believe that she could be so wrong. Something inside her wanted to believe that Jack was exactly what he seemed—kind, honest, strong, true. She wanted to believe that he meant everything he'd said, that she was special to him.

Besides, she remembered, she wouldn't have gotten very far. Her car had a flat tire. She winced.

"I'm coming out, Valerie."

Despite the shiver of fear that ran down her spine at Jack's voice, Valerie got up to let him out the door. He handed her a mug of coffee. "Come on."

They walked down to the lake. In the silence between them, everything seemed louder, brighter, clearer. A twitter of birdsong from over here, a chirp from over there filled Valerie's ears. The sky glowed blue and clear, the water sparkled like diamonds, and the smell of cedar and birch rose sweet and pungent on the breeze. Reddi trotted along beside them, taking off for brief forays into the bushes and open areas.

Down by the water, they settled cross-legged onto the warm beach, already heated by the morning sun. Valerie anchored her coffee into the soft ground and removed her shoes. Burrowing her feet into the warm, gritty sand felt good, somehow making her feel safer.

Jack removed his shoes too and tossed them to one side. He stretched his long legs out before him and took a swig of coffee. He didn't look at her, but instead gazed out at the calm morning waters.

"I stayed in the park all night."

Valerie frowned. She didn't know what she'd expected him to say, but that wasn't it. "Why would you do that?"

"Because . . . I was worried about what would happen."

"Worried?" Valerie turned and watched Jack's strong profile. She loved his straight nose, the full lips and firm chin. The glaring bruise shocked her once more with its vividness, reminding her of all she didn't know about him. "Why would you be worried?" she asked slowly.

He shook his head.

An odd thought struck her then. Jack had no evident bug bites. "I guess you stayed in a cabin there, or maybe a tent?"

"No. Outside. I made a shelter from tree branches."

"Then why aren't you badly bitten? No one can stay outside this time of year without getting chewed up by bugs."

He turned and looked her full in the face. "Bugs don't like me, Valerie. Just like Reddi. They don't like me because I'm not normal."

Valerie's brow furrowed. She tensed. "What do you mean, not normal?"

Jack shook his head again. The green of his eyes deepened. "I've been trying to figure out how to tell you this ever since I met you. I can't think of any good way to do it. So I'm asking you to promise to listen to me, right to the end, no matter how crazy it sounds."

Valerie gulped. Was he going to tell her he was a werewolf, or something equally creepy? She remembered the fake I.D. cards. No, more likely he was going to tell her he was a criminal. Or even worse, he was going to try to convince her he wasn't a criminal—when she knew he had to be.

She teetered on the edge of fleeing. She could still make a run for it. Still get away and report him to the police.

She looked up and met his gaze once more. The pain she saw there, and something else she didn't understand, made her hesitate. Even after all Reed had done, she'd given him a chance to explain. Surely she could do at least as much for Jack. She took a deep breath. "All right. I'll listen."

"Good." He held her gaze for a long moment, then looked out at the lake. "Do you remember the story you read in Art's scrapbook? The one about my namesake, Jack Wilder? The guy who drowned with two other people in 1927, only they never found his body?"

He turned and looked at her again. In the black of his pupils, she saw herself reflected. She nodded.

"And you remember the Jack Wilder that Velma said worked here the summer she was eighteen?"

Valerie nodded again.

He looked at her, his eyes harsh, as if he were challenging her to dispute him. He took a deep breath. "Well, those Jack Wilders—both of them—are me."

Valerie stared at him blankly, not understanding at all.

"I'm the Jack Wilder who drowned in 1927. I'm the Jack

Wilder Velma had a crush on so many years ago. And I'm the Jack Wilder your uncle knew."

Valerie frowned. "What . . . what are you talking about?"

"Don't you see, Valerie? Don't you get it?" Jack's voice rose, more ragged and hoarse than she'd ever heard it.

"I'm a ghost. I'm a ghost who was born in 1895."

Chapter Seventeen

Valerie stared, unable to grasp his words, and what seemed to be their creepy meaning. She felt stiff and floundering, as if she were floating in a sea of batter. She'd expected Jack to tell her something unsavory. That he was an imposter. That he was a thief. That he was a con man.

But a ghost?

The word skimmed through her head, over her thoughts, unable to make any sense or any connection with anything real.

Until it collided with the memory of where she'd found Jack. Here, on the beach, unconscious and covered by sand. Until she remembered his strange disappearances. Remembered the odd way his name came up again and again. Remembered Reddi's dislike.

With the speed and power of a gunshot, panic seized her. She leapt up, knocked over her coffee, and ran.

Only to sprawl face-first in the sand when a hand snapped shut around one ankle.

"Valerie! Don't run. I—"

As quickly as Jack had grabbed her ankle, he released it. From her spot in the sand, Valerie heard Reddi's growl, more menacing than ever. She raised herself up on her hands and knees and looked back.

Jack rolled in the sand, his arms raised to protect his face. Reddi's teeth were sunk into his right wrist, and he wasn't letting go, despite Jack's writhing.

Valerie wavered. Should she run and leave Jack at Reddi's mercy? And what about Reddi? He was still a pup and Jack was a large, strong, grown man. It would likely be only a moment or two before he succeeded in freeing himself from the pup and knocking him away. And then what?

She knelt up. "Stop, Reddi," she yelled. "Stop."

The pup ignored her; if anything, he seemed to bite down harder on Jack's wrist. Jack grabbed the pup by the ruff of the neck and started pulling.

Gritting her teeth, Valerie lunged forward and yanked Reddi's collar. "Reddi, let go. Let *GO!*"

To her relief, the dog released Jack and she managed to pull Reddi away. It took all her strength to keep him from attacking Jack again.

"Thank you." Jack sat up and rubbed his wrist. Blood flowed from a jagged tear in the skin. Even from several feet away, Valerie could see the teeth marks.

"You're bleeding," she said, struck by the incongruity. "If you're a ghost, why are you bleeding?"

"I don't know." Jack pressed down on the wound to stanch the blood. "All I know is I was born in 1895. My name is Jack Wilder, and I'm not dead and I'm not alive. That's what your uncle was trying to tell you."

The raw despair in his voice, combined with the invocation of Uncle Arthur's memory, made her pause. She looked at him hard.

Whatever Jack was or said he was, did she really believe he was a threat to her? That this man whom her uncle had liked and respected might hurt her? That this man who had offered to protect her from Reed, that this man who had made love to her, with consummate gentleness and care, would harm her?

No matter what, she wanted to be fair. She'd allowed Reed, who *had* hurt her, the chance to explain, to make his case. Could she do less for Jack, who meant so much more to her? She took a deep breath. "We'd better get some antiseptic and a bandage on that bite before it gets infected."

"It doesn't matter." Jack rose to his knees and looked at her, his green eyes devoid of emotion, his expression flat. "I'll get my things and leave. When I get to town, I'll go see Grierson and sign my share of the lodge over to you. You can do whatever you want with it."

"Whoa!" Valerie stared at him, uprepared for this abrupt change. "Not so fast." Carefully, she released Reddi's collar. The dog, though still growling, didn't move. "Don't you have something to tell me first? Don't you owe me at least that?"

He shook his head. "What's the point? You won't believe me."

His last words came out with a savageness that startled Valerie. "Believe what?" she challenged.

He ignored her question and rose unsteadily to his feet. Reddi made to leap forward; Valerie grabbed him just in time. "Believe what?" she repeated, struggling to hang onto the dog.

Jack shook his head again. "Haven't you ever wondered about why the bruise on my forehead never heals? Haven't you wondered about how you found me on the beach?"

"Of course."

"That letter that your uncle wrote you, the one he was trying to finish when he died? He was going to tell you about how he's known me since he was a kid."

Valerie swallowed. "Yes?"

"And that book, the brown cloth-covered one I found on your uncle's shelf that first night? Have you been able to find it again?"

"No."

"That's because I took it. I wasn't sure what Art had written about me in there. I know he spent years trying to figure out what I was. Why do you think he had all those books about ghosts, the supernatural, and life after death?"

Valerie shivered. She was starting to feel uneasy again. "So . . . so you are a ghost?"

Jack winced, then regarded her steadily and with a resignation she'd never seen before. "I don't know what I am. All I know is I was born in 1895, and I'm still here, still the same age as when I supposedly died in 1927."

The sunlight glinted off the reddish-gold highlights in Valerie's hair as she sat on the picnic table and put the finishing touches on the cleaning and bandaging of Jack's wrist. Jack had been impressed when, despite her rightful disbelief and leeriness, she had shut Reddi in the house and returned, alone, to his cabin, with bandages and rubbing alcohol.

Now, as she worked over his wrist, he resisted the urge to take her into his arms and bury all his love, his fear, his misgivings in her. Her scent teased his senses; he could almost taste the lips her bowed head kept hidden from him. Only a slight tremor here and there betrayed the nervousness beneath her show of calm. Another man might have been distressed by her disbelief, annoyed by her fear. But the fact that she was willing to listen to his story, despite her doubts and her fear, made him love her all the more. No one, except Art, had ever given him that chance before.

"Well, that's that." Valerie moved away from him on the table. "Now, talk." She smiled with a jauntiness that Jack appreciated despite its falseness. Leaving her now, as he most certainly would, would be far worse than any previous departure.

Jack grimaced and raked one hand through his hair. Good or bad, there was only one place to start, and that was at the beginning. "You already know that Jim and Louise Redden drowned in July of 1927. Supposedly I drowned too, but my body was never found."

He narrowed his eyes and assessed Valerie and her willingness to listen—and to believe. This was where the weird part started, the unbelievable part. "I remember being out on the lake. I remember some . . . some other things. But it's what I remember next that's important. I woke up. It was night, and I was lying on the beach down there." He nodded to the lake. "Naked, and covered with sand, just like you found me. Overhead, the Northern Lights played across the sky in a stupendous show.

"I was disoriented. I thought it was later that same night, after . . . after the fight." Valerie's eyebrows rose when he mentioned a fight, but he carried on. "I crawled into the woods, and slowly made my way up to this cabin. My cabin. But it was occupied, by four men I'd never seen before. I didn't understand. I stayed in the woods all that night.

"The next morning, after the guys went out fishing, I entered my cabin. Everything I owned was gone. Things looked different. I stole some clothes and left. I thought I was dreaming, or maybe going crazy.

"I managed to get cleaned up and dressed. I scouted around the camp. I couldn't understand. There were two new cabins. Another dock had been built. I recognized some of the faces, including the Pembrokes, but something didn't seem right. I couldn't figure it out.

"Finally, the next night, I spotted Art. He was eleven years old, or that's what I thought. I'd been taking him fishing, teaching him to hunt and to whittle, since he'd been four or five. But there he was, bigger and all teenage-gawky, beside a fire built back behind the road, guzzling from a jug of homemade cider. I couldn't believe it. I was ready to tan his hide. But that was before he saw me."

Jack looked at Valerie, who hadn't taken her eyes off him since he'd started his tale. "I'll never, ever, forget the look on his face when I walked up to his campfire. He took off like a madman. I finally tackled him just before he made the road.

"Finally, when I got him calmed down enough to talk, he told me everyone thought I was dead. That it was 1930 and that I had drowned three years ago, along with Mr. and Mrs. Redden. That they'd never found my body. Art was all for bringing me home, but I wasn't sure. Where had I been the last three years? Why didn't I remember anything? Where were my clothes? I was scared, and I didn't know why.

"We decided I should stay in the woods. Art brought me food, and we discussed daily how I should arrange my reappearance. But it didn't matter. Before I could decide what to do, I'd disappeared."

"Disappeared?" Valerie repeated, her brow wrinkling.

"Yes. But I only discovered that later, after I reappeared in 1935. Same thing, same place, me naked on the beach, the Northern Lights overhead. Thank God Art still lived here with his parents, helping out with the lodge. He was nineteen and he found me on the beach, when he was pulling up the canoes for the night. This time I stayed for almost two months before I disappeared. I built a shack deep in the woods on the far side of the road, near a small lake. I didn't see any point in telling anyone I was here. I didn't know what I was or what was happening to me. I felt guilty that I was alive and the Reddens were both dead."

Jack took a breath before proceeding. He couldn't help the bitterness that crept into his voice. "I didn't show up again until 1948. I couldn't believe it when Art told me there'd been another World War. That his parents were dead and he now ran the lodge. That my mother and father had both died before the war began."

He shut his eyes against the grief trying to swallow him. The grief and the guilt he'd never had the time or the means to address. He opened his eyes and forced himself to continue talking. "That was the first time I took a chance on appearing in public. I went to see my younger sister,

Dorothy. She was about fifty and lived in Huntsville with her husband and five children. She recognized me right away, but refused to believe I was her brother. No matter what I told her, she thought I was either a shiftless imposter or mentally deranged. She threatened to call the police. I left, and I never saw her again."

Reliving the painful scene in his head, Jack unbuttoned his shirt. He yanked it open and displayed his chest, its smooth and muscled breadth marred by the ugly scar over his heart. Valerie flinched and he was glad. Would this make her believe him?

"Remember this scar?" he asked. "When I came back from my sister's, I plunged a knife into my chest. I wanted to die. I felt I deserved to die. I didn't know why I kept coming back, why I seemed to be suspended between living and dying, between heaven and hell. All I wanted was to die."

"But you didn't?"

Jack regarded Valerie sharply. Was she asking because she wanted to know, or because she wanted to test just how far his lies would go? Was it too much to hope that she'd believe him?

Warily, he continued. "I don't know. The next thing I remember is coming to on the beach again, the Northern Lights flashing across the sky. Art was forty-nine—forty-nine for God's sake. I still looked exactly the same as the day I died—forever thirty-two."

He clenched his fists. He could feel the gash in his forehead throbbing. "That was the first time I worked at the lodge again. There wasn't as much call for hunting and fishing guides as there'd been years before, so I turned to carpentry and maintenance work. The lake had changed. Cottages had been built along the south and east shore. Electric power lines had been extended to the lake and the lodge and all the cabins were wired. So much about life had changed. Everything but me. I was still the same, still neither alive nor dead." He tapped his chest. "The only

221

thing new was this scar. A glaring reminder that I was powerless to change my situation.

"I don't know how Art did it, but he had a variety of pieces of identification forged for me, with different dates and ages. We both realized that one day, when I returned, he would no longer be here—and then, well, we weren't sure what would happen."

"That explains the driver's licences and health cards I found under the floorboard."

Jack nodded. When he'd seen Valerie's fright, he'd assumed she'd found his hiding place. It was the most incriminating evidence in his cabin. "Art kept having new ones made, as far in advance as he could. You found the ones he must have completed just before his death. He also kept up a bank account for me, making regular deposits, trying to make sure I'd always have a means of support.

"I came back again eight years later, in 1974. That's the summer Velma remembers me from. I remember her, a very shy, hardworking young girl. I helped her with some of the heavier housework around the lodge. She was sweet on me, and I was flattered. But I knew it was useless, and cruel, to encourage her."

Jack paused. "The second-to-last time I returned, until now, was the summer of 1983." His gaze locked with Valerie's. "You were nine years old. One night I took you and one of the other kids staying here out fishing in one of the small outboards. We anchored on the other side of Blueberry Island. You caught a trout. I'll never forget how horrified you were to see the hook poking through the fish's mouth, or how you insisted I free it and throw it back in, though it was definitely big enough to eat."

He watched as Valerie's eyes widened. A moment later she started, her mind having sought and found the memory of that calm and cloudless night. Would the grown-up Valerie remember him too? Or would he be just another faceless adult, forgotten in the void of time?

Valerie frowned. "Why did you keep disappearing? And

is it always when the Northern Lights are in the sky?"

He shook his head. "I don't know. But yes, the appearances and disappearances have always occurred when the Northern Lights are visible. And always in the summer, usually July. The night I . . . I died, the sky was beautiful with light. I remember thinking it was the most wonderful sky I'd ever seen."

He fell silent and gazed at his hands. "I always disappear on nights when the Northern Lights are strong. Sometimes I think I can tell when it's going to happen. I feel . . . funny . . . lightheaded, almost, with an unpleasant sense of foreboding."

He looked hard at Valerie. "That's why I slipped into the bush last night at the park. I started to get that feeling." He paused. "Obviously, I was wrong. But this time back, everything has been different. I've never disappeared and come back again a few days later. Maybe it has something to do with the increased strength of the solar flares . . . I don't know."

"How . . . how do you disappear?"

He shook his head again. "Usually I fall asleep. I don't know what happens next."

"Where are you when you're not . . . here?"

He shut his eyes. "I don't know that either. I don't have any consciousness of anything. It's as if I don't exist. Until I show up here again."

Valerie frowned. She looked up at the sky overhead, now clear and blue. "I wonder what the Northern Lights have to do with this."

"Art and I tried to figure that out. All we can think is that it has something to do with the magnetic fields that cause the lights. Sometimes they're strong enough to knock out power lines over huge areas, like they did in Quebec ten years ago. Apparently NASA doesn't like to send up space shuttles when the magnetic fields are strong, for the same reasons. And Art found some research documenting that homing pigeons and other birds can't find their way home during the Northern Lights."

Valerie regarded him silently for a few minutes. Finally, she asked in a quiet voice, "Is that what you think has happened to you? That the Northern Lights made you . . . made you lose your way?"

Jack winced. "Maybe. All I know is I'm lost, somewhere between living and dying. Maybe this is a sort of purgatory, a way for me to pay for my sins."

"Sins?"

Jack shook his head. "That's a whole other issue." He focused on her face, trying to discern her reaction. "The important thing now is whether you believe me or not. Do you, Valerie? Do you believe me?"

Chapter Eighteen

Valerie tensed, far too aware of the weight of Jack's gaze upon her. Just as she was aware of the grimness of the set of his mouth, the clenched fists at his sides, the stiffness of his shoulders, all of them shouting out his expectation that she would reject him and his story.

What *did* she think? She looked down at her hands, now tanned a golden brown. She wanted to believe Jack because she loved him, and because she could see how much he was hurting, deep inside. She wanted to believe him out of caring, out of gratitude, but also because believing in him, in some strange way, would be believing in herself. Believing in her judgment and her ability to make good decisions.

But a part of her revolted against Jack's story. It was too fantastical, too weird—even if it did explain the strange circumstances of his arrival, his disappearances, the need for forged identification. Everything fit together, perhaps too well. But if Jack was lying, he was a consummate actor, worthy of the most celebrated stages in the world.

Valerie bit her lip. Despite everything Jack had said, the one thing she did believe was that he would never hurt her. If anything, his story had reinforced that belief. But it didn't mean she could accept it either.

She raised her head and looked at Jack, who was stiffly waiting for her judgment.

"I don't know what to think," she said finally, her gaze resting on his clenched fists. "I . . . I don't believe in ghosts. I just can't. But I have trouble believing you're lying. I'm sure you think you're telling the truth—"

"So I'm crazy, then?" Jack's eyes narrowed.

"I didn't say that!" Valerie tried to backtrack, but could think of nowhere to go. "You have to admit . . ."

Jack leaned abruptly toward her. "Valerie, you remember your uncle's journal? The one I mentioned earlier? Let me show it to you. It's the only proof I've got."

Valerie waited while Jack retrieved the book. How could a diary bolster his story? With a shudder she considered another possibility. Might it demonstrate just how expert he was at devising a story with all the trademarks of truth? Her stomach churned at that notion. Oh, she was so confused.

The door to the cottage porch slammed shut. Jack handed her the small, cloth-covered book she'd noticed on her uncle's shelves but hadn't been able to find later.

With shaking hands, she opened the book to the first page. It was dated July 5th, 1948, in a handwriting that Valerie immediately recognized as her uncle's, though it was stronger and bolder than his writing in later years. She took a deep breath and started to read.

This is a factual account of my experiences and meetings with one Jack Wilder, of Huntsville and lately of Lake Aurora, born Feb. 22, 1895, and died July 12th, 1927.

Valerie shuddered. This was right to the point. She kept reading, Jack standing silent guard.

Until his death, Jack had been a hunting and fishing guide at Aurora Lodge. That was how I, as a young child, came to know him. Whenever he wasn't working, he would take me fishing, or swimming, or canoeing. He taught me how to whittle, how to read animal tracks, how to identify trees and plants. Besides my parents, he was my first relationship with an adult. It would be fair to say I idolized him.

But then, in the summer of 1927, he drowned. I couldn't believe it. I blamed the guests who drowned with him. I couldn't imagine what could have happenend. Not Jack. It was impossible. But I was only eleven years old. Eventually I had to accept his death, to go on with my life.

I guess I did, more or less. Until one night, three years later. I was out in the woods by myself. I'd squirreled away some cider, stolen when Pa wasn't looking. I built a fire, a half mile or so on the other side of the road, just far enough away that no one would be likely to find me. I had finished about half the jug when a dark shadow stepped out of the trees and gave me a royal fright. I thought it was Pa, come to give me a whippin'. But then the shadow drew closer. In the light of the fire, I recognized his face, a face I'd dreamed about night after night, though less so in recent months. It was Jack. Jack come back from the dead . . .

Wide-eyed, Valerie read about young Arthur's terror, his pell-mell flight, his eventual relief and delight at the rediscovery of his friend, and finally his sorrow and disbelief when Jack disappeared again. He outlined his shock at finding Jack a second time and his growing awe and confusion over what had happened and who and what Jack was.

In wasn't until 1948, when Jack showed up after an absence of thirteen years, that Arthur made his first entry, and began what was to become a lifelong search for a solution to Jack's dilemma. As she flipped through the closely written pages, Valerie sensed her uncle's excitement each time he came up with a new possibility, only to be followed by disappointment and frustration when it did not pan out. He tried seances, magic spells, channeling, hypnotism, all in the interests of finding a solution, interests that explained his extensive library on the occult and various kinds of therapies and New Age ideas.

As page after page went by, Valerie realized something else. The first was a discomforting sense that Jack, with each new appearance and disappearance, was descending lower and lower into despair. He was coming to accept that he was forever suspended between life and death, and worse, that he deserved it.

Arthur too changed as the years sped by. His regard for Jack remained the same, but evolved subtly, from the worship of a childhood hero, to the friendship of a respected cohort, and eventually to the love for the son he'd never had. And with that love had come an urgency, a desperation, to resolve Jack's plight. Before it was too late. Before Arthur died.

Valerie's eyes widened when she read one of Uncle Arthur's last entries.

I'm getting weaker. I have to face it. I'm not going to live much longer. I shouldn't have left it this long, but I guess I always thought that I would be the one to find the answer.

Now it's too late for me. I know that. But who else? To whom can I pass this task? Whom can I trust with Jack's life? The only one I can think of is my great-niece, Valerie. But I haven't seen her for a long time. Would she understand? Would she listen? Would she be willing to stay here, to run the lodge and devote her life to finding an answer to Jack's dilemma?

Valerie turned the page. There were no further entries. Unseeing, she stared down at the blank sheet.

She didn't know how long she'd sat there, the book open on her lap, when Jack gently tilted her chin upward and used his fingers to silently wipe away tears she hadn't known she'd wept. She blinked, then looked at Jack through moisture-studded eyelashes.

"You were crying." He dropped his hand to his side.

"Yes." She struggled to gain control of her voice. "I . . . it's terrible. Uncle Arthur . . ." Her voice broke and she stopped.

"Art was a wonderful man, the best friend anyone could ever have. The last few times I was here, he was like a father. I can't tell you how much that meant to me. How much it means to me."

Valerie sniffed. Yes, she thought, I do understand. Because you lost everything, everyone. He was all you had left.

For a long moment, Jack regarded her. Finally he asked what was on both their minds. "Do you believe me?"

"Yes." She sniffed again. "I don't want to. It opens up questions about things I don't want to contemplate, places I don't want to go. Scarey things, the boogeyman and all that." She tried to smile, but managed only a lopsided grimace.

"But I believe it. I know Uncle Arthur wrote this. It sounds like him, the kinds of things he would say and do. It's his handwriting, his expressions. His wishes."

She cleared her throat once more and tried to effect a jauntiness she did not feel. "But you can't really be a ghost." She paused. "Can you?"

Jack frowned. "I don't know. Not in the sense that people usually mean when they refer to ghosts. Because when I'm here, I'm real. You can touch me. I have thoughts and feelings. I respond to pain and other sensations." He raised his wrist. "I bleed. I don't know what happens to me when I disappear. It's as if everything stops. I'm in some kind of limbo."

Valerie tilted her head and surveyed Jack through narrowed eyes. "Uncle Arthur wrote that you believed you deserved your fate. That it was your punishment, punishment for something that happened before you drowned."

Jack tensed, his features set in a grim scowl. "It's the only logical explanation, if anything can be said to be logical about what's happened to me. And it's true. I am guilty. Intensely guilty."

"Of what?"

"Of what happened the night I and the Reddens drowned. Of what happened in the days before that. Things I shouldn't have done. Things I knew better than to do."

"What things?"

For a moment Valerie didn't think he would tell her. Then he sighed. "You have a right to know. You've heard everything else. But I don't want to sit here and tell you. Let's walk."

"All right." Valerie slipped off the picnic table and gazed up at the sky, where the sun sat firmly overhead. Noon already, she realized with amazement.

She nodded to Jack. "Let's go."

In silence they walked through the trees to Valerie's house, then around the lodge building, to the office and the parking lot. White fluffy clouds had risen on the horizon, and now sailed lazily across the blue sky. To the left birds chirped happily from their nests in a tall pine tree. Two chipmunks raced down the steps of the office, in what looked like a wild game of leapfrog.

Jack flexed his fingers and tried to calm the churning of his stomach. Somehow, he'd thought telling Valerie would make a difference. That it would relieve the burden of loneliness he carried, the guilt. That it might change what he had to do.

But no. Now, perhaps more than ever, it was important that he make sure Valerie was safe. It was important that he hand the lodge over to her, to do with it what she wished. Because one thing never changed. He would disappear again, and if the past few days were any guide, disappear soon.

But first, he needed to make a clean sweep of the past.

To tell Valerie what had happened, and why it was important he leave now.

Without looking at her, he began. "You remember the Reddens, Jim and Louise Redden from Buffalo? The couple that drowned the night I supposedly drowned too?" He stopped and turned to Valerie, thrusting out the words so painful to him. "It's my fault they died. I'm responsible."

"What?" Valerie's voice rose. "That's impossible."

"Just listen, Valerie. All right?"

When she nodded, he continued. "Jim and Louise had been coming to the lodge for at least five years. I took them out fishing, together and separately, several times each year. Jim was what you'd call a man's man, a big, blustery guy that most people liked. But he had a nasty streak, one that came out only when he'd had too much to drink, or when he was with his wife.

"It wasn't until their second or third visit that I realized Louise was deathly afraid of Jim. It wasn't anything overt—I didn't witness any bruises or threats to hurt her. But the evidence was there all the same. I started to notice how Jim shamed his wife in public, saying increasingly contemptuous and nasty things to her. Making fun of her skill at boating or fishing, her attitudes on politics, how she dressed and did her hair. At first his comments were disguised as jokes. But as time went on, the humor fell away and his comments were plain hurtful, humiliating Louise and embarrassing anyone else who happened to be around."

Jack and Valerie had paused on the crest of a hill at the base of the parking lot. Jack raised his eyes for a moment, scanning the sparkling water and lazy summer sky, drinking in the beauty around him, a beauty that continued oblivious to the human misfortune played out beneath it. He returned his gaze to Valerie's small face and continued.

"But it wasn't until that last year that things really fell apart. On one of the first days of their holiday, I'd taken Louise out canoeing. We stopped at Bald Rock Island to check if there were any raspberries yet. I asked her a question, something simple and innocuous, and she started to cry. She couldn't stop. It all came out. The escalating abuse, both verbal and physical, an abuse that had worsened each year with their failure to produce a child. Jim was furious, and disgusted with Louise, convinced that she was to blame for their childlessness. Louise was upset too, not only at her failure to conceive, but at the transformation of the husband she'd loved into a man who felt nothing but contempt for her."

Jack shifted his weight from one foot to the other. "I don't know how it happened," he said through gritted teeth, "but one thing led to another. I started out trying to comfort her, but then, well—I'd always liked her, right from the start. She was pretty, and slight, and kind to a fault. And like most women of her day, she took what her husband dished out without complaint." He paused. "We made love. Over the next few days, we decided on something quite outside the pale for that time. We decided that she would stay behind when her husband left and seek a divorce. When she was free, we would marry.

"I wanted her to wait until the day they were to leave to tell her husband. We would tell him together. I was afraid for her. I'd seen how possessive he was. I knew that he'd hit her more than once. I wanted to make sure he couldn't hurt her."

They reached the sand beach and Jack turned and regarded Valerie. In some ways she reminded him of Louise, small and slight, yet different too. Stronger, perhaps, better prepared to take care of herself. He hoped so.

He looked into her dark eyes and wished he didn't have to tell her. But he did. He swallowed. "I'd been away for two days on a fishing expedition with some other guests. When I got back, they told me Jim and Louise had gone out canoeing. It was dark and they still hadn't come back.

"I had a really bad feeling about it. Though it was already dark, I jumped into a canoe and paddled like a madman to the west end of the lake. I wanted to find Louise and make sure she was all right. When I got closer, huge green-ish spotlights began to crisscross the sky. A reddish glow lit the horizon and started to pulse as only the Northern Lights can, but I barely noticed. I could hear Jim's enraged voice, carried across the water, with obscenity after obscenity.

"As I approached, under the well-lit sky, I saw Jim scramble to the far end of the canoe. A loud slap, followed by a muffled cry, echoed across the lake. 'Stop!' I yelled, but I could see Jim shaking Louise, and slapping her again and again. I drove my canoe into the side of theirs and whacked Jim across the back of the head with my paddle. All I'd wanted to do was make him release Louise, and he did, shoving her out of the canoe into the water. Then he turned and leapt on me, upsetting my balance and dumping us both into the water.

"Louise couldn't swim. I was desperate to find her. But Jim was attacking me. I hit him twice, but couldn't loosen his hold. Finally I managed to knock him away. I dived beneath the canoe and came up on the other side. The Northern Lights made it as bright as twilight, but I couldn't see Louise anywhere. I started for a cluster of rocks sticking out of the water, hoping she'd managed to get that far and perhaps pull herself up on one side.

"I had just made the rocks when Jim grabbed me from behind. I tried to throw him off, but he was too strong. The last thing I remember is the numbing pain as my head was slammed into the granite."

With an effort, Jack wrenched his mind from that horrendous night. He forced himself to look at Valerie, and prepared to face her condemnation. "That's why I think I keep coming back . . . why I don't just die and get it over with."

Valerie frowned. "I don't think I understand."

"I slept with another man's wife," Jack spat out. "If I hadn't gone after Louise, then neither she nor Jim would have died."

His flat, unforgiving statement was met with absolute silence. Valerie just stared at him, her eyes narrowed, her brow furrowed.

Which was fine with Jack. He didn't want pity. He didn't want forgiveness. He—

"That's not true!"

To Jack's surprise, Valerie straightened and glared at him. Her voice vibrated with anger. "No," she said flatly, "if you hadn't intervened, likely only Louise would have died. Or at the least been beaten to a pulp."

Jack stared at her, speechless.

Valerie continued, her voice taut, the gold flecks in her eyes sizzling like drops of water falling on a hot stove. "Maybe you didn't behave in the most honorable fashion. Maybe the result of your actions was terrible. But do you think things would have been better for Louise if she'd never gotten to experience comfort and joy with you, if she'd planned to stay with that dreadful man? Would you have felt better if she'd been found floating in the lake the next morning, while her husband pretended everything was fine? Or . . . or been choked to death later at their home?" Her voice broke.

"No," Jack answered. "No, but—"

"Maybe you are condemned to this strange series of appearances and disappearances. But I don't believe you're being punished. I don't think that's how God operates. Maybe it has something to do with the Northern Lights, and what you said about homing pigeons not being able to find their way home. Maybe your spirit got disrupted on the way to heaven."

"Or hell," added Jack quietly.

Valerie glared at him. "All right. Or hell. But maybe you keep coming back for a reason. Maybe there's something you need to learn or find out."

Even though she was wrong, Jack was moved by her defense, by her fierce loyalty. No one—not even Art—had believed in him to that degree.

He stemmed the emotion rising in him, the desire to

pull her close and kiss her until they both forgot who and what they were, to kiss her until right and wrong disappeared, to kiss her until nothing was left but the two of them and their love.

But he knew it couldn't be that way. "Maybe you're right," he said quietly, his eyes not leaving hers. "But if that's true, if I'm supposed to be learning something, I'm not doing a very good job."

"What do you mean?"

Slowly Jack reached for Valerie's hand. He raised the warm, supple flesh to his lips and kissed it, briefly shutting his eyes and wishing with all his might that he could stay.

As slowly as he had raised her hand to his lips, he dropped it, relinquishing her fingers one by one. "Valerie, you're the first woman—the only woman—I've gotten close to since Louise. I knew I should stay away from you. I've got nothing to offer, not even a life. But I couldn't resist you. You—you made me feel alive, and for once, connected to the real world. I wasn't alone anymore. For the first time in decades, I wanted to live, not die. You don't know how much that means to me.

"But I shouldn't have overstepped. You deserve better. You deserve someone who can offer you so much more."

"Don't be sorry," Valerie whispered. Tears shimmered in her eyes. "I'm not."

Jack pushed on. "Then Reed showed up. I don't like him. I don't trust him. I know he hurt you. Now I'm terrified I'll disappear and you'll go back to him. And then he'll hurt you again. Or, because of me, do something far worse."

Valerie's eyes widened, the dark brown deepening to almost black. When she spoke, her voice was low and soothing, but filled with quiet strength. "No. Nothing would make me go back to Reed."

She reached up and stroked Jack's cheek, her hand lingering. "I've known for a long time, even before I broke off our engagement, that Reed wasn't good for me. I don't like the person I became while I was around him. Anxious to please. Unsure of myself. Worried all the time. Afraid I'd make him angry."

She held Jack's gaze, her eyes steady. "You know, Reed is very like my father." She shuddered. "Only my father never became physically violent. But I'd never want to live with a man who needed to control everything. I don't know why it took so long for me to see Reed for what he is."

She dropped her hand and shook her head. "And yes, Reed's arrival here upset me. It scared me. He—"

"He tried to strangle you!"

She jumped, then stared at Jack. But this time she didn't deny the truth. "Yes, he did. It was after I'd broken off with him. He couldn't believe that I wouldn't take him back."

"What if he tries it again?"

Valerie shook her head. "I've thought about it a lot. I don't think he will. I think he was as shocked by his explosion as I was. He—he likes his own way, he likes to be in charge, physically and every other way. But I'm sure he doesn't love me. He just finds it hard to . . . let go."

Jack surveyed Valerie. She seemed to genuinely believe what she was saying.

"I can visit him today," he said flatly. "Convince him it's in his best interests to stay away from you."

His gaze locked with Valerie's. "Because you know I won't be here."

"I know." She didn't flinch from his gaze. "Which is another reason why I need to take care of it myself, as much as I might like you to do it."

Jack nodded reluctantly. He understood, even if he didn't like it. He just hoped Valerie was right.

There was only one thing left to say. Jack girded himself to force out the words. "I've got to go now."

"Go? Where?"

"To town. I'll see Grierson. I'll tell him I want to sign my share of the lodge over to you."

"And then?"

"There isn't any 'and then,' Valerie," he said quietly. "I'll take my things when I leave and book into a motel."

"A motel. Why?"

"You know why. To wait. To wait until I disappear again."

Valerie looked more stricken than she had at any time during the revelations of the morning and early afternoon. Jack felt like a jerk. But it was better this way. For both of them.

"Good-bye, Valerie."

Chapter Nineteen

It took a moment for Valerie to find her voice. "You can't go," she blurted out. "I won't let you."

Jack halted but did not turn back. His response was muffled and sounded far away. "I have to go. You know that."

She swallowed, surprised at her stubbornness and the conviction she felt. "No. That's not true. There's nothing to stop you from staying here with me. At least until you disappear again."

This time Jack slowly pivoted to face her. The breeze off the lake whipped his hair off his forehead, exposing the ugly bruise. "It's not—"

Valerie stood on tiptoe and silenced him with a desperate kiss, a kiss in which she tried to instill all her feeling, all the words she couldn't say.

When she dropped back to her heels, she continued to frame his jaw with her hands. She could feel the pulse in his throat, beating strong and steadily. How can you be a ghost? How can you be dead? she wondered.

She gazed into his sea-green eyes, eyes that had once

brimmed with warmth for her but now seemed to be growing more distant. She knew she'd do anything for this man. Anything.

She took a deep breath. "Once you said you loved me. Did you mean it?"

Under her hands, Jack's jaw tensed. For a long moment, he said nothing. Then, "Yes."

"Say it, Jack."

"Yes." He paused. "I love you."

"I love you too," she whispered raggedly. "I know we haven't known each other a long time. I know there are . . . *complications.*" Giddy laughter at the understatement that last word represented bubbled up inside her, but she choked it back. "I just know that I love you."

Gently, Jack grasped her wrists, his touch electrifying her senses. But the eyes burning into hers were steady and filled with sorrow. "Think about what you're saying, Valerie. You can't love me."

"Don't tell me what I can or can't do. What I feel or don't feel." Her voice rose with an unexpected streak of anger. "I *know* that I love you. Reed always told me I didn't know what I thought or felt, what I could or couldn't do. Before that it was my father. Don't you do it too. I'm an adult. I'm a responsible person. And if I know nothing else, I do know how I feel about you."

Jack shook his head. "Valerie—"

She didn't give him a chance to say anything else. Abruptly, she rose once more on tiptoe. Her mouth slanted over his. Where he had been startled and unresponsive to her first kiss, this time he yielded, then slowly began to respond.

His hands dropped from her wrists, sliding down her arms. Suddenly he grasped her and pulled her to him, the heat of his kiss flaring, along with the love and the desire he no longer tried to hide.

Valerie welcomed his embrace with every part of her being. Her lips parted under his and she reveled in the sweet taste of his mouth, the strength and hardness of the body pressed next to hers, and the raw urgency of his wanting.

Finally, she dragged her lips from his and hugged him fiercely. She looked up at him. "When two people love each other, they try to stay together. They help each other . . . they love each other . . . for as long as they can."

Jack set her slightly away from him. He cupped her chin and his gaze locked with hers. "I love you, Valerie. But it's not fair to you. Not fair to ask you to—"

Valerie touched his lips with her fingertips to silence him. "I don't care. It's my choice, isn't it? And I want to spend this time with you. Loving you. Making love to you. Even if it's only for a few days. Or a few hours. I love you. That's all that matters."

For a moment Jack said nothing. Then he grasped her shoulders. "Oh, God, Valerie," he murmured before his mouth descended on hers in a blistering kiss that took her breath away. Body pressed against body, soft curves fitting to hard planes, heated flesh to heated flesh. The kiss went on and on until Valerie thought she would faint from want and dizziness.

It wasn't until her back bumped into the rough bark of a maple that she realized Jack had moved them under the cover of the woods. She leaned against the trunk, glad of the support for her melting bones.

Jack slipped his hands beneath her T-shirt and unfastened her bra, freeing her breasts. As his hands closed around them, she arched into his embrace, rubbing her nipples against his palms. Her body ached all over for his touch, a touch for which she grew increasingly impatient. But she had the same fevered desire to give, to touch him and to taste him, to show him in every possible way how much she loved him. To let him know she wouldn't let him go without a fight. She released the buttons of his shirt, and her hands traced the lean musculature of his chest, then descended along the firm lines of his body.

Locked in a feverish kiss, Jack lowered them both to a

moss-covered mound. The damp ground felt soft and cool against Valerie's back. She sank deeper into its cushioning embrace as Jack positioned himself over her.

Despite the shade, Jack burned with a fiery urgency that grew greater with every breath. He shut his eyes, reveling in Valerie's love, the firm softness of her breasts, the sensitivity of her lips, taking all she would give him and trying to return it tenfold. He had so little to give, and nothing lasting. But for her, he would make these few fevered minutes the most memorable, the most delicious, the most loving of her life. He had his love to give, and that was all.

But by God, he would give it.

The rustling of the leaves overhead and the caress of a cool breeze across his sweat-slicked back awakened Jack from the languorous state induced by their lovemaking. He shifted slightly, removing his weight from Valerie, though he remained inside her.

His movement provoked an immediate response. Valerie's arms tightened around his neck, drawing him closer once more. "Don't go."

He nuzzled her throat. "I love you." He dropped kisses along the line of her chin, then gazed into her eyes, the kindest, most welcoming brown eyes he'd ever seen. "I hope you know how wonderful you are," he said. "How special you are to me."

He paused. "You don't know how much I wish I could stay."

Valerie's eyes shimmered with tears. "No," she said, "don't ruin it by talking about leaving. We need to enjoy the time we have together...."

He silenced her with a gentle kiss. Inside her, he felt himself strengthen and grow as desire flared once more. Through his lips, he sensed her quickening response, which in turn built his own fires. He held her close, loving her, wanting her, thanking her with every motion, with every breath, for the gift of her love. The fact that she knew his story, the fact that she wasn't tied to anyone else, the fact that she gave herself to him, freely and with a passion he had never experienced before, humbled him, and filled him with a desire to please her and love her as no one had before. For now he was content to set reality aside, and live and love for the moment.

But even he, a ghost or some unnamed specter, could only set reality aside for so long. Afterwards, as he held her close, as he buried his face in her silky hair and breathed in her wonderful scent, he knew he had to follow his original course. It was time.

Reluctantly, he released her and sat up. In the dappled sunlight of their forest seclusion, only yards away from the dock access road, her naked skin appeared alternately golden and darkly mysterious, beckoning to him to continue an exploration they had just begun.

"Where are you going?"

Jack didn't look up as he stood to pull on his jeans. "To town. To see Grierson."

"Don't go."

"I'm coming back, Valerie. But I can't put off signing the lodge over to you any longer. What if I disappear tonight? What would you tell Grierson? God knows how long my disappearance would tie things up and prevent you from selling the lodge."

Valerie sat up. Her dark eyes looked huge in her small face. "But . . . what will happen when you *do* come back again? Where will you stay? How will you survive?"

Jack paused in the middle of buttoning his shirt. He'd pondered these questions a hundred times. "I don't know," he said slowly. He knelt down and took her hands in his. "But it doesn't matter. What matters is you. *You* don't want to keep the lodge. *You* have a job, and an apartment, friends, and a life in Chicago. I can't ask you to keep this lodge, to stay here on the off chance I show up again in a few years. What if I don't come back for twenty years? What if I never come back?"

With silence she met the questions to which they both knew the answers. She bit her lip, looked down, then back up again. She sighed. "Okay. I know. . . ."

She stuck out her lower lip. "But I don't have to like it."

Jack's heart swelled. He laughed, then reached out and ruffled her hair. "I wouldn't have it any other way."

Valerie finished slathering suntan lotion over the bare skin exposed by her bikini, then lowered herself to the lounge positioned on the deck to catch the mid-afternoon rays. As she sank into the blissfully thick cushions, she sighed. After a morning of astonishing revelations, followed by emotional upheaval and the most wonderful lovemaking of her life, she was exhausted in body, soul, and mind. Yet more sober, more alert to every nuance of her surroundings and to every passing moment than she'd ever been before. And more anxious than ever for Jack to return from town.

She shut her eyes and concentrated on the warmth of the sun bathing her skin, reminding her of another warmth, a pair of arms, she longed to revel in again.

The phone rang. Grumpily, she opened one eye and regarded the cell phone sitting on the picnic table. Should she answer it? She was about to turn over on her stomach and ignore it when it occurred to her the call might be from Jack, or Mr. Grierson.

She stood up, ambled over to the table, and picked up the phone. "Hello."

"Hi. Is Reed Vogler there?"

"No." Valerie wrinkled her nose.

"Is that Valerie?"

"Yes, it is," Valerie said with more than a little caution. "Who's calling?"

"I'm sorry. I should have introduced myself. I'm Gord Vickers, Reed's lawyer. I've been trying to get him all day, at his motel and on his cell phone, so far with no luck. You wouldn't know where I could reach him, would you?"

"Beyond his motel and cell phone, no."

Silence filled the air for a long moment. Then Vickers said, "You have seen him, haven't you?"

"Yes." Valerie frowned. For her own benefit as well as the lawyer's, she added, "But I expect he's on his way back to Chicago by now."

"Oh." The man on the other end of the phone hesitated. "If you do see him, will you tell him to call me? It's important."

"Certainly. Good-bye." Valerie clicked off the phone and set it back on the table. She pushed her hair back from her face. With all her heart, she hoped that what she'd told the lawyer was true: that Reed had accepted her decision and finally left.

Her calm rattled, she lay down once more on the lounge and tried to sunbathe. But no matter how she twisted and turned, she couldn't get comfortable, couldn't shake the uneasiness that had seized her.

Reddi's barking broke the afternoon quiet. Valerie sat up. Was it Jack? Or was it Reed? Please let it be Jack.

The barking subsided, which told her nothing. Reddi had either been reassured by Reed, or subdued with a mere look from Jack. Valerie shook her head. She would never understand how Reddi, after what he'd witnessed, could greet Reed with such affection, yet hate and fear Jack. Unless, she mused, unless it had something to do with Jack being a ghost, if an unusual one.

She was still pondering that idea when Reed appeared through the trees, Reddi dancing at his heels. With his white T-shirt and olive shorts, his trim build, bronzed skin, and dark good looks, Reed looked strong and vibrant and poster-boy perfect, as perfect as the white teeth that flashed at her from between two perfectly formed lips. It was all perfect, down to the twinkle in his eye as he caught sight of her, waiting on the deck.

But all that perfection hid a darker reality, an appalling and twisted need to control everyone and everything, and a simmering rage, the consequences of which Valerie had

had the misfortune to suffer. The realization, with a clarity she had never had before, freed her from the last of her fear. Instead, for the first time she felt disgust for Reed, disgust and an odd sort of pity. Pity for a man who could not, would not, see the truth, about himself and everyone around him.

As Reed bounded around to the steps, she shut her eyes and thanked God for sending her Jack. She didn't know *what* exactly Jack was; she knew only that she was eternally grateful for his presence in her life, however short that might be.

Reed took her by surprise, before she'd even had a chance to open her eyes. He swooped down and settled a hard kiss on her lips, while his hand slipped under one cup of her bikini top to take possession with a painful digging in of his fingers.

Valerie pushed out of his embrace and knocked his hand away. "Reed!"

Reed grinned, the sunshine glinting off his white teeth. "Ah c'mon. It's a beautiful day. It's hot outside. What better time to go inside and spend the afternoon making love? Or right out here on the deck?"

Valerie jumped up. She'd known getting rid of Reed wouldn't be easy, but she'd never expected it to be this difficult. If he'd only stayed in Chicago, and forgotten all about her. But nothing was easy when it came to Reed. He just didn't hear her. He had his own agenda and wouldn't accept anything else.

She ignored his comment. "Your lawyer called here a few minutes ago. He wants you to call him. He said it was important."

Reed gestured to her phone. "Can I use yours? Mine has run out of juice."

At her nod, he placed the call. A moment later it went through. "Gord, hi, how are you? I hear you've been trying to get me. What's up?"

Valerie sat down. She could hear the other man's voice

on the phone, but couldn't make out the words. Whatever they were, they didn't alter Reed's jovial mood. After a moment, with a nod to Valerie, Reed rounded the corner of the deck out of sight. His voice carried back, muffled, but low and insistent. It came again and again, each question or comment more abrupt than the time before. Finally she heard a terse "Good-bye." He walked around the corner, dropped her phone on the table, and plunked down beside her.

Immediately his arm snaked around her bare shoulders and pulled her closer. Without missing a beat, Valerie lifted his fingers from her shoulder, moved over a foot, then turned and looked at him. The look of calm expectation on his handsome face distressed her.

She took a deep breath. "Reed, this has got to stop."

"What's got to stop?" His smile widened and he reached for her hand.

She pulled it behind her back. "Your touching me. Your refusal to accept that what we had is finished. Over."

His expression transformed at lightning speed into one of solicitude. "Ah, Valerie. My sweet little Valerie." He shook his head. "Is it too fast for you? Because I'm willing to wait. I'd like to get married before the end of the summer, but—"

"You're not listening. *I* don't want to marry *you*. *I* don't want to go out with *you*. It's finished, don't you understand?"

"How can you say that?" Reed looked genuinely wounded. "We're perfect together."

"No." Valerie shook her head. "No, we're not. Maybe it's perfect for you. But it's not for me." She looked hard at Reed, trying once and for all to make him understand. "After what happened, I can't trust you. I don't like you. I don't want to be anywhere near you."

For an instant, Reed's face contorted into that awful expression she had seen only once before, the look of incredulous rage and hate that had haunted her dreams, the look that was burned into her memory for all time. Then the expression disappeared, replaced with the solicitude she detested. "Where's your car?" Reed asked out of the blue, only his choked voice giving his reaction away.

"My car?" Startled, Valerie rattled out the answer. "Jack fixed the flat and took it to town."

"It's him, isn't it?"

"It's him what?"

"It's that worthless freeloader who's turned you against me, isn't it? He sweet-talked your uncle into leaving him half the lodge and now he's deluding you. And worse, destroying our chance of happiness."

Valerie stared at Reed in shock. "If you're talking about Jack, you're wrong. He's not like that at all. That's the last thing he'd do. And you're wrong, anyway."

As Reed's accusations sank in, her anger grew. She raised her chin and glared at him. She loved Jack, and she wasn't ashamed to admit it. But Reed had to understand that, Jack or no Jack, she would never have married him, never have submitted to a control that was destroying her inch by inch. Even if he hadn't almost choked her to death, even if he hadn't terrified her, she would have left him. For herself, for her own self-esteem and confidence. She wouldn't have repeated her mother's mistake of marrying a domineering man and losing herself.

"Reed, listen to me. I don't want to marry you. It wouldn't have mattered whether Jack came along or not. I never could have married you."

With each word, she felt the shackles that had held her for so long falling by the wayside. She felt stronger, braver, and strangely elated. If simply saying the words could make such a difference, how would she react when Reed was truly gone from her life?"

"What do you mean, I'm no good for you? I've never hurt you!"

Valerie gaped. How could Reed continue to insist that he hadn't almost choked the life out of her? Not to mention all the times he had hurt her in subtle yet painful ways. Forcing himself on her. Making her engage in sexual acts she found distasteful. Criticizing her body, her friends, her ideas.

But she didn't mention any of that. "Reed," she said, "we both know you like to be in charge. For the last two years you've tried to change everything about me—what I wear, my hairstyle, how I talk, what I think. I can't help wondering now if you ever liked anything about me."

"That's ridiculous. I love you." Reed's voice had risen slightly, the only sign that he was in the least perturbed. "I'm just trying to take care of you."

"No." Valerie shook her head. "It's not me you love. You're not trying to take care of me—you're trying to control me. You love yourself. You love being in control. You don't love me."

Reed pasted that infuriatingly patient smile on his face. He stroked Valerie's arm as if she'd never spoken. "We'll talk about this later. Let's go for a swim. You'll feel better after you've cooled off."

Valerie shrugged off his hand and jumped up. "I feel fine, thank you. And now I'd like you to leave. Good-bye."

Slowly he got to his feet and regarded her, a mocking smile on his face. "That's my little Valerie. So stubborn. So silly. So lovable."

He paused for a long moment, his gaze roving insolently over her body. Then he smiled and turned away. "See you tomorrow."

"No, Reed. You won't," Valerie called after him.

He didn't acknowledge he'd heard her, just kept on walking.

Jack shut his eyes as his lips settled over Valerie's, drinking in the taste and touch and scent of her, sensations he never wanted to forget. His arm tightened around her shoulder with a possessiveness he knew was foolish, but which he couldn't help.

Finally, with reluctance, he broke off the kiss, but did not remove his arm from Valerie's shoulders. As they sat at the end of the dock, warmed by the last rays of the afternoon sun, their legs dangling in the cool water, he looked out over the clear, deep waters that had played such a big part in his life. On the water he had committed murder, in the water he had died, and every few years from the water he was reborn. Involuntarily, he shuddered. He didn't understand any of it. Only that every part of his body, mind, and soul ached to be alive. To be alive, and to be in love with Valerie, here, at Aurora Lodge.

"What did Mr. Grierson say when you told him you wanted to sign the lodge over to me?" Valerie's question interrupted Jack's somber thoughts. He tried to smile, to concentrate on this moment. He would have told her sooner, but the second he'd arrived back, they'd run hand-in-hand into the lake, laughing like two crazy people. In the water they had celebrated the sheer enjoyment of being alive, splashing and dunking each other like two smitten teenagers. Until their antics suddenly sparked into something much deeper, hotter and adult. In the L of the dock, hidden from prying eyes, they had made wild and passionate love. It was a wonder the water around them hadn't sizzled from the heat.

He turned his mind to Valerie's question. She looked so serious, so earnest sitting there, despite the hair slicked back from her face, the drops of water still wending their way past her cheekbones, the skimpy bathing suit that made him think of chocolate and all things delicious.

He cleared his throat. "Grierson was surprised, no doubt about it. But he didn't ask why. I think he's glad to get things moving, and he doesn't really care what direction they go in, as long as they get resolved before he retires."

Valerie tilted her head. "I've been thinking. Maybe I should keep the lodge. Maybe—"

"How would you run it from Chicago?"

"Perhaps I could get someone like Velma and her hus-

249

band to manage it. Or maybe—maybe I'd stay here after all."

Jack winced. He knew why she was thinking about staying. He knew and he loved her all the more for it. But he couldn't let her do it.

He squeezed her hand. "Valerie, I know why you're doing this. But it won't work."

"Why not?" Valerie's bottom lip set stubbornly. "It's what Uncle Arthur would have wanted. For me. For you. For both of us."

"Valerie, when I leave this time, it may be years before I come back. Once I was gone for twenty years—twenty whole years."

He paused, his eyes burning into hers, making sure she understood the unpalatable truth. "Maybe I won't come back at all."

"That's impossible!"

"Unlikely, perhaps, but not impossible." He continued relentlessly, not wanting to hurt her, but unable to avoid the facts. "I'm dead, after all. Neither of us know why I keep appearing and disappearing. If there are rules for whatever is happening to me, I don't know what they are. And neither do you. I can't let you gamble on something that might or might not happen."

It hurt to say the next words, but he forced them out. "Besides, you have a life, a home, friends, and family. And one day you'll find someone to love—someone who will love you and treat you right, someone who can give you everything you deserve."

Valerie averted her gaze, but not before he saw the tears in her eyes. She played with his hand, slowly folding back his fingers and then pressing them close to his palm, her motions slow and deliberate and full of love. When she raised her head, her eyes still swam with tears, but she looked straight at him.

"I've been thinking about what we talked about. You know, about perhaps there being a reason you keep coming back. That maybe there's something you're supposed to do, or say, someone you're supposed to save or rescue. A way to redeem yourself."

Jack frowned, disturbed that she seemed to have ignored what he'd just said. "You may be right. The only problem is, I don't know what it is I'm supposed to do. Whatever it is, I haven't stumbled on it yet."

Valerie paused. "Maybe . . . maybe you've done it already."

"What?"

Valerie spoke slowly. "Perhaps just loving again has done it. Loving me. But you've done more than that. Knowing you love me has helped me stand up to Reed. It's helped me get over my fear of him, made it possible for me to tell him to go away. Having you around has made me feel safer too. It's like what you tried to do for Louise, only this time it's worked."

Jack snorted, the reminder of his role in Louise and her husband's deaths bringing back the guilt he'd never been able to dispel. "Reed was here again today, wasn't he? If I'm supposed to have helped you make him go away, I haven't been very successful."

"But you will be. That's why I want you to stay here all day tomorrow. Then, when he comes, you and I can tell him together to leave and not come back. He'll have to get the message then."

"And if he doesn't?" Jack was willing to do anything Valerie suggested, but he had deep-seated doubts about whether Reed could be convinced. "Valerie, I think you should tell Reed that you'll call the police if he comes near you again. That you'll tell them what happened in Chicago." He paused, unable to keep the frustration and bitterness from his voice. "I can't even guarantee I'll be here tomorrow."

"Maybe not, but I'm willing to gamble that you will be here," Valerie insisted. "And then . . ."

Jack narrowed his eyes. "And then what?"

"And then you'll have redeemed yourself. Then . . . then you'll live again."

Hope glowed in Valerie's eyes, a hope that Jack was reluctant to crush. He sighed. "Maybe."

"You don't sound convinced."

He placed his hands on her shoulders and turned her to face him. "You're right. I'm not convinced," he said slowly. "Besides, I don't think it matters whether I redeem myself or not."

Puzzlement filled Valerie's eyes. "Why not?"

He paused. "Valerie, if I redeem myself, if my sins are forgiven, what exactly do you think will happen?"

"You'll stay. You'll stop disappearing and appearing."

"That's possible." He tried not to flinch from the optimism in her face. "But did you ever think of the other possibility? The one that's more likely?"

"What other possibility?"

Jack steeled himself to say the words. "That when I redeem myself, my soul will finally be at rest."

He paused. There was no good way to say this. "And then I'll be dead."

Chapter Twenty

Dead!

It was only one short word, but it hit Valerie with the impact of a bomb, exploding her hopes, blasting the shreds of her foolish fantasies to the wind.

Dead!

Her bottom lip started to tremble and her eyes swam with tears. She blinked hard to keep them back, and bit her lip to keep down the cry that rose in her throat.

Dead! She turned away to hide her reaction. How could Jack be dead when she loved him so much, when she—

"Valerie." Rough yet gentle fingers coaxed her attention back to the man who had just delivered those logical, yet devastating, words. The man who had made her face what her mental gymnastics had allowed her to neatly avoid. *Dead!*

Through blurry vision she saw a pain that mirrored her own, a pain reflected in Jack's unblinking eyes, in the set of his mouth, in the throbbing of the bruise on his forehead. The sight of his sorrow and loneliness made her heart constrict.

"I'm sorry, Valerie. I don't want it to be like this." Jack's low voice swept over her, caressing her as his hands had only moments before. "But we can't pretend we're going to be together. One way or the other, I'll be gone. It may only be for a few years, but it could be far, far longer. I might never come back."

He took a deep breath, but his gaze didn't waver. "All we have is now. That's it. Now, and the fact that I love you and you love me."

She shut her eyes, ashamed of her tears, of her inability to accept what must be accepted. "I . . . know. I know you're right."

She wanted to tell him that it wasn't fair. She wanted to rage against the world, against fate, against that long-ago couple who had sucked Jack into their problems. She wanted to strike at Jack, to yell at him because he was some weird aberration suspended halfway between man and ghost. But mostly she just wanted Jack. She wanted him here, now and forever.

But telling him would only hurt him more, would make him feel guiltier than ever.

She felt his hands, rough and firm, frame her face, fingertips wiping away the tears that had escaped to run down her cheeks. She drank in his woodsy scent, the texture of his hands on her face, the reassuring sound of his voice, impressing it into her memory. She didn't want to ever forget.

His lips brushed her forehead. "I don't want you to remember me, or this moment, with sadness. I want you to remember how I love you, and how grateful I am for all you've given me."

Valerie's eyes fluttered open and gazed into a deep green pair mere inches away. "Me?" she asked. "What have I given you?"

"Everything. Love. Laughter. Joy. Companionship. And the most precious gift of all."

She frowned. "I don't understand."

"The gift of life. When I was a fishing and hunting guide in the twenties, I took the world for granted. Then, after I died and started coming back every few years, all I wanted was to die. To die and put an end to my misery.

"But now, for the first time in decades, I want to live, to savor each hour of my existence. What I wouldn't give to stay here, with you, for the rest of my natural days. In this time. A time where I seem to fit so much better than I ever did before."

He smiled faintly. "Unfortunately, I had to die before I discovered the truth. But I don't regret it for a minute. Because if all this hadn't happened, if my destiny hadn't veered off in such a crazy manner, I would never have met you. I would never have had the chance to love you. If only for a moment."

Her eyes brimming with tears again, Valerie flung her arms around his neck. She shut her eyes, letting his kisses whisper over her face, wet with tears. She raised her lips to his, wanting his kiss, wanting to feel the heat and the passion of his body. She would willingly give herself to him, body, mind, and soul.

And if it could only be for the moment, she would make it the longest, most intense moment ever lived.

Reddi's distant but frantic barking brought Valerie to a standstill as she prepared coffee the next morning. She listened, carafe of water in one hand, trying to determine if she needed to go outside to investigate what had sparked the pup's outburst.

The barking ceased as suddenly as it had begun. Valerie shook her head. Likely it had been nothing more than Reddi in mad pursuit of a chipmunk or squirrel. She hoped the prey had escaped without harm. Reddi was motivated more by curiosity than any desire to hunt or harm, but the big pup might inadvertently kill his new plaything out of sheer eagerness.

She returned to her task, enjoying familiar motions of her everyday routine. She savored the aroma of the freshly brewing coffee, remembering her promise to Jack to try to live in the moment. It was a promise she'd found much easier to keep after she'd awoken to find him still in her bed, very much alive and ready to plunge back into the lovemaking they'd interrupted for only a few hours last night to sleep.

Humming, she pulled two mugs out of the cupboard, and turned for an all-over stretch. She heard the shower shut off upstairs. Good. Jack would be down soon, and ready to spend another wonderful day together. Better yet, he would be here when Reed arrived. Together they would be sure to convince Reed to go away, once and for all.

With a whack the screen door slammed open. Valerie jumped and turned. Reed stood in the doorway, waving a copy of *The Forester*, Huntsville's weekly newspaper. "Where is he?" he demanded.

Valerie frowned. "Where is who?"

"You know who," Reed sneered, all pretense of good manners gone. "Jack. Your lover boy!"

"You can't just burst in here like that," she snapped.

"We don't have time to talk. You're coming with me." Reed grabbed her arm and started dragging her to the door.

"Reed, let go of me." Valerie struggled against him, planting her bare feet on the floor. "Have you gone crazy?"

"No, but—"

Valerie felt the swish of air past her before she actually heard anything. Jack smashed into Reed at a run, dislodging his grip on her arm. She stumbled sideways, crashing into the wood stove.

She watched in dismay as Reed regained his balance and struck back at Jack. Jack parried the blow and grabbed Reed's arm, twisting it behind his back. He attempted to open the door, but Reed flung back one of his legs and tripped Jack.

The two men fell to the floor with a thud, a flailing heap of arms and legs, grunts and pants, interspersed with the crack of bone against bone. Valerie edged along the stove toward the woodpile. If she could only get a length of wood—

Two uniformed men chose that instant to crowd through the doorway. Immediately they leapt into the fray, yanking Reed and Jack apart only seconds after Valerie realized they were police—the Ontario Provincial Police.

Reed, sitting up on the floor at one side of the room and rubbing his jaw, pointed at Jack. "That's him, officers. That's Jack Vanderstone. The murderer."

"What? What are you talking about?" Valerie's incredulous gaze bounced from Reed to Jack. Jack stood by the counter, panting, his chest and feet bare, his wet hair askew, the dark bruise on his forehead throbbing, the scar on his chest a livid red. The older of the two policemen stood beside him, gripping his arm.

"Is that right? Are you Jack Vanderstone?" asked the other officer, a blond younger man who had lost his hat in the scuffle.

Jack shook his head. "No. Wilder. Jack Wilder."

"Oh, for God's sake, look at him!" snarled Reed. He dragged himself across the floor to retrieve *The Forester*. With an effort, he pulled himself to his feet, stalked over to the officer still holding Jack, and shoved the newspaper two inches from his face.

"Look at the picture!" Reed gritted out. "Look at it. It's Vanderstone. It couldn't be anyone else. This is your man. The guy who killed his wife and kids."

Valerie's heart slammed into her chest at the brutal accusation. For a moment she couldn't catch her breath.

The older officer, a tall but burly man, looked quickly from the newspaper image to Jack. With one hand he brushed the paper aside. "That's good enough for me." He straightened. "Vanderstone, you're under arrest for the murder of your wife and children."

"I'm not Jack Vanderstone."

Amazed at his calm insistence in this horrific mess, Valerie could only stare. Why didn't Jack do something? Show some identification? No, that wasn't a good idea. His license was false. But there had to be some way to prove he wasn't a murderer.

"Maybe you are Vanderstone, maybe you aren't." The officer shrugged. "All I know is you're the spitting image of the guy on our wanted posters. And until you prove otherwise, you're our man." He nodded to the other officer. "Arrest him."

Jack's mouth set in a grim line and his hands balled into fists. For a moment Valerie thought he would shake off the officer and try to run. But he didn't. "I'll get my shoes and shirt."

"I'll get them," the officer said. "Where are they?"

Valerie watched in horror as the younger of the two officers handcuffed an unprotesting Jack. A moment later the older man returned from upstairs, Jack's running shoes and T-shirt in his hands. "Here, stick your feet in these." He placed the shoes on the floor and Jack complied.

When Jack raised his head, his eyes, clear and calm, met Valerie's. He said nothing, but his look was steady and full of a love and faith that said, more clearly than any words, "Don't worry. After all, what can happen? I'm a ghost."

Valerie's eyes filled with tears. They had so little time and now—now this. It was so unfair.

One of the officers urged Jack to the door, but Jack stopped abruptly as he passed Reed. His eyes narrowed and his body stiffened with a menace Valerie had never seen before. "Stay away from Valerie," he spat out, fire blazing from his eyes.

Reed laughed. "Or what?" He waved at Jack and made a mock bow to the officers. "I give you your murderer, gentlemen. A man who killed his wife and children." He turned to Valerie. "And the only real danger to you."

The officer pushed Jack to the door. Reed's face curled up with hatred as he watched the procession leave the kitchen. Valerie took in her former fiancé's expression, then turned her attention to Jack's retreating back, pain and disbelief combining to break her heart.

"Miss?" She jumped a foot, surprised to realize one of the policemen had remained.

"Yes?"

"You'll have to come with us."

"Why?" Valerie frowned. She felt dazed and confused. Everything had happened so quickly, so unexpectedly.

"We'll need to question you about your association with Vanderstone. We've got two other officers searching the premises. You can go with them."

"That's all right. I'll take her, officer." Reed stepped forward, his voice smooth and firm. He placed a hand on Valerie's shoulder; she was too stunned to shake it off. "I know where the OPP station is and I'll drive right along behind you."

The officer looked from Reed to Valerie. He paused. "All right. But make sure you're right behind me."

The second the door shut behind the officer, Valerie yanked the newspaper out of Reed's hand. "Let me see that."

Shaking with anger, she ripped open the folded paper, and looked at the offending photo.

Her heart sank; she had to struggle to keep the blow to her faith in Jack from showing on her face. Because from the front page of this week's *Forester*, a man who looked far too like Jack stared out at her. The only thing missing was the ugly bruise.

She swallowed, then forced herself to study the picture more carefully, searching for a tiny detail, a mark, something to indicate that the man captured in the photo wasn't

Jack. Because it *wasn't* Jack. It couldn't be Jack. Not her Jack.

Her mouth settled into a grim line. The men were so identical it was eerie. The only difference she could see was something indefinable, the reflection of personality and kindness and love that she had come to know so well. But no one else would recognize that. No one but her. Just as no one else would know, or believe, the real story.

The reality rattled her. What if Jack couldn't prove he wasn't Jack Vanderstone? What if Vanderstone had left no medical records, no dental records, nothing that could be used to prove who the real Vanderstone was? Worse, what if Jack disappeared before he could prove his innocence? When and if he returned again, he'd be a wanted man.

"Valerie." She jumped as Reed tugged the paper from her hands. She'd forgotten he was there.

"You're so trusting, Valerie." Reed shook his head, smug concern plastered on his face. "See what you've got yourself into now? It's a good thing I'm here to help. I should never have let you come up here alone in the first place."

Reed's words pricked Valerie like irritating gnats. She brushed them aside, too busy thinking about Jack, and how she could help him out of this mess, to pay much attention.

"I'm so relieved you're not hurt," Reed continued. "I'd never forgive myself if he'd hurt you."

"What?" Valerie almost laughed at the irony of his statement. She must be suffering from shock. "Jack would never hurt me," she said flatly.

"That's why you need me, Valerie. Your judgment is terrible. You don't see the truth about people."

The condescension in his voice pierced through her numbed state. He spoke as if he were placating a small child.

His hand wrapped around her wrist. "C'mon. Let's go. I'll drive you to the police station."

Valerie ripped her wrist from his hold. She glared at him,

furious with him for what he was doing now, and for what he'd already done. "No. I can drive myself."

"You're upset. You shouldn't—"

"I *can* drive," she snapped. Her gaze sharpened on him. "Or don't you believe I'm capable of that either?"

Reed blinked. "It's not that. You need someone with you, that's all. What if the police suspect you knew who he really was all along? What if they charge you with harboring a killer? You could go to jail for that."

A cold chill raced up Valerie's spine, making the hairs on the back of her neck stand up. She hadn't thought of that.

She swallowed and raised her chin, despite her now churning stomach. She marched to the door.

"I don't care. I'm driving."

Chapter Twenty-one

Valerie squirmed in the straight-back chair beside Detective Lalonde's desk. Through the glass door separating his office from the main reception area, she could see Reed pacing back and forth.

The detective, a beefy man in a medium-blue suit that strained across his shoulders, finished typing in her name and address. He appeared to be no older than his late thirties, but his reddish hair was thinning and what Valerie assumed had once been a trim build had started to run to paunch. But his green eyes were hard and alert, and he surveyed her with clear suspicion.

"So what are you doing here, so far from Chicago, Miss Scott?"

Valerie winced. What was it about the authorities—any authority—that made her feel guilty? She pushed that thought away and concentrated on answering the question. Jack needed her help, and it was important that she provide the information to clear his name.

"My great-uncle Arthur Pembroke left me Aurora Lodge,

on Lake Aurora, in his will. I came up to see his lawyer, and the lodge, and figure out what I was going to do with it."

"And have you?"

"Have I what?"

"Figured out what to do with it?"

Valerie shook her head. She didn't meet the detective's eyes. "I'm still thinking about it."

"How long have you known Jack Vanderstone?"

If the detective had hoped to catch her unawares, it didn't work. "He's not Jack Vanderstone! His name is Jack Wilder."

The detective's cheek bulged slightly as he rolled his tongue and considered her answer. "Whatever. For now let's call him Jack. How long have you known this man?"

"About two weeks."

"When did you meet him?"

"It was the night I arrived at Aurora Lodge. The last Thursday in June."

The detective said nothing and showed no surprise, but Valerie could guess what he was thinking. *That was the night Catherine Vanderstone and her two children were murdered. The night Jack Vanderstone disappeared.*

"What time?"

"I'm not sure. I think it was around ten-thirty at night. I'd just arrived, and walked down to the beach so I could see the Northern Lights better."

Detective Lalonde nodded. "That's right. Quite a show that night." He paused. "Go on."

Valerie swallowed. This was where the story would definitely raise Lalonde's eyebrows, and likely his already well-developed suspicions. "When I got down to the beach, I found Jack lying on the sand, unconscious." And naked too, she thought, but I'm not telling him that!

"Unconscious?"

"Yes. I couldn't wake him, so I assume he was unconscious. I ran up and got the car, and drove it down to the beach. I managed to get him into the car so I could take him to the hospital."

The detective scowled. "The hospital didn't report admitting an unconscious man that night. Especially not one fitting the description of Jack Vanderstone."

"That's because I didn't take him there. He regained consciousness before we reached the turnoff to the highway. He said his name was Jack Wilder and that he didn't want to go to the hospital."

"Hmm." Detective Lalonde's eyes narrowed. "Did he say why he wouldn't go to the hospital?" When Valerie shook her head, he continued. "Or what he was doing on the beach?"

"He was swimming across the lake when he blacked out. That was the last thing he could remember."

The detective leaned toward Valerie, hands splayed on his thighs. "Didn't you find that a little strange?"

"Well, yes," Valerie conceded. "But once he told me he was Jack Wilder, it made sense."

"And why is that?"

"Because my uncle left Jack Wilder half of Aurora Lodge. I'd just been at Ed Grierson's office, and he'd told me that he'd run ads in newspapers in Florida in an attempt to find the missing heir, but so far had heard nothing. Jack told me that he'd just arrived at Aurora Lodge that day, come back to work for my great-uncle, whom he didn't know had died."

"And you believed him?" Skepticism echoed in Lalonde's words.

"Yes." Valerie sat up straighter. "I had no reason not to."

"That bruise on his forehead. Was that there when you found him?"

"Yes."

"Did it look fresh?"

"Actually, it looked about the same as it looks now. It's never seemed to heal properly."

"Did you hear the radio reports of the murders?"

"Yes."

"And you didn't connect it with the mystery man you found on the beach?"

"Why would I?"

"Why wouldn't you? Especially after his picture was aired on television? And in that copy of the *Forester* your friend showed us?"

Valerie gritted her teeth to keep back an angry retort. "My uncle's satellite dish isn't working. I haven't turned the TV on since the day after I arrived. I was trying to relax, get away from it all. And the newspaper—I don't go into town every day. I don't live here. I just didn't pick up a paper."

The detective stared at her hard, then typed a few more lines. Finally he looked up. "Where did you say Jack worked in Florida?"

"I didn't. You'll have to ask him."

"I'll do that."

Valerie realized Lalonde was looking past her. She turned to see what had caught his attention, then frowned when she saw Reed standing outside the door, his arms crossed, the fingers of one hand tapping impatiently against his elbow.

"That your boyfriend?"

"No!" Valerie whipped her head back to face the detective. She could feel the dark flush climbing up her neck.

"Well"—the detective returned his attention to the computer—"he certainly seems worried about you. I'd be too if you were my girlfriend."

Valerie stiffened her spine and raised her chin. "I can take care of myself."

Lalonde rested his suited forearm on the chair arm. He studied her, then turned back to the computer. "I hope so, Miss Scott."

"Have you seen him?"

The question flew from Valerie's lips as she burst into

Ed Grierson's office. Once she'd managed to shake Reed, she'd driven over here like a maniac, leapt out of the car, and pounded up the stairs and past a startled Lynn.

Mr. Grierson motioned her to the chair. "Sit down."

Reluctantly, Valerie did so, but not before she noticed the sorrow in his expression. *Oh, no! Ed couldn't believe Jack was the murderer too!*

The old lawyer shifted in his chair. Suddenly he looked so much older, older and far frailer than she'd thought. She hadn't paid much attention when he'd talked about retiring, but now she wondered if it wasn't past time.

"I just came back from the police station," he began.

"Yes? Are they going to let him go?" Valerie sat forward eagerly.

"No. Not yet." Mr. Grierson's voice quavered. "I've got a call in to a good criminal lawyer in Ottawa. Jack needs a specialist in criminal law, not me."

"But—but aren't they going to let him go? I mean, once they realize he's not Jack Vanderstone?"

"Valerie." The lawyer's kindly voice brought her to a halt. "The only way to tell you is straight out. One of Vanderstone's friends, one of his buddies from the bar he was hanging out in before he went home and killed his wife, has been in to see him already. The police brought him in."

Mr. Grierson paused and Valerie felt a chill run up her spine. *No, it couldn't—*

"Valerie, he's identified Jack as Jack Vanderstone. He swears it's him."

For a moment Valerie thought she was choking. She couldn't seem to catch her breath. The room closed in on her, making her head spin and her stomach churn before it finally retreated. She swallowed hard. "But that's impossible. He can't—"

"That's the premise I'm working on right now. That it's a case of mistaken identity. But Jack isn't making it any easier."

"What do you mean?"

"Well, he's refused to provide any identification, not even the driver's license he showed me. And so far, I don't think the police have found anything in that cabin of his that would prove he's Wilder. Has he shown you anything?"

Valerie froze, remembering the tin box filled with piece after piece of identification, all of it false. Except, she thought, one thing. "I know I've seen his bankbook. That was in the cabin, in a drawer in the table."

"That could help," Mr. Grierson said without enthusiasm. "I expect the police already have it. In the meantime, they've fingerprinted him and are trying to match his prints with some found in the house. They don't have a murder weapon, but they're sure to have at least one set of prints of Vanderstone's from the house.

"I've called Vanderstone's mother in Winnipeg. She should be here tomorrow and be able to identify him one way or the other. In the meantime, I'm trying to find any medical or dental records for Vanderstone. So far, it seems the man didn't frequent the medical or dental professions, at least not around here."

Valerie let out a sigh of relief. "Well, then, it should be all cleared up tomorrow. Certainly Vanderstone's mother will know that Jack isn't her son."

She looked at Grierson, searching for reassurance. When it didn't come, she faltered. "She will, won't she?"

Grierson sighed heavily. He sat back in his chair, and for the first time Valerie thought how unwell he looked, his skin gray and thin as parchment. All signs of healthy coloring had disappeared.

He pressed his knuckles against his mouth. At last he looked up at Valerie again, his eyes shimmering with a deep, deep sadness.

"My dear child," he said, "did you ever stop to think why Jack signed the lodge over to you yesterday? Why he didn't care about any compensation?"

"Because, because . . ." Valerie faltered, knowing deep in

her heart that Grierson would never believe her if she told him the truth about Jack. She rushed on. "It's because he's a drifter. He doesn't want to settle down. He doesn't care about material goods. He—"

"You might be right," Mr. Grierson interrupted. "I hope so. But . . ."

"But you don't believe it, do you?" Valerie finished for him.

He clenched his papery fists. "I'd like to, Valerie. I really would. I've liked that young man from the moment he walked into this office. I had no trouble seeing why Art left Aurora Lodge to him." He paused. "But there's something else."

"What is it?"

"I told you I liked him. But he also seemed very familiar to me, though I knew I'd never met him before. But I was certain I'd seen him before, and often."

The old lawyer looked up, his eyes bleak and beseeching her to understand. "Don't you see? He looked familiar because I *had* seen him before. He looked familiar because Jack Wilder *is* Jack Vanderstone."

His words fell like a bombshell into the room. Finally Valerie managed to choke out, "You can't believe that."

"I don't know what else to think, Valerie. There isn't any other rational explanation."

A thin shaft of light shone through the narrow window near the ceiling of the cell in the basement of the police station. From where he slumped on his bed, Jack watched the dust motes slowly spiral and fall before disappearing into the darkness. Like him, he thought with a snort. Like him. It was like watching the cycle of his life, replayed over and over again.

He turned over his hands, and examined the fingers so recently printed. Solid and strong, and undeniably capable of performing the mayhem of which he was accused. The hands of a man, not of a ghost, no matter what he knew to be true. Because if he was truly an apparition, why was he still here? Why couldn't he fade away at will, moving through walls to freedom and back to Valerie, where he belonged, where he could protect her from Reed?

He clenched his fists. What good was being a ghost if he had no supernatural gifts? If his talents didn't even come close to those of the spirits of movies and television? He laughed bitterly, drawing a quizzical glance from a passing police officer.

Jack shut his eyes against the curious looks, against the bare and slightly dank surroundings. Ed Grierson, trying to be supportive but looking grim, had urged him to tell the truth. But Grierson, despite his protests, believed he was Jack Vanderstone, and had murdered his wife and children. That was the only "truth" he or anyone else around here would believe.

Sooner or later, the police would find Jack Vanderstone's fingerprints, his dental and medical records. Of that Jack had no doubt. Then it would be clear he was not Jack Vanderstone.

But by then a whole new kettle of fish would be boiling. As likely as not, police would have found his cache of identification. They would discover it was fake. They would want to know who he really was. It would throw the whole question of Valerie's inheritance into a legal quagmire.

Only one thing could be worse. He could disappear. Disappear before any of this was resolved. Before the police realized he wasn't Jack Vanderstone, before they questioned the only identity he had. He could disappear, leaving behind a trail of accusations and unanswered questions.

And worst of all, disappear before he could be certain that Valerie was out of danger. That Reed couldn't, wouldn't hurt her.

Jack jerked to his feet and started pacing. He had to do something—and do it now, before he disappeared. He couldn't leave until he knew Reed would never bother Valerie again. That Reed was gone for good, and Valerie was safe. Everything else was secondary, even proving his innocence.

He stopped in front of the window and grasped the bars, staring out blindly. Somehow, some way, he had to get out of here. Before it was too late.

Valerie made the decision as she struggled from an uneasy sleep just before noon the next day. Her confidence—both in herself and in Jack—had been badly shaken by his arrest for murder. And it had been further undermined by the doubts expressed by Ed Grierson, the one person she'd expected to support Jack absolutely.

She gritted her teeth as she tightened the laces on her running shoes and firmly set aside the doubts that had plagued her hour after hour through the long night. She'd finally fallen asleep close to dawn, exhausted from analyzing and comparing everything she knew about Jack Wilder and Jack Vanderstone. Ultimately, she'd been left with two questions, ones she'd been afraid to face. Did she believe in Jack, and in his love for her? And did she believe in herself, and her ability to recognize truth and goodness?

But as she awoke this morning, she had realized it wasn't necessary to keep digging inside herself. To keep analyzing every word and every action of Jack's. Now was the time to show her love and her support, through action, not endless repetitive thoughts. And there was only one thing she could think to do that could possibly help Jack.

She shook her head at Reddi as he danced around the screen door. "I'm sorry, boy. But you've already been out for a while. What I need to do now, I need to do alone."

Holding his collar until the last moment, she shut the door and looked up at the flawless blue sky. How could it be so beautiful, so peaceful and serene, when the world was falling apart around her?

She shrugged. No time for pondering now. She leapt from the deck and raced over to the parking lot. Good. It was empty. She retraced her footsteps, ignoring Reddi's barks when he caught sight of her passing back by the house, and continued along the path.

In front of Jack's cabin, she hesitated. The building looked desolate and unhappy, as unhappy as she felt. She straightened her spine. As that popular footwear ad said, "Just do it."

Looking over her shoulder, she scurried up to the screen door and slipped onto the porch. As she opened the cabin door, she glanced around once more. With relief, she saw no witnesses and, before she lost her nerve, she quickly stepped inside.

Valerie headed straight for the table and pulled out the drawer at one end. Empty. Likely the police had found Jack's bankbook on the first pass-through. But what about everything else?

She closed the drawer, wincing when wood hit wood and the noise echoed through the empty room. She scurried to the fireplace, and the right side where she'd found the loose floorboard. With her foot, she pressed on several likely boards, and then frowned. None of them seemed loose, none particularly shorter than the others. But one of them *had* to be the board under which Jack had hidden all his fake I.D. The question was, which one?

She dropped to her hands and knees, then lowered her head to the floor for a nose-level view. If the police arrived now, her position would do little to support Jack's innocence, or her own, for that matter, as a potential accomplice and aider and abettor of criminals.

Quickly she pressed on the wooden planks with her fingers, looking for some give, watching for a sign of weakness. None of the lumber looked new, so Jack must have propped up the section of floor above the hiding spot in some way.

One board seemed looser than the rest, but for some reason she couldn't pry it up with her fingers. She pulled the Swiss Army knife she'd taken to carrying from her pocket, shoved the short blade between the boards, and levered the wood upwards. She recognized the plastic bag underneath, and yanked it out, but not before she noticed the rocks Jack must have positioned below the board to keep it from wobbling. Valerie replaced the flooring and rose to her knees.

The faint sound of barking broke the noon silence, throwing Valerie off balance. She stretched out one arm to support herself and listened. After three or four seconds, Reddi stopped barking. She sighed, realizing she was shaking all over at the false alarm.

She had started to rise once more when she jerked to a halt. Was that a voice? Men's voices, talking and laughing? She strained to listen, every sense on alert. *Damn!* Maybe it was Reed. Maybe it was the police. Or even worse, both! And they were heading this way.

Chapter Twenty-two

Frantically, Valerie searched the room. The cabin had only one door, the one she'd come in. How was she going to get out without them seeing her? Her eyes raced past the windows, and then she remembered. The bathroom! It had a small hinged window that opened onto the back of the cabin.

With the plastic bag of I.D. in one hand, she scrambled for the bathroom and shut the door behind her. The window, catercorner to the sink, measured about three feet wide by two feet high. It opened easily, but the trick was to climb through it without leaving any signs of her exit.

She glanced around. The toilet was too far away to serve as a launchpad. It would have to be the sink. She hoisted herself up onto the small, free-standing sink, praying it wouldn't collapse under her weight. Listening hard, she yanked open the window. Before she could change her mind, she thrust her head and shoulders through the opening, then shoved off with her foot. The rough wooden frame scraped against her torso as she tumbled through, headfirst into a waist-high growth of weeds she hoped wasn't poison ivy.

She bit her lip to keep from crying out, then stiffened. She heard the squeak of the front door, and the heavy tread of footsteps on the porch. She'd made it just in time. Now she'd better get away from here fast.

She headed for the brush behind Jack's cabin. Thankfully, his was the closest to the tree-lined road and the farthest back from the lake. Once she made it through the fifty feet or so of small sugar maples, yellow birches, and bushes, she'd be on the road.

As she burst from the woods onto the dirt road, she squinted against the full glare of the sun. Out in the open, and away from the lake breezes, the midday heat was brutal, the light blinding. Spikes of magenta fireweed stood in clumps along the road.

The blast of a car horn and the sudden awareness of a gleaming metal monster bearing down on her sent her leaping back into the bushes from which she'd just emerged.

Muttering, she regained her feet and brushed off her dirty, leaf-stained clothing. From the tenderness across her back, she felt certain she sported a crisscross of scratches from the window. She looked at the bag still gripped in her hand. But at least she had the I.D.

She removed the false cards from the tin and stuffed them into her back pockets. She didn't want anyone, particularly not the police, asking her what was in the plastic bag. She stuffed the empty tin and the bag between two tree branches and set off down the road to the Aurora Lodge driveway.

At the entrance to the parking lot, she paused. Yes, it was the police. The white cruiser with the blue OPP logo was parked beside her own, and seemed to regard her accusingly. She winced. Maybe it would be better to go for a walk. She didn't feel strong enough—or guilt-free enough—to face any more questions from people who already viewed her with suspicion.

But where could she go? The road, with the blazing sun, no breeze, and occasional cars speeding around the sharp corners, didn't present a pleasant prospect. If she returned to the house or walked down to the beach, she was sure to run into the police. The only good option she could think of was the nature trails on the far side of the road. They'd been there when she was a kid, and likely still were, intertwined with the snowmobile paths that were supposed to run all through this area. Wasn't there a small lake back there too? Jack had mentioned a cabin on the far side of the road where he'd hidden out the first time he'd come back. Could it still be there?

Actually, a walk seemed like a better and better idea. It would work off the tension from the day's hair-raising activities. The decision made, she crossed the road and began searching for a path.

After a few minutes, she found the remains of what looked as if it had once been one of Uncle Arthur's nature trails. While weeds had grown up in the entranceway, a clearing was evident beyond the road, and she caught a glimpse of hard-packed earth. She waded through the weeds and down off the road into the coolness of the maples and conifers, then caught a glimpse of a jagged piece of wood nailed haphazardly onto a tree and pointing deeper into the woods. Once, it likely had proclaimed the name or the direction of the path; now years of sun, wind, rain, and snow had worn the paint bare and weathered the wood to a gray fragment.

She followed the path, enjoying the shaded coolness, ducking low-hanging branches, and batting at the maple saplings, clumps of wild sarsaparilla, and ferns barring her way. After about five minutes, the trail joined another, roughly adjacent to the road and about six feet wide and recently cleared. The snowmobile route, thought Valerie. She looked down at the faint tire tracks on the muddy ground. It looked as if a car, or perhaps a tractor, had been this way not too long ago, probably for maintenance.

She continued, searching for where the path would leave the snowmobile route again. About fifty feet farther on, she found it, though it seemed to have dwindled to an even fainter trail. Undaunted, she set out along it, hoping it wouldn't peter out altogether.

After several minutes of thrashing her way through an increasingly tangled and overgrown path, she stumbled onto the snowmobile route again, which must have doubled back and cut across this track again, unless her directions were entirely jumbled. She looked around in disgust. She wanted a nature trail, not a superhighway through the woods.

Finally she found what might be a cleared path, though she couldn't be sure. Crushed saplings and snapped branches indicated some kind of vehicle, perhaps an all-terrain vehicle, had come this way recently. She walked on for a minute or more, viewing the smashed and devastated undergrowth on every side until, without warning, the path returned to a narrow and faint track.

Valerie looked around. Whoever had driven in here must have backed out again. Maybe the same person who had driven up and down the snowmobile track. Ah, well. She shook her head and continued. Then a light flashed across her field of vision. She blinked and searched for the source. The sun streamed in through a small hole in the trees overhead, but what had it reflected off? Another blinding flash drew her attention to a tangled mass of greenery. She advanced toward it.

"Ouch!" Her shin hit something hard and unyielding. With one hand she rubbed her leg; with the other, she poked at the offending bushes—only to jump back in shock when the shiny bumper of a car gleamed back at her.

A chill that had nothing to do with the shade shivered up Valerie's spine. Whose car was it? Why would anyone hide a car here? Someone had gone to a lot of trouble to shield it from view.

A vague idea nibbled at the edges of her mind. Hadn't someone—perhaps a radio reporter—mentioned the type of car Jack Vanderstone drove? She racked her brains, trying to remember. At the same time she pulled more branches away from the car, to reveal a dark green, rusting Subaru, but it didn't jog any memories. She squeezed between a towering oak tree and the driver's side and tried the door. It was locked. Peering through the window, she could see that all the doors were locked.

In frustration she kicked the tire, then froze. What if whoever had hidden the car here didn't want it found? What if he was somewhere in the bushes, waiting, watching? What if it was Jack Vanderstone?

She swallowed and edged away from the car. If she were smart, she'd get away from here as fast as she could. If she were smart, she'd run back the way she'd come and tell the police before they left.

But what if this is Jack's car? The mutinous thought betrayed her innermost fear, one she didn't want to admit even to herself. *No, no, it can't be.*

But what if it's true? What if Jack isn't who he says he is? What if everything he's told you is a lie? What if Reed is right, Ed Grierson is right? What if Jack Wilder is an imposter? Or worse, Jack Vanderstone?

The accusations, the horrifying thoughts, all the doubts she'd kept at bay came tumbling in, stronger than ever. She covered her face with her hands, but still they came tumbling in, a dark, horrifying whirl of evil, and deception, and murder.

With a sob, she dropped her hands and ran. She had to get away from that car, from the torrent of horrible uncertainties crushing down on her, making her question everything that was true and good and wonderful about her love for Jack and his love for her.

She ran without thought of where she was going, crashing along the path that led deeper into the woods, not caring who saw or heard. She ran until her breath came in deep, rasping gasps, sweat streamed down her forehead, and her sides hurt with the effort. She ran until, cresting a small rise, she halted abruptly.

Before her spread the calm, blue waters of a tiny, pristine and absolutely deserted lake. No more than three hundred yards across, and perhaps twice as long, the lake sat in undisturbed silence. Near the far end, Valerie could see a solitary duck, floating peacefully on the quiet waters.

She paused, the only noise the sound of her harsh breathing. Gradually, her breathing calmed and grew more regular. With the physical calmness came the return of her logic, and the return of her faith in Jack. Yes, the doubts were there; she couldn't make them go away. But the truths she knew that no one else knew—Uncle Arthur's love for Jack, Uncle Arthur's diary, the newspaper clippings from the past—bolstered her confidence once more. But most of all, her own knowledge of Jack, his kindness, his love, his guilt over those long-ago deaths, his sense of honor and justice surfaced inside her, reinforcing the strength of her convictions and instilling peace, much like the idyllic natural scene before her.

She took a deep breath and began to pick her way along the faint path bordering the shore of the lake. She'd go a little farther before heading back. With the hidden car in mind, she'd be careful, but she wasn't ready to go back to the lodge yet. She needed a few minutes to compose herself before she talked to anyone, especially the police. She stopped and looked around. A sense of déjà vu, that she'd been here before, perhaps on a walk with her mother, came over her. Hadn't Uncle Arthur kept a canoe chained to a tree somewhere near the water's edge?

She paused again and let the quiet sounds of the woods seep into her. The call of a bird, followed by the answering call of another. The buzz of tree crickets. The rustle of leaves. The high-pitched whirring of the mosquitoes hovering around her head, drawn by her sweat.

Ducking away from the mosquitoes, Valerie continued on around the lake. She'd reached the far end when she caught a glimpse of smooth gray wood and moss-covered green shingles ahead. She increased her pace and soon came into a tiny clearing at the end of the lake. A line of birch trees hid it from view from the water, but the path came straight to it.

Valerie looked around. Attached to a white pine, she saw a rusted chain, half buried in debris. Well, there was the chain. No canoe, but the chain was still here.

A long, slow whine made her look around with apprehension. It took a moment before she identified the source of the noise. The door of the shack hung half open on its one remaining hinge. A faint breeze moved the door back and forth, each swing bringing forth the annoying whine.

But the door never quite shut. Valerie's gaze dropped. Something seemed to be propped in the doorway, keeping it open. Maybe a branch or a pile of leaves had been blown or fallen inside. Or maybe . . .

Her gaze fell on something protruding from the door. A running shoe with . . . with a leg attached.

She swallowed. Despite a growing sense of dread, she crept closer. Like it or not, she had to see what—or who—was there.

The door blew open several inches wider just as she reached a spot several feet in front of it. Her eyes widened and her mouth fell open. *Oh, no. Oh, God, no.*

Chapter Twenty-three

Late that afternoon, Valerie stood and watched as the last police cruiser drove away in a cloud of dust, following the tow truck and ambulance that had pulled away earlier. She glanced at her watch. Supper time already, but she wasn't hungry. She didn't think she'd ever be hungry again.

Slowly, she turned and plodded back along the winding road to the lodge's parking lot. Every step took a colossal effort. She couldn't remember feeling this tired, this drained, this frustrated. Her careening emotions, combined with a sense of unreality that had held her in its sway from the moment she'd stumbled over that decaying body, had taken their toll.

Involuntarily, she shuddered. The afternoon had passed like a dream, or rather, a nightmare, alternately racing by or dragging on interminably. In absolute terror, she'd raced back to the lodge, catching the two detectives as they climbed into their car. She'd forgotten about guilt, about the fake I.D. stuffed in her back pocket, about who Jack was or what he might have done. She couldn't blot the specter of those decaying remains from her head.

But ultimately, going to the police had only increased her frustrations. She'd answered every question they'd put to her, and in return they'd told her nothing. Not whose body had lain in that shack for God knows how long. Not whose car she'd found hidden in the bushes. Not whether the discoveries would result in Jack's release from jail. Nothing.

Now, in addition to being exhausted, she felt defeated as she trod back to the house. What was going to happen now? Would she ever see Jack again? Was it too late to visit him today? Why would no one tell her what was going on?

She dragged herself up the steps to the deck and opened the door. Even Reddi, jumping up on her and yipping at his release from the house, didn't revive her spirits. She hugged and petted him anyway, glad for his company, if nothing else.

Reddi seemed to sense her need. Instead of racing from the deck and around the house, he stayed with her, resting his head on her knee when she sat down at the picnic table. Valerie smiled and scratched behind his ears. "Pretty smart for a dog, aren't you boy?"

"Hi."

Valerie cringed at the familiar voice. Reed. Would he *never* go away? Before she could say anything, he had bounded up the stairs, looking trim and fresh, as if he'd come straight from the shower. He carried what looked suspiciously like a picnic basket.

Reed jerked his thumb over his shoulder. "What's with the police car? Were they here looking for more evidence?"

"I guess so." Valerie said nothing more. If she never talked to Reed again, that would be fine with her.

Reed sat down on the far end of the bench. He reached over and chucked Reddi under the chin. Once more Valerie was amazed—and a little miffed—at her dog's continuing friendliness to Reed.

Reed said nothing. He continued to stroke Reddi. I'm

not talking, thought Valerie, her fury at his unwanted visit growing. Except to tell him to go away.

"I'm sorry."

Valerie blinked. "Pardon?" she blurted out.

"I said I'm sorry. I'm apologizing."

"For what?"

"For all you've had to go through these past two days. Being questioned by the police. The shock of Jack's arrest. The way he's lied to you and mistreated you."

His words fueled her growing anger. "Reed," she started.

"No, listen." His dark eyes glowed with earnestness as he leaned towards her, his whole body straining forward in the effort to convince her. "This isn't a good time for you to be alone. Not after all that's happened. I know it's hard for you. I know you're hurting. That's why I came over. I know you're embarrassed, but it's okay."

"Reed—"

"No, let me finish. I'm sorry I had to be the one to bring the police, but it had to be done. Maybe some day you'll understand, but for now, I just want you to know that I'm sorry."

He paused, his dark eyes focusing on her with unusual sadness. "I'm sorry. But I also want to tell you something else: I'm leaving."

"Leaving?" The word leapt out at Valerie, blocking out her other thoughts.

"Yes. First thing tomorrow morning." Reed bowed his head and continued in a low voice. "I don't want to accept it, but I finally realized yesterday I have to face the fact I'm not wanted here. That for reasons I don't understand you can't or won't love me."

He raised his head, and the anguish on his face shocked Valerie anew. "I think you're wrong," he went on, "but I accept your decision. I apologize for following you here. Can you forgive me?"

Dumbfounded, Valerie could only stare. She'd been prepared for arguments, for accusations. But not for this new, penitent Reed.

"I . . . I don't know." She paused, flailing about for the right words. "So much has happened."

His eyes, his demeanor, everything begged her to reconsider. "Please. It would mean a lot."

Valerie eyed Reed dubiously. Dare she believe him and this sudden about-face? Did it even matter? The important thing was that he was leaving. The faster she forgave him, the faster he'd be gone.

"All right. I forgive you." The pardon came out on a whoosh of relief.

"Thank you."

Reed straightened. "Now I'd like to do something for you. I know how tired you must be after the last couple of days." He nodded in the direction of the basket. "That's why I brought a picnic dinner. I thought we could go out on the lake for a bit, maybe stop at a beach and eat. Then I'd bring you right back."

Valerie shook her head. "That's kind of you. But I'm exhausted. It would be better if you left."

"I am leaving. First thing tomorrow. I just want to do this for you before I go."

"I'm really tired, Reed. I know you mean well, but I don't think so."

"Come on, Valerie. I'm leaving tomorrow. You're too tired to make dinner. What have you got to lose? All I'm asking for is an hour or two out in the canoe. For old times' sake?"

Valerie hesitated, suspicion warring with her desire to be fair to Reed, to give him the benefit of the doubt. She didn't want to waste another minute with him. But if he was really leaving . . .

"Okay," she said finally. "But as soon as we're finished, you have to go."

Reed smiled broadly. "That's a promise. Can't interfere with your beauty sleep now, can I?"

Valerie shut Reddi back in the house, and got two paddles from the other side of the deck. "Here, you carry them."

She walked toward the beach, silently dismissing her doubts, telling herself she was doing the right thing by allowing Reed to make amends. Beside her, Reed strode jauntily along, commenting on everything from the view to the cottages.

"I can see why you like this place. Maybe you should keep it. We could hire someone to run it, and then come up here for a couple of weeks every summer."

The words flowed over Valerie like spring runoff. She paid no attention nor felt any compunction to respond. He's leaving tomorrow, she thought, and relief washed over her again.

Reed automatically took the stern of the canoe. Valerie didn't challenge his choice; she was too weary to do more than hold her paddle across the bow.

"So where do you want to go?" Reed's voice echoed over the water as he paddled the canoe out of the bay.

"To the far end of the lake. We pass some interesting cliffs on the way there, as well as sand beaches and cottages. It starts to get swampy down that end, but there's a tiny island, really just a big rock with a couple of trees and a little sand. We can get out and eat there before canoeing back."

"Sounds good. What's that?"

Valerie turned to see where Reed was pointing. A lump filled her throat, making it difficult to respond. "The Tarzan rope," she finally managed.

"Looks like fun."

"It is." Memories of the afternoon spent there with Jack flooded over Valerie, bringing tears to her eyes. Flying through the sunshine and over the water, plunging into the cold clear depths, all the time laughing uproariously. It was the moment, she remembered clearly, when she'd stopped being afraid of Jack. When she'd begun to realize just how special he might be to her.

She swung her paddle deep into the water, wanting to get away from the Tarzan rope as fast as possible. She was glad Reed sat in the stern, unable to see her face. Despite the fact he was leaving, despite the peace and beauty of the lake, she was tired and edgy and worried. Worried about Jack.

By the time she directed Reed toward a rocky island jutting out of the waves, her arms ached and her legs were sore and cramped from kneeling. Listlessly she helped to maneuver the boat around a large outcropping of granite to a tiny white sand beach, barely ten feet across and nestled between two boulders marking the edges of the small strip of land, which appeared be nothing more than a huge, water-smoothed rock. A twisted white pine, a birch tree, and several clumps of blueberry bushes, growing from cracks in the stone or areas where soil had been trapped, completed the scenery.

Valerie jumped out into the shallow water and pulled the canoe to shore. Picnic basket in hand, Reed joined her, and they hoisted the boat up onto the beach. Valerie stretched, then rolled her shoulders. "Paddling is hard work," she commented.

A scowl on his face, Reed examined the landscape. "This is just a big rock." He dropped the picnic basket, then lowered himself to the ground and stretched his legs out in front of him, casually crossing one ankle over the other. He patted the beach beside him. "Sit."

Valerie didn't want to sit down, not beside Reed. *But he'll be gone tomorrow.*

She plunked down a couple of feet away, and positioned herself half facing him. The sand, still heated from the day's sun, warmed her bare legs. She rolled her shoulders again, while Reed busied himself unpacking the basket. He opened a bottle of white wine, poured out two glasses, and handed her one.

He raised his in a toast. "To the future." Reluctantly Valerie clinked glasses with him, then leaned back and looked out at the water. The only future she wanted to think about now was Jack's.

"Valerie."

The urgency in Reed's voice made Valerie jerk her gaze to him. She was surprised by the stern look on his face, a look that reminded her of her father, the first man she couldn't please no matter how hard she'd tried. Her stomach tightened, but she ignored it. *He's leaving tomorrow.*

Reed continued to regard her, his dark eyes growing harsher, his lips pinched together in a thin line. Finally he spoke. "Valerie, I phoned your parents yesterday."

"What?"

"Your father is very concerned about you. He doesn't like you staying here alone, or the fact that you've gotten involved with a murderer."

"Jack isn't a murderer!"

Reed held up his hand. "I'm not arguing that point. It doesn't matter. What does matter is your safety. Your father is worried you'll be hurt. He wants you to go home to Chicago."

Valerie stiffened. "Well, I won't. I can understand why he might be concerned, but there's nothing to worry about. I'll phone him tonight to explain." A phone call, Valerie knew, that would be wasted on her father, though her mother would understand.

"Valerie!"

The urgency in Reed's voice set off a quiver of apprehension. "What?"

"I promised your father I'd bring you back to Chicago."

Valerie stared at him in disbelief. "You had no right to do that."

"Actually, I have every right. It's what your father wants. It's what I want. It's for your own good, and if you hadn't been so muddled by Jack, you'd know it too."

"No, I—"

"We're leaving tomorrow morning. You can follow me in your car to Toronto, where I'll leave my rental. Then we can drive back together."

Anger and shock froze Valerie's tongue. The apology, the picnic—she should have known it was all a set-up. She should have known better than to trust Reed.

As if her silence was approval, Reed continued. "The drive back will give us time together. Time to iron out our difficulties. Time to overcome your foolishness. Time to plan our wedding."

He paused, his features softening. "Valerie, I really want us to get married. I love you. I'm tired of fooling around. You know how I feel about you. And deep inside, you know you need me. It's—"

"No."

". . . meant to be. You and me." Reed ignored her faint denial. He rose on his knees and reached for her. Confident and possessive, his mouth covered hers.

For one confused moment, Valerie let him kiss her. Then the strength that had always been at her core blasted upwards. She struggled out of his grasp and leapt up. "No," she cried. "No."

Reed started to rise. "Stop fighting me, Val."

Valerie heard the censure in his voice, the first signs of his angry, dominating side, a side she had denied for too long. It sparked the fear she thought she'd conquered, and an instant urge to run for her life.

She grabbed the end of the canoe and shoved it into the water, leaping in and snatching a paddle. She started paddling, praying she could escape him, hearing him splashing in the water behind her.

One stroke, two strokes, three, she was getting away. Then the canoe lurched and came to a violent halt. A hand grasped her arm; she yanked away and clambered to the other end of the boat. "Don't touch me, Reed, I'm warning you."

He glared at her from the bow, then eased himself

around to the side of the canoe. "Valerie, I'm getting in. Don't try anything funny."

Valerie stared at the paddle in her hand, wanting to hit him, wanting to escape any way she could. Her fingers tightened around the shaft.

Reed hoisted himself, wet and dripping, into the middle of the canoe, which began to drift from the shallow water around the island, into deeper, rock-strewn waters. He glared at her. "Quit holding that paddle as if you're going to smack me," he commanded. "Put it down."

"No." Valerie's voice rang out far calmer and stronger than she would ever have believed possible. *He can't make me do what he wants.* "I'm not going to hit you. But you're not going to touch me again either. Not ever again, d'you understand?"

"Valerie, you're coming home with me tomorrow. I'm not going to argue with you anymore. You're out of your mind."

"My mind is fine. There's never been anything wrong with my mind. Or my ideas. Or my looks. Or anything else. And I'm not going to let you tell me there is. Never again!"

"Put . . . down . . . that . . . paddle!" Vibrating with barely controlled rage, Reed spat out each word. His lips pulled back, baring his teeth, and his eyes narrowed.

Another spurt of fear raced down Valerie's spine. Reed had looked exactly like this the night she'd refused to take him back. The night he had attacked her and almost choked the life out of her.

The paddle still in her hand, she rose up on her knees. She doubted she could fight him off, but she could jump out of the canoe and swim, somewhere, anywhere, to—

Reed lunged for her. With one wrench he yanked the paddle out of her hands and threw it into the lake. The canoe teetered wildly as Reed pressed his body against hers. She tried to beat him off, but he grabbed a handful of her hair and pulled her face to his, while his other hand circled her neck like a steel band.

His mouth closed over hers in a punishing kiss. She tried to jerk her head away, but he held her hair in a tight hold and brutally jammed his knee between her legs. Desperately she wriggled and fought, distraught by her inability to escape, hoping that if nothing else she could upset the canoe.

"Reed, stop." Her words came out in a harsh gasp as she twisted her mouth out from under his and escaped his stranglehold. But before she could move away, he yanked her back. "Reed, you—"

Her words were cut off as both hands tightened around her throat. He shook her, his eyes blazing with rage, his mouth contorted with hate. "How . . . many . . . times . . . do . . . I . . ."

Valerie scratched and clawed at his hands, to no effect. Panic rose inside her, as Reed's eyes burned feverishly and his fingers continued to deprive her of air. Frantically, she struggled, terror growing with every second she remained trapped, with every second more that oxygen remained cut off. She—

Suddenly Reed jerked; Valerie heard and felt the impact of something hitting his back. He released his hold on her neck and Valerie gasped for breath. The boat rocked violently.

"Get your hands off her!"

Shock, and then gladness, filled Valerie's heart at the sound of Jack's voice. Her eyes sought and found him, paddle raised menacingly, in a canoe that had come up alongside.

But only for a second. Reed retaliated quickly and plowed his fist into Jack's face. Immediately Jack dropped the paddle and leapt across the water onto Reed, knocking them both to the floor of the canoe. They scrabbled from side to side, punching and scuffling, the boat swaying wildly.

"Stop it, stop it!" Valerie croaked, wincing with the sound of each blow as the second canoe drifted away.

The two men ignored her. Valerie tried to pull Reed off Jack, only to suffer a sharp rap in the mouth from his elbow. She backed off, her hand to her lips.

Then an idea struck. Without hesitation, she sat on the right edge of the pitching canoe and leaned out over the water, hoping her weight would be enough to capsize the small craft and throw the struggling men into the lake. But the weight of the two men fighting in its bottom acted as ballast, keeping the canoe upright if unsteady in the water.

She shoved with her feet, and tried rocking the boat to decrease its stability. With her lower legs in the air and her rear end hanging over the side, she seesawed back and forth, growing increasingly desperate. She gritted her teeth, and with a final downward movement, the canoe flipped, throwing Valerie, Jack, and Reed into the lake. A moment later Valerie surfaced and cleared her eyes of water. In the growing darkness, she looked for Jack.

She heard splashing on the other side of the overturned canoe. She swam around it to find Jack and Reed struggling in the deep water. Dismayed, she looked for a paddle, a stick, anything to knock some sense into them and end the fight.

She spotted a paddle and swam towards it. As she returned, she realized only one man's head was visible—Reed's. From here it appeared that Reed was holding Jack underwater, trying to drown him.

"Reed," she screamed, only to end up with a mouthful of water. She swam towards him, trying to wield the paddle. Three feet away she hit him in the head.

The blow didn't knock him out, but it was enough to make him loosen his hold. Jack's head bobbed above the surface, his lighter hair distinguishing him from the dark-haired Reed. For a moment he seemed to tread water, catching his breath. Then his right fist flashed out of the water, connecting with a loud smack to Reed's left temple.

Valerie heard the crack of bone on bone and a sound

like a gasp. Then Reed seemed to slip beneath the waves, as Jack had only moments before.

"Save him," Valerie gasped. No matter what Reed had done, she didn't want him to die.

"It's all right," panted Jack. "I've got him. I can tow him to shore." Reed's head appeared above the water, and Jack's arm snaked around his neck.

"What about you? Can you make it?"

Valerie heard the worry in Jack's voice. She was close enough to see it mirrored in his face.

She chuckled. "I never told you I was on the swim team in high school and college, did I?"

"Thank God."

Valerie knew Jack was thinking about those drownings so long ago. "I'll be fine," she added, then looked around. Her canoe floated about twenty feet away, while the other one had disappeared behind the island. "I'll retrieve the boat—you take care of Reed."

With that, she dove under the water and using quick, efficient movements born of years of practice, headed to retrieve the canoe.

Chapter Twenty-four

"Valerie!"

The moment Valerie stepped onto shore, Jack pulled her into his arms. Despite her wet, chill clothing and his own sodden state, nothing had ever felt as good as holding her, knowing she was there, next to him, safe and alive.

He shut his eyes and cradled her head against his chest. When he'd seen Reed lunge at her in the canoe, the horror of the past had exploded before his eyes, momentarily paralyzing him.

But then his love for Valerie, and his own stubbornness, had broken through. No matter what the destined outcome, he couldn't sit by and watch anyone abuse the woman he loved. Maybe he was a ghost; maybe he was a lost soul forever doomed to pay for his sins; none of it mattered. Only saving Valerie mattered.

"Oh, Valerie," he murmured against her soaked hair. Slowly she drew back and raised her face to look at him. Her hands rose to circle his neck. "Oh Jack," she whispered, before their lips met in a heartfelt kiss that sent warmth tingling through their chilled bodies and made them draw closer still.

The kiss deepened and the warmth spread and Jack felt his manhood grow and harden in response. His heart sang. Suddenly he threw back his head and laughed. He laughed in relief and happiness, reveling in the sheer exhilaration of being alive, here, with the woman he loved.

A moment later Valerie's laughter joined his, ringing through the night air with the same joyous peal. He could feel her shaking with mirth in his arms. Still giggling, she pulled him down to sit in the sand.

"Why are we laughing like idiots?" she asked.

Jack smiled broadly. "Because we're alive. Because we're in love." He paused. "Because I'm a free man."

Valerie started, then began to sputter again. "That's right," she said. "In all the excitement, I forgot. When did they let you out?"

"About an hour ago. That body the police found—you found—it was Jack Vanderstone. He shot himself with the same rifle he used on his wife and children."

Valerie's face twisted in pain. "Oh. That's so terrible."

Jack said nothing for a moment. "It was pretty hard on his mother too."

"His mother?"

"Yes. They flew her in from Winnipeg to identify me. She had just confirmed what the fingerprint evidence had already shown—that I wasn't her son—when the ambulance came back with the body."

Neither Valerie nor Jack spoke for several minutes. Finally, Valerie asked, "So even without finding the body, they would have released you?"

"Yes. Apparently Vanderstone had a distinctive birthmark on his right hip. I don't have it, or any sign that it's been removed. Mrs. Vanderstone also said I didn't sound right, and my mannerisms weren't the same."

Valerie sighed. "Thank God."

"Yes. But you know the weird thing? Jack Vanderstone *is*

related to me. His mother was a Wilder. I found out she's the daughter of my older brother. That's one of the reasons she was so anxious to see me. The Wilder name made her wonder—well, whether her son had taken it to confuse people."

"So Mrs. Vanderstone is your niece?" Valerie mused. "What would that make Jack Vanderstone?"

"A great-nephew, I guess."

Silence fell once again. Holding Valerie's hand between his own, Jack glanced behind him to where Reed lay on his side down on the sand. Despite the knock in the head, he was breathing regularly, and Jack expected him to regain consciousness any time.

"I wonder what made him do it," said Valerie quietly. "Vanderstone, I mean. I wonder why he killed his wife and kids."

Jack shook his head. "Mrs. Vanderstone still couldn't believe it. But she did admit he'd been depressed. Apparently he'd had bouts of depression on and off since he'd been a boy."

Jack deliberated about whether to continue. He looked out at the water and the dark sky. Just above the tree line, a faint flicker of sulphurous green tinged the sky. A tingle of foreboding ran down his spine. He swallowed. "She said it was really strange, but he always seemed to get worse at times when the Northern Lights were really strong. The more beautiful and vivid the night sky, the worse his mood."

"Jack!" Valerie looked at him, amazement on her face. Then she looked out at the sky and her face fell as she too saw the faint green glimmer. "Oh, no, Jack. You don't think—"

He nodded. "I do. I can feel it inside. I can't be sure, but I think this is it. I—I won't be here tomorrow, Valerie."

"Jack—"

Valerie's cry of pain was interrupted by a moan from

behind them. They both turned to see Reed roll over and then groggily raise himself up on his hands.

Jack frowned. "We'd better get him back right away." He looked at Valerie. "Are you going to press charges?"

"Yes."

"Good." Relief washed over Jack. "We'll take him straight to the police station."

He held out his hand to Valerie, and she took it. Their eyes met for one brief moment of longing; then he pulled her close and brushed her forehead with his lips.

"C'mon. Let's get Reed into the canoe and go."

Jack and Valerie stopped on the deck to gaze at the night sky, pulsating with waves of sulphurous green and yellow, and punctuated occasionally with shimmers of red. The light was even more stunning than it had been the night she'd found Jack unconscious on the beach. What had started as a faint glimmer and flicker during the canoe ride back to the lodge had blossomed on the drive to and from the OPP station into a vast, pulsing panorama of color that spread across the darkness like a moving, living stain.

Valerie sighed. She'd been so relieved when Reed had not fought them or tried to press countercharges against Jack. Reed had been sullen, and clearly angry, but he'd seemed to recognize he couldn't avoid the assault charge. Her swollen lip and the fresh bruising on her throat had seen to that. The last she'd seen of him, he'd been quietly following a police officer to the cell block.

Jack touched her hand, bringing her back to the present. He nodded up at the sky. "D'you want to stay out here and watch it?"

Valerie shuddered. "No."

Reddi whimpered outside the door, and Valerie opened it and let them all in. Silently they walked through the kitchen to the living room and sat on the couch facing the fireplace. But the Northern Lights followed them inside, flashes of red and green light illuminating the sky outside the huge picture window, and casting eerie reflections through the room.

Valerie shivered again. She and Jack had changed their clothes before driving Reed to town, but she still felt the chill of the water on her skin. Or was it the chill of knowing that the Northern Lights, for all their beauty, were about to steal away from her the only man she'd ever truly loved?

"D'you want me to shut the blinds?" She turned to Jack, expecting to see misery on his face.

She blinked. He smiled at her, with an open and gentle steadiness that made him look more relaxed and at peace than she'd ever seen him.

He shook his head, blond hair falling over his bruised temple, and his smile turned rueful. He reached out, his broad hand with the long, strong fingers caressing her cheek. "Valerie," he said, "there's no point trying to run away. It's going to happen. I'm going to leave. I can feel it inside."

He paused, his expression growing more serious. "But it's all right. Don't you see, Valerie? Everything's changed now. For the first time—ever—since that night when I . . . I died, I feel good. Good inside. Because you didn't die. Because my actions didn't result in anyone's death, only in helping you, in saving you from Reed. I feel as if . . . as if a huge weight has been lifted from my shoulders. I'm finally free."

Valerie tried to be glad, glad for Jack's release from the guilt that had poisoned every aspect of his life. She tried to hold back the tears pooling in her eyes.

"But I'll never see you again," she cried, her voice cracking, the first tears breeching the dam and spilling over onto her cheeks. "I don't want you to go."

"I know. I don't want to leave you. I wish . . ." Jack's deep voice grew husky. He swallowed and his green eyes clouded. "I wish you were the one I'd met, so very long ago, at Aurora Lodge. I wish everything was different."

"It's not fair." Valerie knew she sounded like a spoiled

child, but she didn't care. Tears ran down her cheeks with abandon now. "I love you. I need you—"

"Shhh." The rough pads of Jack's fingers touched her lips to quiet her. He traced the tears on her face, silently wiping them away. He framed her face in his hands.

"Valerie, you don't *need* me. I hope you love me, as I love you. But you don't need me. You're a strong, wonderful person. You've shown that over and over again since I met you."

He paused, then broke into a heartbreakingly beautiful grin. "And you can swim too. You don't know how glad I am you can swim."

"I—"

This time Jack hushed her, not with his fingers but with his lips, a warm and gentle kiss that steadied her, calming her wildly careening emotions and bolstering her acceptance.

"I love you," he murmured against her ear. "And if this is going to be our last time together, I want to spend it making love—not raging against what we can't change."

He cupped her chin and, nose to nose, stared deep into her eyes. "I want your love now, body, soul, heart, and mind. I want you to remember how wonderful we are together, not how terrible it is to part. I want to give you my love now, and I want you to know every second that you're being loved. And that you'll never forget, just as I'll never forget."

Valerie tried to answer but couldn't. The tears flowed faster from her eyes than before. When Jack's lips met hers once more, her arms circled his neck and pulled him closer. Through the tears she could taste him, and feel him. Despite her tears, her body responded to his closeness, her pulse quickening and a deep liquid heat pooling in her abdomen.

She tried to hurry him along, but Jack would have none of it. He was kissing her, in long, drawn-out bouts that slowly built the fire within her and himself. Slowly he raised her T-shirt, the motions of his rough hands on her breasts repeating the motion of his lips and tongue on hers. Her whole body started to undulate toward him, wanting him, needing him, screaming for release, but gently and firmly he continued to set the pace, a pace designed to draw the most from each of them.

Finally, they were naked, lying on the rug before the bare fireplace. Valerie reveled in the feel of his hard, sleek muscular chest, the saltiness of his skin, his woodsy scent and still-damp hair. The flickering and pulsing Northern Lights flashed through the windows, reflecting off their naked bodies and adding a sense of urgency, of poignancy, to their lovemaking.

Still, Jack took his time, loving every square inch of her with his mouth, with his hands, with the hard planes of his body. And Valerie, loving him and wanting him to know as he'd never known before just how much he meant to her, returned his love with all her attention and fervor, slowly building the fires within them both.

When he entered her, she welcomed him, clasping him to her with her legs and arms, tightening around him. Together they rose on a wave of sensation, the wave rising faster and higher with each thrust until, in a final spasm of glory, it crested, taking them both.

Exhausted but satisfied, they clung to each other, content to bask together in the afterglow of love. With her head nestled against his chest, his arms around her, Valerie heard the thunder of Jack's heart slowly abate to a regular beat, his ragged breathing gradually calming.

Suddenly she remembered—and tensed. "Jack," she whispered.

"Mmmm?" he mumbled.

"Jack. Don't fall asleep. Please. Not yet."

His arms tightened a fraction more around her. "Mmm-hmmm."

Valerie struggled against his grip and sat up. She grabbed his shoulders and shook him until his eyes opened. "Jack, wake up. I need to tell you something."

He blinked. "What?"

"Jack. I'll wait for you. I'll be here when you come back."

Beside her, Jack shifted and blinked again. He appeared only marginally more awake. "You can't do that. We talked about that already."

"Yes, I can. I want to."

Jack's hand closed around her wrist. This time his eyes stayed open and he fixed her with a serious green stare. "Valerie, it might be twenty years before I come back. I might never come back—in fact, that's the most likely scenario after tonight. It's different now. I can feel it. I can't let you sacrifice yourself like that."

"It's not a sacrifice. I want to do it. I've decided I want to stay here. I want to keep the lodge open, the way Uncle Arthur wished."

A shadow fell across Jack's face, a shadow tinged with red from the pulsing lights outside. "If that's what you really want, do it, Valerie. But not for me. For yourself. Because you love it here. Because you want to stay. But not for me. Promise me you won't wait for me. That you'll find someone else."

His grip on her wrist tightened. Valerie stilled. He was right. She knew he was right. But, oh, she didn't want to promise.

Their eyes met and held for a long, long moment. Finally, Valerie swallowed. "I promise. I . . . won't . . . wait . . . for . . . you." Each word stabbed her like a knife. She had to bite her lip to keep from sobbing.

Jack's hand relaxed on her wrist. He pulled her down and into his arms and his warmth once more. He nuzzled her neck. "Just stay with me. Fall asleep with me."

Valerie shut her eyes to hold back the tears. She pressed her head against his chest, and listened tensely as she heard his heartbeat slow once more, his breathing relax into the measured rhythm of sleep.

Despite herself, she started to grow drowsy in the warmth

and comfort of his arms. She fought against it. If nothing
else, she would stay awake, stay awake and with him until
the moment he disappeared. . . .

As the last tendrils of sleep loosed their hold, the first thing
Jack noticed was the warm body within his arms and
pressed hard against his chest. He breathed in, and the
sweet scent of clean hair penetrated his senses. He shifted
his weight, provoking an involuntary groan at the cold and
stiffness in his shoulders and hips.

He shook his head and opened one eye, only to close it
immediately to shut out the dazzling light. Slowly, full consciousness dawned, and with it, a faint but glowing hope.
Could it be?

Taking a deep breath, he opened both eyes wide and
held them open, despite the bright morning sunshine. As
his pupils adjusted to the light and focused, he realized he
was looking straight into the fireplace and the sooty rem-
nants of a fire several nights earlier. He not only could see
it, he could smell the charred wood and ash. His throat
tightened and, hoping against hope, he dared to lower his
gaze.

His heart stopped for a split second when he saw the
chestnut hair he loved so well, the morning light glinting
off it like sparks of fire. Involuntarily, he tightened his grip.

Valerie shifted, and a whimper escaped her lips. Jack
couldn't help smiling when she tried to insinuate herself
deeper into the warmth of his arms.

He leaned over and grazed his lips across her forehead.
"Hey, sweetheart," he said, his voice husky from sleep and
emotion. "Wake up."

Valerie sighed and shook her head. She started to
squirm. "I'm cold," she said.

Suddenly she froze. Her eyes flew open. Without warning
she shot upright like a cannon. The top of her head
crashed into Jack's chin.

"Ouch!"

"Jack!" Valerie's eyes widened in shock, a shock that quickly turned to joy. "You're here. You're still here!"

Jack rubbed his chin. "Well, if the pain in my jaw is any indication, yes, I'd say I'm still here."

"But—but you said—"

"I know what I said. I was wrong."

Valerie's soft pink lips pursed. Her pink-tipped breasts poked toward him, luscious and waiting and as wonderful a symbol of life as anything he could imagine.

He watched as Valerie's brow creased. She bit her full bottom lip. Slowly the light in her dark eyes grew brighter. "D'you think—d'you think—is there any way this could be for good?"

Jack held back the smile fighting to crack his face. "I don't think," he said. "I know."

"But *how* do you know? How do you—Jack! The bruise is gone. There's no bruise on your forehead anymore."

Jack reached up to his left temple. True to her words, the gash was gone. All he could feel was smooth, unscarred skin. As if there'd never been a mark there at all.

Valerie touched his chest, then looked up at him with wonder. "And the knife wound—it's gone too."

His hand still on his temple, he looked down at his chest, and Valerie's fingers stroking the tan skin where no sign of injury remained. He raised his eyes to hers, the smile he'd held back spreading across his face. "You're right. It's gone. They're both gone. Two more reasons why I know I'm here now. Here to stay."

Their eyes met for a long charged moment, his green and electric with life and love, hers dark like the night and full of the love and longing she held for him. Slowly they moved towards each other, their lips parted.

A ball of wet, slobbering fur landed with a thud and a chorus of barks between them. With licks and slurps, Reddi poured out his affection on Valerie, while his wagging tail repeatedly struck Jack in the face.

Laughing, Valerie raised her arm to fend Reddi off. "Down, boy, down. Not now. Down."

Obediently, Reddi left off. He turned to Jack. For a moment, the pup sniffed the air, then Jack's hand. Without warning he leapt forward, his tongue wagging, and started to lick Jack's face.

Unprepared for the friendly assault, Jack fell over with the impact. Laughing, he held up his arm. "Easy, boy, easy."

But Reddi was not to be deterred. His paws firmly planted on Jack's chest, he slathered attention on whichever side of Jack's face was unprotected by his arm.

"Do you know what this means, Jack?"

Valerie's voice, high and excited, cut through the slobbering.

"No," grumbled Jack as he rolled away to escape Reddi. He sat up several feet away and glared at the dog. "Down, boy, down."

"Don't you see? Reddi knows. He knows you're not a ghost anymore. That's why he's not afraid of you any longer. That's why he's licking you."

Jack rose to his knees. In wonder, and dawning recognition, he looked from Reddi to Valerie, and back again. If he'd had any doubts about his changed status, about whether he was still a lost soul, they were gone. Reddi, with his acceptance, an acceptance based on an instinctual understanding and recognition of the most basic elements of nature, had removed the last shreds of his doubt.

Pure, sweet joy spurted through Jack's veins, filling him with a lust for life and love, the very things that had been denied him so long.

Smiling so widely he felt his face might break, he held out his arms. With an answering smile, Valerie moved into his embrace, while Reddi leapt around them.

As his arms closed around Valerie, Jack knew he had finally found his way home.

Epilogue

Christmas Eve

The kitchen door swung open, bringing with it a rush of cold air, swirling snow, dog fur, and a bundled-up Valerie.

Jack dropped the wood he was feeding into the Quebec heater and stood up, only to be almost bowled over when Reddi leaped on him and Valerie threw herself into his arms.

Laughing, he straightened himself, hugging Valerie with one arm and petting the dog with the other. He bussed her red, frosty cheek, and breathed in the cold fresh air that had wafted in with her. "I thought you'd never get here," he said, his eyes meeting hers.

"I was beginning to wonder, especially when it started to snow."

"Here. Take off your coat. And come into the living room. I've got a surprise for you."

Jack helped her out of her coat and she undid her boots. Ignoring the puddles of melting snow on the kitchen floor, he took Valerie's hand and led her into the other room.

"Wow!" Valerie gasped, her eyes wide with delight. "What a beautiful job!"

A huge fire blazed in the stone fireplace, its light reflecting off the old-fashioned glass ornaments and tinsel that adorned the tall and bushy Christmas tree standing regally before the window. The sweet scent of fresh balsam, from the tree and from swags and garlands festooning the mantel and the doorways, filled the room.

"I was going to wait," Jack started, "but I was worried you wouldn't get here in time."

"I'm glad you didn't wait." Valerie dropped his hand and turned slowly, her nose twitching. "The tree smells wonderful, but there's something else. . . ."

"Tortiere." Jack grinned. "Velma stopped by an hour ago with a homemade tortiere. It's in the oven now, heating for dinner."

"Mmmm, traditional Christmas Eve meat pie." As if in response, a loud rumble emanated from Valerie's middle section. She looked at her stomach, then at Jack. They both laughed.

"It'll be a few minutes still," said Jack. "I'll go out and bring your bags in from the car." He paused. "Wait until you see everything else."

"So you've finished the cottages?"

"Yes." Jack grinned with pride. "Four of them are ready for winter occupation. And they're all booked for Boxing Day."

"That's wonderful!" Valerie threw her arms around Jack's neck and gazed up at him with a look of love that meant more to him than dinner, than the lodge, than life itself.

Jack stilled. "You're here, then, for good?"

"Absolutely. My job's wrapped up, apartment's sublet, furniture in storage for the time being. For a while there I didn't think I'd ever get it all done in time." She grinned slyly. "But then I'd think about you. And Aurora Lodge. And how much I wanted to be here."

Jack's arms tightened around her and he kissed her, long and slow. "I'm so glad," he whispered.

"Oh."

He felt her stiffen. He drew back.

"There's something I forgot to tell you. It's about Reed."

He stilled. "What about Reed?"

"Oh, no. It's all right. He hasn't come near me. Not since he pleaded guilty to that assault charge. No, it's something else."

"What?"

"You won't believe this. It only happened yesterday. He's been charged with the murder of his wife."

"What?" Jack repeated. He stepped back from Valerie.

"I guess I never told you," Valerie explained. "His wife died five years ago, after a fall down the stairs. Everyone thought it was an accident.

"But then one of his wife's friends went to the police. They started talking to Reed's friends. To me too. They exhumed the body. And now he's been charged."

Jack frowned. "Do you think he did it?"

Valerie shook her head. "I don't know. If you'd asked me before Reed's second attempt to choke me, I would have said no. But now?" She shrugged. "He—the way he explodes with rage . . . I just don't know."

Jack took Valerie in his arms once more and hugged her. Then he tipped her chin up. "Forget about Reed. We've got a big night ahead of us. Dinner. Unpacking. Then later we can drive into town for the midnight service."

Valerie's lips turned up. "I'd like that."

So would Jack. As he gazed down at her, her warmth and love seeping into him, he knew he had much to be thankful for. Namely, a second chance at life, with a woman he loved more than life itself.

Valerie rose on tiptoe. Her lips brushed his, setting off the first tingles of desire.

She pressed her nose against his and grinned. "I think that tortiere can wait a little longer, don't you?"

"What tortiere?" he murmured just before his mouth captured hers.

KATHERINE DEAUXVILLE
OUT of the BLUE

Maryellen isn't sure whether to call the Men in Black or the men in white coats—all she knows is that she is having an incredibly alien experience. The voice that comes out of her mouth isn't hers (she certainly wouldn't swear like that!) and though the hand exploring her breast is her own, she's never had the urge to do that before.

Her sister says Manhattan is finally getting to her. She claims Ur Targon is simply the last alarm bell of Maryellen's biological clock. But how can either of them deny a golden god who promises to make her see stars? Maryellen has to get Targon out of her body and heart. If he needs her enough, he can find his own way back in.

___52469-4 $5.99 US/$7.99 CAN

WHISPERS ON THE WIND

JUDY GILL

In a secluded cave amid the Canadian Rockies Lenore finds Jon: the lover of her dreams, a man quite literally from another world. In a desperate bid for survival he has sought her out telepathically. Injured and separated from his crew, Jon's success, the future of his planet, his very life depends on Lenore. She denies him nothing, sharing her home, her knowledge, her strength, and eventually her heart. Until what had begun as mere caresses of the consciousness progresses to a melding of not only bodies, but souls.

___52435-X $4.99 US/$5.99 CAN

Alicia's Song
Susan Plunkett

For Alicia James, something is missing. Her childhood romance hadn't ended the way she dreamed, and she is wary of trying again. Still, she finds solace in her sisters and in the fact that her career is inspiring. And together with those sisters, Alicia finds a magic in song that seems almost able to carry away her woes.

In fact, singing carries Alicia away—from her home in modern-day Wyoming to Alaska, a century before her own. There she finds a sexy, dark-haired gentleman with an angelic child just crying out for guidance. And Alicia is everything this pair desperately needs. Suddenly it seems as if life is reaching out and giving Alicia the chance to create a beautiful music she's never been able to make with her sisters—all she needs is the courage to sing her part.

___52434-1 $4.99 US/$5.99 CAN

Susan Plunkett

Bethany's Song

For Bethany James, freedom comes in the form of the River of Time, sweeping her away from her old life to 1895. But on awakening in Juneau, Alaska, Bethany discovers a whole new batch of problems. For one thing, she has been separated from her sisters—the only ones with whom she shares perfect harmony. And the widowed mine-owner who finds her—Matthew Gray—is hardly someone with whom she expects to connect. Yet struggling to survive, drawing on every skill she possesses, the violet-eyed beauty finds herself growing into a stronger person. She is learning to trust, learning to love. And in helping Matt do the same, Bethany realizes the laments of the past are only too soon made the sweet strains of happiness.

___52463-5 $5.50 US/$6.50 CAN

THE DEE DAVIS
PROMISE

The mine calls out to Cara from deep in Colorado's San Juan Mountains. It is rich in ore, overflowing with wealth that can make a family's fortune—or destroy it. In it began the weaving of a murderous tapestry of lies that meant the deaths of many innocents. But its labyrinthine tunnels also hold a magic that can draw a woman one hundred years into the past, into the arms of one who can make her life whole. To right the wrongs already done, to paint a brighter future, Cara will have to unravel its mysteries. She will have to depend upon the rugged man who emerges, trust his vow that he will keep her safe and cherish her forever. Only then will she truly understand the danger—and the power—of the promise.

___52475-9 $5.99 US/$7.99 CAN